CHEST OF
B NE

THE AFTERWORLD CHRONICLES

VICKI STIEFEL

CURIOSITY
QUILLS PRESS

A Division of **Whampa, LLC**
P.O. Box 2160
Reston, VA 20195
Tel/Fax: 800-998-2509
http://curiosityquills.com

Cover Art by Eugene Teplitsky
http://eugeneteplitsky.deviantart.com

ISBN 978-1-62007-741-2 (ebook)
ISBN 978-1-54279-181-6 (paperback)

To my Betas, all superb, who found my story while hiking through the morass of words.

Abby
Alisa
Debi
Ericka
Kathy
Richard

And to Ilona Andrews,
Who found my Betas

"The only way to make sense out of change is to plunge into it, move with it, and join the dance."
—Alan Watts

CHAPTER ONE

The word "former" sucks. *Former friend. Former lover.* *Former astronaut. Former anything implies that the past was better than the now.*

I don't believe that. All you have is now, and maybe a few tomorrows… if you're lucky.

Destined for the Feed and Seed, I turned from pondering "big thoughts" and flicked on my audiobook as my Tahoe sped down Route 202 in Midborough. Stark and lonely in its winter cloak, the road was lined with snow-dusted pines, frozen marsh, and the occasional house. As I crested the rise of the small hill, something down below prowled onto the pavement. And sat. In the middle of the road. I pressed the brake on the downslope, slowed the truck.

I squinted into the bright morning sun. *What the hell?*

A huge black cat sat smack on the double yellow line where the road leveled off. Black cats were bad luck.

And this black cat was the size of a Harley. It was beyond bad luck. It was scary as shit. It also made me question my sanity.

I'd been doing that a lot lately, the sanity thing.

I braked.

From twenty feet away, the cat lunged, a blur, landing inches from my bumper.

I jerked the wheel, careened off the road toward the snowy pines to avoid hitting the humongous black panther that shouldn't exist in any reality, no less New Hampshire's. I flung my sanity worries aside. If I crashed into the fast-approaching pine tree, the point would be moot.

Splatting into a tree... I'd never show Dave my pink-tipped blond spikes... never watch his new mentalism effect... never read that book he'd promised me... never again see *him*. My mentor was "off," something bad going on with him. If the meeting of tree and me happened...

My Tahoe bounced, tipped sideways, and went airborne. The landing thud shook my bones. I slammed the gas, yanked right, avoided an alder stand. And that ginormous pine, looming closer and closer...

I white-knuckled the steering wheel and braced for impact.

Savage anguish lanced through me, a sadist rearranging my atoms. Razors slicing my skin over and over.

No. No. No. Not now... not...

Blind. Blind. Blind. Can't see, can't hear, can't think.

Tried to mantra my way to sanity.

Yeah well, that didn't work.

Being an FBI interrogator sometimes sucked. Being an empath sometimes sucked worse.

Frost iced my skull, my face, my mind, my body.

I blacked out.

I awakened. My head rested on my hands, which curled around the steering wheel. I blinked twice. Vision, check. Fingers and toes, check. Torso and legs, check. Brain, whatever.

The world refocused, a lens iris expanding. The truck sat in the middle of a frozen marsh, banded on three sides by pine, spruce, and birch. I was uninjured, the truck—pristine.

I turned the ignition, and the Tahoe purred to life.

Fucking A. What the hell had just...

Screw it. I was alive. The truck was functional.

My phone read... Damn, Dave's store had been open for an hour. I was late.

The day had grown cloudy by the time I pulled into the Midborough Feed and Seed. In the ashen light, shadows of marsh, meadow, and pine surrounded the large blue building shaped like a U, its "Blue Seal" banner snapping in the wind. No sign of any customers. Bonus. I'd have more time with Dave—mentor, friend, and the only father figure I'd ever known. If anyone could make sense of my latest "adventure," Dave could.

Except a Closed sign hung inside the door. And no twin mutts' noses pressed the glass, awaiting the next arrival.

A terrible wrongness leeched across my skin, coating me like boggy sludge. I jerked the car's door handle.

You're too impulsive. Caution. Always. My foster mother Bernadette's words, carved on my soul.

They'd saved me more than once.

I phoned the store. The machine picked up.

Called Dave's home, hoped he hadn't had to close because of another problem with his teenage daughter, Luzlu. No joy on the home machine, either.

I slipped my Glock from its shoulder holster, slid from the truck, and padded to the door. I listened, massaged my clammy skin. Silence. I pushed down the handle—locked—thumbed through my keyring, found the right one, unlocked the door. I eased it open.

Gun in my two-handed grip, barrel pointed dead ahead, I pressed my back to the wall. Inside, that oily wrongness increased. A grim ugliness pervaded the place, tendrils of it, like dirty smoke, seeping from the sales counter that divided the store, maybe thirty feet away. And that smell.

Rotted geraniums and cat urine. Vile. I swallowed, hard.

If anyone hurt Dave, they were toast. I mean, seriously charcoaled briquettes. He was fine, though. Peachy. And worse comes to worst, he knew how to shoot a gun, right? But how well? How good was his aim?

Someone had moved a display, blocking the aisle. I pushed my senses to feel if anyone else was here and caught a faint echo of... pain.

Crouched low, I moved to my left, up an aisle flanked by display shelves. I heard nothing, until...

"Clea."

A ragged whisper. Dave.

I jerked toward the sound, needed to dash. Bernadette's wall of caution slammed into me. I moved silent and smooth down the aisle, toward the counter, toward...

Dave. His back against the counter, legs sprawled. I ran.

Stumbled to a halt, vision blurred. What...? Red? A Rorschach of red. On Dave, the floor, the back of the counter. Legs, torso, arms, face, coated in blood. Shining. Glistening.

I strangled my scream and fell to my knees beside him.

Eyes swollen shut, breathing shallow. Somewhere under all that blood, naked but for a pair of red-soaked boxers...

"Dave," I said, tone hushed.

CHAPTER TWO

The man I adored smelled of death. Dozens of cuts slashed his legs, his sleeve-tattooed arms, his torso, his face. His discarded clothes lay in a bloody pile beside him. They must have stripped him before "working" him over. *Oh gods.* I reached for him, curled my hands. I didn't dare.

"What happened? What can I do?" I fumbled for my phone to call 9-1-1. His bloodied fingers clawed around my wrist.

His eyes slit open, their soft violet capturing me. "No." A whisper.

"But—"

"No." Firmer. Impossible to ignore. Blood trickled from his mouth to his scruff, beaded there.

"The pups?"

"Fine. Locked away." He panted for a moment.

I breathed in a sob, lifted a hand to caress his hair, the one part of him that didn't seem injured. His pain splintered through me. "What hap—"

"No time." He lifted my hand and pressed it to his ruined cheek. "Listen."

"But—"

A faint smile. "Listen, kid." A wheeze. "I'm your guardian. A Guardian."

"Please—"

"Sshhh."

So soft, I strained to hear. I leaned closer.

"I knew you'd come," he said. "I waited. For you. So much still to do.

Shield Lulu. Protect you. Take the chest. A... thing... of... power." He grinned then. Always so quick with that grin. "I know, crazy, huh?"

"Yes. Crazy. Whatever you say."

"Damn straight. The panther. She arrived in time."

"She did." How could he know?

And those gentle lips melted into an almost-smile. "Good. Would have taken you. Killed you, too."

"Who, Dave?" My voice hitched. With each of his breaths, viscous blood oozed, stealing his life. "Who did this?"

A long silence, then, "The Storybook. Find it. Green cover you bit. Take it. Read..."

"Dave, who!"

His lips barely moved. I leaned closer.

"Spell. Magic." Dave's grip on my wrist constricted.

Psychic pain crashed over me.

"Tell no one what you hunt."

"I won't."

"Promise." He gritted it out between his teeth.

"I promise." Something shifted inside me.

With his free hand, he cupped my cheek, a tear strolling from his eye. "Love you."

My body shook. "I love you *so much*." I almost blurted the word "father," for that's what he was to me. Always there. Always present. I couldn't lose him. I couldn't. *Live, Dave. Live!*

His vise on my right wrist tightened. Electric current zapped up my arm, shocking me.

Pain, so bad my back bowed. As if through a glass, darkly, his sleeve tattoos moved. The Ouroboros morphing into The Dragon sliding into The Eye, then twirling, twirling, a cosmos, a galaxy, a spiral nebula that spun faster and faster, and...

Agony rocked me forward. I screamed, each molecule of my being stung by invisible wasps. *Blind. Deaf. Stop. Stop. Stop!*

A cooling balm washed over me, like a winter's stream burbling over rocks, soothing my pain, again and again, until it dissolved.

I panted, pressed my free hand to the floor, steadying myself. My head was buried in his shoulder, my body flush against his. Gingerly, I pushed off him and sat back on my heels.

"I've unlocked it." His hand fell away. "Good. Acknowledge and accept. You *are* the magic."

My breath stuttered, my wrist burned. I rubbed it again and again, as blood seeped through my fingers. Changed.

It was changed.

I was changed.

"Dave?"

His violet eyes dimmed, he panted, thirsty-dog breaths. "I didn't finish. Forgive me."

I cupped his cheeks. "There's nothing to forgive!"

A susurrus of breath. His essence left his body, hovered, then dissipated, raindrops on a lake.

A blink of time. Now, only stillness. Utter. Infinite.

Clues. Of course, I needed to find clues. Who had done this? When? Why?

I scraped a hand through my hair, then stared at my blood-streaked fingers. I shrugged, singularly not giving a shit, then stood and stumbled, breathing deep, sampling the acrid, coppery scent of Dave's blood. It coated my nose, flavored my tongue.

With a mechanical deliberateness, I pulled the nitrile gloves I always carried from my jacket's inner pocket and snapped them on. I walked around the body, feet squishing in the fluids on the linoleum, to the counter. Must find *why*. Must find *them*.

I sifted through Feed and Seed papers, some dotted with blood, Dave's blood. Huh. Had to be careful. Preserve the scene. I snorted. That ship had already sailed. The papers—invoices, bills of landing.

Behind the counter, I came up empty, walked toward the office, seeking, hunting, which is when the whining of Dave's dogs from behind the storage room door brought me up short. He must have shut them in when he spotted the men approaching from the parking lot. Which meant he knew or recognized his killers.

Mutt and Jeff assaulted me when I opened the door to the storage room. I grabbed their collars and led them into Dave's office, made sure to close the door, then slipped them biscuits from my pocket. I told the pair to stay. If they found Dave in his condition, they'd go nuts.

The office was trashed. Papers and broken mugs and loose kibbles strewn everywhere. File drawers open, emptied. Pens and ink and chaos. The techs would have a field day.

The techs. I hadn't called it in.

I dialed 9-1-1 and in crisp words, detailed where I was, what I'd found, and barked they should get to Dave's daughter, Lulu, fast.

I wet my lips. Such utter *mess*!

Maybe he'd hidden something beneath the kneehole of the desk. A clue that would point to his killers or the reasons they'd come a-calling. Yeah, sure, that would make sense.

I got down on hands and knees, face pressed to the desk's edge, and felt beneath its underbelly. I groped. Nothing. Too obvious, for my clever Dave.

My fingers curled into fists, until I felt the bite of my nails, the pain of control.

After three heartbeats, I flexed them, losing balance, slapping them on the floor.

The corner of something hard rested beneath my palm. I wrapped my hand around the edge as I tipped back on my heels to stand.

I held a book. Mylar covered. Old. No jacket, but the blue cloth-covered boards were near perfect and the spine's gilt lettering shined. The original hardcover of *The Once and Future King*, with a red sticky note: *For Clea*. And then, the joke. Always a terrible joke: *What do you call a big pile of kittens? A meowntain.*

I almost laughed, except my body began to shake. No. No. No. A tear dripped onto my coat sleeve.

Shit! Dave would kill me if I got tears on the book, he...

No, he wouldn't.

As my tears came faster, my hands reflexively tightened on the book.

The brrring of the landline on the desk froze me.

Get your shit together.

The caller ID read "Lulugirl."

Ring. Ring. Ring.

Soon, Lulugirl. Soon.

I snugged the book inside my leather jacket and left the office.

Back out front, I couldn't look at him. I mean, if I didn't look, he wasn't dead, right? Except the place was so absent of sound. Of life. I allowed my eyes to seek Dave.

So still. So quiet. Dave defined energy, life.

Silence was never so deafening.

I walked over to the remains. The corpse. The non-Dave. Crap, I'd made a mess of the scene. I crouched down. Dave's blood covered me, crusted my face, my boots, my jacket. I scraped my hands across a couple clean spots on my jeans, then reached for my phone, tapped out every word Dave had uttered and emailed the note to myself. Done, I photographed the remains, each slash of cruelty, and took closeups of a couple. How bizarre. Almost as if his skin had split apart from the inside.

And then, I sat on the floor beside my mentor's body, held his stilled hand, and waited for the troops to arrive.

I had no memory of my parents. Not the brush of a hand, a cuddle, a scent. No pictures, no tokens, no tales. Just a void.

A family fostered me until they passed me off to Bernadette and her grandson, Tommy, who was four. So was I, and we were best friends from then on. That was when I met Dave.

He must have been in his twenties when he took me on as a "project." I never knew why. He was a merry man, tall, and sapling thin. His tattoos fascinated me, and he'd laugh, making up stories about each one to entertain a kid starved for affection. He read to me for hours. And I could still feel our quiet joy as we hiked the forests and rock hills of New Hampshire.

I brushed a finger across that hand that had held mine so often.

"You're the world's most stubborn do-gooder." I sniffled. "Study your math. Stand up straight. Yes, you *are* taking ballet."

We had pure fun when we practiced magic tricks and mentalist reveals.

I squeezed his bloody shoulders. "You brought out the empath in me. Remember how you insisted we first practice on animals? Did I tell you I thought it was really dumb? Pretty sure I did. And people! Oof. Strangers were okay, friends were embarrassing, but the crowds, they were the toughest."

What are they feeling? you'd ask. Are they angry? Sad? Lonely? Joyful?

"You *made* me open my senses, to feel what others feel, the obvious and the secret. Except, dammit, I feel too much. We weren't done!"

A giggle, then a sob.

"You said it mattered. I should have listened better."

Now what am I supposed to do?

I sat back on my heels and smiled, slow and mean. "I'll catch your killer, Dave. And when I do, I'm gonna skewer him, barbecue him, and feed his entrails to the crows. Yeah, all right, pretty yuck. But I'll get him. First, though, I'm going to go find that kid of yours."

The troops poured in and, per procedure, I was interviewed ad nauseam. I'd put on my FBI persona, which managed to get me through until eyes bored into the back of my skull. I split my focus enough to unfurl my senses. Yeah, a lot of people were surreptitiously watching me, but this was different. One guy's interest was so centered, prickles danced along my skin. As if I were a threat? No, not quite right.

Given my emotionally jagged state, getting a clear read on the watcher was proving problematic. I massaged my still-achy wrist, a physical prompt to aid my concentration, then fine-tuned my senses and lasered my probe.

And gasped, stunned by a mind singular and unique—fierce, calculating, savage in intensity. Other.

Guard. Prey.

A blaze of protectiveness burned me, with low notes of compassion, and higher ones of quarry. Was *I* the prey?

At which point, a detective's ceaseless questions intruded, going on and on and on. Finally, a state trooper interrupted the man. I pivoted just a hair to eyeball the room.

Gotcha. In a corner perfect for observing the scene, a large man in dark clothes, a shock of raven hair, bronze skinned. If he moved from the shadow, I would see him more clearly. And what was with that strange, almost unnatural vibe?

My watcher's eyes met mine—a flash of blue, a tongue of heat—before he pushed away from the wall, headed in my direction. I mumbled, "Be right back," to the detective and went to meet him.

Moments later, the stranger and I faced each other, mere inches separating us. He towered over me, a mountain of a man who dwarfed my petite frame.

Everything receded, the noise, the smells, the emotional chaos. His face was a blur. All I saw, all I felt was the burn from eyes as blue as the Pacific Ocean, and as turbulent.

He cocked his head, confusion darkening those eyes.

An awakening inside me, where memories distant and terrible hid. My yearning reached for that, which was *other* in him, a harmonic resonance that sang a song I'd once intimately known, yet had long ago forgotten. Like electrons orbiting the same nucleus, we circled the source where that arcane otherness lived inside him. Inside me.

The melodic harmony intensified, my song rising in pitch, while his lowered, dancing wisps of melody, complementing, blending, to fulfill that perfect refrain.

The blue of his eyes became a sea as tears blurred my vision, the song's beauty devastating.

He gasped. Or maybe it was me.

"Agent Reese," a voice said.

I raised my hand to touch, to hold that song.

"Agent Reese!" repeated the voice.

I staggered, reluctantly turned my head at the sharp command.

Several feet away, the detective stared at me, frowning. "Are you all right?"

"Yes," I whispered.

I turned back once, just to confirm what my senses had screamed. The stranger was gone. So odd. I couldn't even describe his face.

"Sorry," I said to the detective when I reached him. "Where were we again?"

By the time the police released me, my watcher hadn't rematerialized, but pale echoes of the song stayed with me long after I left the Feed and Seed. I headed out to find Lulu when I caught my reflection in the rearview mirror. Blood all over me, crusted and drying. Crap. I dashed home, set *The Once and Future King* on my dresser, washed the blood off the Mylar, then showered and changed into jeans, a turtleneck, and a vest of my own knitting. I massaged my aching wrist. Thankfully, no damage.

Lucky me, Bernadette was at her weekly Wild Spaces meeting, and I peered out at a drab-gray afternoon sky, determined to get to Lulu fast. I collected my throwing knives, strapped them on, and slipped my small Bowie into its boot slot.

I shrugged into my barn coat, bent on doing a quick check on the animals, my basset Grace trotting behind me.

Frigging magic and chests? What was all Dave's woo-woo talk about? Was he hallucinating? Except Dave knew about the panther, as if he'd sent it to delay me, to save me. And that thing with my wrist felt real, too. I rubbed it. Let go. You could just tell when something was becoming a *thing*.

I stumbled—Dave Cochran, my protector, my mentor, my best friend. Truly gone. I caught myself and reached for the doorknob.

Bernadette materialized behind me, so fast, the pearl-handled derringer holstered at her waist flapped. It might not be loaded, but it packed a nasty wallop if she hugged me the wrong way.

"I thought you were out." My lips moved to tell her about Dave. I smothered the words. I couldn't give life to them. Not yet.

Her willowy form towered over me as she thrust a cup of yogurt-and-almonds at me.

"What?" I asked. "I don't need—"

"Eat." She stood in her fighter stance, legs akimbo, hands on knobby hips. "You don't get enough protein."

Gods. She was forever shoving food at me, as if being vegetarian equaled starvation. "I'm not hungry."

She harrumphed, slammed my yogurt onto the counter, and crossed her arms.

I picked up the cup and spoon. *And here it comes, the bada-bum*. There was always a bada-bum.

"Sit." Her grayed unibrow caterpillared when she pointed at the scarred Windsor chair beside the equally scarred pine table.

I remained standing, spooning the yogurt into my mouth. "I've gotta go, B."

"The captain called," she said.

Shit. "He's a special agent." A hell of an FBI agent, in fact, and aware Bernadette would answer the landline. Why had he called *her*? I slumped into the Windsor. "I'm returning to the Bureau on Monday, Bernadette. The doc signed off on me." I had to tell her about Dave. At some point.

She shook her head. "You're still fragile."

My ass. I smiled, projected comfort and reassurance. "I'm fine. And I'll be there on Monday, B. I need to work, to use my gifts. You've always told me that. I feel—"

"Too much, cookie. I know." She sat across from me and took my hand. "The captain's worried about you. Said so."

"Well, what the hell is he calling you for?" I stared into those knowing hazel eyes. "His worry... I don't like it. Look, I'm twenty-eight, not twelve. I'm plenty strong enough to swim those waters. I've done it for years."

She squeezed my shoulder. "Last interrogation, cookie, those waters drowned you."

"A one-off. It won't happen again." I glanced at my phone. Dammit. I had to get to Lulu. Now or never. "Dave's dead."

She closed those wise eyes, dropped her arms to her sides. Her hands fisted. "I know."

I enfolded her in a hug, and she hugged me back. A quick squeeze, gone in an instant. She stepped away, but I leaned in, kissed her parchment cheek. I turned and twisted the doorknob.

"*Zut!* There's *more!*" She followed me out the door.

"It can wait," I hollered back, my words watery with tears, as I strode to my car.

Effusive swearing in French tracked me.

A "something" pinged my mind. No, not a some*thing*. Some*one*. Bob. Bob? *Nearby*?

Was that what Dave meant by magic? No way. While Dave had honed my sensory abilities, I'd just been given a double dose of what everyone else had.

The crunch and whir of tires lacking purchase on our ice-coated drive broke the winter silence, inciting the birds to flight and my basset to howling. I scraped snow across my face, unwilling to let him see I'd been crying. Didn't want Bob knowing what a hot mess I was.

"Told you there was more, cookie!" Bernadette said. "Now buck it up."

Bob at the wheel. Another, too, in the car, an unfamiliar psychic scent. Feminine and strange.

An SUV crested the drive and skittered into the dooryard.

I *so* didn't need this right now.

The driver's door opened and Assistant Special Agent in Charge Bob Balfour emerged, his blue suit polished and immaculate, per usual. "Hey, Young Pup." His warm smile added wrinkles to his fifty-something face.

I walked over for a hug. "Hey, Old Man."

He puffed out his cheeks.

"What the hell are you doing here in New Hampshire?"

He adjusted his FBI lapel pin, grinned. "Couldn't stay away."

I snorted. "Yeah, like I'm buying that. You hate the country."

His brown eyes sparked with laughter. "Old dog, new tricks?"

"Waterfront in Arizona?"

A door slammed, and a whip-thin woman in a stylish parka minced around the SUV in three-inch heels. Heels? Really? She moved to Bob's left, all bangs-and-bunned hair and steel spine, except for her slightly askew black glasses, which annoyed me for no good reason.

She bobbed her head. "Sorry to interrupt, sir."

Bob gestured toward me. "Not at all. Clea, this is Special Agent Katie Taka, from Washington."

She held out her hand.

I tried to sense her, slammed against shields tighter than Bob's, artfully slithered around them, tasted. Ouch. She'd shoved me out, but I'd felt enough. Oily vibes.

"Nice to meet you," I said as we shook, wondering why Bob had brought her to the boonies to meet me. "Bob, I—"

A door slammed, and my foster mother stood on the porch, one hand on her hip, the other resting on the butt of her holstered derringer. No coat, no boots, she shook like an aspen.

"Clea!" Bernadette said. "*Zut!* Where are your manners? Bring them inside. I've got tea, coffee, and scones."

Oh, swellsies.

I took a step toward the house. Paused. A third presence? Over by the side of the barn, in shadow. Yes, a shadow, who waited and watched. I shuttered my lids and unfurled my mind.

The wash of hatred made me stumble back. But not at me, no. Directed at Taka and Bob. Vicious.

The shadow turned, lasered on me.

Concern, pursuit, determination encased in a shell of fierce protectiveness.

I drifted back toward the barn, as if I needed to check that the doors were closed tight. A pulse within the shadow, warm, inviting—it radiated sympathy and comfort and warmth. My mind stuttered. *Was this the man with the song?*

Adamantium shields slammed me backward, alerted by my clumsiness. Dammit. I raced to the barn, and found empty space and churned up snow. Not even a footprint.

"Clea?" Bob's hand on my elbow. "You all right?"

I hated when people asked me that. "Fine," I said.

The other. He'd stood there. That instant before he'd hardened his shields, I'd sensed fury, and that he'd come for me.

I should be alarmed.

Instead, I felt kinship.

We took over the living room. Me, in my worn red-leather chair, Grace curled at my feet, Bob and Taka across from me on the hideous plaid sofa that backed against the partition to the kitchen where Bernadette bustled.

I shoved Dave's death and finding Lulu aside, shored it up, at least until the grief breached those walls.

A relaxed Bob unbuttoned his jacket, smoothed his silver-and-brown hair, and I mentally searched for where I'd put the sticky dog brush to lift Grace's hair from his suit. The closet, maybe? The bath? Crap.

Taka scooched forward on the sofa. "I'm fascinated that you knit while you interrogate."

"Really," I deadpanned. Her insincerity was blatant. Maybe, I'd put the dog brush in kitchen tool drawer. Maybe, I won't offer it to her.

"Yes. So cozy."

I smirked. "That's me, cozy as Madame Defarge."

"Who?" she asked.

Gods. "My knitting's proven an effective tool."

"Your name is Clea," she said. "And yet your nickname? Another oddity. Do you like being called Sticks?"

For reals? "Years ago, my coworkers at counterintelligence thought it apt. I knit when I interrogated then, too. They didn't find it cozy in the least. It's spelled S-t-y-x, by the way. Like the river to Hades and death and, of course, like the knitting needles so useful as tools to disconcert perpetrators when I interrogate them. But I prefer Clea."

"Ah."

Her clueless act was bullshit. And her chilly demeanor would cripple her interrogation skills. She was a bad fit for that position. So why bring her to see me? Had to be one of Bob's frickin' arcane agendas. My warm smile countered hers. "You'll see it in action come Monday."

Bob cleared his throat.

I turned to him. "What?"

"How goes life on the farm?" he asked.

"Okay, Bob, fess up. Not that I'm not glad to see you, but what's the real deal, huh? Bernadette told me you'd called."

A soft chuckle. "Can't I even make pleasant chitchat first?"

"Sorry, Old Man. Of course, you can. It's just I've got stuff to take care of."

"I'm afraid you won't be back at the Bureau on Monday."

CHAPTER THREE

Took me a sec to get it. **"What the—"**

Bernadette waltzed in with the tea tray, and I lanced her with a pissed-off glance while she served Taka and Balfour. On her way upstairs, she mouthed, *tamp it down.*

Yeah, right.

A low sound from Balfour's throat startled me. "I'm sorry, Clea. Our SAC says it's a no go."

My gut tightened. "It's a go."

He shook his head.

My fists clenched, and I burrowed them beneath my butt so Bob and Taka wouldn't see. Sure, those slivers of damaged lives had changed me. Killers, pedophiles, terrorists, torturers. But my empathy for their victims trumped all that. That I could help the innocent, the missing, and the dead meant everything to me.

How could he keep me from that interrogation room?

"You have no one better," I said.

"That's true."

"I'll talk to—"

"It won't change a thing."

I caged my emotions so I could think. I was so good, the FBI had placed me in the Special Assignments Division. All I did was interrogate. But not originally. "Okay. Put me back on the roster as a plain ol' special agent."

Big sigh. "Can't, Young Pup."

"The doc cleared me."

"The Special Agent in Charge did not."

Screw this. "I need some air."

Outside, the dooryard was empty of life, except for the chickadees swarming feeders crowned with caps of snow. I was so pissed. So frustrated.

I caught that shadow again. Those vibes. Out there, somewhere. "Hello? Who are you? What do you want?"

Silence. Utter. Absolute.

I leaned against the porch's post. A crack in his shields, slight, yet again that harmonic song touched me. Beautiful. Then bitter cold. Burning cold. I gasped.

Emptiness. Yet it was still there, his nimbus of energy.

I focused, and blew out a breath, misting the air. Caught *nothing*. The afternoon sky had brightened to a painful blue, promising a starry night, the crisp, dry kind that accompanied February's weather. Whoever, *what*ever was here, had the incomparable ability to totally mask himself from my senses.

And my anger at Bob cascaded back.

What if he handed me Dave's investigation? Given the horrific nature of the crime, he could massage it to fall into the FBI's purview. Sure. I'd work a deal with Bob and go full throttle for Dave's killer.

Back in the living room, I raised my go-mug and sipped, eyes glued to the pair on the sofa.

"So why'd you bring Special Agent Taka, Bob?"

"She'll be primary on the interrogations until your return."

Nuclear didn't describe my fury. Taka was about as empathetic as a tick. Not only did it bug me that he'd brought her, but the "why" of it was driving me batso.

"Now, Clea," he said in that placating tone of his.

"What, Bob? I'm sure Ms. Taka will do swell. Speaking of swell, I have another idea."

I filled Bob in on Dave's death, at least, the non-promised part, kept my emotions out of it, kept it light, like Dave was just a friendly neighbor, played up the murder-in-my-backyard type of thing. "So, since I'm still on leave, I thought you could put me on the Cochran homicide."

He set his coffee mug on the table with his usual precision, and his warm brown eyes softened. "I can't do that, either."

I gave him my fake smile, and he knew it, winced. But I wasn't going to explode with Taka in the room. "And why is that?"

"You know the Bureau's been tightened, leaned up. I give you that the crime sounds pretty grim, but we can't just go charging in. You are well aware it's within local and state law enforcement's purview."

I leaned back in the chair. Something was going down here. Something other than what Bob was telling me. Something hinky. I cooled it. "All right, I concede." As if I'd pay any attention to *that*.

He slapped his thighs and got to his feet. "You remain on leave, kid, until the SAC gives the go ahead."

As Taka stood, she poked her glasses straight. They tilted again almost immediately. I walked them to the mudroom door, Bob brushing the hairs off his suit. "Thanks for coming all the way out here to tell me. It's good to see you, Bob."

He put his hand on my shoulder, squeezed. "Good to see you, too. You'll be back, Young Pup. Soon."

"Thanks, Old Man. Soon."

I turned away as he reached for the doorknob.

"One more thing," he said.

A high-pitched titter startled me. Taka's. She had the faintest lift to her lips and I saw...

I shook my head.

Affection kindled Bob's eyes. "Perhaps you'll give Agent Taka some time at headquarters next week. Talk to her about your work, your interrogation skills. Help her out."

He simmered with expectation.

More fake smiling. "Of course." When hell froze over.

Dave's death ambushed me when I closed the door. I *needed* to see that Lulu was okay. I scooted out.

As I drove, I swiped at my burning eyes and made an effort to leash my reckless emotions.

Fat chance. I slammed the wheel. "Fuck! Fuck! FUCK!"

Damn Bob for not putting me back on the roster. I didn't buy that shit about the Special Agent in Charge. The doc clearing me—that was golden. Yet Bob hadn't budged. Not a weence. Unlike him. He was all about compromise. Strange. Stranger still was what I'd seen when Taka laughed. That was right up there with weird city.

I'd seen her morph. Yeah, morph. Like a three-D movie without the glasses. Into two overlapping Takas, one the bun-wearing, snarky agent, the other, a lab-coated, black-lipsticked twin. I hadn't imagined it. This had happened before. Rarely, but it was part of my empath skill set, according to Dave. He termed it a Spidey sense. The scientific term was scientific. My lips curved, salty with tears.

Okay, focus, Clea. Why today, of all days? Because that was the oddest conversation I'd ever had with Bob Balfour? Or because a subterranean thread had run beneath their words, a dissonant one that produced a corresponding dread? Or because some shadow had watched the house?

Or, as Bernadette would say, I just needed more protein?

I pressed the pedal to the metal.

The sky dimmed with night's approach as I drove toward Hembrook, to Lulu. A swish of tires on asphalt, and I passed the spot of my earlier blinding panic attack.

A dark chuckle escaped my lips, produced by an ironic sort of relief. Crazy as it sounded, that panic attack had *nothing* to do with my returning to the Bureau and *everything* to do with Dave's murder.

What I'd sensed had to be Dave reaching out to me, his terrible pain hindering his efforts.

Logic said I couldn't have saved him.

Logic lied.

I powered down the windows, needing the bite of cold to still my soul.

So many years to come, ones Dave would never experience with his daughter. With me. Wrong, so very wrong.

Dave had said I was the magic. What had he meant? His words hadn't felt allegorical, but real. Magic, eh? So where was that rabbit when I needed one?

My need to see Lulu, touch her, know she was safe burned hot.

I drove up Bergen Hill, not sparing a glance for the spectacular Mt. Cranadnock. A soft left onto Fantin Road, down the country lane narrowed by tall pines and sporadic houses, across 147. Almost there. The waxing moon lit a good-sized field and the red shed, minus its battered black pickup or Dave's Subaru, the latter probably still at the store. I parked beyond the barn, in front of the small white farmhouse, embellished with a porch and Victorian curlicues, where a giant sleeping lilac almost obscured the unshoveled front path. I walked the few yards down the road, quiet, stealthy, until I faced the side entrance tucked behind a screen of trees.

No lights glowed from inside. Nonetheless, I walked the shoveled path toward the side door, ducked beneath a hemlock's snow-laden branch, and knocked.

An anticipatory stillness said the house was empty, waiting for its inhabitants. A few more heartbeats, and I left.

I'd be back, to search, to hunt.

Hembrook was a sleepy village I voted least likely to host a homicide. Driving down its main street, I passed quaint houses and shops, cozy with lights, dusted with snow, and gleaming with historic auras from the eighteenth and nineteenth centuries. An eatery, a general store, an inn, a library.

It was like a fairyland. Or maybe, Brigadoon.

Minutes after a gossipy fact-gathering trip to the general store, I continued down Main Street. The tom-toms, swifter than the internet, had alerted everyone to Dave's death. Lulu's boyfriend, Ronan, a purportedly nice kid, lived up the street with his not-so-nice father. My bets were on Lulu being at their place.

A right fork took me onto a small road with Station on the sign, and I parked on the street, across from a white farmhouse. As I walked to the door, I took a deep breath, then poked the doorbell. I wanted her at home, *my* home, with me, where I could keep her safe.

I punched the doorbell again, then wove my fingers together. The door opened, revealing a bear of a young man, solid six feet, wearing jeans and a blue DeeVal Devils t-shirt. Blond-haired, a downy soul patch arrowed just below his lower lip. Sad hazel eyes peered at me from his mocha-colored face. His full lips moved, but no sound emerged. Eyes that battled tears peered down into mine, and he held out a hand.

"Hello. I'm Clea Reese. A close friend of—"

"Sure. I'm Ronan." He enveloped my hand in his large paw. "Um, hi."

"I was hoping Lulu was here. I'd like to speak with her."

He nodded and drew me inside.

We entered a hall, with a staircase on the right, before the boy led me into a living room on the left. Lulu sat on the couch, wearing jeans and a pink t-shirt, and stroked a fuzzy grey cat curled beside her. She stood.

Tall and willowy, she beat my five-four by at least five inches. Freckles dotted her finely boned face. Bangs and long straight hair the color of copper gleamed under the muted torchiere floor lamp.

"Hi, Clea," she said. "Thanks for coming."

She had the loveliest speaking voice I'd ever heard. Soft, melodic. Nothing like Dave's rough bass. But her eyes—they were his glorious violet. Today they were puffy and spidered with red.

"Hey," I said.

"I..."

Ronan tugged her down beside him and swiftly laid a possessive arm across her shoulders. She leaned into him.

I ached to go to her, hug her, but she was a near stranger to me. I slipped into the recliner that faced the couch and scooched forward.

"Lulu." I forced out words thick in my mouth. "I'm so sorry. So very sorry."

Lips trembling, fingers fiddling a necklace of silver stars, she stared at me and nodded.

I moved and knelt at her feet, needing her touch, hoping to give comfort. I grasped one of her hands, and my wrist throbbed.

"Oh, Lulu, what can I say? What can I do?" I bent my head to hide my tears.

A shaking hand danced over my short hair. A giggle, a sniffle. "Daddy would've hated those pink tips."

I raised my head and smiled. "Heck yeah. Why do you think I did it?"

I hugged her fiercely, a hesitation, then she hugged me back. When we finally parted, the air had cleared, at least a little. I moved back to the recliner.

"Your dad loved you like crazy," I said.

"I know. He loved you, too."

"Yes. I was lucky."

She bit her lip. "I was jealous, you know. For a long time."

I understood. "You were his world."

"I am... was."

"Forever."

"How can he be gone?"

"It seems impossible."

"I never got why Daddy didn't, y'know, bring us closer."

It would have felt nice, wonderful, to have a little sister. "Beats me. But your dad did everything with a purpose."

A quick smile. "Boy, is that ever right."

I leaned in. "You're not alone, Lulu. You'll never be alone."

She rested her head on Ronan's shoulder.

I hesitated, then, "I... your dad, I believe he wanted me to take you home. Wanted you to stay with me."

Her eyes widened. "How do you know that?" she snapped.

"I was there when he died. I found him."

"I'm not leaving Ronan," she said. "No!"

"Please. You could—"

"You heard her," Ronan said.

I winced. "If I could just—"

She squared her shoulders. "Daddy taught me to be independent. I'm going to go home and live and be the person he wanted me to be."

My chest ached. "How about you hang here for a few days? Settle. Process things." She had to stay safe. Had to. "Please."

An argument sparked in her eyes, but she nodded. "I was going to do that anyway."

"Okay. Good. We'll talk again." I got out my card and wrote my home and cell on the back. I reached to hand it to her.

"I don't need it," she said, sharp, snippy. "I have that stuff from Daddy."

I stood. She didn't look at me. I lay a hand on her cheek, red and swollen from tears. "Lulu," I said softly.

She finally met my eyes.

"If you need anything," I said. "Want anything. Night or day. I will be there. I will come."

Lulu shrugged. "Thanks, but I won't need you."

Chapter Four

My chin trembled as I walked to the truck, but I straightened my spine and did not cry. Did. Not. Cry. I got home late. Bernadette had waited supper. Absurd woman, but it warmed me.

"Tell me," she said. "All of it."

I plunged into it, every minute of my soliloquy—torture. She continued to bustle about the kitchen, her safe place, but I didn't miss the covert swipes of her hand across her eyes.

I rose to comfort her, hesitant. Yeah, that had gone real well with Lulu. But she hugged me back, quick, as was typical, and proceeded to tell me she'd made a delicious lamb stew. Wouldn't I like to try it? Not. Cauterizing her sorrow by teasing me. She was never good with grief.

Yet, naturally, Bernadette had also concocted a savory tofu casserole, so I wouldn't starve. In truth, everything she cooked tasted divine, except for the damned salad. Every single night. A salad.

I was a vegetarian, not a rabbit.

"I'm going upstairs to my room," she said after we'd eaten, in a voice roughened by sorrow.

I put a hand on her arm. "Wait, please. I need to talk to you."

She nodded. "Clean up first." And disappeared into the living room.

She was the cook, I was the bottle washer.

I was putting the final casserole dish into the machine when Bernadette shouted, "*Merde!*"

The dish didn't break when I dropped it, which I thanked the gods for as I raced into the living room. "What? *What?*"

Gun in hand—apparently she'd been oiling it—she pointed to the TV.

Scenes of devastation filled the screen. I lowered myself to the chair and leaned forward. Rain pounded off buildings canted forward, some perched over a black maw in the red-rock earth that sluiced into the chasm. Humans and animals lay on the ground, many bloodied. The cries and screams and blasts of sirens hurt my ears. The scene switched, a different camera panning spires of red rock broken, crumbled, trees flattened, boulders rolling.

"What *is* this?" I asked, my voice hushed with horrible awe.

Bernadette smoothed shaking hands across her apron. "Sedona. Arizona."

"In the town, it looked like a sinkhole, but—"

"Not a sinkhole. *Il se passe aujourd'hui.*" She snapped the remote, and the TV went blank.

"What do you mean, it's happening today?" Things were always dire when Bernadette spoke French. "What is *it*? What caused it?"

She cast me a gimlet look. "Perhaps anger at the passing of David Cochran."

"That's not funny." She'd overindulged on the Bénédictine. Again. "What happened there? Sedona. I don't understand."

"It's a thin space." She shrugged, very Gallic. "A harmonic one."

"That's what they said on the news?"

"*Non.*"

Maybe *I* needed some Bénédictine. This conversation was just adding to the crazy.

I put Sedona aside and reached for the soothing vibe of my knitting, the cashmere scarf near complete. "Dave said…" I chewed my lip. "Dave said he was a guardian."

"He was not your guardian." She slapped her hands on her lap, holstered her gun, and began to rise.

"Wait. Dave also said I was the magic."

She harrumphed. "He found you a magical person, *non*? Which is just foolish."

I rubbed my fingers against the cashmere, feeling twitchy as hell. "No. He didn't mean that. He meant it literally."

Her lids dropped to half-mast, her eyes distant. "A dying man's pronouncement."

I saw where this was going, and it wasn't to Happyland. I'd try one more gambit. "He touched my wrist, and electricity shot up my arm."

Her eyes sharpened, a hawk's on the hunt. "Spit out the rest."

"He said he unlocked it. And to acknowledge and accept. The magic. That's when he said I was magic. And he made me promise to do things."

"Such as...?"

"I can't tell you."

Everything in Bernadette tightened, and I saw her, not as she was now, but a vision of a young woman of preternatural beauty, with an aquiline nose, jet-black unibrow, long hair rippling with waves, and skin smoother than glass. Eyes deeper than eclipsed suns glowed as she stared at a bloodied short sword raised high in her right hand. I gasped.

"Clea!" She bent over me, bony hands grasping my arms, surrounding me with her scent of White Shoulders.

The vision snapped, and she again was a woman with pale, pleated skin and braids grayed by the years. "Yes."

"*Écoutez-moi*, and listen well. Forget what David Cochran asked you to do. Forget it."

A push, invisible, but firm. I remembered other times, other places, pushes from Bernadette, sensing them through the fog of blurred memory, where I bent to her will. I pushed back. This time was different. This time, I held her off.

"So," she finally said, more to herself than me. She straightened and the pressure vanished. "This is dangerous ground, cookie, and you are not ready. Cochran failed to finish, so dismiss his words, turn away from those promises, and listen to me if you wish to stay safe."

I grinned. "And when, Bernadette, have I ever wished for safety?"

She didn't spare me a glance as she walked from the room.

I ached to review my notes and photos of Dave's death. Not yet. Instead, I headed for the basement, followed by a gleeful Gracie.

"Shut the door," Bernadette barked from upstairs.

"I always do," I sing-songed back, swiping a towel from the linen closet.

Grace curled on her dog bed, while I loosened up, shaking my arms, legs, rotating my head. I began my Krav Maga defensive moves. Centered, balanced, I kicked, twisted, turned, punched. Sweat coated my sides, glazed my face. I stopped, toweled off, then toed off my sneakers and slid off my socks.

I slipped on my ballet slippers and pressed play on my iTunes Tchaikovsky mix to begin my *pliés*—first position, second, third, fourth, fifth—and stretches, *combre* forward, side, back. *Plies, tendus, releve.* A few more moves, and I balanced in *sousous*, suspended, yet grounded into the earth, connected from the turn out in my calves to my inner thighs. Did a few center splits, deep lunges stretching the psoas muscle, calf stretches, quad stretches, deep hamstring stretches, piriformis stretches. Finally the butterfly position where my feet pressed against each other sole to sole, and I bent to touch my nose to my toes. Fail! I was too impatient.

I removed my ballet slippers and tugged on my newly broken-in, shiny pointe shoes. Tightening my core, I imagined pulling up and out of my shoes. Lower abs engaged, I flew into a waltz step.

Then *precipite, pique arabesque, balance en tournant, tombe pas de bourree* to fourth, *double pirouette en de hours* landing in a generous, joyous lunge. A sequence of *fouettés en tournant*, threw my right leg toward *croisé devant en l'air*, swept it *à la seconde*, then launched into a series of *pique* turns, my favorite.

I closed my eyes. Dance, dance, dance…

"Together!" barked the voice.

I faltered, but regained my balance just as Bernadette joined me. I laughed. "You are *awful*."

She clucked. "I am."

I flopped onto the chair and tugged off my shoes, while Bernadette did the same with hers, followed by her socks and holstered gun.

"Ready?" I asked, barefoot, toes curling. Her nod had me pressing Stravinsky's *The Rite of Spring*, and we were off. I couldn't dance half, no, a quarter as well as Bernadette, who transformed into air and movement and emotion.

Thirty minutes later, Bernadette stopped, and, okay, I staggered a little. I snared her eyes, waiting, hoping for the nod.

It didn't come. "Why?"

"Your body must be stronger, more fit, a tool."

I wanted to snap, *Goddammit, I am a frickin' tool*. Which almost made me giggle.

She laid a bony hand on my shoulder, her voice quiet and dangerous. "Do you blame yourself for Dave?"

"If I'd gone earlier this morning, maybe—"

"What is, must be," she said. "When will you learn that?"

I moved to put away my gear.

"Tommy," she said.

I froze, turned back to her.

Hazel eyes drilled into mine. "If he hadn't joined the Army—"

"—following my path."

Her lips tightened at our familiar exchange. "He wouldn't have learned to fly helicopters."

I curled my hands to fists. "He wouldn't have died in the canyon."

"And that guilt, that softness in you, is your terrible weakness. *Quel est, doit être.*"

What is, must be. My breathing slowed.

"You are *not* the choreographer of everyone's lives," she said.

I plumbed the depths of those hazel eyes. "And what about their deaths?"

She sliced a hand. "Bah! Dave always moved too slowly. I say again, you are not ready."

"Ready for what the frig, B?"

Her scowl caterpillared her unibrow. "It will kill you."

"Then help me. Help me get ready, whatever that means."

She shrugged. "I've tried. I am not enough."

"Who the hell is?" Anger glazed my vision. By the time it deflated, she was gone. The woman could move like lightning or the wind, or maybe she just dematerialized.

I laughed. This was so frickin' absurd. I was living some Beckett play, waiting for gods-knew-what. I bent down and scratched behind Grace's ears. "The stories you could tell, girly."

An hour later, I was ensconced in my comfy red leather chair, having pulled on a pair of sweats and a flannel shirt. Bernadette was nowhere in sight.

I rubbed my wrist. Changed. I was changed. And Bernadette knew it.

Was she right? Was I "not ready?" Could she *be* more ambiguous?

If Tommy were still here... But he wasn't.

For all she drove me batshit, I loved that cranky old woman.

I plucked my knitting from its bag and picked up my sticks. Knit, purl, knit, purl, knit, purl. My wrist tingled. I slipped into a place out of time.

A man stands over me. He's tall and slender, wearing ripped jeans and a black turtleneck. He crouches down, so we're eye to eye.

"Have you been avoiding your schoolwork?" he says.

Nooooo. "Yes."

"How will you learn to master your talents if you don't do your work?"

I'm sad. My lips wobble. His kiss on my brow is gentle and kind.

"Why do I have to study?" I say. "I don't like it."

"We've told you over and over. You tell me."

I pout. That's what Mam and Da call it.

"Clea," he says.

"Because the magic and the mun... mun..."

"Mundane."

"Mundane worlds are mushing together again," I say.

His eyes crinkle almost closed and he laughs. "Retwining. Or replaiting."

I giggle. "Like I said, mushing. See, I can do this." I hold one hand up, palm out and...

He enfolds my hand in his larger one.

Warmth embraced me. And love. I didn't know the man, but I knew I loved him.

My chest ached.

What was happening to me? My hands shook so hard I had to stop knitting.

Forty-five minutes later, I tapped out a few desultory notes about Dave. My office computer read 9:00 p.m. I would just lay my head on the desk and rest. Lids heavy, I cradled my head on my hands. Just a few minutes. Lulu, Lulu, what to do about Lulu. I sank into a doze, deeper, deeper.

Eyes that glowed amber stared into mine, impatient eyes, intelligent eyes, waiting eyes full of age and humor and sentience.

Waiting for what? Me?

I jerked awake.

Was that magic? Was *I* magic? Absurd. So why did my gut say go with it? Okay—I definitely didn't have glowing eyes. Like a vampire's? Was I one? I almost laughed. No way. Maybe a fairy? Like Bibbidi-Bobbidi-Boo? Gods, no. A witch? A road trip to Salem might help. Not! Was this how Alice felt when she'd tumbled down that rabbit hole? Shit, was Alice real, too?

"Cookie, get to it!"

I hissed out a chuckle. Bernadette. It didn't get realer than that. No member of our household went to bed disheveled and dirty. Ever. How had she known that's exactly what I'd planned to do?

Paranoid, I snatched my gun from the closet and dragged myself up the stairs followed by a sleepy Grace. I ran the tub in the main bathroom, preferring that to the shower in mine. The full bath experience was very, very much called for.

As the tub filled, I worked some antihistamine cream across my itchy "magic" wrist, and it thankfully quieted.

We had a deep drilled well that produced enough water for the whole Sahara. My years at Fort Huachuca, the U.S. Army Intelligence Center in Arizona, gave me an abiding lust for baths, and I loved to run the water endlessly. If awake, Bernadette would chide me, but I was confident she'd traipsed off to dreamland once I started the bath.

I added a touch of eucalyptus oil and sank into wonderfulness. Water embraced me to my neck, the sound mesmerized me, and I closed my eyes.

Cheers, no amber eyes appeared.

Minutes later, Bernadette's virtual *tsk, tsk* impelled me to twist off the tap. I stood, flicked off the bathroom lights, and submerged again. The darkness soothed me. Steam rose, brushing my senses, a moist cloud of down.

I leaned back, closed my eyes, and sank deeper into the silence.

If magic is real, Dave, why didn't you tell me? Why?

Caressed by darkness and water, I sank into a meditative state. Calm. Deep. Endless.

Tap, tap, tap.

Great. Now I was reliving Poe's "The Raven."

Tap, tap, tap.

34

I blinked my eyes open. Not a raven. Just an idiot tossing pebbles against the bathroom window. Anger and anxiety fizzed my brain. I rose from the tub. And here I'd thought the day couldn't get any worse.

Without turning on the light, I dried myself, slipped on my nightshirt, and groped for my Glock. I tiptoed to the window and peered into the night.

Below stood a man. He leaned down, picked something off the ground, and tossed it up. Classy. Tall, big, the moonlight carving half his face into planes and angles, the other half shaded by a hat. I reached out sensory feelers, and failed to find his psychic signature. Dammit.

Back flat to the wall by the window, I awkwardly slid it open. A frigid wind gusted inside.

"What do you want?" I asked.

"I want to come into the house, obviously." His voice was more growl than speech.

"Who are you?"

"Special Agent James Larrimer, and I'm fucking cold."

CHAPTER FIVE

I **peered down. He peered up.**

"You're the idiot standing outside in this freezing weather. Come to the side door."

I pulled on some jeans and shoes, then sped down to the mudroom. Flicking on the outside light, I eyeballed the peephole. A billfold showed a gold badge bearing the words "Special Agent" and "US" topped with an eagle. It also held a photo ID.

It looked real. My gut said it was.

He lowered the billfold. "Well?" Still pissed.

"Who am I?" I asked, knowing he would have been briefed.

"Special Agent Clea Reese. FBI interrogator. Former CI interrogator. Farmer."

"What's my middle name?" It was in my files, but I never used it.

"Artemis. For Christ's sake, open the—"

I unlocked the door and backed away, gun aimed at his heart.

Hands raised, palms outward, a large man with unreadable shields stepped inside and kicked the door closed.

The mudroom shrank. Gods, he was a mountain, maybe six-three or four. Not like Ronan. I mean, Ronan was big. This guy was *big*. That made no sense. Gurrrr.

Was this the man from the Feed and Seed? My watcher? He felt different with those shields in place, the upper half of his face shadowed by the dim light and his battered Indiana Jones fedora.

"Chill," he said.

Mr. Laconic. "You chill, asshole."

Even shaded, I caught his expressively raised eyebrow.

I always wished I could do that. "Let me see your badge again."

He drew out a bi-fold, flipped it open one-handed. I reached for it, gun holding steady.

Department of the Interior, U.S. Fish and Wildlife Service, Special Agent. A duck and a fish stamped the center of the badge. I'd never seen one like it. To the right of the badge, his ID read James Larrimer, like he'd said. The picture sure didn't capture that "Danger, Will Robinson!" vibe.

I focused on him again. *Shit.* I hadn't even seen him draw his 9mm.

"Put that thing away," he said.

"Not yet."

"I'll do mine if you do yours." Said with acerbic dryness; the whiff of laughter lurked underneath.

Cocky bastard.

I needed to see his face, his eyes. "Take off your hat."

He nodded, complied.

I sucked in a breath. Eyes of blue Pacific waters blazed, only softened by their frame of laugh lines.

"I know you." My senses jacked up to high alert. "You were at Dave Cochran's crime scene."

"Yes."

"Watching me."

"More," he said, his tone honeyed granite and dark mystery.

Yes, *more.* That song, the harmonic resonance we'd shared—I caught not a trace coming from him now. Could he possibly be that deft at shielding? And if so, why? Or was it even real? Whatever the case, I had no intention of bringing it up and sounding like some woo-woo weirdo.

I waved my gun toward the kitchen door. "Go on in."

In the kitchen's brighter light, I caught the worn-at-the-heel boots, the crisp jeans that defined massive thighs, the beautifully knit Aran sweater. I directed him to a kitchen chair. He dropped his backpack to the floor and hung his parka on the back of the Windsor.

He slid his gun into his shoulder holster, then spread his arms,

VICKI STIEFEL

hands palms up. "See, trust." He bent down to pet Grace, who offered him her belly for rubs.

Traitorous dog. Was he early thirties? Older? Hard to tell. He sat, but I remained standing.

Even seated, an imposing man, built like a boxer, a heavyweight, but minus the fat. He leaned back in the chair, relaxed, almost smiling, but not quite. Like I amused him. Smug. I felt like punching him.

Raven hair cut raggedy several inches below his ears, tucked behind them. His face, all chiseled and tight and bronzed, but for a disfiguring crosshatch of scars on his cheekbones, and a sinuous scar that traced from his temple to the left side of his jaw. A bladed nose, squared chin. Somewhere along the line, American Indian had melded with Anglo. Not a handsome man, but an arresting one.

A sharp twinge. My electrocuted wrist ached from holding my gun. Not ready to put it down, I again focused my mind, and was finally able to sense hints of the man beneath the undoubtedly deadly exterior.

Self-possessed, confident, intense, but quiet. Oh, so quiet. Like a still lake just before the monster bursts out and eats you.

One scary dude.

"Why were you there, at the Feed and Seed?" I asked.

"Investigating."

"Why are you here now?"

He cocked his head as if I'd just uttered a non sequitur. He sat there, calm, loose, but energy simmered beneath the surface.

We'd segued into a staring contest. I was heart-bruised and exhausted and so frigging annoyed I could scream. A perfect competitor, in other words. Go me!

I leaned back against the counter. "Let me repeat, what the hell are you doing here, Mr. Fish and Wildlife?"

That's when he arched that eyebrow again. "ASAC Balfour said you'd be expecting me."

Bob? How could he? And he hadn't said a word. I hesitated, then lay my gun on the counter within easy reach. "Is that so?"

"So," he said.

He eased the chair down, stretched out his long legs, and crossed them at the ankles.

"How about I put on some coffee?" I sighed.

"Tea, if you have it."

That voice shivered through me. I'm a sucker for voices.

"Sure." I reached for the upper cabinet, got out the Earl Grey, held it up.

"Excellent," he said.

A ping inside me, of familiarity, or its illusion. But I wasn't a dumbass, didn't give him my back as I put on the water for tea, then did up Mr. Coffee for me. What I saw, what I *felt*, was a man riddled with contradictions, most of him hidden beneath strong shields. Fascinating. Bob, huh. Larrimer was so not Bob's buttoned-down type.

I reached for my iPhone that I'd left on the table at dinner. Gone. I'd swear, Bernadette spent her life tidying up.

"Who comes to a person's house at night like that?" I opened and closed drawers. Damn it, Bernadette.

"My orders were to come now."

"So why didn't you knock?" I asked.

"I did. Nobody answered."

"And the dog didn't bark? Really?"

His eyes gleamed a challenge. "You tell me." Again, he tipped the chair onto two legs. It creaked.

"You're going to break the chair," I said, all snippy. "Believe me, you don't want to tick Bernadette off." Now *that* would be something to see.

I was angry... that he'd interrupted my bath... that he'd drawn on me when I hadn't seen him... that he'd... crap, just because.

He lowered the chair. "Sorry."

He looked sincerely chagrinned, a choirboy caught stealing a smoke. Except his eyes laughed. Who *was* he?

I kept him in focus while my hand crawled around the junk drawer hunting for the phone until I felt the smooth silicone of its case. *Finally.* I speed-dialed. "Hey, Bob."

"Christ, Clea, you okay?" Sleep scratched his voice, and worry.

"I'm fine." I lowered my voice and slid onto a stool. Larrimer's eyes tracked me. "I've got a Fish and Wildlife Special Agent sitting my kitchen."

"Tarnation."

"You were supposed to tell me, correct."

He sighed. "Sorry, Young Pup, I forgot."

Bob *never* forgot. "What's up with you lately, Old Man?"

"Nothing. Never mind."

"Have you met him?" I asked.

"Yeah. Big. Black hair. Asshole."

Larrimer all right.

"One more thing, Clea," he said. "He's investigating the Cochran homicide."

"*What*?" Dave was mine. Mine. "Dammit, Bob, you know I want that case. What makes Larrimer—"

"He's a pro."

"That's obvious." Phone white-knuckled in my hand, I left the kitchen to walk deep into the living room's gloom. I lowered my voice. "The Cochran case? Fish and Wildlife?"

"I don't have details," Bob said. "Just orders." He coughed. "I've, uh, I've talked to Witzel."

"Who?"

"He's our new SAC."

Whoa—special agent in charge and head of the Boston bureau. So, there'd been a change of the guard, what do you know. "You're still the assistant?" Bob desperately wanted the SAC post. And here he'd been passed over again. Damn them. He must be devastated, but he'd never show it. He was a good man. An ache bloomed in my throat.

"Yes, I remain ASAC. Anyway, I felt bad, real bad about our conversation, so I went back to Witzel. Hell, I knew you'd investigate no matter on leave or not. The SAC approved you working in a limited capacity, as an adjunct under Larrimer on the Cochran case."

Under Larrimer! As an *adjunct*! What the hell did that mean? But still, I'd be official. My assent died on my lips. My gut, that ever-present nag, tightened like a Tupperware seal. I flopped into the red chair. Alarm bells clanged loud enough to still my knee-jerk reaction, to make me think.

Something was hinky about this offer. Very hinky.

Search for the mysteries beneath the surface, Dave always said. It felt like a set up. *Why?*

I gnawed my lip.

Gods. Working Dave's case *under* Larrimer. But what choice did I have?

Bob grunted. "If you don't want—"

"Okay, I'll do it," I said. "And you'll do your best to fast-track me off this leave crap, right?"

"Good," he said, his tone pleased. "Of course, I'll get you back on board ASAP. You're missed."

"Thanks, Old Man."

"Take care with Larrimer," he said, a bite in his voice.

He'd sounded almost jealous. "Will do."

"Now I'll excuse myself to get back to business."

As if on cue, a background titter of high-pitched laughter.

A ping of recognition, and as I disconnected, the ping solidified. Taka. That laugh was frickin' Taka's. Dear gods, was Bob doing friends with benefits?

I raked a hand through my hair. *Geesh*. Nothing for it. Now I had a man to deal with who took up way too much space in my home.

I walked back to the kitchen. "Sorry about the mix up."

"Point of fact," he said. "Balfour's an asshole, too."

He'd heard that? "Don't go there. Period." Shit. Had he heard the "under Larrimer" comment, too? One snarky comment, and he was dead meat.

All he did was nod.

I fixed his tea and my coffee and handed him his mug.

"I hear you knit when you interrogate. Interesting. Clever." His hands enveloped the mug, hands cut with those same faint crosshatched scars.

A memory jogged my brain. Larrimer. Sure. Something about him leaving the Bureau under murky circumstances and Afghanistan. "You used to be with the FBI."

"I was." He nodded. "How about you take a seat. Relax."

And that's when I realized I wasn't wearing a bra. Blood charged to my face. My boobs are ample, even if I could still pass the pencil test. I scooted into the mudroom, grabbed an old chamois shirt and slipped into it.

My brain swirled around Larrimer's FBI connection. He'd been legendary. A hunter. A man who cleaned up others' messes. Was called a shooting star. Then he'd... What? Afghanistan. Something had happened there. Maybe five years ago, before I'd joined the bureau.

When I returned to the kitchen, my face felt normal. His, on the other hand, looked impassive, except for those half-lidded eyes.

"I could have lent you my coat if you were cold," he said, voice flat, but underneath... the jerk thought I was a-laugh-a-minute.

I speared him with a look. "What was with the stupid rocks at the window?"

He frowned. "Who has all the lights off at nine-thirty?"

"New Hampshire farmers," I said.

"It's freezing out there."

"Oh? You noticed? You could have waited until tomorrow. That would have been the genteel thing to do."

He grimaced. "Actually, I couldn't."

"Sure you could."

"The Old Crows Motor Inn is full."

I saw the impending train wreck. Not happening. "Some B&B's are—"

"I tried several. Most are closed for the winter. I found one open in Shannon, but it's full, too."

"Keene."

"Too far."

I mentally gnashed my teeth, did the verbal sweetness-and-light thing. "It's not too far."

"It is for what I need to learn about Cochran's operation."

"Operation? You mean the Feed and Seed?"

"No."

I'd had it. "I am *not* a hotel."

He shook his head, an almost-smile toying with his lips. "I told Balfour you'd have none of it."

I'd kill Bob, and enjoy it. "You told... Damn him! He said you could stay here, right?"

He tugged a finger down his scar. "He did."

"There's always the barn," I said.

Those blue eyes glimmered. "Cold. Way too cold."

He was playing with me, and I was living *The Man Who Came to Dinner*, that old movie where the pain-in-the-ass guy breaks his leg and stays and stays. I chuffed out a breath. "Fine. You can take my office. There's a daybed."

"Thank you." He reached for his pack.

"Not yet. Not by a long shot."

"But it's bedtime, for you, at least."

"My ass. Dave Cochran is a friend." My heart thumped. "Was a friend."

He nodded. "I'm sorry for your loss."

Startled by his sincerity, I waited for the bada-bum. Silence. "And...?"

He leaned forward and crossed his arms, biceps bulging. "You're not going to like it."

We moved to the living room. I took the red chair and reached for my knitting. He took the couch and stretched out his legs.

I began to knit, my critters' cashmere sliding through my fingers. I just knew what was coming. He'd yammer on about how I was his *underling*, had to obey his every word. Yada yada yada.

Larrimer swiped a hand across his face, as if regretting the words to come. "Cochran was trafficking in animals, endangered ones. Importing them and selling them to the highest bidder."

My released breath became a laugh. "That's the dumbest thing I ever heard."

He retrieved his pack, extracted a MacBook Air, and tapped a few keys. "I can email you some of the evidence. Enough to convince you. Some photos of our undercover man making a deal with a Cochran lackey and taking possession of an endangered Santa Catalina Island fox."

I shook my head. "I don't care what you show me, tell me, Dave would *never* do something like that."

His face tightened. "Honestly? I don't give a shit if you believe me or not. You're my adjunct, and this is our trajectory. Remember that."

"Bite me."

He leaned forward, forearms resting on his knees. His words were clipped, his voice dark and low. "Believe this. Someone in his organization killed him. Tortured him."

My eyes lost focus, again saw Dave's bloodied corpse. "I saw."

"Clea." He infused my name with warmth. "I know you and he were close. And, again, I'm sorry."

"Forget it. Go on."

"We believe whoever killed him wanted something from him. Supply routes, money, sources. Maybe all three. Cochran's setup was as elaborate as it was well orchestrated. It was only luck we chanced on it two months ago. One of the flunkies messed up. I'd been trailing him and found him badly injured with a dead Canada lynx on his hands. While they're on the threatened, not endangered, list, it's still illegal to hunt, capture, or sell them. He didn't know the guy heading the organization, but he gave us a name, and from there..." He paused. "We followed the crumbs to your friend."

I stilled. "I'll work with you. No problem. But Dave Cochran was a good, good man. Nothing you can ever say will convince me that he did this thing. Nothing."

His eyes deepened to a murky blue. Startling and strange. "That's your choice. We will shut the organization down tight, lock the perpetrators away, keep the animals safe."

"What about Dave's killers?" My voice spat only a fraction of my fury. "What about *them*?"

"We want them, too."

Chapter Six

When my head hit the pillow, sleep plodded on leaden feet. I picked up my go-to "blankie," a ratty copy of *The Fellowship of the Ring*, and started to read. My lids finally grew heavy when Merry and Pippin were trapped by Old Man Willow in Tom Bombadil's wood.

I put the book aside and turned out the light.

The helicopter smells of leather and tobacco... excitement!... fear. I don't want to do this! But, I do. I do.

Glass curves in front of me and beneath my feet, and as the impossibly small machine rises, Tommy's copter, the one in front of ours, lifts up, too.

Dust whirls and soon the tips of conifers slide below us. And then, the canyon. Ohmygod, it's beautiful. The earth vanishes, the canyon's maw sucks us in. We dip! I clutch my thighs, sweat coats my body.

His copter drops, too.

In my mind, Tommy laughs, calls me a scaredy-cat.

Our copters rise, and with the thud-thud-thudding of blades, we stream along the canyon, a river of glorious blue gliding below.

Beautiful. So beautiful.

But, wait...

I lean forward, seatbelt tugging. Are the blades of Tommy's copter slowing?

Slowing and slowing...

His copter tilts left, right... a drunken sailor just before...

I lift my right hand, palm out, trying, trying...

The tail flies up, nose plunging down and down.
A jagged boulder... reaches up... stabs the fragile metal.
Shards of silver exploding...
I scream.

"Hey! Hey!"

"Tommy!"

"It's Larrimer, and you were screaming your brains out."

My fingers pressed against closed lids, expecting the greasy feel of blood. Except hands banded my upper arms. Large. Calloused. Alive.

Not Tommy's. Sticky tears pulled at my eyes as I blinked them open. I stared down at the quilt, waving a hand at the stranger holding me. "I'm fine. Let go."

An exhale. "You want some coffee?"

"Yes, no, I'll make it." I pushed to a sitting position.

"Already made. I'm going out. I'll be gone all day."

The door groaned, then clicked closed. He'd slipped from the room on silent feet. Woozy as always after Tommy's Dream, I pinched the bridge of my nose. My heart squeezed.

The down comforter landed on the floor when I left the warmth of my bed. Cold pine boards slapped me further awake. I tugged on my cargo pants, pulled a sweater over my tank, slid on the socks I'd finished knitting last week for Bernadette, ones she'd rejected as too hot.

The dream was the same as always. I paused. No, something was different. I'd held up my right hand, palm out. Tonight was the first time I'd ever recalled that. I'd done it right before Tommy crashed. Just like in the memory with the kind man. I'd been trying to *do* something. What?

The sky still dark, I made my way to the barn. We'd had an overnight dusting of snow, and it flew every which way as I did my chores.

Sorrow draped my shoulders, a sodden shroud. But the chores helped. There was order and peace to the routine of the farm. I loved the snuffles of the beasts, their sighs and chatters, the smells, too, of heat and mulch and fecundity.

Tommy knew that, knew how I loved the place and its animals. Maybe that sense of life was why he'd gifted me his half of the farm.

Or maybe it was to needle me with the responsibility of his grandmother. I smiled. Yeah, that would be typical Tommy.

I might have grown up here, but I had never been a part of it. Now it was a part of me.

Time for the tiny violin? Dave would say.

Hell no, I'd answer.

Young ladies don't swear, he'd reply.

This one does, I'd say.

We'd both grin.

Goddammit. Goddammit!

This time yesterday, Dave was alive.

Chores complete, I worked in my office gathering the elements of the case. If I was to be an adjunct, I'd be a damned fine one. So who wanted Dave Cochran dead? I Googled, and found stuff on Dave and Lulu on the Web. Not a single thing related to magic or murder, and zero on Dave's wife. Curious. Like she'd been erased.

I called a friend at the state lab. With Dave's prints and DNA, a pal at the Bureau could run them through the law enforcement databases.

"Marcia," I said when the lab's assistant administrator answered.

Chitchat, then I gave her Dave's name.

"No got 'em," Marcia said.

"How's that possible? I understand his DNA might not be back, but his prints—"

"I'll look into it. Promise."

As we clicked off, a mosquito of unease buzzed me.

I grabbed an early lunch at the computer, and while I ate, reviewed yesterday's notes and photos and made two piles, one related to... can't believe I'm thinking it with a straight face!... magic and the other, to practical.

Dave: "I'm your guardian. *A Guardian.*"

No, he wasn't my guardian. But "A Guardian?" I added it to the "magic" pile.

He'd held back death until I arrived. Could I have saved him if I'd gotten there earlier, driven faster?

Stop!

Dave: "Shield Lulu. Protect you."

So whoever had killed Dave would threaten Lulu and me, too. Craptastic. A major practical pile.

Dave: "Take the chest."

No clue, so I tossed it into the "magic" pile. Why not? *Oh Dave, you never said a word about things of power and guardians and magic.* You were never a woo-woo guy. *Just what gives?*

Dave: "The Storybook. Find. Green cover you bit. Take it. Read."

I'd bitten the cover. Yeah, I was a biter for a while there. Into the "practical" pile it went.

Dave: "Spell."

I knew what pile that puppy was going in.

Quick check of my phone. Nope, couldn't call Marcia back yet.

Dave had no arterial bleeding, so I Googled Death by a Thousand Cuts. Huh. Slicing chunks of flesh off? That was so not what had happened to Dave. I enlarged his cuts. It was like his skin had ruptured from inside out.

Here goes—I Googled "magic." I didn't need to look up The Tarot, divination, necromancy, or dowsing. I knew stuff about them. Sympathetic magic used an imitation of the environment or person being magicked. So you'd do the magic on the doll, and it would affect the real person. Creepy. Contagious magic, on the other hand, was when the magician used a person's hair or clothing or fingernails as a conduit. Even creepier.

The definition for psychic felt eerily familiar—perceives things, information hidden from the regular five senses. Gods, I didn't want to be a psychic. I'd have to get a storefront. A neon sign. A crystal ball!

Okay, so I sensed things, felt things from other humans beyond the normal ken. Animals, too. Objects? Not so much.

At lightning speed, I was getting nowhere.

I snapped my computer windows closed and paced, reached for my phone to call the lab again, except it chimed.

Lulu. "Hey, hon," I said.

A voice muffled by tears, stuttering sobs.

"Lulu, what's wrong?"

"They... they won't let me have Daddy's body." More sobs.

"Ssshh. I'm here. Please explain."

Gasps of breath, then, "I called Mr. Shatzkin. He's the funeral guy. To find out when we could, you know, plan."

"Okay."

"He... said they didn't know when... that... that..." She broke down.

"How about I call one of the medical examiners? She'll be able to tell me approximately when your dad's body will be released. How does that sound?"

"Oh." A sniffle. Another. "Oh, all right. That would be good."

"I'll get back to you as soon as I know. Would you like to come here maybe and—"

"Ronan's here. I'm fine."

Sigh. She sure didn't sound it.

As soon as we clicked off, I called Sue Parker, deeply pleased Lulu had turned to me.

I waited through handoffs, aware that it was early days—they had to perform Dave's autopsy, troll for clues, and determine the manner of death. But Sue could guesstimate the release date. When she picked up, I explained the problem. And met with silence. "Sue?"

"He was a friend?" she asked.

Warning bells. "Yes," I said with caution. "A close one. What's up?"

"You always could read my pauses." Her chuckle was bitter.

"What's going on, Sue?"

"Nothing I can talk about."

"Hey, you've always been straight with me. I've got a girl here who's frantic to bury her dad, a man who was horrifically murdered."

"I know. I saw him before..." Another pause.

"Before what?"

She sighed. "You still good at keeping stuff to yourself?"

"As always. What's the deal?"

"The remains are gone. They—"

"What do you mean 'gone'?"

"Two medical examiners showed up this morning. Yards of paperwork to shore them up, and off the body went."

I needed to ask the right questions, unsure of what they were. "What agency?"

I could almost hear her shrug. "No idea. No one knows, except the chief. He okay'd it. And if you say a word to anyone, ask the chief anything, I'm toast."

"How about ASAC Balfour? Can I talk to him?"

"I don't know—"

"I won't. I'll keep you out of it. Safe. What about Dave's prints? DNA? The ME's report."

She snorted, sounding pissed as hell. "They cleaned house."

Having reassured Lulu that we'd get her father's remains back for burial—how, I hadn't figured out yet—I itched for action.

Fine. I'd search Dave's home for "the chest" and the Storybook. Bernadette was out, as was our unwanted guest. I couldn't wait to see my foster mother's reaction to him. Whooeee.

I changed into my black cargo pants, a black turtleneck, and my shitkickers, then armed up with my gun, a couple throwing knives, and reached for my small Bowie.

Tires varoomed on our driveway. *Crap.* I slid the Bowie into its boot sheath, then accompanied a howling Grace to the mudroom door.

With much revving and smoke, a Mercedes finally floundered its way into the dooryard and came to a halt. The door opened.

Now what?

Forty-five minutes later, I sat at the kitchen table, still punch-drunk, the Mercedes taillights disappearing down the drive. Guardian. I was Lulu's legal guardian. I'd also signed the paperwork that made me the executor of her $12 *million* estate, and the inheritor of $3 *million*, all courtesy of Dave's last will and testament.

Still reeling from the profound trust Dave had placed in my shaking hands, I called Lulu on her cell, said that I'd be over in a bit, that we needed to talk. The unaccustomed weight of Dave's bequests scared the shit out of me.

Snap out of it!

Ah, that line from *Moonstruck*... Wasn't helping.

I could do this. *I could do this.*

Coffee.

I glanced at the coffee pot, except a massive golden bird, head tilted, eyed me with impatience.

What the *hell*!

With deliberate care, I drew my gun from its holster.

It stared at me with narrowed gold eyes, glowing ones. Mesmerizing, like the ticking of a clock before a bomb goes off.

Tick tock, get going. Tick tock, get your ass in gear. Tick tock, hurry.

I scrambled out of the chair. Blink. Gone.

Of course there was no frickin' bird.

I zoomed for Ronan Miloszewski's. And had a fender bender on Glade Street in Midborough.

The car came out of nowhere. Well, actually, the street by Glorious Chocolates. Plowed right into Fern's ass. Temptation said to just keep going, but too many years in law enforcement made that impossible.

After a not-so-speedy exchange of info, not to mention a broken taillight, I drove on, thankful today's predicted snowstorm had passed us by. By the time I pulled onto Ronan's street, it was mid-morning, the air a damp chill that carried the fragrance of woodsmoke.

Ants in my pants, I rang the bell. Three times. A physically small man, bowlegged, with a weathered face and gray-stubbled chin answered the door. Ronan's dad, I presumed.

"I'm here to see Lulu."

Although he tipped his John Deere cap at me, eyes the color of blackberries scrutinized me with suspicion. He smelled of English Leather, of all things, and with obvious reluctance, waved me inside.

He scraped a hand across his stubble. "Not here."

Well hell, he could've told me that outside. Unease hammered me. "Oh." I feigned a composure I wasn't feeling. "Did she and Ronan go somewhere?"

"Boy's in school, where he should be. That Lulu girl left."

The hum became a shriek. I dug for casual. "Any idea where she went?"

He crossed his arms and shoved his hands under his armpits. "I don't keep tabs on the girl."

You should, you prick. I didn't say it, but instead raced to my car.

I kept it at thirty through town, then sped up Evergreen toward Lulu's home. She had to be there. She just had to.

She was fine. Of course she was fine. So why did I feel I was in the race of my life?

I screeched to a halt before the red shed, forcing calm through my veins. She was probably here, getting some things. A wild woman tear-assing around would scare the hell out of her.

White and black chickens clucked in the yard as I walked the path to the side door. And paused. A jumble of footprints churned up the snow, two pair—I walked closer—large, men's, smooth-soled—they'd slogged around from the front door through the unshoveled path. Most locals used their side doors and wore shoes with traction in winter.

Whoever had been here was from away.

I stood in the shade of the snow-laden hemlock and listened. The place was quiet. The wooden screen flapped in the breeze, every so often slapping the frame. An unwelcoming sound.

With my leather jacket unzipped, cold slithered up my chest. But I had easy access to my shoulder holster.

The air felt thick, ominous.

The senses I'd expanded outward prickled me with goosebumps. Violence had happened in this house.

Gun in hand, I used the corner of my jacket to turn the knob and pressed open the unlocked door. Emptiness, yes, coupled with that same sinister prickle.

"Lulu?"

The hall was trashed. Drops of what could be blood dappled the floor. Throat dry, I padded to the living room. Frigid air swirled through the room, now a chaos of books and cushions and a splintered flat screen. An explosion of some sort had left a jagged hole where a window had been. I took a step closer. My wrist throbbed.

I quickly cleared the rest of the house. All trashed.

Where was Lulu?

The barn? Empty. Maybe the red shed. Someone had returned Dave's old Subaru, but his black truck was MIA.

Where had Lulu driven? Not to Ronan's. The Feed and Seed. I holstered my gun, then reached for Fern's door. A UPS truck pulled up behind the Tahoe. Crap.

"Hey, Clea!" the driver said.

"Hey, Todd. I didn't realize you delivered here."

He shook his head. "Sometimes. The regular driver's sick today. So, this package. Think I should leave it? You know, with Dave and all."

"I'll take it. I'm meeting Lulu later."

He disappeared into the back of the truck, then handed me an eight-by-ten padded envelope. "You doing good? Car trouble?"

I smiled. "No. Just stopped to see the chickens." I turned toward my truck. I had to get out of there.

"They're different than yours. What kind?"

"They're Jersey Giants. Pretty cool. Mine are Rhode Island Reds. Sorry, have to run! I'll make sure Lulu gets her package."

He winked, put the truck in gear, and drove off.

I hightailed it to the Feed and Seed.

CHAPTER SEVEN

Ten minutes later, which felt like fifty, I peeled into the parking lot.

In the daylight, grasses and brown cattails poked from the frozen marsh. A lone Canada goose honked overheard. The lot was empty, the "Closed" sign still in place, but today, two noses pressed against the glass.

Dave's twin mutts, part Brittany, part mystery, observed me. I relaxed a fraction and drove around to the rear of the store. Dave's old Dodge pickup sat to the right of the back bay doors. I parked beside it, wishing Dave hadn't put off installing a smaller entry door.

Back out front, both mutts stared back at me, ears flat, wary, where they normally barked with exuberance.

I peered inside, saw no one, tried the door. Locked. I withdrew my gun, unlocked the door, and stepped inside. Deja vu.

I pulled a handful of treats from my pocket, and when the pups inhaled them, their normalcy reassured me. A calico kitten wove between my legs. A shimmer. A ping of memory. Gone.

Rows of pet food and toys and collars filled the barn-sized room. I sampled the air. Strong bites of fear, with hints of anger and anticipation. I let the quiet settle, then, "Hello! Lulu?"

She didn't answer. But some human was watching me. I crouched behind a row of Eukanuba bags. It didn't help that Mutt and Jeff were nuzzling me, tails wagging and tongues lolling.

"Anybody here?" I listened.

"I've got a gun," screeched the high-pitched voice. "So don't move. I'm gonna shoot you and... well, shoot."

I dove behind an aisle of chew toys. Craptastic. Lulu'd been scared enough to wave a gun around. At least, she sounded okay.

She was somewhere behind the counter, so I stayed low and listened. Nothing.

Here goes.

"Lulu, it's Clea," I shouted. "Put down the gun."

"Really?" squeaked the voice. "How do I know it's *really* you?"

Groan. "I'm going to stand up, where you can see me. I'd rather you didn't shoot my head off."

No answer. I slowly straightened, hands raised, Glock in my left. "See? I've got the safety on." Glocks don't have an external safety, but she didn't know that.

"You're not going to kill me?" came the disembodied voice.

"I wasn't planning on it. And I fervently hope you won't kill me."

"Oh... okay. I'm not in trouble, am I?"

I ran a hand through my hair. "Not yet. But you're working your way there. C'mon, Lulu, it's me."

Lulu bobbed up from behind the counter, eyes bright as amethysts, hair a blaze of copper, wearing a baggy black NYU sweatshirt. An immense gun quivered in her outstretched hands.

"Lulu," I said.

She dropped the gun on the counter, and I was thrilled the damned thing didn't fire.

"It is you!" she said. "Daddy's gun's heavy."

I squeezed my eyes tight, opened them, tried to smile. I holstered the Glock, walked to Lulu, pups faithfully trailing after me.

"Don't be afraid." I walked over to the counter and picked up the giant .357 Magnum revolver. "This thing is dangerous." Once I emptied it of bullets, I finally relaxed.

I took her hand. "I've been worried sick, sweetie. We had an appointment, and you weren't at Ronan's. I saw the house. What happened?"

"I'm sorry. It's been really bad. I'm really sorry. Really. I..." A spike of fear. Lulu rested her head in her hands.

The calico kitten jumped on the counter and began cleaning itself. "Sshhh." I ran my fingers across the back of her hand. "It's okay now." The girl raised her face. No tears, just moist eyes. "No, it's not."

In the store's back office, I took in the cranked wood stove, the rumpled bed and pile of clothes, the end table's box of tampons and blush case.

She'd moved here. Damn.

I started to speak, but her eyes pinballed with terror. "Be right back." When I returned with my knitting from the truck, she was seated in a threadbare wing chair. I took its twin and began to knit. She smiled and out came her own knitting, a green-and-red object.

"It was for Christmas," she said. "For Daddy. A scarf. Except I didn't finish. I'm not very good."

"Looks great to me." I smiled. "It's the process."

We fell into a rhythm. Back and forth. Click-click, click-click, click-click. Her neck muscles relaxed, and she eased deeper into the chair. "Why the gun, Lulu?" When she finally made eye contact, her gaze crackled with fear and anger. I held it, and she quieted.

"I won't let anyone hurt you," I said. "You'll stay with me."

She shrugged, a lock of red hair sliding across her face. Big breath, then, "I went home. Well, see, Ronan's dad said he had to go to school today. He's a senior. And I didn't want to stay there alone... with *him*."

"Good call," I said.

"I took Mutt and Jeff and... It felt so weird, being at home knowing Daddy..." She shrugged. "I expected home to look different. But it didn't. I did some stuff. I don't know. Then I went into the living room and sat on the couch." She smiled.

Gods, it was a sad smile.

"I tried to read, *The Fault in Our Stars,* but I fell asleep."

"You must be exhausted." I rested a hand on her knee.

"Yeah. I don't know when, but Mutt and Jeff crawled around me on the couch. They always do that." An idle hand reached down to pet the closest mutt.

I smiled, and knit. Here it comes.

"I woke up when they moved. Someone was in the house. Mutt and Jeff's fur, right on the backs of their necks, stood up straight. That's how I knew it was bad. We have a secret place."

"Okay."

She fingered her star necklace. "I wanted to see who was there, but Daddy said not to do that, even if I wanted to really bad. So I opened the window nice and quiet. I took the wand, too."

"The wand?"

She grinned. "That's what he called it. It's got a button. Mutt and Jeff knew the drill. They leapt out first, and just as I was almost out, two men in long black coats came into the living room. They had guns. And they shot at me!"

"What! Are you hurt? Were you hit?"

"Nope. The bullets just stopped. It was awesome."

O-kay. She was fine. That's all that mattered.

"I jumped out the window and pushed the button! The window exploded, just like Daddy had shown me on our practice runs. All red and blue and yellow sparks! Way cool. Daddy called it our secret spell."

A spell. My reality was warping like wood in water.

"I ran to the barn. We scrambled down the hatch in the floor, and I clicked the lock. Daddy promised no one could break that lock. I was to stay there until I was sure I was safe." She nodded. "And I did."

"You did so good," I said. "Wonderful."

She straightened, shoulders back, proud. "I heard them. Well, one of them, anyway. He came into the barn. It sounded like he was limping. I liked that, that he'd been hurt. He was looking around. I could hear him! But he didn't find the hatch. And I waited a long time after I couldn't hear him anymore."

"Good for you. Patience pays off."

She bobbed a nod. "Yeah. But it's hard. We have food and water down there, and food for Mutt and Jeff and books, too. So I read and read. And then, I came here."

I took her hand in mine, sent waves of love and care to her, hoping she'd feel them.

"I wanted to go to Ronan's," she said. "But *he's* there. He's creepy. And mean."

Ronan's father. But she hadn't come to me, either. I banished the sting. She was a kid. She hardly knew me. I'd have to earn her trust, not expect it as a gift.

"I'm here now," I said. "And I know how to use my gun."

Her lips burst with a grin. "You're a badass."

Laughter bubbled out. I might not be a badass, but I'd be good enough.

"Tell me, Lulu, did your dad ever talk about things of power or guardians or magic?"

Eyes wide, she dipped her chin, bit her lip. "No."

A lick, a touch. I stood. I squeezed her hand and released it. Someone was here, outside. A "someone" with a nasty psychic scent.

"Get in the bathroom," I said, wishing there was an exploding window here for Lulu's escape. I gripped my gun in my left hand. "Take the mutts and call 9-1-1."

"But—"

"Do it." A command.

Lulu and the dogs scuttled into the bathroom, and I closed the office door behind them. I swept Lulu's Magnum and bullets under the counter and waited. No time to load the revolver.

A man limped toward me across the central aisle. He wore a ballcap, but as he neared, it failed to hide the cuts on his face and hands, one of which was wrapped in white gauze. Whatever Dave had rigged had done a damned fine job.

He approached the counter. Florid complexion, beefy hands, and I'd bet a shotgun caused that bulk under his coat. A boil of anger and belligerence. I could use that. Nice.

I coated my fear with a smile of welcome, my left arm at my side, gun aimed right at the bastard's thighs. The counter was thin enough for the bullet to pierce his flesh. I hoped.

I forced my face to keep the smile, too aware of never having fired a gun in live combat. Lulu called me a badass. Time to prove it.

He reached the counter. "Greetings."

"Can I help you?"

He smiled. Bad teeth. "Nice place."

"It is."

He reached into his breast pocket, and I tensed. He drew out a photo. Lulu.

"I'm looking for a girl. This girl. Her pop died couple days ago. I was a friend of his."

I tilted my head. "It's kind of you to call, but she's not here." A trickle of sweat down my spine.

"You know where she's at?"

I shook my head. "I don't. Sorry. She's pretty broken up about her dad."

He gave a jerky nod. "Bet she is. I'll try again. Hey, thanks, ma'am."

"Sure. Maybe I can help you with some pet supplies?"

He shook his head. "Nope. Don't have any." He turned to walk away.

Nothing was that smooth. A ping of violence. I flattened to the concrete, just as he whirled on me, shotgun glinting.

"Fuck," he said. "Can't we do this easy?"

I held my silence and listened, nerves sizzling, slowed my stuttering breath. I centered my mind, and the world sharpened. I began to carve out a knot in the wood with my Bowie.

"I just want the girl. I don't even want to hurt her. Just talk. I won't hurt you, either."

And Christmas came in July.

I pried and poked at the knot. "I told you, she's not here."

"Saw the truck, ma'am."

"She's *not* here."

"Look, lady, you got two days before the shit hits. Two fucking days before—"

"What happens then?" I'd added some whine to my voice.

Silence. Guess he wasn't going to tell me.

He was out there. A killer in a swirly coat.

He would kill me, Lulu, the animals, too.

I wished I knew why.

My knife broke through, and I pried out the knot, peered out the hole. A squeak of leather. There. A foot. Maybe two yards away. Could I hit it? I visualized all the targets I'd bullseyed in practice. Hell, yeah. Sure. Maybe.

Then the blast of the shotgun, a pump, another blast. The counter held.

I moved into a crouch, peered out the hole, aimed for the foot, squeezed off a shot. I hurtled from the counter just before another spray of shot splintered the boards.

I rolled toward the metal shelves. One, two... I bounced up, blasted five rounds. A bark of pain. *Yes!*

His shotgun splintered the silence as I jumped. Pain bit my arm. I hissed, slid around another row of shelves.

Shit, shit, shit. My arm was on fire.

Adrenaline mixed with fear into one hell of a cocktail.

Silence. Then a moist wheezing. A curse.

He might not be down, but he was hurt worse than me.

Now was when I'd get him. I pulled shreds of courage close, positioned my feet beneath my thighs, and pushed hard up and out, gun pointing, spraying the store in a 180° motion.

The front door flew open. I'd missed. Hell.

I raced after him, he swiveled back, and I flattened in time to avoid his shotgun blast. I rolled, sprang up again, fired as he hopped toward a BMW parked out front.

I ran forward. The kitten! At my feet, in the line of fire. I scooped her up as I dove to my left.

A blast of his gun barrel, glass shattering.

Gods!

I landed hard. A display of dog biscuits collapsed around me. I rolled off the pile onto my belly, shooting again and again and again.

Pebbles peppered what was left of the window as the guy peeled out of the lot. The car wove, straightened, then was gone.

The kitten. Where was the calico? Gone, no blood, safe.

Ohboy, ohboy. Chest heaving, like I'd gone ten rounds with Ali. I sat up, hand against my wound, frustration melting my bones. With great care, I lay down my gun. Held onto it, though. I gasped. *Just a reaction. Everything's fine. Yup. Just peachy.* I laughed. I hadn't even gotten his license plate.

CHAPTER EIGHT

Lulu!" I shouted, my voice bubbling with panic. "Are you okay?"

"I think so!" the girl hollered back. "Wow, that was *awesome!*"

It was frigging scary. "I told you to keep the door closed!"

To hide my shakes, I leaned casually against the counter. My arm throbbed. A flesh wound. I'd deal. But the rip in the leather. Dammit it, I loved that jacket.

She stood framed by the office door. "I did... mostly. How did you do that?"

"Practice." I pumped my voice with strength. I honestly had no idea. Scariest thing ever.

"Are you all right?"

No, no I wasn't. As I'd reached for the kitten, I'd seen instead a huge golden bird, like the one I'd imagined in the kitchen.

What the hell was wrong with me?

The hurly-burly of cops and forensics hadn't been as bad as when I'd found Dave. The police assured me they'd keep an eye on the store and Lulu's home.

When we arrived at Sparrow Farm, Bernadette fussed over Lulu and tended my wound with her usual efficiency. She wasn't gentle, but the former nurse was sure thorough.

Mr. Fish and Wildlife hadn't returned, and I was thankful for small favors.

After I settled a somber Lulu, the two dogs, and the kitten, which was just a kitten, in the spare room beside Bernadette's, the three of us sat down for one of my foster mother's overabundant meals. Cornbread, steak, veggie burgers, green beans, acorn squash, garlic potatoes, and three kinds of desserts. Enough calories to kill a rhino.

"I don't like green beans." Lulu's lips quivered with nerves, while violet eyes sparked with petulance.

"Eat half, please," I said and softened it with a smile.

"No."

I didn't have the energy for that battle, given the larger battle to come, when I told Lulu I was her legal guardian.

After dinner, she plucked at a sofa cushion, not making eye contact, while Mutt and Jeff curled at her feet. Grace crawled onto the sofa, and Lulu giggled, a watery sound.

I sat across from her. My twenty-eight years felt like dandelion fluff, wispy and inadequate.

"What?" she asked, voice breathy.

"Um…" Wasn't I full of witticisms? My stomach churned. What if she refused to live here? Or ran off and married Ronan? What if she said I sucked, or that she hated me?

"What's wrong," she said, face so tight, her freckles stood out like constellations.

"Nothing, sweetie." I squeezed her hand. "You're wonderful. Perfect."

"No, I'm not." She bowed her back and crossed her arms over her chest, as if embarrassed by her small breasts.

Well, that told me volumes. "I just need to tell you something, and I'm scared."

Her head jerked up. "Scared? You're a badass."

I shook my head. "Here goes. Your dad made me your legal guardian."

She wrinkled her forehead, as if processing lousy news.

"I'm, um, sorry it wasn't someone else, but—"

"No. No, I think it's cool."

"Cool?"

"Yeah." She grinned. "Well, I'm almost sixteen, and I really don't *need* a guardian or anything. But I guess, if I have to have one, you won't be so bad. You'll let me do lots more than Daddy!"

"No way I—"

"Psych!" She kissed my cheek and bounded upstairs. I wiggled my fingers a goodnight and released the breath I'd been holding for hours.

Since Larrimer was still out, I typed up today's events, complete with expletives, onto my office computer. Exhausted, I forced myself to do it now, or they'd be confetti on the wind. I sent a copy to Bob, like the good little adjunct I was.

After I bathed and cleaned the tub—Bernadette was killer about that stuff—my arm was on fire. I went hunting and found Larrimer bent over the fridge, trolling.

What a gorgeous ass. "Geesh, you're snoopy," I said.

He closed the fridge and pivoted. Even with jeans slung low on his hips and a rumpled white tee, he looked ready for battle. Then his lips softened, and I caught the exhaustion bracketing them.

"Long day?"

He nodded. "By the time I finished up, everything was closed. I need food."

I waved a hand at the fridge. "Plenty of leftovers. Feel free."

"Veggie burgers? Green beans? Tofu? I need meat."

I shrugged. "Sorry, steak's all gone."

"Steak," he said with longing. "Heard you had an interesting day."

"News sure travels fast."

"That it does." He spread his hands. "And...?"

I was dying to tell him, except at the same time I was getting "Danger, Will Robinson!" warnings. Geesh. I was turning into Sybil.

The snapping of his fingers ruptured my reverie. "Oh, right. So I went to meet Lulu." Yup, I spewed.

He snagged me with those Pacific blues. "You don't look... right."

"I'm right as rain." I set my jaw. Yeah, my arm hurt, but I was fine. Well, sort of fine. Since the shootout, I'd danced around my feelings, a boxer too scared to take the first punch.

I *interrogated* people. I understood the twitch of an eyebrow, the tap of a finger, the ooze of pain. I'd trained in the Army and at Quantico, studied Krav Maga. Knives. Guns. I'd even once fired a bazooka.

But before today, I'd never shot a living thing.

He tilted up my chin, forcing me to make eye contact. "That first gun battle with it all on the line, knowing death might be a kiss away? A truth better left unknown."

I steeled myself. "The guy I shot said it would be two days before the shit hit."

His eyes narrowed, and he punched his hands into his pockets. "What shit?"

I gave him that cocky grin that drove Bernadette nuts. "We never got that far. Verbally, that is. But I'm good to go."

His lips quirked. "I just bet you are." He paused, and thankfully I didn't rise to that bait.

"They went after the girl," he continued. "Did she tell you anything? Give you any hints?"

I shook my head.

"So what does she know about her father's operation?"

"There wasn't any 'operation' like you mean. And if it's anything, Lulu doesn't know that she knows. Dave would never involve her in something dangerous."

"You admit he had something illegal going."

"Of course he didn't. How about I fix you a ham-salad sandwich?"

His near-silent chuckle said we weren't done with our tête-à-tête. "Sure. That would be great."

"Sit." He sprawled at the table while I built his sandwich, then handed him a plate and a bottle of lager.

He bit down on my creation, and his features stiffened. He swallowed. Hard.

"What's wrong?" I asked.

"Worcestershire sauce with ham?"

"Sure. I love it."

He frowned. "Worcestershire sauce has anchovies in it." Nostrils flared, I'd swear he exhaled smoke, just like a dragon.

"So?"

Then, he blew out a breath and said, "Thank you for making this."

"My pleasure."

Eyes steeled with determination, he took another bite.

My cell bleeped, and I left an unhappy Larrimer to his ham salad, while I snatched up my phone in the living room.

"Bob?"

"Hey, Young Pup, are you okay?"

"Apparently that's tonight's topic, and, yes, I'm fine. I emailed you about the incident. Didn't you get it?"

"I did. Word has it you're looking for something."

"Whose word?" Shit, he couldn't know about the Storybook and chest.

"A missing body."

"Um. How did you—"

"No need to prevaricate. I talked to Sue Parker at the New Hampshire medical examiner's office. I'm cleared for convo."

My pressure-cooker tightness eased. "Oh, well, good. So where is Dave's body?"

He snorted. "Can't you guess?"

Why would no one ever give me a straight answer? "Stop with the games, huh? Just spill."

A feminine voice said, "Quack, quack, quack" and then Bob's, "Dammit, Taka," and he disconnected.

I tossed the phone down on the table, livid. That dragon who stole the body sat smack in the middle of the room. Its name was Larrimer, with a frickin' flying duck on its badge. Quack. Quack. Quack.

I stormed back into the kitchen. The empty kitchen. When I peered down the hall toward my office, all was dark. Larrimer had gotten out of there fast.

I wagged my finger. "Just wait until tomorrow, dude. Just wait."

Except I awakened in the morning, a silent scream on my lips.

The hand I raked through my hair shook. I'd had Tommy's Dream again. The copter tilting, plunging, me raising my right hand, the jagged boulder, the fragile metal. The explosion.

I reach for him, and...

The bite from my wounded arm dragged me back to the now.

He'd been gone so long. His smell, his laugh, his scowl. The texture of his hair. The bristle of his beard. The warmth. A best friend's love. Yet now, after four-plus years, time had stolen the innate sense of *him* that once was a part of me.

If I was magic, shouldn't I have been able to save him?

4:00 a.m. was still too early for my barn chores, but I wouldn't fall back to sleep, not after The Dream.

I opened *The Fellowship of the Ring* and was transported until my phone's alarm told me it was time to care for my critters. I pushed back the covers and sat up. Chill air feathered my skin, waking me further. Through the window's sheer curtains, night still blanketed the farm. 5:30 a.m. was *not* when I loved farming. I crawled out of bed, toes scrunching on the cool floorboards. I retrieved the clothes I'd strewn across the floor, crept out of my room, and down the stairs, where Larrimer sat curled over his computer, brow furrowed, pounding keys.

Grace trotted over to me, her exuberant barks destroying any hope of stealth.

He looked up. No acknowledgement. Nothing. The machine's glow sculpted his face like a mask.

He looked otherworldly, possessed of an essence I didn't understand. I itched to ask what he *was*.

He resumed his tapping.

A quiver inside me, a string that pulled me toward Larrimer.

I shook myself. Tommy's Dream always rattled my senses.

"We need to talk." About Dave's body and that the facts about Dave were only part of the story.

"Fine. Twenty minutes."

Could he *be* any more terse? "Sure." See, I could be terse, too. Gods, I was reacting like a teenager.

I bent and scratched Gracie's chin. "Where were you last night?"

"With me," he said in that sorcerer's voice, part stone, part honey. No innuendo, just alluring as hell.

I gave Grace the long stare. *Traitorous pup.*

In the kitchen, tongue aching for coffee, I lifted the pot. Damn. Last night, I'd polished it off. I'd wait.

Grace at my heels, I tugged on my mitts, coat, and boots and opened the mudroom door to the proverbial winter wonderland. I pulled the snow shovel from its wall clip and dug a path to the barn.

Dave, where are you?

My chickens out in the pasture spotted me and in a cacophony of clucks, they rushed to their barn stall. Pandemonium from the rest of my beasts.

"Hi, girls." I grained up the chickens, tossed their old water, and added fresh to the waterer sitting above the heating stand.

"This is pretty cute."

I whirled. "What happened to twenty minutes?" He wore his Aran sweater, ratty jeans, and no coat.

"I finished." He hitched a hip against a stall door. "Thought I'd meet the animals. And I brought you this." He handed me my go-mug. I inhaled. Yum. Mixed with the coffee, hints of cinnamon and honey and a pleasing something I couldn't identify. I sipped. I sighed.

"What?" he asked as he raised his own mug to his lips.

"Ambrosia."

"I made it for you." No irony. Straight. Serious.

"Thank you." I sniffed at the steam coming from his mug. "What's that?"

"Tea."

"Nice," I said. "Smells fancy."

He crooked an eyebrow. "That's me."

His serene face fascinated—no, tempted—me. I would trace the scar on his jaw with my finger. Would it get a rise out of him? Or would he like it? *Whoa.*

"C'mon." I led him to Claudia's stall. Her straw bedding looked good, but her small hayrack needed topping off, so I fetched her hay and added in some nuts and fresh apples for my immense Pig of Substance. "Isn't she majestic?"

He crouched down and scratched behind her ears, which made her snuffle with pleasure. "They say pigs are more intelligent than dogs."

I grinned. "Don't let Grace hear you say that."

Next, I led him to the stalls where I kept my ten cashmere goats.

"These are Odin, Freyja." They had ample grain and hay, but I topped them off. "And Nanna and Balder." I freshened their hay and added some grain.

He smoothed his hands down their long, silky coats. "Luxurious."

"I sell most of it, but some I spin and knit."

When I moved to the next stall I said, "Thor and Sif, Nott and Delling." He took one of my grain buckets and started to fill it.

"Just a little." I peered into the adjoining stall and chuffed with annoyance at Loki and Lofn's empty feeders. "We'll need those next door."

He nodded, a lock of hair brushing his forehead.

Delicious. Oh, hell. *Focus*, girl. "Loki, did you eat Lofn's again, too?" Inside the stall, Loki butted my belly for head scratches. When I spotted Lofn chewing Larrimer's sweater, I huffed, "Stop that, girl!" and grappled it from her teeth. "Sorry!" Utterly mortified, I fingered the ruined stitches. "I'll fix it."

He examined the gnawed trim. "No. It adds character. Wabi-sabi."

I was charmed by his response. Yes, wabi-sabi—the beauty of imperfection.

We proceeded to fill their feeders and freshen their water buckets.

"Have you lived here long?" he asked.

"Always." I turned away and clicked the stall door closed behind us.

As we moved down the aisle, I took pleasure in his warmth. He seemed comfortable in the barn, natural. He fit.

We finally came to Clem, Bernadette's old chestnut horse, and I fetched the hay for his feeder.

"You don't feel like New Hampshire," Larrimer said.

I never had. "And you're from...?"

"Montana. Bozeman."

Easy to picture him in a cowboy hat and boots, riding like the devil on a huge bay horse.

"You're smiling," he said.

"I imagine Montana to be wonderful."

"I haven't been back for a long time," he said. "So tell me, anyone in your life?"

Was he asking me about *men?* "Not for a while." Not since a guy I dated forget to mention he was *married*. I wouldn't ask Larrimer. I wouldn't. "You?"

He looked at me with sleepy, heavy-lidded eyes that even in the dim light gleamed Pacific blue. "No."

The elastic moment stretched and stretched, until he finally said, "Why cashmere goats?"

"Dave gave me my first pair. Hey, buddy." I scratched Clem's nose. "You want to feed him?"

As he reached to take the hay with those big, scarred hands, Dave's bloodied ones superimposed on his.

"Are you aware of how he died?" I asked. "You have Dave's... you have Dave, don't you?"

He took the bundle of hay from me. "We flew Cochran's body to our Oregon lab."

So far away. "Why?"

"Clues. A path to the traffickers."

He took his time with Clem, scratching beneath his muzzle as he spoke low and soft to the old horse. When he left the stall, I gave Clem a carrot. "I'm determined to prove to you that Dave wasn't trafficking in endangered animals, but right now I'm thinking about Lulu, and how much she wants to bury her dad."

He chuffed out a breath. "His autopsy's incomplete."

"And when it's done, you'll return his body?"

"Perhaps. It's hard for me to say."

I shot him a sharp look.

He shrugged, his face bland. "Not my purview."

This was getting me nowhere. "I'll see Dave's autopsy report when it's complete?"

"I don't see why not."

Our conversation was off. But it was subtle. So, what was he hiding from me? I found my center, let it warm me, opened myself to it. And almost exploded. "You're not here for Dave, but for the girl. For Lulu!"

He crossed his arms, eyes narrowed. "You see more than you should, Clea Reese. Thanks for the tour."

It took patience, a quality I was woefully short on, to watch him lope away and not tear after him. But I needed to calm down, to diffuse my pissyness. I performed the rest of the chores with determined deliberateness, said "Bye, kids," as I closed the barn doors. Patience. At a slow simmer, I cleared the dooryard with the snow blower, then practiced throwing my knives.

I finally boiled over. *Screw this.*

CHAPTER NINE

Why in hells bells was he here for Lulu?

As I stormed inside, I grabbed a couple pieces of wood from the porch's tarped pile, joggling my now-empty go-mug. I ass-closed the door and said, "So what's this evidence you have on Dave?"

He moved from where he'd been working at the kitchen table and reached for the wood.

I hugged it to my chest. "Answer my question."

"I'll put the wood in the stove, and you can grab some more coffee."

It looks like you need it. Good thing he didn't say it, or I'd explode. But, yeah, I did need more coffee. I released my death grip on the wood.

While he replenished the stove, I washed my hands, snagged my knitting bag, and filled my mug from the penguin-shaped French press. He must have brought the fancy gadget with him, since we sure-as-heck didn't have one.

I sat at the table and knit a row, then another. My own personal valium. I began to weave patterns with my thoughts. Larrimer reappeared, stretched, then shoved his hands into the pockets of his tight black jeans.

Bet he had a great package. Damn, a dropped stitch.

"Come sit here." He pointed to the chair he'd just vacated.

He was relaxed, waiting, his stance commanding, like he owned the space, *my* space.

He was so contained, so deadly, so... broken? Where had that come from?

I didn't know if I wanted to flee him, fix him, or fuck him.

"You just emailed it to me?" I asked.

He nodded.

"I'll read it on my tablet."

He shrugged, and before I could snag my iPad, he took took his computer into the living room, where he folded his large body into *my* red leather club chair.

I tried not to be annoyed. Okay, so I'm territorial about some things. Childishly so. I swiped the iPad from the table and took the chair across from him, the ancient one covered in flowered chintz. An errant spring poked my butt. Damn.

A floorboard creaked. Bernadette. Ohhh, this would be juicy. She'd fry him but good.

She descended the stairs like a queen.

He stood.

"This is Special Agent Larrimer," I said. "He's investigating Dave's death."

She iced Larrimer, giving him one of her long frosty stares, took his measure up, down, and back again. "You've invaded my home."

He took a step forward and offered a slight bow. "I have, Lady."

Bowing? Lady?

Her eyes flew wide. Blue and hazel clashed in some silent dialogue that careened right over my head.

After long moments, she nodded once, said, "Welcome," and vanished into the kitchen.

Well, holy shit.

I moved to the couch, bent my legs into a half lotus, and sat the wafer-thin iPad on my lap. "What was that?" I asked.

"It seems she likes me." Larrimer's lips twitched, an almost-smile.

Damned dragon dude. And why the hell had I thought of him that way? I would not get annoyed. Would. Not. "Why are you really here? Why *you*?"

"Because I was sent."

Had I imagined that friendly man in the barn? "What are you, Mr. Fricking Miyagi?"

He nodded, all sage. "*Karate Kid*. Good movie. The first one."

Gurrrrr. I unlocked my iPad and read the emailed files on Dave.

My heart plummeted. I scanned the information, the photos, forced myself to look at the bloodied lynx, read on, my mouth desert-dry.

Damning evidence. Dave looked like the top-dog choreographing a vicious illegal operation that took animals from the wild—tigers, bears, more—and sold them to...?

"Who's on the receiving end?" I asked.

He wiped a hand across a face dark with stubble. "We don't know the big player. Some recipients were individuals, the kind who get off on owning what no one is supposed to possess. But that's just a trickle. A significant someone is buying these animals. We haven't found who. But big money's coming from somewhere. We'd targeted Cochran and set a sting into play."

"And then, he was murdered."

"Yes."

I poked the bear. "I called Bob Balfour. He confirmed he'd send me a copy of Dave's autopsy report. So you needn't bother."

His eyes, half-lidded, held secrets. He threaded his hands behind his head. Nodded.

Round two. "So you've set your sights on Lulu."

A trickle of annoyance. A small leak in his stoic carapace. "I don't intend to endanger the girl, but she knows something. Or has something."

"Lame."

He leaned forward, elbows on knees. "Not lame. Your assailant said, two days before the shit hit. Makes sense they might try to take the girl with something big."

"You're trying to wind me up. It won't work."

He rotated his shoulders, stretching the muscles. "It's worked so far. Entertaining."

I almost exploded out of the chair, which was exactly what he wanted.

He brushed a finger down his temple. "You're never easy, are you?"

"Thank the gods." I rubbed my wrist. "I know Lulu's a target. And it sucks. The Gunfight at the OK Grain and Feed, the guy was a pro."

"With a sawed-off shotgun, I hear."

Whoa. I'd forgotten to tell the cops about the shotgun, hadn't mentioned it except in the report I'd written up and copied to Bob.

"You're awfully cozy with Bob Balfour."

"We're the opposite of cozy." He threaded his hands behind his head. "You want my honest evaluation, here goes: You found Cochran's body. You protected the girl yesterday. It's simple. You've become the prime target. They don't know about me, so take you out, get the girl."

"That's absurd."

"Is it? You're the impediment, one that needs to be removed. Don't worry, I've got your back."

The phrase flung me into the past.

I sit on the fresh-mown grass, on a lonely hill with a view of Mt. Cranadnock.

Tommy. I feel him at my back as he strolls up.

"Hey, Clee."

"Hey, Tom." I miss our longer names that aren't cool as teens. Tommy and Clea somehow sounds better, fits better.

He sits beside me, uncaring that his favorite pair of jeans will get grass stains, and I love that about him.

"I heard you bombed out with Jen," he says.

I did." I make my voice assured, confident in ways I don't feel. "I was performing at that kids' party. Like I always do. You know, where I was doing Dave's mentalism tricks. The kids were eating them up."

A sidelong smile. "You're good at them."

"Thanks. But they're tricks, practice, nothing more. I'm no shut eye. I was in the middle of a cold reading. Jen was there, with her little brother. And I looked at this kid, Luke, and blurted out that his mother was hurt." I shrug. "I didn't mean to."

"Yeah, yeah, sweetness." He pushes my lips into a smile.

I slap his hand away. "Stop it. One of the adults called home. Turned out, Luke's mom had fallen down the stairs that morning. Luke was shocked. The kid hadn't known. Everybody got really quiet then. Spooked. Jen... Ever since then..." I puff out a breath. "I really stink at friendships."

He winks. "Not with me."

"You're special."

"Well, natch. But so are you." He tugs my hand to his lips and kisses my palm.

I chew on his words for long moments. "I scare people. Sometimes... I know what they're going to say or do next. I feel their emotions, too."

"So keep it to yourself. Your empathy gene is in overdrive, kiddo."

I pluck a couple blades of grass, toss them. "It's more than that. You know it."

"Jen hurt you, huh?"

I shrug.

He massages my shoulders. I feel his caring, his love. He comforts me in ways others can't.

"I'm going to fuck her over good," he says.

"Tommy, don't."

"Tom."

"You're going cold, Tom." The sun shines so bright today, so dazzling. I shiver. Beside me, Tommy gets colder and colder, smoky, like dry ice. He burns. "Please don't. It's cruel."

He notches his head. "So? Look what she did to you."

"That wasn't cruelty. Just human nature."

"Yeah, well, this human's gonna nature her but good."

And he did—dated her, bedded her, and dumped her. And whatever else he did, whenever I'd see Jen in school, she'd shoot me a wary, almost frightened glance, and give me a wide berth.

If that was what my magic produced... Revulsion tremored through me.

The memory of Tommy, vivid, alive. At times like this, I felt like an amputee, missing an arm. Tommy'd always had my back, sometimes to the detriment of others.

"Clea?" Larrimer said. "Clea?"

I shook off the memories and snapped, "Thanks, but I watch my own back."

"As you will." In one liquid movement, he unfolded himself from the chair. "I'm heading out."

"Not without breakfast," came the steel-laced voice from the kitchen.

"Of course, Lady," Larrimer said.

Bernadette—I'd swear she could command battalions. *That* was the strength I needed to acquire. Except it wasn't me, not who I was. If only she'd see that.

Larrimer straightened, all six-foot-plus of him, then gestured toward the red chair. "You can have your property back now."

I narrowed my eyes at him.

His deep-chested laugh erupted.

He was one of *those*. "Don't. Just don't."

A board creaked. Lulu stood on the stairs. The two mutts ran to her.

"How'd you sleep, kiddo?" I asked.

Her shrug said it all.

"This is James Larrimer. I'm working with him on your dad's case."

Larrimer crossed to her. "I'm sorry about your dad. I know how hard a loss like that can be."

"Thank you." Lulu looked up at him all googly eyed. "Nice to meet you, Mr. Larrimer." She beamed.

Oh, dear, a crush.

He crouched down to pet the dogs, scratching beneath their chins. "Handsome. Part Brittany, aren't they?"

She giggled, blushed. "Yes."

A spark of irritation, and I'd almost blurted *What about Ronan?* Geesh!

We sat around the dining table while Bernadette buzzed about the kitchen, putting out steaming pots of coffee and tea and laying platters of biscuits and ham and eggs in front of us.

When she finally joined us, she gave me a wink. Oh, that devil. She knew how shocked I was at her welcoming Larrimer and Lulu. Understatement. Some Candyland golem had replaced my Bernadette.

I leaned toward Lulu, a brief touch to her hands. "It's been a scary time for you, sweetie. We're trying to understand why your dad was killed and why those men came after you."

Her puff of breath ruffled her bangs. "A few weeks ago, Daddy started acting funny."

"Funny how?" I asked.

She kneaded her napkin. "He sort of, well, got all closed up. I tried to get him to talk to me, but... he kept saying I was his first treasure, he had to protect me."

That made me smile. "Well sure. That's what dads do."

"His other treasures?" Larrimer said.

She shrugged, began to play with a long strand of copper hair. "I don't know."

"Did he do anything unlike himself?" I asked. "Go anywhere unusual?"

She shrugged again.

When I'd visited Tibet, I met a young girl with a loving spirit and many secrets—Lulu reminded me of her. I searched for the path inside her, found a maze of wants and needs, fears and secrets, all twisted together, constantly shifting.

Larrimer leaned his chair back onto two legs.

Bernadette's unibrow rippled as she frowned, and he lowered the chair to the floor.

I lifted my work from the knitting bag beside my chair. "Feel it," I said to Lulu.

Lulu reached a tentative hand toward the mushroom-colored scarf. "Oh. Wow. It feels like butter, no, velvet."

I smiled. "It's cashmere. From Loki and Lofn."

"You mean...?"

"Yeah. Two of my goats."

Lulu laughed, a sweet chime. I knit, and as I did, Lulu relaxed as she fingered the scarf, rubbing the cashmere over and over.

"The lace edging," I said, "Is called a Fir Cone stitch. Easy to knit."

"I could never knit anything that pretty," she said.

"Sure you could." I snared her eyes, but didn't stop knitting.

"After Daddy died, and I was home—"

"Alone?" Larrimer said.

"Yes. We don't have any relatives." She twirled her hair, dipped her chin. "And I'm almost sixteen. I didn't know Clea was my guardian. Daddy never told me. Then Ronan called and said I should stay with him. But then later, I went home again." She turned to me. "You know why."

"I do. And those men came."

She sighed, looked away. "I don't want to remember."

I couldn't blame her. I was so tempted to give her a pass. Instead, I ran the back of my hand across her cheek. "I wouldn't either. Except, it could help find your dad's killer. And it can be better to get some stuff out."

"I guess."

"The men, Lulu," Larrimer said. "Did they say anything before they came into your living room?"

A one-shouldered shrug. "Maybe. Sort of." Her voice lowered to a whisper. "One said if they didn't find it, The Master would kill them."

Chapter Ten

The Master. **I shot Larrimer a glance, and he shook his** head, the barest movement. But his eyes gleamed like a cat's when it spotted a mouse.

"I don't know what they were looking for," she said. "It was all fast and icky. And then they came into the room, and I escaped."

To the secret room under the barn. But what did Dave foresee to prepare that room, the exploding windows, Lulu's "trial runs?" If there was such trouble brewing, why hadn't Dave talked to me about it?

"Is there anything else you can recall?" Larrimer asked, his voice a deep caramel. "A small thing, perhaps?"

Her cheeks flushed. "I disobeyed Dad. He told me never to look back, only to run. And I did. Except, I looked back once. And in front of the red shed, I saw that big hearse thing."

After we cleaned up, Larrimer vanished into my office, and I changed and got my stuff, preparing for a little road trip. I expected Larrimer would join me. He'd be ready fast, so I'd have to hustle as I planted a few seeds. I made a dozen calls around town—shops and eateries, the police and the selectmen's office. All schmoozing, sure, but I carefully mentioned *"The Master,"* to see if anyone reacted. No one had, but the trees would start clacking. If I shook enough branches, a juicy morsel might fall out.

Larrimer reappeared wearing all black right down to his thin leather gloves and began to strap on a dual-pistol shoulder harness. Two guns, knife slots. Impressive and useful. And all cold predator.

"I'm heading over to Lulu's place," he said.

"Ready when you are."

He straightened. "Not a good idea."

I smiled.

"What?" he asked.

"I think it's a very good idea. In fact, that's exactly where I was headed." With a stop in between.

Grim-faced, he crossed his arms, all bulging biceps and rigid resolve. "You're injured. Tired. And you're a target. I don't need to be worried about you while I'm examining the house."

I tilted my head. "Like you have charge of me. Right."

"You're my adjunct," he said, words spat like BBs. "I make the decisions."

"Okay, then." I nodded. That was my windup. Now I slammed him with the pitch. "Except, as Lulu's guardian, the house is mine now. Step one foot in the place without the proper paperwork, and you're toast." I smiled, sweet as pie.

The temp in the room definitely dipped. He could freeze me all he wanted, we were going as a team.

With his "okay" nod, I relaxed.

Then a finger poked under my nose, and he bent until his eyes were even with mine. "You don't ever threaten me again, Clea. Not ever."

I might have shivered a little as I shrugged on my leather jacket. I slid my Glock into its shoulder holster and my Tru-Bal throwing knife into its boot sheath, added an extra clip, and tugged on my leather fingerless mitts.

After yesterday, I wasn't going anywhere unprepared.

From his pack, Larrimer pulled out some fancy-assed gun I didn't recognize. Intense. "Ready?"

I nodded. "We can take my truck."

I reached for the mudroom door, and heard Lulu say, "Wait!"

"I'll warm up the truck." Larrimer plucked the keys from my hand.

"Coward," I mumbled, as Lulu appeared in the mudroom.

"Wow, you look..." she said.

"Badass?" I grinned. "We're just doing a little reconnaissance."

"Where?" she asked.

Crap, I'd hoped to avoid this. "Over at your place, hon."

She clasped her hands, a smile on her face. "I'll come! I can be ready in a sec."

I hated turning her down. "I'm sorry. No."

Her eyes welled with tears.

"We'll take you back there," I said. "Just not today."

She spread her arms, palms up. "I want to go. The stuff I have here, well, that's what I kept at the store and in the back of the pickup. At the house I've got—"

"Not today. I'm sorry."

Her chin trembled.

In so many ways, Lulu's life had been stolen. I rested a hand on her shoulder. "Maybe we could bring you something from home?"

She cocked her head to the side, eyes brightening. "Okay. That would be good. Um. I know! My pink dress in the closet. And my bras. I really want my bras. And the picture album next to my bed. My jewelry box. It's on my dresser. And there's Blue Monkey. Dad gave me him for Christmas. Mutt and Jeff tried to steal him before… I think he's under the bed." She flapped her hands. "I mean, he's got slobber all over him. Gross."

I winked. "We can handle Mutt and Jeff's slobber."

A giggle. "Thanks. That'll be good until you can take me back."

"Consider it done."

Larrimer grudgingly relinquished the wheel when I insisted on driving, and now sat in the passenger seat, bubbles of annoyance floating around him. Tough. It was my truck, my roads, my dead friend.

Snow flowed across the landscape and softened the world like a white drop cloth. The town plows hadn't yet made a second pass on the backroads and the going was slow. Larrimer's displeasure finally dissipated, which was when he said, "I know where you're going, and it's not to the house. Not right away."

Smarty-pants. "Shatzkin Funeral Home is the only game in town. So Shatzkin's hearse parked outside her home when she was attacked bugs the hell out of me."

"Could be nothing," he said.

"True. He could've simply been paying her a condolence visit. I thought we might stop and ask him on the way to the house."

"Good."

As we turned right onto Main Street, my phone chimed *Beethoven's 5th*, while Larrimer's played Clapton's cover of "I Shot the Sheriff."

I looked at Larrimer and smiled. "Nice ringtone."

He grinned, all white teeth and bronzed skin. Given the heat pooling in my nether regions, that smile should be banned.

"Bob," I said into the phone.

"How's it going with Larrimer?" he asked.

Exasperation made me want to snark. He hadn't told me about Larrimer's arrival, and now was acting all paternalistic, something he hadn't done in years. "Fine. He seems competent."

Bob snorted. "That's one word for it. We've made some progress on Carney. I could use your expertise today. Special Agent Taka would benefit from an observation."

I almost asked if she benefited from his banging her. Almost. "Give it up, Bob. Carney's a minor-leaguer. Taka will handle him fine, and you know it."

Shatzkin's Funeral Home appeared around the bend, and I slowed. "Gotta go," I said, and clicked off.

I pulled into the driveway next to the large gray Victorian with the wide pillared porch and parked beside a hearse. My wrist started to itch like crazy, and I scratched. A signal of some sort?

Larrimer stilled my hand with his gloved one. "Don't do that. You'll make yourself bleed."

"Thanks, Mom."

His chuckle irritated me. I felt smothered. First Bob, now Larrimer.

"Let's go," he said.

No cars were parked out front, so no funeral in progress. As I punched the back doorbell, I tried to ignore Larrimer's intense presence behind me. *Fail.* Good thing he'd covered his array of firepower with his jacket or he'd scare the hell out the funeral director.

I gripped my knitting bag. He'd better not make any cracks about it.

Boy, did I have my grouch on.

Sonorous chimes rang, and soon a large-bosomed woman with gray hair opened the door. She wore a gray dress, too, that matched her hair and the house. Nothing like color coordination.

After we showed her our badges, she led us down the hall, where we passed a large man smelling of Listerine heading the other way. Apparently not Shatzkin. She ushered us into a small waiting room and opened the door to an office that once must have been a back parlor.

"Visitors, Terrance," she said, and turned to us. "He'll be with you in a minute."

Once she left, I peered into the office. Heavy oak lined the room; papers—stacks of them—were strewn about in a seemingly random fashion, along with hole punches, notebooks, binders, and a sleeping, ancient Great Dane. He was gray, too.

A blue leather wingchair facing the desk on the far wall hid the occupant, but not the sticky psychic scent that perfumed the room. To the chair's left on the floor, my eyes snagged on what looked like an invitation, calligraphed in red atop a pile. Too far away for me to read, it pulled at me as if it were magnetized, and that wrist itch worsened. Interesting.

I moved closer, trying to get a peek at the card. The Great Dane chose that moment to totter over and butt its head against my hand. I hunkered down to pet him, drifting ever closer to the invitation. What I got was a face bath from a humongous pink tongue. Larrimer cleared his throat, I stood, and he waved a blue-dotted handkerchief. I retreated to where he sat and wiped my face.

"Thanks," I said.

No hint of answering laughter except the eyes. Damn those laughing eyes. Warm and bright and thrilling.

He leaned in close so his breath warmed my ear. "You realize you crawled halfway across his office floor."

Well no, I hadn't. Guess I'd have to wait on Mr. Shatzkin to get close to the card.

I sat beside him and took out my knitting.

We waited. Larrimer cleared his throat again, this time louder. No response.

I'd had it. "Mr. Shatzkin, we'd like to speak to you about Lulu Cochran."

Silence.

I stood, but Larrimer was across the room faster than The Flash. His face hardened. "He's dead."

We were back on the road two hours later, leaving behind one dead funeral director, the Gray Lady, who was Shatzkin's wife, the dog, and the usual hullabaloo of cops, ME's people, and forensics. We were questioned about everything, in particular the guy we'd passed in the hall. We had little to tell them, and the Gray Lady knew nada.

Shatzkin hadn't had a mark on him.

And I'd forgotten to get an up-close look at the damned calligraphy card.

Silence enveloped the truck as I powered down 202, then turned left up Bergen Hill. I told Larrimer about the calligraphic invite.

"And you know this how?" he asked.

"I sensed it, felt something."

I expected him to laugh or make a woo-woo joke. He simply nodded. "Happen much?"

"Enough." I didn't want to talk about it. "That was certainly strange and disappointing."

"I agree."

"Your knitting is interesting. Tell me about it."

"I intended to use it on Shatzkin. It confuses people that I knit while I interrogate them. Scrambles their perceptions. It's a tool."

"A good one."

"Thanks. It works."

I took a left onto the mighty Bergen Hill Road and Fern thundered onward. The roads were nasty, but I'd driven worse. I hooked a right onto Fantin, took the corner too fast, and the truck's rear fishtailed.

"You practice that?" he asked.

"Yup."

We drove toward Lulu's home. It wasn't even four, but the day was gently dying.

I had told Larrimer how the home had been trashed, so we both knew we'd find chaos. We entered through the side door into the small hall, guns drawn.

Dave's home was freezing. The petite phone table lay on the floor, its contents spilling onto the blue Oriental rug.

The cops had told Bob that Lulu's attackers must have policed their brass, and the bullets found so far had led nowhere. Fingerprint powder dusted the table, the door frames, the bannister.

The place felt violated and claustrophobic. Yet beneath that, I caught a lingering resonance of love, and my heart tripped.

We cleared the house fast, then separated. Larrimer took the dining room, and when I stepped into the living room, as if on cue, my wrist itched like crazy. I shuddered anew at the destruction and at the gaping hole where the window had been. The invaders' knives had gutted the blue sofa and chairs and littered the room with broken paintings, ripped photos, and despoiled books. I'd spent hours in this home, and the wreckage shook me.

Thank the gods Lulu hadn't come with.

Hundreds of books remained in the bookcases. A quick survey, and I found the children's section. Golden Books, a collection of Pooh, dozens of others. None had a green binding. So I started at the beginning, on my left, up and down, through science, nature, fiction. None of the green-bound books I found had teeth marks.

I looked in cabinets and under what was left of the sofa and chairs.

"I'm doing the kitchen, then upstairs." Larrimer stepped inside the room. "Anything?"

"Nothing so far," I said, frustration leaching out of me.

"Frantic," he said.

"Yes. Those creeps."

He disappeared, and I gave the room another once-over.

Out of curiosity, I walked to the blasted-out window and laid my hand on the splintered jamb. A pulse. Electrical. It didn't hurt, but beat in time with my heart.

The residue of magic made real?

I turned away, then trotted upstairs. On the landing, I jerked to a stop and again opened my senses. Larrimer and I were alone, but as I settled, I tasted that same sticky psychic scent I'd encountered in Shatzkin's office. Not as intense, but present in the air. "There's something."

Larrimer joined me on the landing. "No one's here."

"No. But there *is* something. Be careful."

He raised an eyebrow. "Will you bite me if I say the same for you?"

"Maybe."

He grinned.

Gods. "I'll take Dave's bedroom," I said, voice hushed.

"Bathroom's clear," he said. "I'll tackle Lulu's."

"Look under the bed for her blue monkey." I listed her other requests, and he disappeared. "And her bras!"

Bet he loved that one.

Inside Dave's room, my sense of dread grew. But no itching wrist.

I circled his bed. Mattress slashed, covers and curtains piled on the floor. Pens, pads, and letters, broken glass and photos. Cracks spidered an old tube TV atop the dresser. Feathers from ripped pillows attached themselves to me as I walked by. In the closet, clothes and the scent of anger. I rummaged the shelf and the floor. No chest. No book.

Help me, Dave. Please.

Maybe *they'd* found them. What would Dave's killers do with them? That fetid taste of danger increased, and a buzzing, like bees. *Focus, dammit, on what's here, not what you're sensing.*

I picked up a curled photo of Lulu and her dad, ink splashed on its corner, slipped it into my jacket for her. Frustrated, I stepped to leave—and my eyes snagged on the oddest thing. Against the far wall stood a shoe polisher with a tall chrome handle so you wouldn't lose your balance.

The buzzing increased, and I almost laughed. Dave and a shoe polisher *so* didn't compute. And tucked beneath it on the wood floor sat what looked like a thin book, its green spine facing outward.

I raised the heavy polisher, slid out the book. The minute I touched it, power, like the charge in the air just before a massive thunderstorm breaks, prickled my skin.

As I lowered the polisher, I smiled. The book bore a child's tooth marks on its well-worn leather cover.

CHAPTER ELEVEN

The Storybook was smaller than I expected, only about five by seven. No title on the spine or the cover.

I raised it to my nose. It smelled…

I snuggle next to Dave as he reads me the Storybook. It's so good! I love the princess and the queen, but I love best the little girl in the forest. She's like me! That's what Dave says.

He closes the book.

"Why do I feel sad at the end, Dave?"

He puts an arm around me, and I snuggle closer. "Because something important is lost."

"Oh." I still don't understand.

"Someday you will, Clea."

"How did you hear my mind?"

"Because I can, little one. Sometimes."

I move my fingers across the marks on the book. I feel guilty. "I'm sorry I bit the book."

He smiles. "I'm not. It's your book, after all."

"Mine?" Excitement! "Can I take it home?"

He shakes his head. I think he wants to laugh, but he doesn't. "Not for a long time, sweetheart."

I cross my arms, huff. "Humph. I want it now.*"*

"I know, my little hasty Clea." He tucks a finger under my chin, tilts my head so I look at his pretty eyes. So serious. "Someday, it will be your task to find—"

"There you are!" says Cruella. Well, that's not her real name. She stands all tight and bright in the living room door.

Dave tucks the book behind his back. "Hello, darling. I thought you'd gone out."

"Were you reading again to that child?" She flicks a finger at me.

She doesn't like me at all, and I don't like her, either, especially not her pointy ears that hear too much.

"I was." He holds up The Jungle Book.

I love those stories, but Dave is fibbing. Why?

"How come you have pointy ears?" I say. It'll make her mad. And she'll go away.

"That child!" She pulls her hair over her ears.

After she leaves, I giggle.

Dave leans forward and kisses my forehead. "Quite the mischief maker, aren't you?"

I throw my arms around his neck and hug him. "I love you."

I held the book close, the Storybook, with a capital "S," and again inhaled the leathery scents of age and use. I felt joy.

The magic... Dave was teaching me all those years, and I never knew it. That's what he'd meant by not finishing. *Oh, Dave.* I was alone on an uncharted plain. *Why* had I been sheltered from it all my life? Bernadette said I "wasn't ready." For what? Would I ever be? How would I know?

I unzipped my inner jacket pocket and slipped the book inside.

"Anything?" Larrimer called from across the hall.

"A jumble," I said. "Stuff ripped, torn, stained." And no chest.

He walked into the bedroom, face stiff with anger. "Bastards." He carried Lulu's things. "We shouldn't be taking these." He dangled the monkey from his fist.

"They've already processed the house."

"Yeah. I'll call that prick Balfour to—"

"He's not a prick, dammit! Why did—"

A crunch downstairs, then a splash. I'd dampened my senses while I'd searched Dave's room. Stupid.

Larrimer raised a finger to his lips. "Hush."

I closed my eyes, scented the air. Sourness, death, urine, geraniums... Synapses clicked. "Larrimer, run!"

He grabbed me around the waist, and suddenly we were airborne, his back shielding me, hand covering my head as we crashed through the bedroom window a heartbeat before a deafening blast propelled us straight toward a giant pine. In an impossible move, he flipped me around so he'd land first, and somehow we thudded into the frozen snow, saving us from death-by-tree.

We landed hard, and he flipped me again, his body draping mine as heat billowed and debris rained. I shielded his head with my hands, terrified he'd be injured.

Vibrations and noise whizzed through me, except cotton wadded my ears, and then something whammed my temple.

A flare of pain.

A shape hovered above me, blocking the sun. I blinked and blinked again. I pushed at the face, but hands held my wrists. What was wrong? Where was I? Why was I trapped?

A weight pushing on me. I pushed back, but it didn't budge.

My ears... I couldn't hear! Blood inside my mouth. My stomach heaved. I spat.

The man's lips moved, like he was talking, but what was he saying? Who the hell was he?

"Let go!" I screamed, but I was mute, my words stolen. Once before. Yes. *Oh, gods.* There, watching the helicopter crash, unable to help, floating inside myself, dribbles of blood, gouges of pain.

Suspended. Was I there? No... not desert hot, the ground cold with snow.

And the man still looked at me. The bluest of blue. A Pacific Ocean of it. Soothing. Cradling.

I sniffled, blinked, squinted.

A trickle of memories, a blast. My head throbbed. And he was holding my wrists, keeping me prisoner. Let it go! Let me go! Can't escape, can't escape! *No, no, no!* Panic!

You can *escape. Remember your magics. Focus. Do it now.*

I press my mind toward the voice, like I'd been taught.

That's right, focus, little Mage.

But he's holding my wrists. Red teeth, hands, claws. The Bad Meanie! Let. Me. Go! I uncurl my hand, and glowing lights swirl from my palm... scents of citrus and cedar... fireflies pushing out, glorious patterns expanding, almost doing it, doing it.

... everything collapsed.

Trapped! I cranked back a leg to kick the bastard in the balls. Except he wasn't there. *Fuck.*

"I heard that," came his muffled reply.

I heard him, too, though he sounded far, far away.

What had happened? I shook my head. What had I been doing? Panic and pain and...? Remember, remember. But I couldn't grab it. A wisp of memory. Damn.

My head killed. My face, my arm. My wrist *burned*. A memory, a shred, a thread. I tried to unwind it. Dissolved. Smoke.

I coughed, craned my head back, and looked into a bronzed face, scarred cheeks, startling blue eyes.

Larrimer. He stood above me, arms at his sides, calm, serene almost. Really? We just flew out a fricking window. And here I was, and here he was, and we were *alive*. Hoorah for that one. And I'd been about to kick him in the balls. Well, damn. Shame on me.

I rolled to a stand, hating my Lilliputian-size to his berserker's, except the earth shivered, and I began my descent.

Larrimer caught me around my waist. He was being way too touchie-feely helpful. I shoved at his chest. "Cut it out! I'm fine." I spat more blood on the ground, just to prove it.

"Glad you're back," he said.

"Me, too."

"Come on," he said.

"We need to—"

"—do squat. I called our techs."

"Gee, they'll get here quick. Not." My mouth full of marbles. I slid out my phone, thankful for its protective cover, and walked a few steps away. When I dialed headquarters' tech division, Berti answered. They'd come. By the time I hung up, a smile ghosted my lips. Now I *knew* the scene would get a proper investigation.

His jaw clenched—all pissy—he didn't bother to comment.

I looked around. Blood dotted the snow. So did a million

photographs. Oh, Lulu. I was amazed we were alive. Larrimer had shielded me, saved my life.

I looked him over. Was he hurt? His black sweater was shredded, a couple bloody scratches marred his face. "Are you okay?"

"I'll do."

"Thanks," I said. "Thank you."

I ignored his answer as I spied a piece of Blue Monkey, a leg. Somehow, that was too much. I turned so he wouldn't see my tears, and began picking up remnants of the stuffed animal. The head. Two arms. The leg and another. His furry blue body.

I slid them into my jacket pockets, and started on the photos, what was left of them. Larrimer helped. Now my nose was running. Crap on that. A hand waved a maroon handkerchief in my face. I took it, blew my nose, and pushed the thing into my back pocket.

Miraculously, draped across a bush, one of Lulu's bras was pristine. I picked it up and sniffled again at the heavy padding that spoke to a girl's poor body image. The bra went into my pocket, too.

"Her jewelry?" I asked.

He pulled a T-shirt-wrapped box from his jacket pocket. "It made it."

Maybe the pink dress... No, it hung in tatters from a tree.

When we were done, I stumbled to Fern. Larrimer limped beside me. I said, "Are you sure you're—"

"I'm good."

I gave the house one final look. Well, it wasn't really a house anymore. More like a pancake of wood, as if a giant had smooshed it, leaving scattered clapboards, a tilted chimney, and not much else but unidentifiable debris on the ground and in the trees. Fire burned, low and smoky, feeding on wood and clothes and unnamed treasures. Sirens screamed in the distance, growing louder. What a disaster.

Lulu had not only lost her father, but now her home, too. And if Dave's chest had lain undiscovered inside, it had been blasted out of existence.

That evening we dealt with Lulu's renewed grief and Bernadette's tsk-tsking as she patched up Larrimer and me. Arm bandaged, wrist bandaged, purple-and-green forehead butterflied with bandaids, I looked like a refugee from a bad bar fight. At least, Larrimer's leg injury was relatively minor.

Aching to read the Storybook, I'd wait until I was alone.

After I showered, I slipped into Lulu's room and laid the bra on her dresser alongside a small plastic jewelry box that Larimer must have put there. I sighed. Minutes later, I gratefully sank into the sofa's softness. Larrimer's eyes followed the Celtics' game on the flat screen, which was muted. Warmth and calm surrounded us. Home. I closed my eyes.

The cushion next to me moved with another's weight.

"Did you..." Lulu asked, hope warming her eyes. "Did you find Blue Monkey?"

I cranked my eyes open to see her mingling of hope and fear. My heart stuttered. I didn't know what to say, but I got up, retrieved my jacket and pulled out the remnants of Blue Monkey. I cupped them in my hands like some damaged offering.

Lulu just stared.

I didn't know where to put the parts—on the table, in Lulu's lap—and I just wanted to scream that none of it was fair. Not any of it.

Bernadette took the pieces of Blue Monkey from my hands. She smiled at me, a gentle smile. "You did good, cookie."

I shook my head, but said, "Thanks."

Then she wrapped an arm around Lulu. "Ça va. I'll fix your creature right up. Better than new." And Bernadette, arm still around Lulu, clutching Blue Monkey's pieces, led the girl away.

"Clea," Larrimer said.

I turned to face the man sprawled at the opposite end of couch. "Yes?"

He frowned. "You're hurting."

"I'm fine."

"You say that a lot."

"You say it a lot, too."

He scraped a hand through his shower-damp hair, then switched off the game, opened his laptop, and tapped a few keys. He handed me the computer. The screen held an image of an invitation. My breath caught.

Written in sweeping calligraphy the color of red wine:

You are invited to the Midborough Policeman's Gala

February 27, 7 p.m. to 11 p.m.
Semi-formal to formal attire
Midborough Country Club
49 High Street
Midborough, New Hampshire

It looked an awful lot like the card in Shatzin's office. "How did you get this?"

He reached to reclaim his laptop. Our hands brushed, and he stiffened as he took the computer. That's when I realized we'd never really touched, skin to skin.

"You mentioned the invitation you saw in the undertaker's office," he said. "*This* was found on the floor beneath Cochran's body."

Dave. He foresaw his death. Maybe not that day. Maybe not the next. But soon. He knew. And planned.

Why hadn't he run with Lulu? Had death rushed too quickly? Perhaps he couldn't leave. Or maybe he'd made a conscious choice, knowing his end was inevitable.

"Dave put it there," I said. "For a reason."

Larrimer nodded. "I suspect so.

"I'll be going to that gala." I gave him my hard stare. Had he any idea how much I hated the idea of attending pretentious crap like that?

"And I'll be escorting you, of course, Ms. Clea Artemis." His lips twitched.

Yeah, he knew. Bet he didn't much like galas either. I relaxed, and every aching muscle screamed back to vivid life. "Yes, you will."

He traced his index finger down that long sinuous scar that ran from his temple to his jaw. "There's an ugly coda. According to Fish and Wildlife's lab, the calligraphy ink's composition is unique. Part commercial, but a good portion was made of animal blood."

I winced. Gross. And oh, so bizarre.

"Someone's idea of a joke, perhaps?" he asked.

"You don't believe that."

"No."

I stared at the invitation on his computer screen. "A power thing." If I could touch it, would I feel its power? They'd never let me near it. Bob could get ahold of it. So what would I say to him? Let me at it, so I can feel its energy signature? Oh sure, he'd buy into that. Right.

Larrimer's eyes gleamed. "Yes, a power thing. Hundreds of these were sent. Except for the few in the know, it's pulling the wool over the eyes of the clueless. A nasty bit of work."

His striking visage hid a sharp mind, which made for a dangerous and near-irresistible package. "Taunting the pathetic saps who'd be horrified to know what they were touching. If that's how this guy thinks, the invitation is ideal. I've never gone, but the Policemen's Gala is a big 'do.' All the muckety-mucks in town go."

"Mixing with a bunch of pompous assholes," he said. "Save me."

I almost groaned. "If only I could."

At 1:00 a.m., the house finally asleep, I fetched the Storybook.

Back in my room, I slipped on my bunny slippers, dragged my ancient cashmere blanket over me, and sat up in bed, all cozy.

I stroked my hand across its cover and felt a tickle of strength. It feathered my fingers, reached up my hands...

To evaporate. All I held was a slim volume with a worn leather cover. But Dave's hands had known this book intimately. He'd read it to me, and, perhaps, to Lulu, too. The small tooth prints on the cover brought a smile. He'd found my sampling funny, as if I'd wanted to taste our book.

I went to open the cover. It didn't. Open, that is.

Chapter Twelve

The cover would not open, as if it had been glued to the pages. I tried the back. Same deal.

Now what? Was I supposed to say some magical incantation or something? Wave my hands? Use a wand?

"Abracadabra."

Yeah, well that didn't work, not that I'd really expected it to.

I waved my hands over the book. Right.

Next, I pressed my wrist to the book, right where it always itched. Still stuck.

I pried, pulled, pushed. Okay, maybe I shouldn't have, but dammit, I was going to get this book open. I stopped when I ripped a nail, not that I cared about the nail. The damn thing wasn't budging.

Dave said the book was mine. *Mine.*

It sure didn't feel like mine.

My jaw hurt. I'd been clenching my teeth.

Calm. Quiet. Patience. Yes, Bernadette. I almost said it aloud.

I needed a distraction, so I reached for *The Fellowship of the Ring*. As they were climbing Caladris—problems, problems, problems—I recalled their arrival at the gates of Moria and the whole ferdazzle that happened because they couldn't unlock the doors.

I put LoTR aside and reached for the Storybook.

Calm. Quiet. Patience. I took a breath, deep and slow, and said, "Open."

And nothing happened.

"Please open."

Nope.

And then, I knew. Just as Frodo realized the truth of the doors.

"I Acknowledge and Accept."

Feathers across my fingers, and again something changed. I easily lifted the cover.

The endpaper and the facing page swirled with gold and purple, the gold reflecting the light. I turned the page. Plain cream vellum, rich and thick, and on the right-hand page, an inscription.

I fy mab, Dafydd y Mage~
Ti yw fy drysor. Drysor y llyfr hwn yw o ddoethineb a chariad.
Felly mae'n fod.
Gyda llawer o gariad,
Mam

The language. Uncommon, yet familiar. Maybe Gaelic or Welsh. And "Mam." Mother.

The word resonated, deep inside me.

I'd used that name for my mother. Yes.

So long ago.

I rolled it along my tongue. *Mam.*

The memory of the man in ripped jeans, my father, I'd called him... Da. Yes, he was *Da.*

And Dave, whom his mother termed a Mage in the inscription.

I flipped pages, velvet beneath my fingers.

I read.

THE MAGIC BOX

Alone in the forest, a fine little girl stored her magic in a small box. She found the magic when the world was born, and she loved it.

She would wave her hands, and the magic poured out.
The dead grass greened.
The muddied stream turned crystal.

The withered flowers bloomed.

As she grew, so did her magic, and she crafted animals, both four- and two-legged. Beings to wield magic and those who sparked with magic. Creatures who shifted shape and those who lived on blood and breath. She used her magic often to create many, many things. And it thrived.

She became a princess, then a queen. They called her Evermore. And she protected her kingdom, and her box, for there were those who would steal her kingdom and her magic.

One bright, sunny day, a young man came to her and said, "May I borrow your magic box, to guard and protect and share?"

"Why?" the queen said.

"Because you have an abundance of magic, and if you lend me the box, then more magic will grow and blossom like yours. And your Beauty and Strength will be shared with the world."

The queen saw goodness in the young man, so she placed a tiny fragment of her soul in the box, and leant it to him.

And for many long eons, as others used it, they, too, gifted the box with fragments of their souls and passed it on.

And the magic grew and blossomed and multiplied.

But one day, the queen, alone in her room, felt a change, a lessening.
She traveled to the forest, where she'd first felt her magic. And there, too, her magic was less.

And she sensed an unraveling.

Soon, evil sprouted and grew, and the queen was unable to hold it back.

The evil shriveled the world. The evil shriveled her.

The queen sought out the young man to whom she'd given the box, but he had since died, ages past.

She built a fire, for she had power still.
She sang to the winds.
She called forth the water.
She dug the earth.
She scoured the bones.
Then she magicked the ashes, and delved.

She delved deep, deeper, down through the years, searching out his sons and his daughters, and their sons and their daughters.

And one day, the queen met an old woman, the many-greats granddaughter of the young man.

The old woman told the queen that the box was lost.

And the queen cried stones of silver.

The queen continued to seek the magic box, but all she heard were whispers she failed to understand. For the world was unplaiting.

As days and months and years wove through time, the queen remained in this world, but her magic waned until only a small trickle endured.
Finally, she gathered all that was left of her magic and, with great sadness, she passed from this world to the Other Side.

What once was will be again,
That which has unwound will again wind.
Find The Key,
And the box will be found.

Where is the Box?
Who is The Key?
Can you find what is lost?
Twine what is found?

I closed the book and ran a hand across its cover. What happened to the queen, to Evermore? Did she travel to a place like Valinor, in Tolkien's world? Was she The Mother, the embodiment of Earth itself? Rather than a tale for children, the book read more like a prophecy.

And didn't that just answer everything.

Not.

I'd know more if Dave's wife hadn't interrupted. Cruella and her pointy ears. Pointy horns would be more apt. I almost giggled, which spoke to how tired I was.

The Storybook didn't read like anything for a child, not really.

Could the box in the Storybook be the chest? Why not? Except the Storybook asked more questions than it answered.

I swiped a hand across my face. I needed Cliff Notes. No, I needed Dave. But I was fried. A puzzle best left to tomorrow.

Just one more thing. I flipped to the book's inscription, lifted my iPad, and Googled a translation page. I bet the queen would have really liked Google. I first tried Gaelic, then Welsh. Score.

You are my treasure. This book is a treasure of wisdom and love. So be it.

Dave had called Lulu his treasure. Another puzzle piece?

A blanket of dark forced me to let go.

The following day, moving was not pleasant. In fact, it was deeply, bone-wrenchingly *un*pleasant. I forced myself to do stretches, and thanked the stars and genetics that I was a fast healer.

We were all here, the second day after the attack at the Feed and Seed. I planned to keep it that way and to study the Storybook further.

Except Bob insisted I come to Boston, allegedly to complete my old paperwork on a case. His tone, however, said that wasn't the real reason. He'd never admit it, but he was worried about me, wanted to see for himself that his "Young Pup" was in one piece.

At headquarters, I could beard the SAC in his den and learn what it would take for me to get reinstated to active duty. A plan.

Larrimer hitched a ride with me to attend a meeting about another Fish and Wildlife case. My crankiness didn't enhance the trip. Someone had told Bob that I'd been at the Cochran house explosion. Larrimer denied it was he, but smoke signals had puffed.

Upon arrival, Berti informed me the SAC was out of the office. All day. Figures. Even grouchier than before, I hightailed it to a cubicle to demolish the dreaded paperwork. Bob's warm eyes narrowed with concern when he found me tapping away on the case. I almost blurted, "Why are you screwing Taka?", but wisdom prevailed.

"Clea." He pulled a chair up to my loaner desk. "Jesus. You look like you've been through a war."

"All superficial. See, I'm doing my duty," I said, all chipper. When his frown deepened, I went for gravely reassuring, "I'm fine, Old Man."

He nodded, expression pinched. "This Cochran business. It's damned dangerous. Life-threatening. You've been shot, blasted to wherever. These men aren't playing tiddlywinks."

I rested a hand on his forearm. "I agree. And I'm a trained special agent." I shot him a smile. "Or have you forgotten that itty bitty fact?"

His brown eyes softened. "Be safe."

"Now where's the fun in that? Why aren't we more involved?"

"We are." He winked. "We've got you, and Fish and Wildlife has it in hand."

That was *so* not Bob Balfour.

"Your hair?" he asked.

"Huh?" I swiped a hand across my hair. It felt peculiar.

"How about dinner after you finish?" he asked.

"Sorry," I said. "I can't."

"Come to my office before you leave?"

"Of course," I said, his dissonance a tart taste on my tongue.

I slipped into the lav to pee before rejoining Bob. When I looked in the mirror as I washed up, I stilled. My spiked hair had grown at least two inches. I closed my eyes, opened them, squinted. Yup, still there. My spiky hair *drooped*, with hints of curl!

I tried to perk it up with gel, "tried" being the operative word, then finger-combed it back, left the lav, and entered Bob's office.

Crap. Taka sat poised in a chair beside his desk, ankles demurely crossed, tapping the iPad on her lap.

I tamped down my annoyance and took a seat across from Bob.

"You perplex me," Bob said.

I shrugged. "So what else is new?"

"An ant on the move does more than a dozing ox," he said.

Taka stopped typing and raised her head. "Lao Tzu."

"Yup," I said. "ASAC Balfour loves pulling the Lao Tzu card."

She tittered, high-pitched, almost strident, just like on the phone. Not gonna go *there.*

"So what am I, Old Man?" I asked. "The ant or the ox?"

He laughed. "Definitely the ant."

Balfour's door opened, no knock, and James Larrimer prowled in with that surpassing grace, like he owned the room and didn't care. Pleasure startled me. *I* was glad to see him, Bob, not so much. A sour scowl bowed his lips, whereas Taka's expression remained guarded as ever.

"Agent Larrimer." Bob nodded.

Larrimer strode to the desk and held out his hand.

"Sorry," Bob said. "Got a cold."

"A shame." Larrimer turned to me, eyes dancing with glee, the kind just before two guys go at it.

Animus perfumed the air.

Bob stood so fast, his chair hit the wall. Larrimer shifted to the balls of his feet.

"James." I tried to cut through the testosterone. "Everything good?"

A toxic wave crested, then ebbed. "Yes." Larrimer notched his head. "Let's go."

He didn't spare Bob or Taka another look.

Bizarre. The whole scene was bizarre.

I rose, equally eager to vamoose. "I'll be seeing you, guys."

Larrimer's hand pressed the small of my back, and we turned to leave.

Powerful threads of emotion shot through the room, so many so fast, they were beyond untangling.

Bob halted us with a, "Clea, wait up."

"Hum?"

"Are you stopping by the hospital to visit Juan? If so, we've got some cards for him."

"What are you talking about?"

He puffed out his cheeks. "I'm sorry. I assumed you knew. The ME, Juan Rankin. He's in ICU over at Mr. Auburn Hospital. Heart attack."

I drove, and on the way over, Larrimer said, "I lied. Things are bad."

"What—"

"Every golden eagle we track has vanished."

I almost swerved into the opposite lane. "Vanished?"

He rubbed the back of his neck. "Other countries have reported the same. Gone."

"A mass extinction?"

"We don't know. No corpses." Suppressed fury darkened his voice. "And from what we can ascertain, the un-tracked goldens have disappeared as well. It's North America's largest bird of prey, the national animal of five nations, historically profound and symbolic. Gone."

I focused, tried to make sense of it. Failed.

We stood next to Fern at the hospital entrance and kept her running because Larrimer had asked to borrow the truck for another briefing.

"I'll meet you here in two hours," he said.

"Make it the Mt. Auburn Cemetery entrance. If I have to leave early, the cemetery's pretty beautiful. I'll wander around." I bit my lip. "I suspect I'll be in a dark mood."

He peered up at the impossibly blue sky, then at me, shoved his hands into his back pockets. "Now don't go off on me, but are you aware it's two days since that guy's threat? I've got a friend watching Lulu and Bernadette. But you." He frowned.

"I won't go off on you." I rested a hand on his forearm and smiled. "And I'm aware. I've got my knives and my gun, and I'll take good care."

"Keep your senses out there. Don't bottle up because of your friend's condition. Stay alert."

I saluted. "Yes, sir!"

He skimmed a hand across my hair and was gone.

Juan was dying. Heart attack and stroke.

I stood alone atop a hill in Mt. Auburn Cemetery trying to collect myself. I had an hour before Larrimer returned.

I was right—after visiting Juan, I needed the quiet. Hospitals were the worst for me. The fear, the pain, the sorrow. They scoured my emotional bones.

And I'd just tasted my friend's impending death. Juan was a wonderful man. Sharp. Witty. Caring. His leaving, a heart-wrenching thing. Unfixable.

So I walked the paths amidst the trees and gravestones.

Far more than a resting place for the dead, Mt. Auburn was home to sculpture and gardens and nature. Carved angels, dogs, a sphinx. Interred Civil War veterans, African Americans, average Joes. Flowers, ponds, paths. And wildlife in abundance.

Today, ice draped the trees and statues. It fit my mood. Crystals danced on the oaks and maples and spiked from myrtle and rhododendron. A shocking flash of red from a cardinal. Paw prints of deer, fox, and raccoon.

If elves were real, they'd live here, in this landscaped ice palace that eased me in ways beautiful and terrible. Hell, maybe they *were* real.

I leaned against the trunk of a beech tree, the stone sphinx crouched before me, and stroked the cashmere of my fingerless mitts until it soothed me.

I walked on, toward a more heavily forested area, more private and a favorite of mine. Icy wind buffeted me. I couldn't feel my cheeks, couldn't feel my lips, couldn't feel my tears. I liked it that way.

Death came to all. Was Juan going to meet his Jesus? His Buddha? A white light? Or did we just end? Like in End? Perhaps, there existed truths out of time and imagination our minds couldn't process? If the body...

Eyes brushed over me. Close. I rubbed my arms, deliberately expanded my senses. Nothing. Mt. Auburn could do that. I took another step. Except the feeling intensified. I turned.

A white wolf the size of a pony padded toward me at a bouncy trot. I blinked. Still there. Still pony-sized. About six feet away, it stopped.

Chapter Thirteen

I **stayed cool. Sure I did. Right.**
Its head came even with my chest, the breeze ruffling long fur the color of new-fallen snow. Eyes like ancient gold coins. Magnetic. Otherworldly.

There are *no* wild wolves in New England. None.

Terror leeched onto my skin, into my blood. I hadn't factored in a huge wolf when I'd geared up that morning. My gun would damage it, sure. But unless I could make a kill shot... Oh, *hell*.

I didn't want to kill a wolf.

My damned heart did the conga, my breath—clouds of fear—mist in the cold.

The wolf didn't growl, didn't bare its teeth.

I bit my lips. What the frig!

Juiced with adrenaline, I calmed my heart, corralled my fear, cast my senses outward.

The wolf's vibe—I caught no malice or hunger. Only waiting.

His golden eyes held mine. He didn't move closer, just stood there, a cool silence.

I'd once stumbled on a black bear in the woods. I'd made lots of noise, and it had lumbered off.

A bear was not a wolf.

I backed away from the wolf, slowly, carefully, and he mirrored my movements, like in a dance.

I couldn't take my eyes from him. Nor, apparently, he from me.

I lost time. Seconds? Minutes?

Sounds became muffled, as if a shroud lay across the cemetery, the wood, the animals.

I stopped, as did he, and I cast my senses.

Waiting. Dread. Fear.

The wolf's nose twitched, and his eyes slid to the right.

Mine followed.

A presence, just beyond the heavy screen of trees. Not the same as the wolf. Nothing at all like the wolf.

Cloying. Hungry. *Evil.*

Rotted geraniums and cat urine. I'd smelled it before. At Dave's abattoir.

Smoke swirled around the trunks of trees to coalesce by the path's edge. It glistened, syrupy now, wove forward, and as it undulated, it darkened from grungy white to gunmetal gray.

I stumbled back, and the lupine closed on me, my eyes bouncing from him to the thing that slimed closer and closer.

Was the wolf part of that *thing* or... No.

My mind hamstered around in a vain attempt to process.

If this was magic, I didn't like it one bit.

I kept backing up, knowing that *thing* meant me harm.

Warm breath on my thigh. I bumped into the wolf. "Shit!"

He glided around me, brushing my jeans, halted before me and sat, cool, calm, his muzzle pointed straight at the slime.

The ooze paused. Drew closer. A large clump differentiated into a woman's face—high-cheekboned, deep-set eyes closed, gray skin mottled as if with shiny burns, a full-lipped mouth tilted upward as if in bliss. A plain red circlet on her crown pulsed, banded around her bound and tendriled hair as it lengthened and grew, undulating and moving of its own accord. The snaking coils solidified further—a chittering sound filling the air. They dropped to the ground, then rose, opening red cobra-like hoods, eyes black and bulbous, black forked tongues flicking, tasting.

The chittering stopped.

That couldn't be good. I whooshed out a breath. Holy moly, what the hell was that thing?

My mind fogged, and I swayed, stumbled forward.

The wolf's head shot around and snapped at my legs.

Shocked to my senses, I froze, then oh-so slowly slid out my gun, leaned down for the Bowie knife in my boot. Even if my hands trembled, just a bit, the gun in my left hand, knife in my right, grounded me.

The nest of hooded cobrathings slithered closer, but slowly, as if breeching a resistant barrier.

Bullets and cold steel might do nothing to the creature, but they felt so good.

I aimed my gun at the woman's head and fired. The bullet pierced her forehead, but left no mark. Shit.

The cobrathings hissed. Their red hoods began to pulse like malignant hearts, their heads swayed and tongues flicked, jaws yawning to reveal one immense dripping fang.

Oh, gods. I staggered, found my balance, and moved into a crouched stance.

On my left, a cobrathing shot forward, fast, prepared to strike. Reflexively, I slashed out with my knife.

The head fell, separating from its snaky body, and yellow pus splattered onto my hand, bubbling and burning so bad, my eyes watered. Foam erupted from the headless stalk as it continued to sway, obscenely alive, until it finally plopped to the ground, where it compressed and retreated, sucked back into the woman's head.

Golly. One down, a bazillion to go. That was all I could conjure, when what I really wanted was a one-way ticket out of Oz.

More eyes, behind me. I stole a glance. Five more white wolves crouched, fur bristled, eyes agleam.

The immense wolf in front of me raised his head and howled.

The others joined in. A chorus. A battle cry.

Whoopdedo, I liked it!

The cobrathings paused, and the wolves charged.

Screw this; here we go. I ran forward, too, slashing, cutting, shooting my Glock, biting with my knife at those cobrathings, over and over and over. Burns on my hands, my cheeks, my scalp. My adrenaline-fueled cocktail of fear and fury didn't give a shit.

Growls and yips and screams.

Cut, slash, rip, rend. Blood, pus, and clumps of flesh coated the earth. I slipped, fell, came face-to-face with a hooded cobrathing pulsing death.

The wolf leader ripped the head off that sucker and tossed it.

I punched to my feet and began again.

An eon later, a roar deafened me, one of pain and petulance and hatred.

Time stopped. Sound. Sight. Scent. The Void.

Flux, an ebb, a flow, then pain burst through my body, endless, eternal, until a brush of warmth, of fur brought me back. Panting, bent in half, hands on knees, I raised my head. I was covered in blood and pus and the scarlet of my burns.

The ooze, the cobrathings, the woman, gone. Vanished.

Six white wolves faced me in a semicircle, chests heaving, coats dappled in red blood and yellow pus. They raised their muzzles and howled in triumph.

I howled, too. Hell, yeah!

I gasped another breath. Another.

The wolves' howls expanded, the rhythm building to a mighty crescendo. They ceased.

At the edge of the wood, movement. I raised my knife and gun. All I saw were luminous amber eyes that wove between the lustrous white of the trees.

Five of the wolves turned and padded toward the eyes into the wood, soon hidden by the ice-coated trees.

Relief jellied my legs, but I held my stance.

The magnificent wolf who'd never left my side, muzzle wide, teeth and fang gleaming with blood, peered up at me.

I dared stroke his massive head.

"Thank you." Gratitude knotted my throat. "Thank you so damned much. I wish you could talk."

He yipped, and I'd swear it was a laugh, then he nudged me down the path to where the vegetation thinned and, in the distance, a couple walked hand in hand, heads close in conversation.

The wolf's gold eyes again captured mine, as if he wished to impart prophecies I couldn't grasp.

He blinked, then bounded off after his pack.

Somehow I managed to stagger down the path, past the handholding couple, chatting, all gestures and smiles, toward people and cars and skyscrapers. As I walked, the pain eased, the blood faded and disappeared, as did the yellowed pus, and my burns smoothed to pink, then to normal-looking flesh. My clothes, again pristine.

On putty legs, I made it to a granite bench beside a small birch. I swiped off the snow and lowered myself to the seat.

I hugged my knees, teeth chattering, body shaking, tried to stop my tremors. My mind faltered, struggling to process what had just happened.

A shadow, the one from days ago at the house. Again, someone was watching me. I grasped my knife, my gun, unfurled my mind, and surfed a gentle wave deeper inside the shadow. Walls slammed me backward.

Snap. Gone.

Time passed, the cold—a numbing companion.

A crunch behind me. Weapons up, I pivoted.

"Promise I won't bite," Larrimer said, hands up, palms out.

I replaced my gun, slipped my knife into its sheath.

A frown. He slid off his sunglasses and sat beside me on the bench. "Are you hurt?"

When I shook my head, black spots swam in front of me.

He slid an arm around my shoulder, muscled and hard, and pulled me close. I stiffened.

"Sshhh," he said.

Comfort. Concern. I'd be churlish to refuse. I wanted this, so I relaxed, absorbed his warmth, his reality. He held me, and for eons we sat there, the beat of his heart a mantra of calm.

"Were you attacked?" he finally said. "Clea?"

I sloughed out a breath, got it together. "I'm okay." I pushed away, examined my clothes, my hands.

Nope, not a thing. I even checked my knife. Clean.

Another form of fear stabbed me. Had I just lived some kind of freakish mental episode?

No, it was real. Wasn't it?

Later. I'd deal with it later.

Larrimer's brow furrowed.

"Something scared me," I said, aching to tell him everything, knowing he'd think I was nuts. "That's all. How did you find me?"

"You're easy to spot." He smiled. "You okay to walk?"

I nodded, tucked my hands into my jacket pockets. "You're early."

"Briefing done."

"The golden eagles?"

He shook his head.

Again, he wore no gloves. I'd knit him a pair of mitts.

We circled a frozen pond.

"You've been crying," he said.

Juan. A lifetime ago. "Um, the ME, my friend, he's dying."

"You feel too much," he said. Cold. Dark.

"I'd rather that than too little."

"Feelings cloud thought."

A gust of wind. Icy. Alive. I was alive. I grinned. "Hell yeah. Like a shot of Jim Beam Black."

He barked out a laugh. "I prefer Blanton's Original, myself."

A flurry of wings, and a hawk burst from the trees. Hunting.

After long moments, he said, "What happened?" He stopped and raised a hand to my shoulder. "Something happened. Tell me."

I shook my head.

He peered down at me, the dying sun carving his face. "I'm glad you're safe."

Those eyes. A blue flame. I wanted to stand on tiptoe and taste those lips. But even on tiptoe, I couldn't reach them. He'd have to bend down, and I sensed the man before me seldom did that. Would he bend for me?

"You're cold," he said. "I would warm you." He started to remove his jacket.

Oh, he would, this man I barely knew. But no doubt I'd get little more than the physical. "No need. I'm warm enough. Let's go. I have stuff to do."

CHAPTER FOURTEEN

I insisted on driving—I needed to be in control of something, anything—and I made him belt up. He slept, slouched in the seat, again taking up more room than any person had a right to. I refused to think about the woods, the wolves, the glowing eyes, and especially that snaky *thing* that tried to end me. Damn, she made Medusa look like a garter snake.

I focused on the road, the tarmac, the potholes, the reality. Yeah, right. Like I knew what reality was anymore.

Cars and trucks jammed Route Two, and we varoomed around the Fresh Pond circle and over the bridge. We soon passed Belmont's immense Mormon temple, then through Lexington and round the Concord circle, toward home.

A niggle distracted me. It grew, and I glanced at the speedometer. I was hitting eighty-plus. I slowed to seventy-five, but whatever gripped me, remained. Lulu? Had someone gotten to Lulu?

"I Shot the Sheriff" fractured my thoughts. Larrimer answered his phone, and a few terse words later he ended the call, then pecked out a number and put the phone to his ear. When he disconnected, he turned to me.

"She's fine," he said, his tone mellow. "The girl."

How...? But I didn't care about the how. "Thanks."

"It was your face," he said. "All scrunched up. And your driving. Christ, you're scary."

"A thrill a minute." I glanced at him, a tad annoyed at how well he read me. But I felt better. "The call you took?"

"Headquarters. Some place called Bronze Printing. They're the ones who printed the invitation. We'll pay them a visit in the a.m."

Good thing he said "we."

Lulu and Bernadette were fine, excepting Bernadette's newest accessory—a turban. A black tapestried one. It sure complemented the derringer at her hip. *Oy.* She was turning into the eccentric grandmother I never had.

After I'd tucked in all the critters, we chowed down on Bernadette's divine dinner. Then again, given my day, PB-and-J would have tasted extra special.

Later, I stretched out in bed, massaging my aching muscles with Bag Balm. Good enough for a cow's udder, good enough for me.

The Storybook called.

Not gonna think about that woman's face and slimy cobrathings crawling over me. Nope, not.

Hell. If this was magic, it should be prettier. And if that thing was after me, what else was?

I shivered.

No thinking. Forbidden.

I read the Storybook again. And again. Until sleep took me.

Dammit, people were yapping in the kitchen, waking me and interrupting a perfectly yummy dream. My phone read 3:00 a.m. Who the hell... Just in case, I slipped my hand around my Glock and padded into the darkened hall.

The voices—Bernadette's and Larrimer's. Bizarre.

I tiptoed down the steps, avoiding the creaky places, to the third up from the main floor, and peeked through the railing.

Yup, there they were, sitting across from each other at the kitchen table, sipping what looked like bourbon and chatting away. I'd seen stranger things, but not by much.

"You realize what's going on, don't you, sonny boy?" Bernadette said.

"I don't know what you mean, Lady."

She snickered. "You don't know."

A rumble, low in his throat. "I do not."

She picked up her glass, swirled the liquid around, took a long swallow. "Ahhh. Well then, if whoever you're *really* working for didn't tell you, I will."

Larrimer waited with that perfect stillness of his.

"What's inside you." Bernadette pointed a long finger at his chest, her tone deadly serious. "The same thing's inside her."

His lips twitched. "Lungs? A heart?"

She pressed her hands to the table and straightened her spine. "You know, you understand, so don't play games."

"Not a game, Lady," he said, his voice molten granite. "You have no idea what's inside me."

She leaned back, took another swig. "Bah, of course I do. Some of it, at least. Do you think I don't hear the song, too?"

The boil of Larrimer's fury nearly knocked me backward.

The song, Bernadette had said. The melody I'd shared with Larrimer when we'd first met. Not possible. I'd never reacted to Bernadette like *that*.

She waved a hand. "*Calme-toi.* I hear it, yours, Clea's, but they don't echo within me. My type is quite different from yours and hers."

His brow furrowed. "Type?"

"Type, um, subspecies or family. *Merde!* I don't have the words."

He tipped back his glass, polished off his drink and pressed his hands to the table, as if to get up.

"Not yet." She waggled a finger. "This, you must understand. Your very essence is growing her abilities. And hers are growing yours."

His face tightened, his cheekbones stark in harsh relief. "I would know if that were happening."

Bernadette downed the last of the bourbon and stood, looking down at Larrimer's now grim face. "Would you?"

I squeezed the baluster. Questions like bees buzzed my mind. They wanted me excluded from their conversation. Now wasn't the time to ask, but what mattered was *why?* I flew up the stairs on what Dave called "silent feet."

At eight the next morning, the world looked normal, if Larrimer inhaling steak and eggs and waffles constituted normal. Had I imagined that tête-à-tête in the middle of the night? No, no I did not.

I toyed with my waffle as I watched his single-minded food focus clear the piled-high dish.

I'd bet he'd be like that with sex, too.

"That man knows how to make coffee," Bernadette said, pulling me back to reality. "Lotta fuss, since you're the only one who drinks it."

"Um, Larrimer..." I said, near-bursting to ask him and Bernadette about their conversation. I *knew* Bernadette would tell me nothing. But Larrimer might. I'd frame my words with care.

Lulu wandered in. Damn. I stuffed the questions down deep, along with the urge to tell Larrimer about yesterday's cobrathings.

I needed to think, to *understand*. It was like I was in a dingy drifting further and further from reality's shore.

Larrimer finished smearing jam on his English muffin, looked up, and I became his singular focus. "You started to ask...?"

I speared another waffle. "Pass the maple syrup, please."

Soon after, Bernadette and Lulu took off, and when I emerged from my shower, I found Larrimer gone, too. He returned that afternoon, and we drove to the putative breadcrumb that might lead us to Dave's killers and the endangered species traffickers, Bronze Printing in Fantin, a small town just north of Hembrook.

When we left the car, he leaned in, close to my ear. "Looks like you survived the thug's two-day deadline."

I grinned, fake as a stripper's smile. "Looks like. How about I take point?" I asked as we entered the small brick-and-wood building. "Fish and Wildlife strikes fear in the hearts of few." Of course, Larrimer could strike fear in the heart of anyone he chose. But I wasn't about to tell him that.

He half-smiled back. "I'm the one with the warrant."

"True. But I'm the one with the interrogation cred."

He held up a finger. "Point." Then he did his faux laconic lean against the far wall, giving him a view of the entire place.

I approached the counter.

From the back, a blonde with bee-stung lips and pneumatic breasts waltzed up to us wearing a black sheath skirt and a barely buttoned blouse. Her wide eyes glommed onto Larrimer, where they stuck like suckers. Cute.

I cleared my throat, held up my FBI badge, and offered the woman my hand and an open smile.

Hers appeared slowly, reminding me of yesterday's snaky things. Her handshake was dry and assertive. Her vibes? Those reminded me of yesterday's cobrathings, too, except she was hungry for Larrimer, not me.

"How can I help you folks?" She produced a toothy grin.

I placed the printout of the blood invitation on the counter. "I understand you did this work."

She glanced at it. "So? We print lotsa stuff. It's what we do here." She rested her head on her hands and winked at Larrimer.

I cleared my throat. "We'd like to know who ordered and paid for the printing?"

"I'm sorry, but that's private." Big smile again. I couldn't see it, but I would bet Larrimer was smiling back.

I offered my own big-ass smile. "We'd *so* appreciate it."

Her eyes frosted, and I caught the meanness in them. All for me. Yum.

Larrimer stepped over, face dazzling with sexy intent. He smiled. Her chest surged.

I was going to puke.

He flashed his credentials.

The woman froze, licked her lips. "You, uh, you got a warrant?"

Larrimer withdrew it from the inside of his jacket pocket and handed it to her. Nice.

She didn't bother to read it, but slid off the stool showing lots of shapely leg. Her glance at Larrimer could have fried eggs. Minutes later, she returned clutching a file. She held it out—pointedly not to me.

I swiped it out of her hand. "Thank you. Do you remember anything else about this print job?"

"Nope," she said.

"Do try."

"Like I said, nope." She leaned forward and slid a card toward

Larrimer. "In case you think of any questions *you'd* like to ask me."

He slipped it into his pocket.

I turned to him. "Time to go."

"Wait," she said, a sharp note in her voice. "You can't take that with you."

I grinned. "Oh, but we can."

Outside, I tried not to fume. "That was disgusting."

"What?"

"Oh, right. You and that obviously sex-starved piranha."

He stepped closer, eyes half-lidded. "Catch more flies with honey."

I held my ground. "Careful. Your teeth might rot."

A spark in those Pacific blues. "Watching your slow burn was my fun."

Ten… nine… eight… gurrrr. "Oh, *really*."

His soft chuckle. "Babe, sometimes you're tough as jerky, but sometimes you're so easy, it hurts."

I would not rise to the bait. I would *not*.

A text chimed.

Come home now, please. Hurry. From Bernadette's cellphone.

Bernadette never texted and never said "please."

Something bad, something *very* bad was coming.

I texted back, *On my way.*

Ice momentarily stole Fern's wheels, and I did a 180 at the top of the farm's drive.

"Jesus Christ, woman!"

"Nothing to worry about." I pulled the steering wheel and narrowly missed the left corner of the barn. I said thanks for small favors and hopped out.

Larrimer was beside me in a flash.

"I don't see Bernadette's Jeep," I said. Time slowed.

He notched his head toward the single-bay garage. "Maybe inside."

"No, she only parks there in a bad storm."

He cocked his head. "It's too quiet."

No cluck of the girls. No bark of Grace. No birds at the feeders.

I bit my cheek, checked the time. 4:00 p.m. The day was beginning to fail. Yet no lights glowed from inside the house.

I slid my hand onto the solid presence of my Glock. If I lost one more loved one...

We eased behind Fern as Larrimer pulled his gun.

"You take the lead," I said, the words out before I could think about them. Something unfamiliar settled deep inside me. Trust.

Gun in hand, I followed him toward the house. The *house*. No. My senses screamed...

"Wait," I whispered. "The barn. Whatever it is, it's in the barn."

He stood stone-still, nodded, and pressed a finger to his lips. "Let me clear the house. I'll be fast."

Fast wasn't the half of it, then he hunkered close, and his warm breath licked my ear. "All clear, except for the kitten. She's fine."

I swallowed. "Good."

We ran in a crouch toward the barn. Quiet. Too quiet.

The pastures to my right were clear of animals. In the one on my left, two goats lounged. Larrimer slid inside the partially open barn door, and I followed.

A foul aroma perfumed the cold air, the coppery smell of blood and feces. Ah, geesh.

I moistened my lips, senses humming. Only the gray rays that filtered through the stalls leant any light. My eyes adjusted, and I moved forward.

Larrimer's arm jerked out, hand fisted.

I stopped, then saw. Decapitated chickens lay scattered across the aisle. My girls! I counted. "Rosie and Rocket and Redeye."

I closed my eyes, just for a second, felt him in front of me. My eyes flew open. His back was to me, his gun at the ready, shielding me.

"I'm okay," I whispered.

He moved away, and I sidestepped down one stall and peered into the girls' winter coop. Four red hens hunkered down. Alive, but silent and afraid.

Death awaited me further inside the barn. Heavy. Crushing.

Larrimer signaled he would take the barn's right side, while I took the left.

My gut was so tight it ached. Clem whickered as I passed him.

Claudia was asleep in her stall, puffs of hot breath stirring the air.

Larrimer's movements paralleled mine as he checked the opposite stalls, and we reached the back of the barn simultaneously. I peered up the stairs to the second floor. I sensed no one, but if I were wrong, whoever had done this would be up there.

As I took the first step, Larrimer blocked me.

"Wait," he said, hushed. He pointed to the wooden crate near his feet, then the square opening to the hayloft above one of the empty stalls. I gave him a thumbs up. He tucked his gun in his waistband, carried the crate into the empty stall and set it on the ground. He climbed up, bent his knees and sprang, rocketing up to the opening, which he gripped with his hands. He pulled his torso up, just enough to peer around the floor of the hayloft. Then his body slowly disappeared from view.

I stayed put, back to the barn wall, gun pointed downward alongside my leg. Long minutes drizzled by.

He finally dropped down through the hayloft opening. "Clear. No one's here. Not now."

A shiver of relief. "Good." I holstered my gun and started back down the aisle.

"Wait," he said.

"No. I need to see all my goats are safe." Nanna and Balder, Odin and Freyja were now out in the pasture. I'd seen Thor and Sif in the other one.

Larrimer moved, a blur in front of me, denying me access to Loki and Lofn's stall.

"What is this, some do-si-do?"

He wrapped his hands around my upper arms.

"Don't," he said.

"Move!" I pushed at the wall he'd made with his body.

With a dragon-sized chuff of frustration, he stepped aside.

CHAPTER FIFTEEN

I unlatched the stall door and walked in.

Red. All I could see was red, from their slit throats to their guts spread across the fresh straw.

I fell to my knees.

They lay on their sides, my gentle white fur babies, wearing giant red smiles, throats slit, blood splattered, *eviscerated*.

Those sweet, funny people, gone. I inhaled a sob, leaned against the stall wall, head bowed.

I sensed him reach for me.

I held up a hand and shook my head, again looked at the two bodies. Steam didn't rise from the entrails or the bloodied bellies. They'd been dead a while.

"Nott and Delling are fine," he said.

I gripped the wood, peered over the stall's half-wall. The pair munched some hay, hanging out, but quiet, as if they knew one of their bleats would break me.

Outside, the backfire of a truck. I flew to the barn doors.

I prayed that it was the assassins, come to check on their grisly handiwork. My bloody dead animals, my girls, my goats, lay in heaps, robbed of life just because they were *mine*.

Mine, you fuckers!

Arrogant creeps. Didn't they realize they'd offered us clues?

My knowledge tasted bitter.

Larrimer and I stood shoulder to shoulder at the barn entrance. The shriek of tires not finding purchase on the ice, and soon Bernadette's dilapidated Jeep hoisted itself into view, as if using its last reserves of energy to land on a horizontal surface.

My spirits lifted when a slim, booted foot peeked out the open passenger door. Soon all of Lulu appeared. She opened the rear door for Grace, who tumbled out and bounded toward me, Lulu's mutts not far behind.

And there, Bernadette's turban bobbed as she pushed open the driver's door.

So relieved. Yet it felt as if someone stood on my shoulders, pressing me deep into the earth.

I ran to them—Bernadette and Grace and Lulu and Mutt and Jeff—skidded to a stop. Oh gods, they were safe. *Safe.*

I hugged them all like crazy.

They looked at me like I was knitting with one needle.

Yeah, a part of me was.

I waited for Larrimer in the mudroom with my smaller version of a tech kit and my Nikon DSLR. Outside, icicles draped at the edge of the barn roof like daggers.

When I felt his presence, I turned. He stood there in fresh pair of jeans and a black t-shirt with golden leopard spots, holding his evidence kit. His hair was mussed, his face an impenetrable mask. He was beautiful. How had I ever thought him not a handsome man?

"I'm sorry, babe," he said. "Very sorry."

I raised a hand to his face, but he shook his head. "I'm not big on skin to skin."

"All right."

"When I checked out the hayloft," he said, his voice sandpapered with razors, "I found the killer had rigged an old chair with filament. He'd trip-wired the steps and attached the chair to a shotgun aimed downward. I snipped the filament, emptied the shotgun of shells, including the chambered round meant for you. If you'd kneed it or stepped on the pressure point, the gun would have blasted you to a bloody pulp."

"Nice." I chuckled. "I'm going to cut off their balls."

"What did you say?"

"I said, I'm going to cut off their balls." I smiled. "I'll use a dull knife."

He crossed his arms. "I thank God I'm not the perpetrator."

"Yup."

"I'll process the scene."

I shook my head. "Not alone."

"You'll be in the way," he said, his tone cruel.

His meanness froze me. He slipped into one of Tommy's old barn jackets, lifted his kit, and reached for the door.

And then I got it. Not cruel, no. He was trying to shield me from more pain.

"I'm coming," I said, voice soft. "I must."

The smell hit me, and I faltered, but just for a moment.

"What they've done here." He notched his chin toward the stairs. "They planned for you to be so distressed, you'd walk up those stairs and boom."

"So I'm a target, too. Big whoop. It doesn't change anything."

"It should."

If he only knew about that thing at the cemetery. "Show me the shotgun setup."

Upstairs in the barn, while I took photographs, he examined and printed the scene, bagged the gun and other detritus.

A shiny "something" glinted in my peripheral vision. "Shoot your flashlight over there, please." I scooched down.

His light illuminated a small silver lapel pin.

"Strange-looking thing," he said.

"Not so much. It's the Old Man of the Mountain. The rock formation's gone, but we New Hampshirites still revere it. I've seen a lot of guys with these lapel pins. It's awfully small, but maybe there'll be prints on it."

"Maybe."

Downstairs, we processed the chickens next. My girls.

He took samples, bagged and tagged those, while I again shot photos.

Finally, we got to Loki and Lofn.

After we processed them, today's event a movie etched in my mind, I crouched down and said my farewells, petted each of their heads, their eyes no longer glowing with silver, but glazed with a milky film. So changed, so uninhabited. They hadn't deserved this.

I whispered words of love and thanks until I felt Larrimer's living heat behind me, then a hint of warm breath on my neck.

"We should finish," Larrimer said.

My strength failed. I couldn't bag them, not the girls, nor Loki and Lofn. I walked to the barn doors while Larrimer took care of it. He said he'd arranged for their pickup. They'd go to the lab in Oregon, folded into the ongoing investigation.

I watched as he carried them in bundles of plastic to the shed. The temps were so cold they'd stay preserved until retrieval.

It was time to tell Lulu and Bernadette.

Nobody said much at first, our group solemn. Bernadette loved my animals as much as her own, and her red eyes and tight lips betrayed her grief, as did the petting of the pearl handle of her beloved double-barreled derringer. It didn't take a psychic to know what she was thinking.

The text wasn't from her. She had no clue how to text. She'd lost her cell phone, wasn't sure where. Possibly Barlow's, where they'd eaten lunch. Stolen, more likely.

With Larrimer's man watching them, the theft had been clever.

No dummy, Lulu shot me a look of pure fear.

Larrimer took up the slack. "In a twisted way, Lulu, this will help us find your dad's killer."

"I don't understand," she said.

"The more they do, the more they show their hand, the more we learn about them. The better to track them."

She twirled a lock of copper hair around and around. "Were they after me, do you think? When they killed the animals?

I'd heated some of Bernadette's onion soup for everyone, and placed the bowls on the coffee table. "I don't believe the barn killers were after you, Lulu."

"You don't?" she asked, her voice rice-paper thin.

"Why's that, cookie?" Bernadette's was stiff with concern.

"Larrimer here believes this was aimed straight at me. I'm forced to agree. Whoever's after you, Lulu, doesn't want me involved."

She smiled. "Because you're baaaad."

I snorted a laugh.

Bernadette harrumphed, her unibrow scrunched.

"They need Lulu alive." Larrimer lasered the girl with a sharp look. "The question is why."

Lulu's chest puffed. "I don't know!" Her eyes blazed, then dropped. "I don't know anything!"

And I'd caught Lulu's lie. She reeked of it. Lulu, indeed, knew something, and had no intention of telling us what it was.

Like the bread Bernadette was so fond of making, I'd let her rest some before I started kneading.

Larrimer took a deep breath. "We'll relocate you two temporarily."

Bernadette snorted. "I'm going nowhere."

"What about Lulu?" I asked. "You want to stay here while she goes somewhere else with an outsider to protect her?"

Lulu offered a hormonal fifteen-year-old's smirk. "I'm not going anywhere, *either*."

"Christ in a crapshoot." Larrimer raked a hand through his hair, his frustration palpable. He turned to Bernadette. "You can have my shotgun. I'd lay money you know how to use it."

Bernadette's eyes glowed. "Don't need yours, sonny boy. Got my own."

He chuckled, which did funny things to my body.

"We're partners, Lulu," Bernadette said. "Right?"

"Right!" Lulu said, then giggled.

Great. I'd lost complete control of the people under my care. Just great.

The following day, I sat on my bed and tried to look *objectively* at the shitstorm that was our lives. One attack was all woo woo, the other, too real. They felt disconnected. Two attacks in two days? Lady Luck might be fickle, but the grain-store shooter had been right. The shit had hit.

That vision I'd had of my Da. He'd said the magical and the mundane were, what was it? Retwining. So how were my animals' apparently non-magical deaths connected to my magical snake-creature opponent? And what did either have to do with Dave's homicide?

Damned if I had a clue.

What was Dave's connection to all this? I'd lay money that he was trying to track the same bastards we were. So how had he insinuated himself into their organization? Offered to sell them some seed?

That line of thought got me nowhere, as did my review of the Bronze Printing paperwork or my Internet searches. All dead ends, except for the invitation. Possibly. Talk about vague.

My phone chirped. Ronan Miloszewski.

"Ms. Reese," he said.

"Clea, please."

"Ma'am, I, um, I'm sorry about your animals. Lulu told me. People like that. They're evil."

"I agree, Ronan. Thanks for your kind words. What's up?"

"I've been talking to Lulu. A lot. She, um, wants to go back to school."

Why hadn't Lulu said something? "I'd like that, but—"

"I'll pick her up and drop her off."

"What about practice?"

"Yeah, but, um, if I can't, I'll have somebody else watch her, like on the bus. I'll make sure she's not alone."

A smart, caring boy. I was tempted. "I don't know if it's time yet, Ronan."

Silence.

"Ronan?"

"She really, really wants to, ma'am. I won't let anything happen to her." His voice rang with sincerity.

"Let me think about it, and I'll get back to you ASAP. Okay?"

Downstairs I hunted for Larrimer. While it was my decision, mine and Lulu's, I'd like his take on it.

Nobody was in the living room, and as I headed for my office, the phone chirped again. The Cranadnock paper. I declined.

And again it bleeped. I sighed. There was something to be said for the days before we attached cell phones to our navels.

A text this time. From a number I didn't recognize.

3 p.m. at the diner if u want to learn about The Master. Sit at the counter. Come alone.

I reread the text. "Huh." My calls stirring the rumor pot had done their work.

When I looked up, Larrimer stood before me, silent, one eyebrow raised.

"I heard your 'huh,'" he said.

The guy was a phantom, I swear.

Could he be the shadow? I had no way of knowing, since every time I probed his shields, they were laced tighter than a Victorian corset.

I filled him in on the text and didn't even argue when he said he was coming with me. In fact, I felt positively saintly.

Late February at the Midborough Diner defined slow. The day was cold and damp, nasty, with just a hint of spring to come. We parked next door, at the Truffles Bookshop, and I walked to Station Square's silver diner. In spring, they'd bring out the round umbrellaed tables. Today, a few desultory piles of snow banked the split-rail fence that fronted the sidewalk. The tang of woodsmoke and almost-rain sang to my senses.

I left Larrimer in the parking lot. We'd agreed he would wait five minutes before following.

I slipped beneath the green awning, and when I opened the door, a bell tinkled. As I stepped further onto the checkerboard tile, a suited customer in a booth to my right, briefcase open, studied paperwork while he ate. To my left, two girls, high-school age, texted as they sipped what looked like ice-cream sodas in a corner booth. No one at the counter.

Like I said, winter-slow.

Adrenaline bubbling, I slid onto a counter stool and plucked a menu from its stand, my ears tuned to the noises coming from the kitchen.

Minutes later, a six-foot chocolate-skinned woman stood before me. I'd guess in her thirties, she wore leggings and a black t-shirt printed with the diner's logo. Ebony hair fell to her shoulders in wild curls, lush lips and arresting sloe, blue-black eyes far older than her apparent years. Those eyes stared at me, deeply curious.

"May I help you?" she asked, her voice smoky, each word enunciated with precision, as if English wasn't her first language.

I didn't need to "read" her. Intensely strange vibes poured off her like a waterfall. "I'd like a coffee and the strawberry-rhubarb pie, please."

Her closed-mouthed smile climbed to those exotic eyes. "Of course."

She retrieved a cup and saucer, poured my coffee, and vanished, and I wondered how that uncommon creature had landed in a rural New Hampshire town. Seconds later, she set down a large wedge of pie in front of me.

"Thank you." I held eye contact.

A gleam. She touched her chin with a long, elegant finger and leaned forward. "Are you Clea?"

The bell tinkled behind me, and she looked up, eyes cat curious. Larrimer.

"Yes," I said, drawing her attention back to me. "I am."

"One second." She came around the counter and headed toward Larrimer's booth. Much as I wanted to watch their interaction, I kept my focus on the pie and coffee. It was delicious pie.

I'd eaten half when she returned. "More coffee?" she asked.

"Sure."

She poured. "It's my break. Meet me in the alley beside the diner."

"Here would be better," I said. "Less notable."

She puckered those lush lips. "But I need a smoke. Drop your wallet to the platform where you rest your feet. Then meet me outside."

My wallet—insurance that I'd return inside. When she disappeared, I glanced sideways. From where he sat, Larrimer could see the small alley. Good.

I waited a heartbeat or two, while a sandy-haired man replaced the woman behind the counter. I lay several dollars next to my cup, dropped my wallet to the foot support, and walked out. As I left, I finger-waved Larrimer to stay.

If he trusted me, he would.

CHAPTER SIXTEEN

O nce I made it to the alley, I spotted the woman standing in shadow by the rear entrance. She punched a cigarette from a pack, lit it, and inhaled deep. I walked over, feeling a pygmy compared to her tall elegance.

"The Master," I said as I faced her. Too quick, but I was in no mood for small talk.

"Ohhh, the niceties. You are Clea. I am Anouk." She leaned against the diner's outer wall.

"I apologize," I said. "I didn't mean to be—"

"—quite so precipitous? But you can be, can you not?"

I smiled. "Sometimes."

"Yes, I see that." She drew out the words, her acerbic tone laced with irony.

A damp gust slithered beneath my coat. She wasn't wearing one, her skin smooth, unpebbled with cold.

"Much as I'd like some girl talk," I said. "I need information. Not games."

Her smile meandered across her lips, all sharp canines. "All right. Perhaps another day we will play. The Master is all about control."

The way she'd said it, as if it were a title. "What kind of control?"

"He seeks to be a big player in the unfolding game."

"Game of what?"

A quick shake of her head.

She was going to dole out info in her own time. Talk about a game player. Fine. "He lives around here?"

"I do not believe so. But he has based himself in this area."

"He's importing—"

"Yes, importing." She waved a hand. "You were going to say what? Dangerous things? Illegal commodities? Drugs? I know you would never tell a lowly waitress about the endangered animals."

Lowly waitress, my ass. More like an Amazon warrior.

Smoke curled from her lips. "Think what you will, but those poor creatures are not his end game. He is looking for treasure. Searching for it with his web of contacts, which is extensive. It will be very bad if he finds it. You must not let him find it. It will be the queen on his game board. It will change everything."

"He killed Dave Cochran," I said.

"Of course."

"What kind of treasure?"

"So hasty." She inhaled a puff, exhaled it through her nose. "Ahhh. The sin of smoking. Not money. No." Silence.

"Anouk."

"I am unsure if I will tell you."

Dear gods, I would scream. "You want to."

She flared her nostrils. "Magic treasure. Millennia ago, the two—"

"He wants to control the magical treasure?"

"The magic," she hissed.

I crossed my arms. How could anyone *control* the magic? "Right. The Magic. So how come everybody doesn't know about it, see it?"

She chuffed a laugh. "How would they see what they do not believe? And we who are here are proficient at disguise."

"Sounds like more hoo-ha to me."

She curled her upper lip. It might have been a smile. "Does it? You fought the *Cardillo* with the wolves."

"You know about that *thing*?"

"How many do you think would have seen her? As they say in your realm, it takes one to know one."

"Gimme a break."

"You *are* young. Attend me. Simply listen. Many thousands of years ago, the two essences—what you see as the 'real' world and what is the magic world—were intertwined, much like the braid on a woman's hair."

126

"*Really?* A history lesson? I need to know about the treasure."

She pinched my cheek, her lips an inch from mine. "In good time. You want to be ready? This matters. Whether you think it does or not.

I nodded, and she released me. "Apologies. I'll try to be patient."

"*Be* patient. All right. Where was I? Yes, the braid on a woman's hair. Your 'real' world and the magic world, together. An upheaval—"

"What upheaval?"

"By Garuda's wings! An upheaval, where the magical and your world unwound, the binding fabric shredded."

"Why?" I waited.

"You are as annoying as they said. I am giving you thousands of years of history and events in a few short sentences. Deal with it!"

I laughed. "And here I thought you hadn't a sense of humor."

"The magic and the 'real' world began to unravel," she said. "Until the braid, as you were, became two separate locks. The Guardian lost the chest—"

"The magic treasure?"

She blinked. "Which chose your real world. And no, we do not know why. We paid little attention—much to fury of some of us—because in the 'real' world, the chest was inert. We grew accustomed to—many even relished—the separation. And so it was lost in the mists of time and place."

"Who are '*we*?'" I asked.

A sound at my back. I twirled, went for my gun. A man, reaching inside his jacket... to pull out a pack of Marlboros.

"Hey," he said. "Hope you don't mind."

"Of course not." Anouk dropped her cigarette and ground it out, then pocketed the butt.

"I must get back." She turned toward the rear entrance.

"You're not done, not by half," I said.

"I am. For now."

"I've got your number," I said. "We'll text."

She shook her head, but I caught her soft laughter. "Naturally I used a, what do you call them? A burner phone."

"Dammit, Anouk."

"I will be in touch."

127

When I reentered the diner, Anouk stood behind the counter. Larrimer dutifully manned the booth.

"I forgot my wallet," I said as I walked up to her, seething at her peremptory dismissal.

She nodded.

Movement in my peripheral vision, and I leapt across the counter, pushing her down in the process.

A flashing pain in my neck, then more gunshots as a blur of Larrimer pursued the man who'd fled out the side door.

My neck burned, and liquid warmth oozed down my neck. Blood. I pressed my hand to my neck as I eased back from my awkward position and thumped onto a counter stool.

Anouk glided to her feet in one smooth movement, her eyes glowing amber. I blinked. No, they were blue-black and furious.

"You protected me." Her eyes flashed amber again. Right.

Wet seeped through my fingers.

"You!" she said. "You protected *me*."

She sounded indignant.

I shrugged, pinned like a butterfly by her angry stare. "Um, would you get me something for my neck?"

She did so, and as I waited, I hoped Larrimer had caught the shooter, thought about the businessman with the open briefcase that artfully concealed a gun.

Three days. Three attacks. A bit much, *goddammit*.

A sound. I looked up, expecting Anouk, but the man who'd been her replacement handed me a warm, wet towel. He put a dry one on the counter.

"I called the cops."

"Good. Where's Anouk?"

"She left."

Got out of Dodge. But I knew what I seen. Her eyes gone amber. I'd seen those eyes before. They'd glowed as they'd woven between the white of the trees at Mount Auburn Cemetery.

Seconds later, Larrimer stood beside me, doing a slow burn. "Let's go."

"Did you—"

He clamped his hands around my upper arms and lifted me away from the counter.

Startled, I didn't fight him. But, geesh, he was annoying.

"Later," he said.

"You don't get—"

"Christ almighty, woman." Icicles. "*Later*." He tore the towel off my wound, grabbed some fresh napkins, and pressed them to it.

Not in a talking mood, eh? I took over the napkin holding duty. Damn, but my neck ached.

We didn't wait for the cops, and when we arrived home, Bernadette patched me up, *again*, tut-tutting all the while and readjusting that bizarre turban.

Larrimer had peeled out after he handed me off to Bernadette, and the screech of tires prompted my snort when he'd zoomed down the driveway.

Apparently, it took a bullet to ignite Mr. Dragon Dude.

Surrounded by Gracie, Mutt, and Jeff, their warmth making me drowsy, I waited on the couch for Larrimer's return. And waited. And waited.

Finally, I dragged myself upstairs, long after Lulu and Bernadette had gone to their rooms.

The world chorused to the beat of my injured neck and a blazing headache, so I downed four ibuprofens. I squeezed out a cool washcloth, got in bed, and laid it on my forehead. It felt good. Not much else did.

I closed my eyes, desperately eager for sleep. Except my thoughts raced in a hedged maze. Anouk. Who was she? *What* was she? My senses said nothing I'd ever seen, ever *touched* before. She couldn't possibly be a cat, a panther. Could she?

Calico Kitty jumped on the bed, her eyes, happily, a normal green.

I felt like a stranger in my own personal strange land. One of mystery, of magic, of things my mind couldn't grasp.

I hadn't missed how she'd asked if I wanted to be ready. Oh, no, hadn't missed that one.

The Master. Anouk said if The Master found the magic treasure, it would change everything. What was everything?

The Storybook. It all seemed to come back to the Storybook and its magical box. Had to be Dave's chest. Didn't it?

Great, I was living inside some hellish Disney movie.

Anouk said the worlds were twining together again, which reinforced that vision I'd had of my Da. What had happened to him? To Mam?

Why couldn't I remember, dammit! And why did the world look the same as always. Where were all those magic critters, hiding under rocks? What were they?

Anouk. A panther? Could *she* be the black cat I'd seen in the road? No way. Way?

Fairies? Succubi? Dryads? Vampires? They were magical, right? Were they? Trolls. Unicorns. Witches. Dear gods, how was I supposed to know? I needed a guidebook. Anouk would give me one. Of course she would. Along with my new magic wand and a pair of sparkly red slippers.

I blew out a breath. Ouch. My head killed.

Again, I closed my eyes, and Loki's and Lofn's corpses wrapped in slithering tentacles appeared.

Larrimer. So grounded, so *present*, he'd help sort things out. When I needed him, where was that contrary man? How could I possibly miss him? Because I liked running things by him, hearing his take, his sharp mind knifing, his carved body...

A tap on the door. Larrimer. Finally.

"Go away," I said, wanting him to have to work for it.

"Clea?" Lulu's voice was soft and reed thin.

I sighed. "C'mon in, kid."

The dark felt so good, I kept my eyes closed for a few more moments. Soft footsteps padded across the wood floor.

A hand touched mine. "Are you angry at me?" Her voice was tentative, scared.

"Angry? No. Not even a little."

The wet cloth disappeared from my forehead, replaced by an icy bag that sounded like pebbles. Peas?

Deliciously cool, it softened the stiletto in my head. "Playing nurse, are we?"

"Agent Larrimer said it would help."

So he was back, and I stifled my disappointment that he hadn't come to check on me. "It does. It's not bad, really."

"But it could have been bad."

"Well, yeah." I cranked my eyes open. Lulu looked panicked, pale eyes fearful. I inched a hand over to grasp hers. It trembled. "I'm fine. Just got a lousy headache is all. I thought you were asleep."

She chewed her lip. "I couldn't. I asked Agent Larrimer, and he said it would be okay if I sat with you for a while. If something happens to you... I... I want to stay here. With *you*. You make me feel safe. Please?"

I smiled, even if it did hurt. "Of course you're staying with me. That's what kids do with their guardians."

She punched out her chin. "I'm not a kid."

This time, the smile was easy. "I know."

She skimmed a hand across my hair. "It's longer. Fast growing and sort of curly, too."

"Weird, huh."

"I like it. It's pretty."

I relaxed back into the pillow, frozen peas soothing. "Thank you, Lulu. And thanks for sitting with me."

And she began to sing "Twinkle, Twinkle Little Star," her voice low and impossibly sweet. Beyond Adele. Beyond anyone I'd ever heard. A magic voice. Oh, I was so not going there.

She segued into "What a Wonderful World," and tears burned my eyes at the beauty of it.

On her final heart-stopping note, emotion filled me so completely, I couldn't speak.

"Did you like it?" she asked.

I nodded.

"My dad," she said. "He called it a talent. I don't sing for most people."

"I'm so glad you did for me."

"Me, too."

As sleep embraced me, a girl held my hand and stole my heart.

The next morning, creaky body and all, I did some stretches, then began typing a quick report to Bob about yesterday's diner "episode," leaving out the magic stuff from my convo with Anouk. My fingers slowed, became deliberate. I double-checked each word I lay down on the page. My trust in Bob Balfour—my old friend, my FBI mentor—had begun to erode. This care I took with something that used to be second nature showed just how much.

Task complete, I trotted to the barn, further loosening my cranky bod and mulling over Larrimer. Again. Him not filling me in the previous night, that *stung*! He hadn't even come upstairs to give me the once over.

Was I sulking? Dear gods.

I made sure all our animals were safe, no more corpses. Except someone had fed and watered them. Not Bernadette. I'd passed her baking pies in the kitchen. Lulu still slept.

He'd done it. Warmth blossomed at his kindness. Maybe I wasn't completely annoyed with him.

It took all my energy to slide the barn doors closed. I could not get sick. I turned and stared at my home. Home. It had never really been that. Well, when Tommy lived. Yeah, then, it had been a home, with a sprinkling of laughter, the voices of Tommy and his friends playing video games, Bernadette constantly on the move. She was softer then, less idiosyncratic, before her grandson's death had peeled away any normalcy, leaving only the shrapnel of sorrow.

Funny, but now the ancient post-and-beam building felt sort of like a home again. Bustling with purpose and people. Noise. Comings and goings. Laughter. Sadness. Energy. Family. Love.

Back inside, I hung up my barn coat. When I turned, Larrimer handed me my go-mug. A truce, except when he glanced at my neck, his body hummed with anger.

But I was in a mood, too, my bad elf perched on my shoulder. There he stood, all bronzed biceps in his tight black t-shirt. So he didn't much like skin-to-skin, eh?

"Let's talk." I smiled and hooked an arm though his.

"Don't touch me." Startled words ground out likes rocks.

"Grouchy, are we?" But I let him escape and as he walked away, was surprised to see him brush his fingers across the spot where I'd touched his flesh.

He took the red chair, another salvo. I took the ancient one, trying to ignore that spring poking my butt, and picked up my knitting, the mitts I'd started for him. I fired back, all dulcet tones and smiles. "Thank you so much for doing the barn chores. Hope you didn't get too much chicken poop on you."

His lips twitched.

I grinned. "You're fun."

"You're more fun."

"But you're still madly inscrutable," I said.

He raised that eyebrow. "Whereas you're simply maddening."

"It's good for you," I said. "Given you try to bulldoze your way most of the time."

He started to speak, almost smiled, then, "I'm more subtle than that."

I nearly blurted *my ass,* but then we'd be off again. Instead, I told him what Anouk had said, again editing out the magic, and he listened with that intensity that hallmarked his skills.

"Control's a funny thing," he said. "Elusive. It can shift in an instant."

Didn't I know it. I sounded him out about Lulu and school, and he thought it was a wise idea.

"Now it's your turn." I cut his questions off at the pass.

"I lost him," he said.

"Not buying it. You're faster, cannier than any man I've ever seen."

He pulled back, his face a blank slate, his body language relaxed. "He's dead."

"Did you—"

"No."

I tilted my head. "Why can't you be forthright with me?"

Statue still, he leaned forward, reached out a hand as if to caress my cheek. He fisted it. "Simple. There are things I won't share."

Frustrated, I hid my disappointment. "All right. For now." I waited a beat. "When I entered the diner, I glanced at the shooter. I sensed nothing. No anger, no toxicity. That bothers me."

"His training."

I shook my head, my new curls tickling my cheeks. "I should have sensed that layer."

"I believe we can disabuse ourselves of any notion that you are safe."

CHAPTER SEVENTEEN

T he day dragged, the ache in my neck slowing me down. Larrimer had taken my truck to the Hadley, Mass., Fish and Wildlife headquarters. A briefing, he'd said, about the eagles. I was concerned about him, a faint hum in my head saying he might be in danger.

I surfed the net, dithering about his return. I found nothing about The Master except for the 2012 movie and several Dr. Who references.

The Master. What a dumb name. Maybe it was an acronym. People loved those. Like Menace After Stupid Thing. Crap. That was silly.

Luscious cooking smells finally distracted me—hoorah—and the murmur of low voices. I tested my shoulder, which was way better, as were my other nicks and bruises. Or maybe it was the throbbing in my neck that drowned them out.

I fast-walked to the kitchen, and spotted Lulu in the living room, glued to the TV while she munched a sandwich.

"What're you watching?" I asked.

"A new reality show. 'Real Magic.'"

My eyes crossed. Could I *not* get away from this? "Oh?"

All excited, she took another bite. "Yeah, it's so cool, like... real stuff."

"What stuff?"

"Like videos of jackalopes and fairies riding mice and this thing called a Hodag in Wisconsin." Her eyes widened. "It's got two tusks and spiky things on its spine. It's really gross."

I could only imagine Anouk's take.

At dinner, Lulu bubbled about her return to school the following day. She flew from the table to call Ronan, not even bothering with her dirty dishes.

A healthy sign. She was home. Even if Larrimer wasn't.

When he finally blew through the door and looked to be in one piece, something inside me relaxed, which, oddly enough, made me feel physically crappier. Bernadette handed him a mounded dinner plate, and I decamped into the living room, having been ordered not to clean up.

Minutes later, Bernadette carried a tray of steaming tea, bourbon, scones, and what looked like two stainless devices of torture and set it on the sofa table.

"Time to fix your dressing." She frowned, worry pleating her wrinkled face.

"Are you magic, Bernadette?" It just popped out.

She glared. "*Mon dieux!* You've lost your mind."

"Probably."

Larrimer ambled around the corner, and she notched her chin. "Sonny boy here says he wants to watch. Check out the wound."

Face canvas-blank, he eyeballed my neck.

"What am I, some medical experiment?" I asked, grumpy as hell.

He snapped on a pair of gloves. "You're oozing."

Gross. I poured two fingers of bourbon into the tea and drank, manning up.

Bernadette grinned and tore off the bandage.

"That hurt!"

"Tough it out," Larrimer said. But at odds with his words, he gently rubbed a thumb back and forth across my shoulder. My clothed shoulder. Damn, I wanted the man to touch me. Even more, I wanted to touch him.

"So what are you going to wear?" he asked.

Bernadette's hand flashed as she swiped Betadine across my neck. "Wear?"

"To the Policemen's Gala," he said. "My agency's replicated the invitation. We're good to go."

What the frig *was* I going to wear?

"Ah, you're opting out." He nodded like some Buddhist sage.

"Never. It's just goat farming isn't conducive to owning anything frou-frou." None of my clothes would cut it. "I'll figure it out."

"I'll take care of it," he said.

"You're deranged."

"I thought we'd already established that." His eyes took on an animal sparkle.

Bernadette dabbed on a gob of salve, then pressed a new bandage to my neck.

"Ow!" I said.

"Poor baby," Larrimer said, looking all faux sad.

"It's a good thing you're a man," I said under my breath.

"What does that have to do with anything?"

"If you weren't, swear to gods, I'd take you out."

"You mean like on a date?" he asked.

"No! I mean like in a fight."

"What," he said, face stoic, but eyes laughing. "You don't fight men?"

"Of course I do! Just stop bugging me." I turned away, pissed. I didn't want him to see me grinding my teeth.

Larrimer twined gauze around my wrist. "Don't scratch it."

Gurrr.

As I pulled a new skein of yarn from the closet, Larrimer's voice came through the closed door to my office. Had to be on the phone. I inched closer. Impolite, but irresistible.

"She looks lousy," he said. "Bastard shot her."

Pause.

"He's dead, chomped on something in his mouth, foamed, and died."

The shooter committed suicide. Extreme.

Pause.

"Why send an incompetent?" Larrimer's voice, cold enough to freeze the Sahara.

Pause.

If only I could hear the other end of the conversation.

"The Anouk woman? So they'd been after *her*. Yes, she talked to Clea. So?"

Anouk was in their sights, too. Little wonder she'd scooted so fast.

Pause.

"That's a fucked-up reason."

Pause.

"What was on that bullet?" His voice, a hot growl.

Pause.

"That's fucking deadly. Fix it. Use the wyvern's blood."

Wyvern?

"I don't give a shit if you were saving it." Pause. "No, not even for my men. She needs that fucking antidote *now*."

Pause.

I raised a hand to my neck. Sensitive and sore. But I felt okay.

Pause.

"If anything happens to her..." he growled, his voice near feral. "Pray that the courier arrives in time. Pray hard."

A whine at my feet. Grace, wanting to go out. Larrimer's footsteps. I vamoosed, fast.

Wyvern? That was a *dragon*. Holy shit. Larrimer wasn't just hiding a secret, but a whole grab-bag full. He knew more about Dave and the magic world then he'd let on. At the end, his psychic scent spoke of fury and desperation, and underneath it all, care. For me.

Back in the living room, I scooched forward on my chair, in an effort to grab Bernadette's attention, which was stapled to the TV. "I was serious before, when I asked you about magic."

She waved a hand to shush me. "Not now. I'm watching my story."

No one but Bernadette would call *Game of Thrones* a "story." "You've seen this episode."

She fussed with her turban. "This is On Demand. I want to see it again."

I couldn't help myself. "Reliving old times?"

She jabbed the pause button. Her hazel eyes blazed. "I can't help you, Clea. I told you, you're not *ready*."

I swept my fingers through my hair. They came away greasy with sweat. "When I'm ready, will you answer me?"

"I already told you, I *can't*."

"Why, Bernadette? I don't—"

"I made a *serment*."

A vow. Except she was lying. No. Rather, she was speaking half-truths. Lately, my senses were refining, grasping even subtle nuances from peoples' emotions. "You took a vow."

"A sacred one, cookie." She pursed her lips. "Sure as shootin', you don't want me to break it."

"But..." I shook my head, which felt like a bag of rattling rocks.

She turned from me and pressed play.

Dismissed, I walked toward the stairs, stumbled.

"Clea?" she asked.

I forced myself to straighten. "Just tripped."

She pinched the loose skin at her throat. "I worry. I don't want the wolves to get you, cookie. That Larrimer's one of them. You'll get eaten."

Smiling, I winked. "I've always liked lupines."

Upstairs, I spun to shut the door, got dizzy, and leaned against it. My room swirled like a mad funhouse, and I squeezed my eyes, tried to still the vortex. Fail.

All I had to do was get to the bed. I took a step, stumbled, reached out, and belly flopped onto the floor, a handful of bedspread cascading over me. I pushed it away, tried to holler for Bernadette. What came out was soft and breathy. My phone. I fumbled in my pocket, and the walls of the room shrank, then bowed.

I pushed the phone's buttons, tried to find Larrimer's number. After a couple of breaths and blinks, I stilled the crazy enough to press the buttons.

"What?" he asked.

"I have a problem."

"On my way."

"Just you." Cold flash-flooded my body. My teeth chattered.

He strode in seconds later, his unease caustic on my tongue. I must look like shit. Either that, or I was about to die. Bad thought.

He lifted me onto the bed.

A stab in my belly. Dizzy. I puked.

Tommy yammering. "Look out!" "Don't go that way!" "Check the stirrup!"

I mean, really. Get a grip, Tom. I'm not a baby.

He keeps yelling at me. Why isn't he shutting up?

"Clea! Stay with me!"

More orders. I'd had it with orders.

Ohhhh. Cool liquid against my lips. Heaven. So hot in here. Broiling.

"Clea. Open your eyes."

I lay cradled in someone's lap. "Where's Bernadette?"

"She looked in on you. Now we wait. Open your eyes."

I did. Blinded by the light, by the song. "Where are we?"

"On your bed."

"No I'm not!" Crawled my fingers to his shirt, fisted it. "Don't take me to the hospital, Tommy."

"I'm not Tommy."

Panic! I blinked. Larrimer came into focus. "I insist we go home. Who will look after Lulu?"

"Ssshh. We *are* home, Clea. I told you I've had someone watching the house. Jason's outside now."

"Ohhhh. That's good." Words slurred. "More water?"

As I drank, he kept glancing toward the door. He wasn't paying attention! What would he say if...? "I'm magic."

"Yes, you are." His eyes bored into mine. He was always so serious.

I wiggled my fingers. "See."

"I do."

A belly cramp. I curled into a ball. Another. Maybe I *was* dying. Lights out. Gonzo. "Am I a goner?"

"Not an option." His arms tightened around me, his voice low and *mean*.

"If I die, I trust you. To keep Lulu safe. Find Dave's killer. I trust you, James." I grabbed his hand. He tried to pull it away, but I hung on. "Why don't you like me touching you? I like when you touch me."

He growled. "You're being a drama queen."

I laughed, and started coughing. Spittle on my lips. He wiped it away. Red dotted the tissue he clenched. Blood. My blood. "Am not. Not scared to die. Maybe I should be. Huh. Or maybe I'll never know, and it'll just happen. Boom. Dead."

A beast boiled the room, filling it, consuming it with rage and fear. Larrimer.

So *that's* what he felt like when his shields were down. Epic. "I'd rather not. Die, I mean."

"You won't," he ground out.

I poked his chest. "You can't hold back death, mister."

"That remains to be seen." He smiled at me. Gods, he had a fine smile. I hoped I wasn't drooling. Was I drooling?

He wiped my face with a cool cloth. That came away red, too. "Can I run my fingers down your face?"

He looked like he'd sucked lemons, but nodded.

I touched him, and he winced.

"Hurt you?" I asked.

"No."

But his hands, white-knuckled on the mattress.

Another cramp, so bad I screamed.

"He's here!" came a shouted voice from far away. But loud. So loud.

The ambulance. He *was* taking me to a hospital. I tugged at his shirt. "James, please. No hospital. *Please.*"

My gut spasmed. *Knives, spreading, slicing, expanding.*

CHAPTER EIGHTEEN

Yuck crusted my eyes, so I rubbed them clear, saw my quilt, my Nantucket baskets, Kermit. I was home, in my own bed. And, of course, there was Larrimer sprawled in my reading chair, a magazine covering his face, hands on flat belly, taking up enormous amounts of bedroom space. I reached for the water glass. It had a bendy straw. Sweet.

My head ached and my neck throbbed, but only a little. My right wrist, re-bandaged, itched like a son of a bitch. But overall, I felt pretty fine. Almost too fine.

I shouldn't wake him up, but, "Am I about to croak?" My voice, sandpaper.

He awakened with a jerk, the magazine sliding to the floor. He looked awful. His bronzed skin pasty, his eyes shot with red. "No."

"No, really."

He walked to my bedside and did the looming thing. "You're fine."

"Oh," I said. His beard had grown, more than a day's worth, his shirt rumpled and half hanging out of his jeans. "You have one too many tequila shots?"

"If only." He tucked in his shirt.

How long was I out? How long had he watched over me? "I have to pee."

"I live to serve." Hand on waist, arm out, he bowed like a cavalier of old.

"Dream on, buster. I'm going on my own."

"If you insist, as you always seem to." His eyes hinted laughter, that almost-smile. Those eyes, starlight on the Pacific. Spectacular.

"Why did you stay with me and not Bernadette?" I staggered out of bed.

"The thought of you waking to her gave *me* nightmares. That turban and derringer. Plus, she'd pepper me with that shotgun of hers if I left you alone."

A twinge. I'd hoped for... more. Made it to my bathroom door. Panting hard, but I just had to turn the knob. I looked over my shoulder. "Bernadette's a crack shot."

"I run fast." He grinned, all teeth. Manical.

I took care of business, but back in bed, I failed to keep my eyes open. Later, I half-awakened to a whispered voice. Secretive, covert. Larrimer, over by the window, on the phone.

"She has a right to know," Larrimer hissed as he looked out at the night. Then, "I won't keep quiet forever."

Another pause. Larrimer laughed softly. "You really think you can stop me, Balfour?"

Bob?

"Freak?" Larrimer said, voice a low rumble. "Yeah, man, I've always got my freak on."

Pause.

Bob must be talking. Again, I wished I could hear both sides.

"She should know," Larrimer said. "What you've done. The Union. She's a human being, and we're tracking a monster."

Larrimer, hand pressed to the window, listening, then his fingers curling to a fist. "I don't give a flying fuck *what* she is. You tell her. Or I'll do it myself."

What was The Union? What were Bob and Larrimer keeping from me? What *was* I?

Two days later, surprisingly hale and healthy, I poured myself into a slinky black dress with little halter straps, the sweetheart neckline making me look like boob central.

Earlier, I'd gotten nowhere with the "What am I" when I'd asked Larrimer and reacted poorly to his "provocative." When I'd threatened to ask Bob, he shot me one of those "you poor sap" looks. He knew I no longer trusted Bob, not the way I'd always done. Which sucked. So I tabled the conversation. At the moment, we had bigger fish to sauté.

Finally, we were about to follow a strong lead on Dave.

Mr. UPS had delivered The Dress, overnighted, courtesy of Larrimer. I seriously didn't understand the man at all. Larrimer, a fashionista? Boggled my mind.

I twirled. The dress was stunning. I ran my hands down the soft black velvet, reminded of Sargent's *Madame X*, minus her nose. I laughed, took a breath. Would Larrimer like it on me? Crap. I was all nerves.

A faux-diamond choker hid the bullet wound's bandage, the earrings matched. All Larrimer, my personal shopper.

"Ouch."

The clasp had caught in my hair, which now reached below my ears, curly hair, Lorde-like hair, wild and savage. My heart stuttered. Was it because of my magic? Dave's shocking my wrist? Ah, yes, my hair, just another weird thing to add to my bizarro bouquet.

Once I'd slipped into my strappy heels, I took a final peek in the mirror. *Holy shit.* I looked regal. Who was that woman?

"Almost ready?" Larrimer called from downstairs, frustration tinting his voice.

"Coming!"

My gun slid into my thigh holster, and I dropped the skirt. Invisible. Confirmed the pocket I'd slit to reach the gun worked. Perfect. Ditto for my right thigh, with my knife.

Things felt smooth, like well-oiled gears. Good.

I snatched my bag, and when I stepped off the stairs into the living room, Lulu and Bernadette gasped in unison.

"Do I pass muster?" I asked.

"You rock, Clea." Lulu and Grace bounced around like Mexican jumping beans. "Wow."

Bernadette crossed her arms and nodded, as if to say "as it should be." Then Larrimer strolled into the room, graceful as liquid glass.

He'd combed his midnight hair straight back. Bronzed face against the white collar, tall and broad, lean and mean, he wore his tux as if he'd been born in the thing. I swallowed. Hard. Gods, he was sex on a stick.

I did a pirouette.

He took me in, from the top of my head to the tips of my toes, those damned blue eyes ice-hot. "You look nice."

Nice. *Nice?*

I insisted on driving, which I knew would annoy him. I wanted him to react to me, to show some, *any*, emotion. Nope, sealed tight. That stoic façade had to go.

Freezing rain pelted the truck as we headed down the driveway. Careened, more like it.

"Clea." Larrimer's low voice cracked like a whip.

"No worries." Just as I said it, I realized the truck disagreed, unwilling to stop at the end of my ice-coated driveway. I pumped the brakes and prayed no car appeared as we skittered onto the two-laned road.

"The *hell*." Larrimer said.

Finally, some emotion, just not the one I craved. "Sorry. Sometimes, the ice. It's challenging."

"Challenging. We could have been killed."

"But we weren't," I said, deadpan. "Cheers to us. And to finding a killer."

We turned onto the curved drive of the Cranadnock Country Club.

"Do you have a plan of attack?" I chewed my lip. *Remember to reapply lipstick!*

"Nope."

"Well, that's just swell," I said. "Mine's to schmooze."

"Try to be nice."

"I'm always nice."

He raised an eyebrow. "You're a wisenheimer."

"Who says 'wisenheimer' anymore?'"

"Obvious, isn't it?"

I pulled into a space on the outer rim of the lot. "Prepping for a quick getaway."

"Good."

I laughed. "Of course, I'm not sure there are any quick getaways in Midborough. Look, tonight, don't go all He-Man."

He leapt out and opened my door. "I'm that clumsy?"

"You're never clumsy, just intimidating."

He laughed softly as he slid my shawl across my shoulders. A shiver raced down my spine, of the uber sexy kind. That laugh. I heard it so seldom.

"We've got to find something concrete," I said, my voice unintentionally sharp.

"At your service, ma'am." He air-kissed my hand, then took it in his.

He wore thin leather gloves, black and buttery soft. "You really do hate skin to skin."

His face was in shadow. "Yes."

"Why?"

"Secrets make the world go round, little Clea."

"Secrets enable you distance."

"The way I like it."

With Larrimer's duplicate invitation, we walked into the gala, no problem. While Larri... *Remember to call him James.* A niggle... *Lipstick!* Once I'd swiped my lips with Killer Coral, I checked out the ballroom.

Little had changed since the last 4-H meeting I'd attended twenty years ago. Pine-paneled walls, wood floors, a blazing fireplace, and a curtained stage. Not the glitz of Boston or New York, but it would do.

The emotional vibe of the room was raucous. I'd have trouble filtering out individual feelings. Nothing for it.

Larrimer held out his arm, and I took it as we entered. At least a dozen people I knew mingled inside. What would he think when I was assaulted by...

"Hey, Clea!" Jeb Barlow beelined toward us.

Here we go.

"Who's that buffoon?" Larrimer nodded toward Jeb.

"You disdain most people, don't you?" I draped my shawl across the back of a chair.

"Most are users. Exploiters."

I turned. "Hi, Jeb."

He kissed my cheek. "You look lovely."

"Thanks. You clean up nice, too."

He beamed. "Want to dance?"

"Not quite yet. We just got here. Raincheck? Meet my friend, James Larrimer."

Jeb pumped Larrimer's hand, then he nodded sagely. "So what is it you do?"

Larrimer gave him a crooked smile. "I'm an engineer. How do you know Clea?"

"High school."

"Ah." Larrimer shot his pearly whites at Jeb, who beamed. "So what's your line of work?"

"I sell feed. King Brand. It means quality, for sure."

Larrimer grew solemn. "You must have known Dave Cochran."

Jeb crossed his arms. "Well. I knew him well. One of my best customers. A good man."

That do-se-do continued all night—introductions, chitchat, mentioning Dave—with Susie Dinkins and Ted Le Blanc and Peppy Zakowsky. People from grammar school and high school, from performing at parties and babysitting and a million other places. And yet, I didn't really know them, or they, me. I'd called one or two "friend," years ago. Now, they were just acquaintances. For all that I'd spent mere days with Larrimer, and he remained an enigma, I felt closer to him than any other in the room. I'd always wanted to fit in, yet I was different, a touch too idiosyncratic to blend.

Not to mention, one of them may have murdered Dave. A hundred tiny cuts. I zapped the image away.

Larrimer inhaled it all like a fine Merlot, a Sphinx-like smile playing around his damnably handsome mouth. The women, on their part, inhaled *him* like so much eye candy, birthing a green-eyed monster I didn't know I possessed.

Froggy Balder took my hand. "Over at the VA, we still miss Tommy and his jokes."

"Me, too."

"So what are you working on?"

Froggy always was a nosy soul and fascinated with my FBI work. "Oh, this and that." I smiled.

He wagged a finger. "Meaning secret stuff."

"Of course!" I hooked an arm through his skinny one. "C'mon. Let's dance."

He led me onto the floor. "Yeah, yeah. And you pretending you're a farmer."

"I don't pretend. I am a farmer." Froggy squeezed me tight, and I gasped, almost suffocated by his aftershave. I leaned back, trying not to inhale the fumes. "Pretty shocking about Dave Cochran, wasn't it?"

Froggy frowned. "A real shame."

Kip Alvarise tapped Froggy's shoulder, and I was handed off to a barely familiar selectman. He was tall, handsome and knew it. Word was, he imagined himself a player.

"You're looking glamorous this evening," he said.

"Thanks, Kip." We made small talk until I mentioned Dave.

"That Cochran," he said. "I heard he was up to something not so good."

"Really? I didn't think he was the type."

Kip shrugged. "Lotta people don't fit the type, do they now?"

"What exactly was Dave into?"

"Don't know. I'd like to, though." He gave me a sly wink.

"Me, too." I lowered my voice conspiratorially. "Who might have some info?"

"I'll have to think about that one."

I offered him a blazing smile and pondered Kip's words as I watched Larrimer waltz Lucy McGraw, all the while expecting Lucy's thong to make an appearance, given the mile-high slit in her sequined dress.

Kip frowned.

"What?" I asked, concerned I'd pushed too hard.

"You, ah, you remind me of my wife when she... before... Aw, damn." His face crumpled.

I tilted my head. "Kip?"

"I'm okay." His eyes stirred to life. "I just miss dancing with her. She's got MS, but we're doing good."

I twirled with many I knew, some I didn't, and a bunch of town muckety-mucks prone to preening. With each dance, I asked about Dave, but Kip's gold was the only nugget I mined.

From my brief encounters with Larrimer, he wasn't getting very far either.

Larrimer danced the way he wore a tux. He glided across the

hardwood, leading his partners with effortless grace. With all my ballet training, my body did fine. My head? I felt awkward and out of place. I was sure my Killer Coral was gone, having the lousy habit of chewing my lips while on the hunt. The fashion show was fun, all sequins and velvets and satins, but my gala costume had begun to constrict and my high heels killed. The worst was the chatter, dislikable gossip, superficial town blather that drilled holes in the skull. Folks whirled around the room, sipped champagne— the evening's one positive—ate, and acted in no way suspicious that I could see. Well, hell.

While I made frequent trips to the ladies' room to chat up the women, Larrimer made small talk with dozens of couples, often with me acting as arm candy. Definitely a new role for me, one I didn't much care for, except for the steel of Larrimer's forearm beneath my fingers.

The gun strapped to my thigh was the only thing in this disagreeable world that felt normal.

After a fast dance, with Jeb sweating like a leaky hydrant, I strolled over to Larrimer, who rested an elbow on the bar and surveyed the room.

"Gods, I'm bored," I said.

"Not having fun, are we?" He smiled as he stared at a blonde with a dress cut to her navel.

I snorted. "It's all those flashy babes holding your attention."

"No." Eyes fierce with heat caught mine. "I like watching you."

I shook my head, ready with a snappy retort, when a fresh breeze announced new arrivals. The room's atmosphere changed, the air thickened, electrified. All heads swiveled to the entryway.

"You feel that?"

"I do," he said, eyes tracking to the entrance.

A group spilled into the hall, led by a portly man in a tux with a crooked nose and a rolling gait. Two curvy women flanked him, a blonde and a redhead, each with a matching glam "do." The three men around him—two brunette bruisers and a tall, fit blond—seemed like satellites, until I caught the blond checking out the room. He was no satellite.

I knew power when I felt it.

Larrimer took my hand in his, wrapped an arm around my waist, and whirled me across the ballroom, close to the newcomers.

"Finally," he said.

"I know. They're different."

Strong fingers caressed my waist. "That's not what I meant."

I glanced up, but he was watching the new arrivals. "I wish you'd take off your gloves."

He peered down at me, eyes a cosmos of darkest blue. "Not tonight, but soon."

When, I almost said, because we weren't just talking about gloves. We finished our twirl, and Larrimer led me back to the bar, ordered me a Coke, then strode purposefully across the ballroom.

As he bowed over the redhead's hand, then guided her onto the floor, I itched to do the same with Blondie.

The portly man's lips pinched as Larrimer stole away the redhead. Then Blondie rested a hand on Mr. Portly's shoulder, leaned in, and spoke. Portly nodded and arrowed across dance floor toward me.

And off we go.

CHAPTER NINETEEN

Mr. Portly took my hand. He smelled of cigar smoke, but it wasn't unpleasant. His bespoke tux was a thing of beauty, but I'd swear his bowtie was a clip on.

"Might I have the honor?" His accent was all Boston Brahmin. A put on. His vibe shouted "small."

I smiled up at him. "I'd be delighted."

"Call me Roberto." He held out his hand.

I placed mine in his, gave him my name, and we embraced. I expected us to move, but we didn't. He stared at my cleavage, and I knew how horses felt at auction. He'd better not massage my withers. Then he pulled me tight, too tight, and his hand crawled from my waist to cup my ass.

"I wouldn't do that." Larrimer, who'd materialized from the ether. He smiled, all predatory male. "She's *mine*."

Roberto took a step back, scared eyes peering up at Larrimer.

What the hell? We were working.

"Sorry." Roberto moved a respectable distance from me. "Mind the dance?" he asked to Larrimer.

"Not in the least." Larrimer nodded, and disappeared into the crowd.

I might never achieve Pavlova artistry, but Roberto moved like a twelve-year-old in dance class, clumsy and uncertain. I caught him shaking his head at the blond man. What was that about?

"What's your line of work?" I asked.

"I own The Fish Dish."

One of Dalesboro's best restaurants. "Yummy."

"I am."

Ick. He kept turning his head toward the blond, and what I first thought was a hearing aid was a wireless earpiece. Interesting. Expensive.

Roberto earned a zero as a conversationalist, but he sure had an agenda and was by far the night's most fertile prospect.

"You're fascinating," he said.

I wasn't. Certainly not that night. Even his vernacular sounded phony. "I'm a farmer. I raise cashmere goats, among other things."

"You'd never know," he said.

Swear to gods he sniffed my shoulder. *What? He expected I'd smell like goat?*

"You ever sell 'em for meat? We serve a mean rabbit, too."

My hand jerked, and I covered by flicking an errant strand of my Medusa-mane. I forced my jaw to unclench. "I sell their cashmere."

"A shame. If you're ever interested..."

His words trailed off and he stumbled. Maybe it was the death stare I stabbed him with.

Someone caught his elbow, and he spun.

"My turn," Larrimer said to Roberto.

No, I mouthed.

But Larrimer twirled me away.

"Dammit, dude, why did you do that?"

He grinned. "You looked ready to gut him."

"Well, yes, I was."

We whirled around the ballroom, and he stole my breath.

Eyes burned my shoulder, and as we twirled again, I saw the woman from Bronze Printing. When I smiled, her eyes spat hate and she looked away.

As we neared Roberto's crew, another young woman, in a slinky midnight-blue number, joined the group.

I quickly filled Larrimer in on my Roberto haul.

"I agree," he said. "Blondie's the one in charge."

"So what's their deal?" I asked. "Roberto's a restaurateur. Not exactly *I Spy* material."

"No." He narrowed his eyes. "Then again, nobody here is. The girl didn't have much to say, either. Not a lot going on upstairs."

"I got yucky vibes from Roberto," I said.

"I get those vibes from a lot of folks here. That girl in the blue dress is new. Maybe they're collectors."

"You mean, prostitution?"

"The type of men who'd buy exotic animals for bragging rights could collect women, too. Same impulse."

"Maybe. Except this is Midborough. I mean, *really*? And where's that power vibe coming from? If only someone would wear a sign saying, 'I killed Dave Cochran.'"

He nodded, eyes alight. "Yes, that would help."

The dance ended. "Would you get me some champagne?"

He tilted his head, a silent question. "Your wish and all that."

When he made it to the champagne table, I trotted across the floor and asked Blondie to dance.

"So, pretty lady, who *are* you?" Blondie took a proper distance, not too close. I appreciated that. But his scent, faint. I'd smelled it recently. It was antiseptic and... Listerine.

At Shatzkin's. The guy we'd passed in the hall wearing a ball cap. Same height and build. It fit.

Holy moly. Larrimer was on the other end of the room, and while I was jumping out of my skin to tell him, no way was I passing up this dance. Had Shatzkin been silenced because Lulu spotted his hearse?

I looked up and smiled. He was shorter than Larrimer, but not by much. Handsome in a Nordic way, with chocolate eyes, and he returned my smile with teeth bleached to ultra-white.

Oh yeah, this guy was the leader.

"You smell like apricots," he said. "I watched Roberto. He has the manners of a pig."

"Now you're being unkind to pigs."

He laughed, and his hold on my hand pinched. I felt like a bonbon about to be consumed. His practiced look of hunger would appeal to many women. It didn't to me.

He pulled me closer, so my nose pressed against his lapel and moved both hands down to encompass my waist. I lay my arms across broad shoulders bunched with muscles.

"Do you have a name?" I asked.

"Ivor."

"Clea."

He squeezed. I felt trapped, and tamped down the feeling. "So tell me about yourself," I said.

"I like you."

A non-answer. I leaned my head back, so it strained my neck. I wanted to see his eyes. They were warm, inviting.

He playfully tugged one of my curls. "Maybe you're not too skinny."

"For what, Ivor?" My words dripped molasses.

We danced near one of the large hall's side exits. He was steering me somewhere, his vibe ugly and hungry.

Yeah, not gonna play that game.

I surfaced from his shoulder and came to a dead stop. He overbalanced, then corrected.

I drew away, except he didn't loosen his hold.

"What, pretty girl?" He kissed my bare shoulder. "You taste sweet."

Larrimer better not come to the rescue. I laughed. "C'mon? You're going with that one?" I moved to step away again. His fingers contracted. Pain shot through my waist. Nasty bastard. I wasn't afraid, just pissed.

I could easily kick his legs out from under him, but I wanted to see what he'd do next. "Are you about to waltz me outdoors?"

"I thought you could join our little party."

"I'm not much of a party girl." I tittered.

Again with the snarky grin. "I bet you know how to play."

Still smiling, I shook my head. "Oh, I never play."

His muscles relaxed, and the pain in my waist became an ache. Obviously, he failed to get the point of my banter.

"You'd play with *me*." His jaw hardened.

Damn me, I wanted to laugh. Compared to Larrimer, he felt like a minor leaguer, albeit a nasty one. "Would I?" I flowed my hands forward to his waist, as if to hold him, then down and inside his front pant pockets, seemingly hungry for him. I touched what felt like a card, palmed it, and slid my hands back out.

In time with the music, he slow-walked us back into shadow. I snagged his eyes and fluttered my hands to my breasts where I tucked the card into my dress.

He nuzzled my neck, and I made a soft noise while I dipped my hands into his front jacket pockets then around to his back trouser ones. Nada. One hand caressed my throat above my necklace. He chuckled and squeezed. Tight.

My wound screamed, not that I would give him the satisfaction. Calmly, I said, "You're hurting me." Twice now. This guy enjoyed inflicting pain. I forced myself to lean into him.

A wave hit me. His thrill of victory, his joy of my pain.

"Did I mention you're hurting me?"

"Only a little." His hand tightened.

I stepped on tiptoe. "I'm not much for S&M." He squeezed my chin with this other hand, and I felt his cock as he shifted his hips, so he could rub it against me.

Bad idea, bub. I raised my fingers to the wrist that held my chin and pinched his median nerve, hard.

He barked, "Fuck!"

I shoved him. "I see you don't like pain either, asshole," and whirled away, right into another couple. "Oh, excuse me." I walked on, aching to rub my neck, forcing myself not to. Then, Larrimer was there, taking me in his arms, and we danced toward the thicket of other couples.

"I was on my way over to murder the prick," he said.

"I took care of it." I smiled.

I peeked around his arm and saw Blondie rubbing his wrist, shooting daggers at me, teeth bared.

I told Larrimer about the Listerine, Shatzkin's, and my suspicions as we spun around the room, my eyes on Blondie. Done rubbing his wrist, he crooked a finger at Roberto, who hustled over.

Larrimer gripped my arms. "Don't ever do that again. Taunt someone like that."

"Let me go," I said, trying to control my temper. "I've been mauled enough for one night."

Instantly released, I felt for the card I'd shoved into my cleavage. Still there. He jammed his hands into his pockets, and we walked toward the bar. "Swear to God you need a keeper."

"I'm not yours to keep."

"You risk things you don't even know you're risking."

"I'll take that chance."

The air crackled between us, and I had the terrible urge to stand on tiptoe and meet those lips head on, to suck on them with my mouth, to tug on them with my teeth, to lick them until he licked mine back.

Snapping around to take my eyes off Larrimer, I discovered the merry band had decamped.

"Time to go," he said, calm as can be.

Damn him. The volcano inside me felt like it'd blow any minute.

A heavy hand thudded onto my shoulder. "Hey, Clea!"

I whirled. A big-boned man with a ready grin and pale lashes pulled me in for a peck on the cheek.

"Mr. UPS! Todd, hi! Uh, Bernadette's waiting up for me. Have to run. Sorry!" I gave his arm a quick squeeze as Larrimer steered me away. Off we went.

We stood just outside the clubhouse. The cold air, a balm.

"I don't see the crew," I said.

We'd walked halfway to the truck when Larrimer whispered, "Stop."

Cold wind hissed around us, and I caught a scent. Listerine.

Blondie, I mouthed.

He nodded. We circled back behind a row of cars toward the truck and waited. Pebbles sprayed and footfalls sounded. The scent intensified. A whistle.

I slid my hand through the slit in my dress and pulled out my gun, keeping it parallel to my leg. Larrimer reached beneath his jacket, and a Beretta appeared in his hand.

Then Froggy and Diane erupted from the clubhouse along with several other couples. Flashlights bobbed in the parking lot as folks made for their cars.

I stilled, tried to catch Blondie's antiseptic scent. Seconds later, we were at the truck. I opened the passenger door with a near-silent click, glad I'd disabled the interior light. Larrimer did the same on the driver's side.

Breathing hard, tense, riding that juice of adrenaline, I slumped down, as did Larrimer, so we wouldn't be overtly visible. Larrimer turned the key, and all she gave were a few pathetic cranks.

Bad luck, or someone had fooled with the truck. Luck? Yeah, right.

Larrimer tried again. Same deal.

Around us, car lights were popping on. I imagined Blondie's crew, out there in the darkness.

I leaned over the seat back and groped.

"What are you doing?" Larrimer said with a whisper.

"Boots." I doffed my heels and laced them up. "I wish I'd brought more firepower."

"Always fun to go out guns blazing."

"Let's go after them."

He shook his head. "Much as I'd like to, too many bystanders around."

"Yes, okay, collateral damage. How about we pretend I'm drunk?"

He nodded. "We'll hitch a ride."

We waited until the next rush of partygoers poured from the country club. I cracked my door and we crept out my side. He wrapped an arm around my waist, and I staggered toward a down-coated couple.

"Can you help us?" Larrimer said. "My wife had a bit too much to drink. She lost our keys."

"Ummmm," the man said.

These dudes were drunk for real.

"We'd be happy to give you a ride," came the voice from the darkness, one I recognized.

Blondie appeared, grinning.

Why did they always grin?

"You're not going our way," Larrimer said.

"We'd be happy to make an exception," Blondie countered.

The other couple said, "Great!" and vanished into the night.

Partygoers streamed around us.

Phantom-quick, Larrimer had Blondie on the ground and out cold. Just as swiftly, he pushed me down so I flopped onto Blondie like a beached fish. A near-silent muzzle flash sparked the darkness.

From where?

I could fire back, we could take them, dammit, but in this crowd, the risks outweighed the gain.

He grabbed my hand and said, "Run."

We rolled off Blondie, and took off for the woods, ones I knew so very well.

Larrimer moved like the wind, silent, swift. Me, after him. Behind us came the herd of elephants. Two, maybe three followers.

Ice and snow hindered us, and he dropped behind me. I felt him stop, and paused. He turned, fired at our pursuers. A shout of pain.

"Go!" he said.

I ran in stealth mode over snow-covered ground, and Larrimer, he was a ghost. We hugged the tree line, close to a field that sparkled in the moonlit night.

"If the blond was The Master—" Larrimer said as we ran.

"He's not," I hissed.

"You can't know that."

But I did.

We passed a pine marked with a tripod. I felt it, a pull, a tug I hadn't sensed in almost fifteen years. My steps slowed.

"Clea, dammit! Hurry!"

I ran.

Breath chuffing, picking up the pace, sliding into a rhythm, except I wasn't there, but nine-years-old again, at the cave.

Chapter Twenty

C'mon, Clea, you gotta see this.*

I want to see it, but the day we'd hiked up here, Dave said it was a no-go zone.

Except Tommy says it's so cool.

I run, leaves slapping me, Tommy in front of me, darting in and out. He's so fast!

I giggle, laughing for the joy of it. "Tommy!"

He doesn't pay any attention. When we're on a mission, he never does.

We're being bad. Dave would be angry. But Tommy's right, sometimes being bad is fun.

Faster, faster, breath coming harder and harder, like I'm running through jello, which is sorta freaky.

And I get to the big rock, but he's not there!

"Tommmmy!"

I hate when he does this. Teases me. Scares me. When he hides or like when he stuck that snake under my nose. Ewwww. He better not...

He peeks around the big rock, laughing with his hand covering his mouth, his whole skinny body shaking.

I slap my hands on my hips. "You're mean."

He holds out his arms, and I run to him.

"Aw, Clea," he says, "You're so fun to scare. I'm sorry."

His hand smoothing my hair feels nice.

He leads me around the rock. "Look."

"A cave!" I say.

"Yeah, cool, huh?"

"Have you been inside?"

"Nope. I wanted to explore with you, sweetness."

"Thanks." I kiss his cheek.

"Jeez, Clea." He swipes it away. "Cut the girly crap."

"Sorry." I giggle, feel like slobbering kisses all over him, just 'cause he'd think that is gross.

He tugs my hand. "C'mon."

The entrance is really big, ginormous, and covered in thorny vines.

We step closer. Pins and needles all over my skin, like when your leg wakes up. I go to tell Tommy, but he doesn't sense things like I do. I don't want to hurt his feelings.

He's brought his favorite knife, and he starts cutting the vines. When a bunch fall to the ground, I move in front of him and lift my foot to step inside.

Something I can't see pushes back, more pricklies. Ohboy. I shake my head. Fizzy. I peek in, where there's some light, except only a little ways. The walls curve up high into blackness. I shake my head. Just plain spooky.

This has to be the coolest. I step again, and again, and my red Cons feel like they're pushing on Play Doh. I lift my hands, and that same thingie pushes back on them, and I...

But something pulls me, too. Calls me in the prettiest way. Not a voice, but a song, yeah, in my head. And I see...

"Clea! Clea!"

Dave! I jump back, twirl around.

Tommy stops, knife at another vine.

"We're screwed," he says. "We're so screwed."

I chew my lip.

"Clea! Clea!"

"He's getting close," I say to Tommy, his face all scared.

I don't understand why Dave doesn't love him like he does me. He never gives Tommy a pass. Never.

"Okay," I say. "Here's what we're gonna do. You hide inside the cave."

Tommy folds his knife and slips it into his jeans, face tight and brave. "I'm not afraid of Dave."

But he is. "I know that! But he's better with me."

Seconds pass, and Tommy gives, and I'm so glad.

"Yeah. Yeah," he says. "All right."

"Clea! Clea!"

"He's close!" I mouth. "Hurry."

Tommy dashes to the cave. "Hey, what's with this way-out…" And then, he's inside. I look over my shoulder to make sure I can't see his hiding place, then I walk in front of the granite rock.

I wave. "Over here, Dave!"

Soon, he stands in front of me, really mad. He puts a hand over his eyes, sighs, then gives me a long hug.

Dave's shaking, but he's not mad now. Fear. He's scared. "What's the matter? I was just—"

"You're all right?" he says.

"Sure!" I grin, so glad he hasn't seen Tommy.

He brushes hair from my face and scooches down, so we're eye to eye. He doesn't say anything for a long time, and that's when I realize no birds are singing and no little animals are making noise. And Tommy, he's always so noisy, but now I don't hear him, either.

Dave's pretty eyes soften. "Honey, I told you never to come here. Remember that hike?"

I bob my head. "I remember."

"Please. Never come here again. Promise."

I don't want to promise. I never break my promises to Dave, and he knows that. And I want to explore the cave with Tommy. Those prickles and oohh, it was cool.

But Dave's eyes, so scared and puddled with love.

"I promise."

It's around ten, and I'm in my bed, drinking water to stay awake, and I'll have to pee soon. I just know it.

Bernadette's up way late for her, and I'm really pooped. We have school tomorrow.

The sound of the door, doggies yipping, Bernadette's happy cry. Tommy's home. Yeah.

Boy, I bet he had a really great adventure. Without me.

Can't keep my eyes open, but it's okay now, he's home. I really wish I didn't always keep my promises to Dave. I wish I was a badder girl.

Maybe someday, I will be.

I was back in the forest, running beside Larrimer, no longer spring, toes numb from freezing cold. Running, running, chased by thugs.

Tommy had carved that tripod long ago, marked the tree on the path to the cave.

A surge of energy, a drug through my veins, but *more*. I slowed, a terrible compulsion pulling me toward that tripod, that rock edifice, that cave.

"Almost there." Larrimer wrapped his hand around mine. "C'mon."

"Right." It came out breathy, distant. "Right."

We stood on the edge of the trees by the highway. I sucked air into my lungs, trying to catch my breath. Silence behind us. We'd lost them.

I tucked away that strange-sad memory of the cave and thought about Blondie.

Larrimer shuddered, as if shaking off some warrior fever.

"James?"

His long stare smoldered with cold fire.

"He's not The Master," I said. "I just know."

"You're freezing, aren't you."

Somewhere along the way, I'd lost my shawl. Damn, I loved that thing. "So are you."

He took off his tux jacket and laid it across my shoulders. "Call."

I shook my head. "It's one in the morning. I hate waking her." She'd rip me a new one, too.

"Just do it."

"What are you, a Nike commercial?"

He smirked. "That's so yesterday, babe."

I ground my teeth, then spoke a name into my phone. It dialed.

"What mess did you and sonny boy get into now, cookie?" Bernadette said.

Worse than death.

Five-thirty came early the following morning. On my tablet, I fired off my latest report to Balfour. Not that it would do any good. Without putting too fine a point on it, his silence was deafening. Normally, I'd call, go all, "what the hell's up with you?" Normally.

Today, my gut was screeching, "Danger, Will Robinson!" My confidence in my greatest cheerleader and sounding board had officially eroded to a pinhead.

Downstairs, I slipped on my boots and jacket and walked to the barn.

I hoisted the grain bucket through Nott and Delling's stall door, and as I poured the grain into their feeders, they bumped and nuzzled me with affection. They'd recovered, thank heavens.

I scratched their favorite places, freshened their water, and moved on to the next stall, knowing a certain bliss. Last night, it was ten degrees, today it had warmed enough that I didn't need the rubber mallet for their water. Spring was coming. At least, that's what I told myself when the grind of winter got me nuts.

The animals centered me, calmed me, reminded me of things free of violence and evil.

Then thoughts of Loki and Lofn burned away the peace. And of Dave. The killers had taken him from me, but, more importantly, from Lulu. I wanted to peel them from the inside out, to watch them suffer, to carve pieces out of them.

A cleared throat.

Lulu stared at me, eyes wide. "You're looking, um, a little bloodthirsty."

I blinked. *What was she doing out here at five-thirty a.m.?* I smiled. "Sorry, kiddo. In spring, we'll get six new chicks, and I'll purchase a pair of cashmere kids, too."

"Will I be here in spring?" she asked.

"Of course."

Her earnest face, white with fear, made her freckles stand out in high relief. She looked me in the eye. "Are you sure?"

I cupped her cheek. "Yes, Lulu, I'm sure. And I'm glad."

She turned away, wagging her hands. "I *think* I am. Mostly. Yeah, I am. Where's your family?"

"Long gone," I said. "I don't talk about them much."

"Why not?"

I inhaled the sweet scents of the barn. "Because I was so little when they died, I don't remember them."

"That's weird," she said. "How can you not remember them?"

"It just is." Claudia oinked in glee as I poured food into her bucket. "I wanted to—"

"You and Agent Larrimer are hunting my dad's killer. I can help, you know."

I peeked over the stall. "How?"

She gave me a thumbs up. "I'm great with computers."

"Super. But you're hiding things from me, Lulu, and that makes it hard for me to confide in you. Won't you talk to me about it?"

"I... I've... But I deserve to help! He was *my* dad. You're just jealous."

I squeezed my eyes tight, shook my head. "I was never jealous, Lulu. Love isn't expendable. The more you give, the more exists. Your dad loved me very much, but *you* were his treasure. Nothing and no one could ever change that."

She slammed her hands on to her hips. "*You* don't love me. You won't let me help."

"I don't want to be glib or easy, but you're in my heart. And that's the truth. But you are keeping secrets that might help us find your dad's killer. How am I supposed to get past that?"

Fear in those amethyst eyes of hers. Fear of change, of aloneness. And anger. "I can't. I *won't*."

Shoulders hunched, she stomped off, copper braids trailing from the green cabled beanie.

Perhaps Lulu guarded her dad's secrets so closely because, to her, they were the only private things left of him she had.

When I walked into the mudroom, she was waiting for me. I started taking off my boots. "You'd better get ready for school."

She kicked a nonexistent speck of dirt. "I'm sorry. Dad always said I had a temper. He hated when I 'flounced' out. That's what he called it."

"It's okay." I gave her a quick hug.

Her eyes probed mine.

I held them, saying nothing, waiting for her to pursue the silence, to open up.

She kissed my cheek and left, and I inhaled a long, stuttering breath.

Larrimer had made me coffee again. Small kindnesses. Yeah, talk about getting to my heart. I carried my mug to my office, intent on inputting my notes from the previous night. Ha. Some gala.

The door to my office was open maybe three inches, and a funny squeaking came from inside. I toed the door a hair wider. Larrimer had shoved all the furniture against the walls and rolled up the carpet. He danced around the room, feet shoulder-wide, elbows bent close to his body, barefooted, barechested, rocking black flowy pants, a stout sword in his right hand. In the early morning light, sweat glistened on that intense face, sheened his shoulders, and covered his broad chest. He lunged and thrust, parried and twirled and leapt, all while wielding a blade maybe two feet long, carved at the end like a Bowie knife, with a curved hilt.

His form of ballet.

He plucked a second, longer sword off the day bed and continued the dance.

Back and forth, around and around, the blades blurred as he moved faster and faster. I focused my senses, and his intensity arced through me. No thoughts, no words, his mind a laser on an invisible opponent more real than I. Long moments passed as the power, the grace, the *man* held me spellbound.

Otherworldly.

He perceived a watcher, started to turn.

I shielded my senses and backpedaled down the hall.

CHAPTER TWENTY-ONE

An hour later, Larrimer and I were headed to Dalesboro and The Fish Dish. On the way, we stopped to retrace our steps from the previous night, hoping to find some evidence dropped by last evening's nasty group of predators. We separated, Larrimer at one end, me at the other, to meet in the middle. When he was out of sight, I took a small detour by the tripod tree. Soon, I came upon the big rock, far closer to the path than I imagined, and smiled at the child's memory. I walked around the rock and just stared at the same immense granite outcropping. I took a few minutes to search, but found no cave. I ran back to the path.

No clues, no cave, no joy.

The Fish Dish's site said the place served breakfast, as well as dinner. On the way over, after Larrimer handed me the ripped shawl he'd found on the path, I'd shown him the card I'd snuck from Blondie. All it said was, *Wild Things*. Short and well... short.

"No hits on the Web relating to anything that might interest us." I handed it over to him. "Maybe your techs will find something."

"I'll recheck my notes," he said. "But I don't remember that phrase."

"Anouk said the trafficked animals aren't The Master's..." I did air quotes. "End game."

"And what if that woman's purpose was to put you off the trail?"

"In her own strange way, I think she wants to help. Are you a *Game of Thrones* fan?"

Up went the eyebrow.

"I love it," I said. "Especially the dragons. You remind me, sometimes, of those dragons. Which is why I think of you as dragon dude."

His lips twitched. "I'm not a dude."

"So you admit you're a dragon." I sipped my coffee, thought about it. "Most of the time, you're like a sleepy one. All banked fire."

"And you know dragons how?"

I laughed. "I have my ways."

"Most would bite your head off."

I pictured all sorts of interesting things. "You wouldn't. You're one of those gimlet-eyed, secret-hoarding breeds."

Just like a dragon, he huffed out a breath. And the coffee I was swallowing spewed through my nose and onto the dashboard. "Gross."

"Precisely."

We turned onto Dalesboro's West Main Street and parked in front of number eleven, a small building with a painted rainbow trout on the window.

Inside, intimate tables flanked red walls, with an aisle down the middle. The sign said Seat Yourself, and we took a table by the window.

The server left after he'd poured Larrimer's tea and my coffee, which couldn't hold a candle to his. Larrimer frowned at the menu.

"You don't like fish?" I asked.

"Not much."

"They have steak and eggs."

"Which is what I plan to order," he said, stoic-faced, but eyes smiling.

"If Roberto's here, he might poison us."

He shook his head. "Too subtle."

I chuckled. "An understatement. I'm going for the bagel with cream cheese and Nova lox. Technically, I'm a piscatarian."

"Nasty."

He turned away, watching the street with that intense concentration of his, while he stroked a finger down his long scar. I studied him. He'd showered, donned a fresh button-down shirt and jeans. I stretched my mind to sense him, and found twilight waters, a tranquil sea. How could he shield so well?

Most people I instinctively sensed, for good or ill. With others, I had to make a deliberate effort. But I seldom had to work hard at it. Larrimer was an odd man out. Twice, I'd glimpsed conflict, shocked at the cauldron boiling beneath the surface. Now all I felt was that contained calm. Before the storm? The thought came unbidden.

He shied from my touch. I was a touchy-feely kind of girl, I missed that skin-to-skin contact, particularly since we'd formed a friendship of sorts. Did I wish for more? Yes.

Sometimes, I'd catch him watching me in that way a man's eyes follow a woman, a woman he craves. Did he desire me as much as I did him? But if I were honest, the pull reached deeper, beyond sex, beyond friendship. And yet when his flesh met mine, he bristled.

He shifted his focus back to me. "What?"

I shook my head. "Nothing." I smiled.

He didn't return it. Dragon dude was back.

As we finished our meal, I spoke to the server. "I'd love to meet the owner. Compliment him on an amazing breakfast."

"I'm afraid that's not possible," he said. "Mrs. Krupnik isn't here."

"I thought someone named Roberto owned The Fish Dish."

The server sniffed. "You probably mean our line cook, Roberto Peres." His description of a portly man fit "our" Roberto.

"Likes cigars?" I asked.

"That would be him. I should have said, former line cook. He's no longer with us." He piled our plates into his hands and cleared them away.

Larrimer tossed a fifty onto the table, and when the server returned, said, "Keep the change."

The tip was more than the meal, and the server's mouth dropped. He scooped up the fifty.

"Where did Roberto go?" Larrimer asked.

The server grimaced. "Who knows?"

"*You* do." Larrimer's eyes snared his.

And whatever the server had seen, he took a clean napkin from the stack and wrote.

The Adept's Den.

"You didn't hear it from me. More coffee?"

"No," I said. "We're all set."

Back home, we sat in the kitchen while Larrimer phoned Bernadette's and Lulu's invisible watcher and I did a Web search for *The Adept's Den* on my iPad.

"Bernadette's upstairs," he said. "Lulu's at school. All's well."

"All's not well here." I turned to him. "I got nothing."

He pulled his chair closer and looked over my shoulder. "Businesses have to file permits, liquor licenses."

"Like I said, nada. I'll put out some feelers around town."

"Don't. It'll connect us too closely," he said.

Minutes later, he left for Boston. *To meet Bob?* Another question that went unasked. I wanted Larrimer to open that spigot.

Hours later, Bernadette's nagging about the coating of ice made me put on my YakTrax to muck out the stalls. Once engaged in that timeworn task, instead of contemplating The Master, the chest, and magic treasure, I kept mulling over questions I'd like to ask Larrimer, like why he'd left the FBI, what were his favorite foods and books and movies and did he ride horses. Totally off-topic. I spread more of the fresh straw and pictured his big body covering mine, him touching my hair, my breasts, licking and lapping and me touching his shoulders, his chest, his... Hell, that was off topic, too.

I checked my phone. Larrimer had texted he'd be back in a few. I began pitchforking hay around the next stall.

A laborious sort of grinding alerted me to someone struggling with our icy driveway. I leaned the pitchfork against the wall and went out to help.

Wheels spinning, the UPS truck was stuck mid-way.

"Hey, Todd!" I trotted down the drive, my YakTrax keeping me on my feet.

"I hate winter," he said.

"It's who we are."

He wrinkled his nose. "Still hate it, though."

"I've got some sand in the shed. Let me—"

"Don't bother," he said. "I'll back down." He handed me a brown envelope, the return address a scribble, then gave me his machine to sign.

"Thanks." I turned to go.

"Wait up, Clea. You looked pretty last night."

I smiled. "Thank you. I'm sorry we didn't get to dance."

"You, ah, you going to the contra dance down to Nelson next Monday night?"

I rocked back on my heels. "Um, I don't think so, Todd. Sorry."

He flushed. "No point in feeling sorry. You sure?"

"I'm sure."

Nice guy, no chemistry.

I headed for the house. Grace tumbled around the corner, right into me. Flew onto her back.

"Gracie! Geesh!"

Bang! And then, the wail of brakes. I spun around. Todd's truck was sliding down the icy driveway, one of its tires blown, headed right toward the school bus stopped to let out some kids, including Lulu.

"Shit!" I shouted. "Turn the wheel! Turn the wheel!"

He was, but the truck twisted, still screeching, still moving, now perpendicularly to the drive.

The bus screamed a prolonged honk, air brakes hissing. It tried to back up, except there wasn't time or room, with a line of cars idling behind it, in front of it. It was trying to turn, but couldn't.

I ran, kept running, but I could do nothing, *nothing* as the UPS truck become a metal avalanche.

Like a burst hive, yellow- and blue- and pink-jacketed kids erupted from the bus, scrambling away, out of the path of the truck.

And there was Lulu's red hair flaming behind her as she half-dragged a boy in a cast.

I wanted to shout her name. But that would only make her pause, make things worse.

A shouted, "No!" behind me. Bernadette.

I could do nothing. *Nothing.*

And then the truck was crashing into the bus, first the right fender, then in slow motion pushing the front of the bus away from the side of the road.

I stopped, horrified, as the bus veered toward Lulu and the boy.

Screeching, incredible noise, the bus relentlessly swerving closer and closer, and Lulu diving for the boy, using him as sort of a sled, trying to push them out of the bus's path.

Panic consumed me.

The world stopped. Time stopped. The bus slid toward the two kids on the ground.

Remember the Magics. The Magics. Trust your feelings. Bold, like a Jedi.

And the world vanished. The bus, the kids, Bernadette, the truck.

Right hand, thumb out, palm open, open to the magics. Gather, gather. I hold out my hand and push.

I scream as a chain of fiery spirals encircles my wrist. I ride the panic. And then I see nothing, feel nothing, but swirly lights. White-gold fireflies swarm from my palm, forming the classic Waterlily lace pattern, scents of citrus and cedar, and thousands of lace Waterlilies surround the truck, the bus, and I pull with my mind, tight, tighter.

Nothing happens! The slide continues, relentless toward Lulu, the boy.

I gasp, stagger. Fight! Gather! Or Lulu will die!

And the UPS truck stops. But the bus continues on and on and...

I pull, muscles straining, pull at the fireflies, and the Waterlilies web and tighten and close, and the bus slows, slows. Stops.

I blink, I breathe, and Lulu moves. Alive!

Scorching pain arched my back. I fell to my knees, hands slapping icy ground, wasps stinging up my arms, enveloping my head, my torso, my legs. Blinding, cutting, consuming. It hurt so bad. Yet the power had felt so damn *good.* I swayed, the world a mirage, distant.

"Clea!"

A shout. But, oh gods, I burned.

I was scooped up. I screamed, skin on fire, head lolling.

I can't see. I can't see!

"Lulu," I said, voice thready.

"She's okay." Larrimer, moving lightning.

I hurt. Everything hurt. Midges biting, prickles everywhere.

He laid me on something soft. "Can't... catch... breath."

Larrimer's fury surged over me.

Pain. Pain!

Gone. A hand smoothed my hair again and again. "Ssshh."

Calm. Yes. Calm.

My breathing reset, pain receding, and it was better. Soothing.

A cool cloth wiped my forehead.

"There," he said. "There."

I opened eyes weighted with lead. "Better."

Larrimer, stroking my face with the cloth. "Jesus. Your tears. Blood. They were *blood*." Larrimer, face taut. "What the hell did you do?"

"Do?" The taste of blood in my mouth. I reached for the towel, wanting to wipe it away.

Instead, he smoothed it over my lips, my nose, my cheeks. "You're bleeding everywhere, for Christ's sake."

"I'm better." Sort of.

He cupped my head and kissed me fierce and hard and long, tasting my blood, tasting me, tasting everything.

I hung on to his storm, gave mine to him, and when he released me, I felt bereft. I opened my eyes to see his, tempests of blue.

"James, I'm okay." My right hand, where I gripped him, had bloodied his shirt. I ran a palm down his arm, and a Celtic spiral, black and dotted with blood, twined around my wrist. "James?"

Bernadette appeared carrying a bowl of water. She got down on her knees and stared, a bright white towel draped across her arm.

Larrimer dampened the fresh towel, went to wipe my face, but he shoved the towel into her hands and strode from the room.

I sat up, too abruptly, and dizziness nailed me.

"Lie down!" Bernadette ordered.

"James," I croaked after him.

"Leave him be. Sonny boy needs to release his personal pressure cooker." She wiped my face, strokes slow and even.

I'd think she was all business if her hand wasn't trembling.

Long minutes later, I pushed myself to a sitting position.

Bernadette held up a finger and took my pulse, nodded. She reached for her blood pressure cuff and took that, too. "Open your mouth."

I did as commanded, and she searched with a tongue depressor until I gagged.

"Here," she said.

I drank the water she handed me, cool, with ice, the way I liked it.

Next, she flicked on a penlight and pointed it at one eye, then the other.

She snapped a nod. "You'll do."

"The accident?"

"No one hurt badly, thank the gods." Bernadette folded the bloodied towels. "Bus stopped just in time." She packed away her emergency kit.

Hadn't she seen the fireflies? Had Larrimer? Had anyone? My mind fissured.

I rubbed my hands up and down my arms. The burning, the prickles had subsided. Other than feeling like I'd been flattened by a truck, things seemed to be in working order.

"I wouldn't look in the mirror if I were you," she said.

Her frown told me it wasn't good. "Because...?"

"Your eyes are blood red. Like a manticore's. All the vessels, burst. I assume you can see well enough."

"Yes. Fine."

She tsk-tsked. "You look like the demon spawn."

"You should know." Which just popped out for some reason. I found that funny, giggled.

She did, too, which might have been the oddest thing all day, and pushed to her feet. Minutes later, she returned with my sunglasses. "Here. You'll scare Lulu."

I slipped them on. "Better?"

Her fingers wrapped around my chin. "You're closer than I suspected. Almost cooked, cookie." Her voice, soft and dark, with a deep French accent.

"What's that supposed to mean?" I asked, mesmerized.

She took the dirtied bowl and towels to the kitchen.

I recalled scents of citrus, cedar, and the *fireflies* as they'd formed the Waterlilies pattern. I ran a finger across my wrist, no longer spirals of fire. Smooth, the tattoo faint, but visible. I reached in my pocket and retrieved my phone, thankfully still in one piece. I took two photos of the spiral. Larrimer *must* have seen *that*.

The dogs barking, hurting my ears. Larrimer's footsteps accompanied by... "Lulu!"

She raced to the couch and kneeled, putting a scraped hand on my knee. "Are you okay? Why are you wearing sunglasses? What happened?"

Pure joy. I hugged her tight.

"Talk about exciting! And this guy, he's a football player, a friend of Ronan's, and he had a broken leg." She chattered on. "Scariest thing *ever*!"

My fingers feathered her cheek. "Are you hurt? Tell true."

She shrugged. "Couple scrapes. And this. Ouch!" She leaned her head forward.

"Where? Let me see."

She pointed to a spot between her bangs and hairline.

My heart seized.

A Valkyrie appeared beside us. Bernadette took Lulu's hand, tut-tutted. "Let me take care of that, dear."

"Did Larrimer see?" I asked Lulu.

"Yup. I showed him! It's not *that* bad."

"You're right," I said.

"In the bathroom, please," Bernadette said, taking her kit and steering Lulu.

"Wait!" Lulu reached for my hand, my right one, and she stared at the tattoo.

Even as Bernadette tried to lead her away, I clamped Lulu's hand and whispered in her ear. "What is this spiral on my wrist, Lulu? Tell me."

She whispered back, tears in her voice. "Daddy had one just like it."

When Larrimer reappeared, my lips throbbed, the remembered passion of his hungry kiss. I hoped for one of his rare smiles. Nope. He was buttoned up tighter than a straightjacket. I patted the seat beside me, but he chose the red chair.

"Feel better?" he asked.

I lowered the sunglasses and pointed. "Demon eyes, according to Bernadette."

"Scary."

I found myself tearing up, which was really dumb. "Thank you." My voice wobbled.

"At your service, ma'am."

"You kissed me. You touched me."

"Yes. I apologize. A mistake."

A simmering anger dammed my tears. That he would deny this feeling between us burned like acid. "Don't. Just *don't*."

His stare was cool, distant.

A knock at the door startled me, then footsteps, and a man stood in the doorframe between the kitchen and living room.

All in black, from his sweater to his boots, he was older, maybe fifty, of medium height and burly, with a clean-shaved chin and outrageously bushy sideburns that I loved.

"Jason," Larrimer said. "Meet Clea."

"Hey," I said. "Thank you for keeping an eye on Bernadette and Lulu."

He flashed a warm, inviting smile, then shrugged. "Not much to it."

"I disagree, and it's appreciated," I said.

His gray eyes cut to Larrimer, and he unwound a fisted hand. In it sat a small plastic bag containing two spent bullets.

Those furrows in her scalp were just what I'd imagined. Someone had fucking *shot* Lulu.

CHAPTER TWENTY-TWO

Jason tossed the bag to Larrimer.

"I'll send these to the lab," Larrimer said. "I don't expect much will come of it."

"Didn't find the brass, boss," Jason said. "Gonna look some more."

Jason left, but my eyes were all for Larrimer. White lines bracketed his mouth. "Dead men walking."

"Larrimer."

Power boiled, and heat. It poured from his fingers, his arms, his chest. The air seethed. The dogs tear-assed out of the room. The man I knew went missing. That *thing* was death.

"Larrimer. *James!*"

He blinked twice, and clamped on the calm like Iron Man dons his armor. Gods, if the switch ever failed.

He whooshed out a breath. "Sorry."

"What was *that*?" I asked.

"My stupidity."

The dogs crept back into the room. He reached down and ruffled their fur.

To avoid foot-in-mouth disease, I nipped my urge to probe. "Did they *mean* to shoot her? Kill her? I just can't see it."

"Maybe to rid themselves of old business?"

That shook me. "Perhaps they messed up. If our driveway hadn't been so iced up, the UPS van wouldn't have lost control."

He ran a hand across his chin. "They may have factored in the crash."

"They *want* her. The Feed and Seed, her house. She would have been an easy grab in the chaos of the crash if stuff hadn't gone wrong, like Lulu helping that kid in a cast off the bus. If she hadn't been helping him, she'd have easily made it out."

He stared. "The bus was inches from killing her."

I bit my lip and started to talk about the hand-sparkly thing. But the words stuck in my throat.

I dragged a shaking hand through my Medusa hair. Change, evolution.

How to control what was happening? I *needed* control.

Larrimer would listen. I should talk to him. Except he hadn't talked to me, and he *knew* stuff.

"I smell those wheels turning and burning." That voice, honey laced with concern.

"That's me, a smelly wheel."

That evening we were all tense. Ronan stopped by after dinner, and he and Lulu vanished into her room. Larrimer disappeared into my office and closed the door. Bernadette called a friend on the landline.

Grace velcroed to my leg, I entered our main bathroom, carrying my phone and wine, which was when I finally looked in the mirror. And bit back a shriek. My eyes were slasher-movie red. Hideous.

My trademark fast healing better crank it up a notch.

Giving several minutes over to my awful eyes and my vanity, I swirled the bath oil around the tub, and then climbed in, clutching my Vinho Verde. After much maneuvering, Grace settled on the flokati rug beside the tub. She wuffled a sigh of joy, unabashedly happy to be sharing these moments of intimacy with me without the intrusion of chickens, goats, or Mutt and Jeff, not to mention the kitten.

The water ran, a mantra of calm, and setting my wine beside the tub, I settled into the porcelain curve, the heat soothing my battered body. I could doze off right here.

Instead, I began to shake.

Shit.

I drew up my legs and rested my head on my knees. Everything felt so *wrong*. Maybe it was PTSD. I held out my palm, the one that had stopped a school bus from crushing Lulu. The Celtic spirals were gone, the skin clear and unblemished.

My phone.

I lifted it, clicked, and sucked in a breath.

Blurred. All the shots I'd taken of the wrist spiral were out of focus. Impossible.

"Shit!"

Apparently nothing was impossible. Since Dave's death, I was living on some magical moonscape. Senses heightened. Visions, magic fireflies, voices in my head.

Maybe "magics" were simply a different system, one we humans didn't understand, one our brains had to unlock?

Gather. Gather. "Got it, Da!" My body shuddered. *Da.*

I snagged my wine and downed it. Bourbon would've been better. The whole damned bottle.

Perhaps...

I held up my right hand, palm facing the box of cotton balls on the shelf, thumb out, just like that afternoon. Cotton balls. What could be easier?

I pushed left, aiming to knock the box off the shelf. I imagined the box moving. I pictured pushing the box. Then pulling the box. Roping the box into a net.

Not even a wiggle. I stared at my palm. No glowy things, no fireflies, no pain, no pleasure.

And I'd stopped a bus with this hand?

Saturday morning, I sat at my desk amidst a sea of papers trying to make piles so I could actually work. So I could think. I'd been to the barn, Larrimer had again made me coffee, and I'd savored its hints of cinnamon and honey between nibbles of Bernadette's scone.

I snugged my flannel shirt around me, then used the Flair pens to mind-map a diagram of all that had happened.

Wow. Looked like a frigging solar system. I balled up the paper and tossed it. Score!

Simplify.

Larrimer and I were hunting Dave's killer. The Master was searching for a treasure, one bound by magic, which equaled Dave's chest.

So *where* the hell was the damned chest? I sighed.

And called the diner. Anouk was on extended leave. Well, whoop-de-doo.

I pulled up the image of the invitation, the one with the animal blood in the ink.

"What?" said the sleepy voice at the office door.

I turned. Lulu. "What what?"

She snorted. "You said, 'the ink.'"

I hadn't realized I'd spoken aloud. "Oh, this invitation to the gala." Found beneath Dave's body, a fact I'd never tell her.

She appeared beside me, milk and PopTart in hand, face bruised and scalp bandaged, vivid reminders of yesterday's near-miss.

"You look—"

"Awful." She winced. "I'm glad prom's not tomorrow."

"I was going to say 'okay,' but that would've been a lie." I smiled. "Good thing my prom isn't tomorrow, either. Pull up a chair."

As she did, she said, "Your eyes are scary."

"Boo!"

She laughed as she leaned toward the screen and took a giant bite of PopTart. Then, her face flushed bright pink.

"Lulu?"

Tears tracked down her face, and she made little mewls. I ran a hand down her arm. "Hon?"

The creak of a floorboard, and Larrimer emerged from the hall, barefoot, in jeans and no shirt, drying his hair with a towel. Muscles carved his torso, his arms, flexed as he moved them. I wanted those arms around me, wanted another kiss, just wanted.

"What's going on?" he asked, his voice rough with sleep.

I shook my head. No clue.

Lulu's tears continued, and I held her tight while Larrimer stood by, looking awkward.

The girl abruptly straightened. "What am I, a baby?"

"No, you're not," I said. "Hon, what is it?"

"Nothing." She jerked out of the seat and turned away.

I snagged her hand. "Lulu, it's *something*."

"*What*?" she snipped.

"Don't—"

"I wasn't flouncing," she tossed over her shoulder.

Teen hormones were a bitch. "What's *wrong*, dammit?"

She sucked in a jittery breath. "I saw what was on your computer. I *saw*. That's my dad's... That's my dad's writing."

It took me a minute. "Dave was a calligrapher?"

She nodded, sniffled, then tossed her head. "Just 'cause he ran the Feed and Seed didn't mean he didn't do other stuff."

"I know that, Lu."

She turned her head away. "But he was secretive, Daddy, about some stuff, like his Guardian—" She slapped a hand over her mouth.

She knew about Guardians. She *knew* stuff, dammit. "Did his calligraphy relate to—?"

"No!" she said. "But he made good money doing it."

"Okay." I nudged the chair. "Why don't you sit back down? Look at this. Do you recall seeing him write it?"

She tilted her head. "Maybe."

I looked at Larrimer, who quirked a brow.

I knew what he was thinking. Animal blood. Confirmation of Dave's complicity.

Lulu's face had frozen into stubborn mode. I wanted to hug her or strangle her. "You're a good kid, Lulu."

She frowned. "What's that ever gotten me?"

"Lots. Is this what you've been hiding? That your dad was a calligrapher?"

"Not exactly. Part of it." She stroked Gracie. "Daddy was gifted. He did a ton of fancy invitations and stuff. He used a different name and everything. A secret post office box." She brightened. "He liked it a lot. But then these men came to the store and, well, it wasn't ever the same. After that, he'd get, I don't know, dark when he got out his calligraphy case. And he stopped talking about it, the styles and stuff. It became *more*. He said it had to be our secret." She jumped up. "And you ruined it!"

Don't explode. Do. Not. Explode. I stood, too. In for a penny, in for a gazillion pounds.

"Is this how your dad found out about the animal trafficking?" I stood, eyeball to eyeball with Lulu.

Her eyes widened. "I promised I'd never say anything about that to anyone."

"Tell me about the men who came to the store, please."

"I don't know!" she shrilled. "I was there, but in the office. Daddy shut the door."

"Do you suspect his calligraphy has something to do with his death?"

She hunched, crossed her arms over her breasts, something I hated. "Lulu."

"Maybe."

"*Why* have you been hiding this?"

"Because it's none of your business. He said never to talk about the calligraphy or the animals to anyone, including *you*. That he was investigating some bad people, and it would be dangerous if anyone knew."

The breath I drew was deep and long. "I thought you trusted me."

"I don't want to talk about this anymore." She swung away.

I put a hand on her shoulder. "Lulu, you said you wanted to help. We're trying to find the people who are doing these things, who killed your dad. Our animals. We *need* to know."

"I…"

"Leave the girl alone!" Bernadette swept into the room, an avenging angel.

"We need her help." I tried to grab those flashing hazel eyes.

Lulu flung herself into old woman's open arms.

"*Ça va*, Lulu." Bernadette speared me with "the look." "You always need someone's help."

Anger pushed me out the door, out the house, out the friggin'…

When I entered Nott's stall, I braced my back against the wall and exhaled a long, slow breath… and got treated to an affectionate head butt.

Nott's wuffle when I scratched the sweet spot behind her ears eased me.

So. *Why*? Why did Bernadette pick at me like that? She'd say I needed more calluses. Except, I already had more than two handfuls.

"Clea?"

The voice, honey and granite. Larrimer. He'd seen it all. Bernadette's jab, my reaction.

I got it together and stood. "Yeah?"

Larrimer, arms and legs crossed, eyes sleepy, leaned against the stall door, all giftwrapped like a pretty package in that damned shield of calm.

Those eyes changed, drilled into me deep, deeper than anyone's since Tommy's. So deep, down to my soul. How could he find that place in me?

He clicked open the stall door.

I gave him my back. "What's up?"

Rough arms entwined my waist and pulled me tight against his chest. Hot breath on my ear, then a whisper. "It wasn't a mistake."

He turned me, bent his head, and kissed my neck, melting me, warming me, his lips a trail of fire on my throat, my chin, my cheeks. I touched his waist, felt the hard muscle beneath his chamois shirt, ran my hands up his chest, around his shoulders. Held on tight.

"Why now?" I whispered.

"Because I must. Because you're hurting. Because it's you. Only *you*."

He kissed me then, so different from yesterday's kiss, his lips soft, then iron hard, his tongue probing, hands in my hair, pressing me to him. Those callused scarred hands cupping my head, his tongue hungry. Mine was, too, as I answered his kiss.

That song, so faint, soon drowned by the assault on my senses.

His hands slid to my ass, pressing me closer, against his hard cock, and I burned, wet and hot, and I wanted that hand sliding down to my crotch, his fingers touching me there, pressing me, pumping me, inside me.

I drowned in the pleasure of his tongue and lips, his body mashed against mine.

He bent me to him, and one hand moved slowly, way too slowly, to caress my shoulders, an aching breast, my hips. Touch me, touch me *there*. Him, iron-hard against his jeans, against me, and I stuttered in a breath.

He released me, backed away, eyes hot and angry, so angry, raked a hand through his hair, shook his head back-and-forth.

"What is it?" I asked.

He barked a laugh. "Too much." And he turned and loped out of the barn.

I grasped the stall door for balance, crazy with need and

disappointment. I smoothed a finger across my lips, swollen and warm and ripe, moved my hand lower.

Why had he stopped? What was too much?

Twenty minutes later, wind bit my cheeks, and I hustled toward the house. I focused on Lulu. She had so much to tell us, but she was afraid. She'd promised her dad. But Dave was gone.

Maybe she'd talk to Bernadette. A part of me was glad Bernadette had assumed the role of protector. But a part was jealous, too. Shame on me.

Larrimer was waiting when I walked through the mudroom door, arms folded, face closed and tight and purposeful.

"Where do you think they went?" he asked in a clipped, demanding tone.

My breasts ached, and the juncture of my thighs. "What?"

He pointed out the window. Bernadette's Jeep was gone.

"Was there a note?" I frowned

He rubbed a hand across his chin. "No. I called Jason. Got voicemail."

I pulled my phone from my pocket. No messages or voicemails. No Jason.

My gut quickened with a sense of dread. "Let's go find them."

CHAPTER TWENTY-THREE

Larrimer slid behind the wheel, while I took shotgun. He'd grown taciturn, but the way he ran his finger down his long scar said my urgency was shared.

"You call them," he said. "I'll call Jason again. He'll be tracking them."

He varoomed to Midborough, while I bleeped out numbers, first Bernadette's, then Lulu's.

The second he disconnected, I said, "Jason?"

He shook his head.

"All I get is voicemail, too," I said. "I'll keep trying. Lulu's phone is sewn to her hip. But I'm going to call a bureau tech. Both Bernadette's new phone and Lulu's have GPS."

In Midborough we checked out Lonie's and Barlow's, the diner and Bishop's Tables, then on to Mandolins in Hembrook.

Dave's house was gone, scraped away by someone to protect its neighbors from the smoldering fire. I hoped Lulu hadn't seen this.

"This is all helter skelter," Larrimer said. "Your brand of crazy's bleeding over onto me. Use that sharp mind of yours, Clea. What are you feeling? Describe it."

I looked away, toward the sky that spat a few flakes through the roiling gray. "I don't know. I can't. I've always been sensitive. But this is more."

"Be precise."

"I don't know how!" And the fear crested over me. "It's like a wave, an electric wave that twists through me. That's the best I can do."

On our way to Ronan's, Beethoven's Fifth rang out.

"Balfour," Larrimer said.

"Yes." The man who'd avoided my contact for days was suddenly in touch. Pissed me off.

"You going to answer?"

"No."

"He's a dick." He stared down at me. "Give me the phone."

"He's not. Stop it." That's all I needed, some macho confrontation. The least he could do was tell me how he and Bob were connected.

There wasn't enough air in the car, and for a few moments, I stuck my head out the open window.

We drove past Ronan's house—no Jeep—which was when the tech called.

"Anything?" I asked.

He gave me the coordinates for Bernadette's phone.

We headed up Bergen Hill, past the apple orchard, past the old Christmas tree farm, and down the undulating hill.

A black Explorer, dirtied with winter, sat canted on the side of the road. Larrimer careened behind it. "That's Jason's car."

He climbed out, and I reached for the door handle.

"Stay," he said. "Please."

I settled back into the seat, and sat frozen by the white noise in my head. Larrimer tucked his hands into the pockets of his jeans as he reached the Explorer. The darkened windows made it hard to see inside, but the driver's seat didn't look empty. Larrimer stiffened, but didn't open the door.

The white noise increased. I didn't want to hear, didn't want to know.

Back in the truck, his eyes were flat, then his firecracker of pain stole my breath.

"Jason's dead," he said, voice cool. "Bullet through the temple. Another through the forehead."

Bernadette's and Lulu's protector. A man with a warm smile and bushy sideburns. "I'm so sorry."

"He was hardcore," Larrimer said. "But righteous, solid. Whoever did this was clever."

My hands turned clammy. I fisted them. They were all right. They *had* to be all right. "Bernadette's cell signal is right down the hill."

Larrimer whipped the truck back on the road, and we continued down the near-vertical hill, my nails digging into my palms. At the dip, I spotted the orange Jeep half-on, half-off the other side of the road.

We screeched behind the Jeep, anti-lock brakes thudding the pedal. He jerked it into park and we leapt out.

Bernadette sat slumped against the wheel, a trickle of blood running from the corner of her mouth. She was alone.

"She's breathing," he said.

Relief, a cascade. She wasn't wearing a seatbelt, per usual. *Oh, B, I could kill you.*

I tried the door. Locked. Rapped on the glass. Bernadette's eyes fluttered open. She spotted me, frowned, and rolled down the window.

"Are you okay?" I asked.

"I think so," she said.

"Where's Lulu?" I kept my voice even and slow.

Bernadette cocked her head, shook it, then lifted the manual door lock.

Larrimer carefully opened the door, while I made sure she wouldn't fall out of the Jeep.

A nasty bruise bloomed above her eyebrow.

What if she were badly hurt? So of course, I said, "Why the hell don't you wear a seatbelt?"

She hissed, then straightened her turban.

"I'm sorry. We're worried. Lulu's not with you, and we find you on the side of the road with a bloody lip and a bruised head. What happened?"

"Skidded. Black ice."

"And Lulu?"

"She's at a friend's." She sighed.

A friend's. Lulu was at a friend's. Except Jason was dead.

Over Bernadette's protests, Larrimer helped her out of the Jeep. I supported her other side as we limped over to Fern.

Larrimer got Bernadette situated in the passenger seat and buckled her in. I got in back, he put Fern in drive, and we headed down the hill.

I leaned forward. "Just tell me where you dropped Lulu off, and we'll go get her."

"Here," she said. From her pocket, she pulled out a pair of red cashmere mitts, the ones I'd knit for Lulu. "Lulu forgot them. Foolish girl."

Her speech was slurred, quivery.

Silence. The air thickened.

So I could see her eyes, I leaned forward, clamped my hands together, and forced a smile.

"Which friend's, Lady?" Larrimer said. "Where is she?"

She bit her lip, her forehead crinkled. "Can't remember."

I put an arm around her and hugged her to me.

"She needs a hospital," he said.

As he drove, he called his agency about Jason, while I rang up the bureau.

My fingers hovered over an extension, Bob's extension. Instead, I tapped out the digits for Mary Conroy, not really a friend, but a rock-solid gal who worked in our Boston office. I detailed today's events and requested she send the report to both Bob and the SAC.

"Not just Bob?" she asked.

"No. Not just Bob."

Thankfully, the waiting room at the hospital was deserted. Fear rode me like a sadistic jockey. Larrimer sat beside me, still as marble. I thought I'd jump out of my skin. *They* had her.

The doctor appeared and told us they were keeping Bernadette overnight. She might have had a mini-stroke or she could be concussed. When we went to say goodbye, we found her asleep.

I kissed her cheek, and we left, almost unbecomingly quickly.

But that *thing* inside me, it kept building and building and...

At a friend's. At a friend's, at a friend's, atafriend's.

Arms around my shoulders, pressing my back to a rock-hard chest. "You're shivering," he said.

I stared straight ahead. "She's not at a friend's."

"I know," he said.

A text pinged, and I fumbled for my phone. The tech had sent me a screenshot with the words, *Just got a read on second phone. Location...*

Numb, I texted a thanks.

"The MacDaniel reservoir," I said. "In the middle of the frozen lake. Let's go."

We stopped at the house and loaded the snowmobile into Fern. We both changed, geared up, and headed for the lake.

Neither of us said it could be a trap. Neither of us cared.

I'd been to MacDaniel reservoir many times, in many seasons. In winter, the lake's pristine, icy cloak shrouded reeds and rocks and froze the lake into folds. As Larrimer drove, the snowfall became more insistent, the sky's gray blended with the snow on the trees and the gunmetal shades of the earth.

I input the coordinates of Lulu's cell into my phone's nav, and directed Larrimer. We turned right, wound up Binder Street, then past the row of small houses, past the dam, to a lone two-story white house, and a little further on, where a brown wooden swing gate blocked the road. We parked in the small plowed area to the left of the gate, and I jumped out.

Larrimer was geared up by the time I retrieved my shotgun, knife, monocular, and an extra magazine for my Glock from the bag I'd packed. I checked my gun, sheathed my knife, and slipped my monocular into the breast pocket of my down vest.

"Let's leave the snowmobile until we need it," he said. "Noise. I'm a strong tracker. We'll find her."

I nodded, nerves bow-string tight.

My boots offered solid purchase as we walked to the gate, padlocked and chained, and climbed over.

Quiet shrouded the world. He paused, cocked his head, listening.

Few sounds—the swoop of a bird, the sigh of the wind, the tink of the snow as it hit the frozen earth. My staccato breath.

Larrimer led us deeper down the road as snowflakes danced. The storm held off. The further we went, the more closed off he became, as if he were a machine honed to a single purpose.

In my pocket, my fingers massaged Lulu's mitts.

He picked up the pace, and we trotted down the snow-packed road and found a rhythm. Every so often, I'd check my phone to make sure we were headed in the right direction.

Woods flanked us, mostly pine, but maple and oak and beech, too. Larrimer angled left, toward the thick pines, and hissed.

I froze. Here, footprints churned up the snow, ones that had come from another direction.

Larrimer pointed to a small evergreen bush, then plucked something from a branch. A necklace of stars.

"It's Lulu's," I said. "I've seen her wear it."

"It's fresh. Not covered with snow. Nor is the clasp broken."

Smart girl.

He slipped it into his pocket, held up a hand for me to stay and ghosted out of sight.

Several other access points existed, and they'd come in from another direction. Didn't matter. My mouth watered. *Soon, Lulu. Soon.*

Larrimer reappeared. "The lake."

I followed him until we crouched by the shore of the immense frozen lake, dotted with a few islands that sprouted thick stands of pine, its borders fringed by forest.

Bootprints in the snow, and an ice boat's runners. They usually held one person, but perhaps they could hold two. I didn't know.

I did know they were fast.

I shielded my eyes, scanned the lake. Nothing as far as I could see. I pulled out my monocular. A clear trail showed the iceboat heading north up and across the lake. I handed it to Larrimer.

Google Maps showed no roads flanking the opposite shore. Just forest for miles.

"While you get the snowmobile," I said. "I'll keep watch here."

He cut me a sharp look. He didn't like leaving me alone. I knew that. But he could get the snowmobile off the truck on his own and drive it here. The man had skills. "I'll be fine. Badass, remember?"

His eyes skimmed the lake once more, and then he vanished into the trees.

Sweat dampened my temples, and I moved backwards toward the cover of trees. A crack, like ice failing.

I crashed onto my belly, swinging my shotgun off my shoulder. My monocular had flown out of my hand. Damn.

Another shot, and a spray of ice stung my forehead and cheek. Way too close.

I pumped the gun, returning fire, then rolled toward the cover of trees that looked miles away.

Was the ice boat a ruse? I was pinned near the frozen lake, a lying duck for the shooter. I blew off another round, belly crawled right.

He had to be using a rifle, and he wasn't such a great shot or he'd have hit me by now.

I sprayed blasts in an arc, and flattened again. Gah! Still hideously exposed.

A snowmobile's roar broke the silence.

"Stay down!" Larrimer shouted from behind me.

Then a red laser beam, just before the repeats of a semi-automatic shattered the world.

A tinkling, like breaking glass, a bark of pain, and a moan from across the lake. But that might have been the wind.

I retrieved my monocular and hoofed it across the lake to the far shore. No movement, no sound.

Then a helmeted Larrimer was beside me on the snowmobile, one hand wrapped around his semi-automatic. I donned the second helmet, took out my handgun, and slid behind him.

"We're going to go in low and slow."

Lulu's smile flashed in my mind, then her smile, her walk, her russet braids, bouncing.

I tightened my hold on Larrimer, gun firm in hand, and scanned right to left as we drove across the ice, following the ice boat's tracks. When we came to a small island in the middle of the lake, he parked the machine just above the embankment.

Given our noisy arrival, the shooter might be gone, but we climbed the small slope, hunkered low, guns at the ready. We entered the stand of trees accompanied by silence. Snow now fell in a steady stream.

Lulu's hands must be cold without her mitts.

We walked on, and he motioned we should circle the shooter's possible locale and come out above, then signaled, you, me, together.

I nodded.

The snow came faster, almost white-out conditions. The pines helped, but not enough.

I caught myself wondering just how many covert ops had he led to grow so skilled and assured, as if it were second nature? Ten? Thirty? A hundred?

A crack and boom. We stopped.

"Not from this island," he whispered.

The trees were black soldiers, night sneaking in. We slipped through the darkening forest, and spotted a break in the trees. He glided forward, hands lightly wrapped around his two drawn guns.

It felt like I walked through static electricity. Tingly. Inert, but still present.

Just before the tree break, he gestured we move to our bellies, and we began inching across the snow, headed back toward the lake. He slipped over a small rise. We'd covered the island, come across the ice boat. Empty.

Impending dark gloomed the world, the three-quarter moon painting the snow a grayish white, inky patches scarring the hill.

"A body," he said.

Please no. Please.

As one, we moved until Larrimer flowed forward to hunch over the pieces. "It's not her."

His face was in shadow. But the pieces, the torn flesh, the string of entrails. A foot. Part of a hand. A head. Turned away from me. Wearing a navy knit cap.

I chewed my lip, snow bitten and raw. *How could he be sure?*

He crouched over the remains. "Clea. It's not—"

"Don't say it," I hissed. "You don't know."

"It's a man. Look at the length of the fingers, the foot, the size. It's one guy, and it's not her." He kept his voice just as low.

He was right. Of course he was right. My chest contracted, expanded. A sharp pain stole my breath.

I crept closer and got to my knees.

What was left of the shooter in the snow, we hadn't done that with our weapons. He'd been ripped apart. By whom, or what, I couldn't imagine.

Closer. I needed to see the face.

Eyes wide. Mouth agape. In a scream? I knew this man, but...

Long, long ago, I'd cradled another head. Da's head.

I dizzied, stuttered in a breath. Da. Had I held my dead father's head? *Oh gods.*

"Clea."

"It's Harry Rosdale. He was an artist. A potter, maybe. We should keep looking for her. The other islands and—"

"I'm sorry, but they're long gone."

"How can you know that?"

"The ice boat's here. No tracks leading away. However they managed it, gone."

Yes, how?

I walked to a granite outcrop and sat, back against the stone, legs stretched out. That memory. The head. My Da. I shook it away. Harry Rosdale. Why would a man like him be involved in this horror?

Larrimer crouched before me. "I'm going to circle the island again. On the off chance."

With a curt nod, I called up my contacts. "I'll buzz this in to the state cops. Balfour, too."

I dialed Bob first, who snapped his concerned anger at me, telling me he'd take care of the state and the search-and-rescue dogs. I answered in clipped tones, then stabbed the phone off. A bitter laugh flew from my lips. The one good thing about Lulu's kidnapping was it guaranteed the FBI's full engagement. Then I searched, too, and found a smashed phone. Lulu's? I sensed Larrimer near. A few more steps toward the clearing, and a stolen glance showed him lifting some samples of Harry Rosdale's flesh into a plastic bag. Silent. Efficient.

We'd learned all we could with approaching night. I swiped the snow off a boulder and sat, butt freezing, chilled from the cold sweat I'd worked up.

Lulu had been here. How many were with her? Two, three?

And just what had torn apart Rosdale? He wasn't cut, but *ripped*. And not by animals.

Larrimer walked over to stand beside the boulder, arms relaxed, waiting, anticipating.

"Maybe Lulu escaped." I looked across the expanse of reservoir.

"She didn't," Larrimer said.

I kneaded my hat in my hands. "No."

"The rifle. The casings. Whoever did this took them from the scene along with Lulu."

"I'll go get Grace, see if she can't track—"

"Stop." Larrimer squeezed my shoulder. "This isn't you. You're not thinking, and you're always thinking, Clea. The SAR dogs will be here soon."

"I can do this."

He hunkered down in front of me and took my hands. "You can do many things. But you're fogged with emotion."

He was right. Still grated to admit that. I squeezed his hands back and looked into his eyes, and though it was too dark to really see them well, I knew he was looking at me, too.

"I'm scared," I said. "I'm really scared. Of what they'll do to her. How they'll frighten her. If they might hurt her." I sighed. "I don't like being scared, this feeling squeezing my heart. Do you ever get scared?"

"Yes. Not often enough."

"What do you mean?"

He chuckled. "I was a reckless kid. Gave my mother plenty of heartache. She was a good, good woman, and I terrified her with the stuff I pulled. I didn't understand what that meant then, not until later. Later." With a rock-steady hand, he traced my cheek, my jaw, slowly, as of memorizing me, moved his thumb back and forth across my lips. "Yeah, I finally got it. But it was too late, way past time."

CHAPTER TWENTY-FOUR

The house was quiet when we made it back. Mutt, Jeff, and Gracie did their exuberant thing, but soon curled up near the woodstove. I expected another call from an apoplectic Bob. Lately, the old man had been acting with such damned inconsistency. So unlike himself. I chewed my lip.

It was six. How could it only be six o'clock?

At least, Bernadette was safe. I'd called, and the doctor said she might be released tomorrow. No stroke, no concussion.

After I fed the animals, I started to nuke us leftovers, but Larrimer pushed me out of the kitchen, insisting he'd make froufrou veggie burgers with chutney.

"We don't have any chutney."

He started searching the cabinets.

I pointed. "What about—"

"No Worcestershire!" He ended up using salsa, and he looked at home in the kitchen, movements economical, hands efficient. The burgers were delicious.

After I cleaned up, I hunkered into the red leather chair, tipped my head back against the smooth leather, and lowered my lids.

"Da! Da! Look what I did! Help, Da."

Kitty floating on the ceiling. How come? I stamp my foot. "Come down now, Kitty!"

My calico kitty doesn't come down. No, she is stuck up there, and Mam will not be smiley at me when she gets home from taking Apol to the doctor. No, she will shake her finger and say, "Bad, Artie."

"Da! Da!"

Kitty floats, up high, legs going all which ways, like when I take my swim lessons. She is making that mew sound, the scared one.

"Da! Da!"

Where is my daddy?

I walk, bold like a Jedi. That's what Da always says. Maybe in his room, where he reads smelly old books that I cannot touch. Forbidden, he says.

Precocious, Mam calls me.

He is not in the room with the fuzzy carpet.

But, Kitty.

Yes. I must find Da.

Maybe in Mam's office. I run to the door, reach high, turn the knob. Locked. Shucks. I giggle. Funny word.

I thump down on my bum. Think. Feel. Da's always telling me to Feel. Okey-dokey. I take a breath and push out my feelies. Da says to push hard.

He is not in the kitchen, where he makes yummy... Stop.

Focus, Mam's always, always, always saying that.

Da, too. Focus, focus, little Mage. And feel.

Feel. Ohhh, they're smooth, soft, like Kitty's fur. I push the feelies all over the place to... Da!

I leap up and run, fast as I can to the living room. "Kitty!"

Da's looking out the window. Doesn't see me. He needs to look at me. He has to get Kitty down.

"Da!" I say. "You need to—-"

Da scoops me up, opens the door under the stairs, puts me inside! The no-go place. "No, Da! Mam will—"

"Hush. Hush. Not a word, love."

He shuts the door, and it's dark, and there are scary things in here. Things that prickle and bite my skin with Power. I cry. Cry, cry, cry. I do not want to be in here, and Mam will be unhappy. No, mad, that I'm in the No-Go Room. I cry more, a storm inside me. Da doesn't like it when I storm. Why did he plop me in here?

Hush, Hush, in my mind.

I get all quiet, for Da. Now I hear them. Voices. Da and another. Climbing. Louder. Bad. I know they're saying bad things.

I Feel, pushing feelies...

Oh! Bad. A Bad. Talking to Da! Oh, bad. Bad. BAD.

I touch the door handle. It burns!

Da! I say in my mind.

Hush. Hush. Stay.

No, no, NO. Have to get to Da!

I kick and kick and...

A BOOM outside the door!

I kick more and more, and oozy goop beneath the door, on my hands, my underpants. Smelly. Yuck.

The door boings open. The Bad Meanie! Scooching down to me. Big teeth, grinning teeth. Red teeth.

"Da! Da!" I scream.

I kick the man hard as can be, hit his penie place! And he tilts over like my roundie toy, and I'm fast, scrabble out, hands and knees zooming over the sticky and...

What...? I stop.

Da's head, eyes big, mouth big, neck all jagged and red and gooey. Ugly. All wrong.

Da? I say in my mind.

No Da. Humm.

I scoot to Da and pick up his head and cuddle him, hair so soft. The Bad Meanie rolling around, grunting. Good! And by the sofa, Da's other parts? So still. Red glop on them, too. Why? Why is he over there, too, wearing the jeans Mam hates, the ones with the hole in the knee?

Focus.

I cuddle Da's head. Have to put him back together. I'll do that. Yes, I will.

The Bad Meanie, laughing. Laughs, laughs, laughs.

He's evil. I know Evil. Da and Mam taught me.

Trust your feelings, Da always says.

I scrunch my face tight, clinging to Da's head, fingers playing with Da's pretty gold earring. I know what I'll do.

I look, higher and higher, up to the Bad Meanie.

He's mad, growling, licking red teeth with a big pink tongue, hands, claws reaching, reaching for me. Oh! For Da!

No! No! NO! NEVER!

I raise my hand, all red and icky—hug Da with my other. Raised hand, palm out, just like we practiced. And I picture that pretty knitting thing Da taught me, the one he called "arrow," to help against the Bad Meanie.

The Bad Meanie walks funny. "Mage bitch."

My flickery lights in my hand. Yipeee! I Gather... Gather... Gather...

The Bad Meanie growls. "What the..."

My swirly lights! Wheee... on my hand... arrows... Da's head... my body... out bigger and bigger, more and more and... A big, fat storm of swirly! The best ever! And...

Dark. So dark. Warm. Feels good. I sit up and rub my belly. I'm hungry, sitting on my bum out here. Where?

Mr. Moon shines down. I squish my eyes, try to see better. Dust. All over me, around me. I wiggle my fingers in a pile. Sneeze. Scratchy funny dust.

A meow. A kitty walks toward me. Calico. Silly word. Whose kitty? Maybe I can keep her. I reach for the kitty and hug her close. She purrs. Nice. She's got that icky dust on her, too.

Meow.

Where am I?

Meow.

Can I keep her?

Meow.

Who am I?

"Clea!"

Reeling from that dream, that incredible, terrifying dream, I blinked. His Pacific blues on fire, squeezing my shoulders, warm, caring.

I stuttered in a breath, ran shaking hands down my cheeks. "What?"

"You wouldn't wake up. You were moaning."

"As long as I wasn't drooling." I offered a jaunty smile. A dream. Just a dream.

But not.

He didn't smile back.

Well, why should he. I probably looked like a corpse. I unfolded myself from the chair and stood to face him, my fingers laced together so as not to touch him, when all I wanted was that.

We looked at each other, two stick figures numb from the day's events.

He reached for me, iron arms drawing me close, slowly, so very, very slowly. He was warm comfort and hunger in a way I understood. My fingers dug into his broad back, aching to obliterate the day's agonies, the dream, the *memory*, aching, aching.

He surrounded me, erasing everything.

"You could have been shot today," he growled.

"I wasn't."

He brushed a finger across a scratch on my face.

"It's nothing." On tiptoe, I tilted my head up, but couldn't reach his lips. "Kiss me, you stubborn man."

His lips twitched, then met mine with violence. We devoured each other. My arms around his neck, his banding my waist, wrenching me impossibly closer, one hand stealing to my throat, the other clenching my hair.

My phone bleeped, and again, and he stepped away so fast I got whiplash.

I stared at him, the demanding phone—background noise. "I don't get it. Not any bit of it."

Cheeks flushed, chest heaving, he said, "If we don't stop, I'll have you on the floor in seconds."

I slapped my hands on my hips. "Well hell, Larrimer, what's wrong with that?

"Just about everything." He notched his head toward the phone. "Speaking of *that*, you better answer."

"Ha ha funny." I waited for a heartbeat, then did.

I paced as I talked. The SAR dogs had found nothing. With full dark, they'd stopped the search. They'd take the dogs out again in the morning, but the handler wasn't optimistic.

How had Lulu's kidnappers gotten her off the lake after the gunfight?

I climbed back into the chair, heat burning my eyes, panic skittering across my shoulders. And fury. At Special Agent James Larrimer, a man who was making me ache. Damn his mercurial nature.

Well, I was *done*. I stomped down the hall to my office and pounded on the closed door.

"Larrimer, you let me in!"

Nothing. He made me feel things for him. Wormed his way inside. I cared for him. Well dammit, I was not some faucet you could turn on and off.

"Open up!" I said.

Silence.

That was it! I punched open the door.

Empty. The room was empty.

He'd flown, yet again.

I awakened the next morning stiff and cranky, having slept all night in the leather chair. I assumed Larrimer had reappeared at some point, since the afghan covered me, and I hadn't pulled it on. James. That was so *him*.

I checked my phone. No calls. The FBI had set up their command center at the police station downtown in Midborough. They had no news on Lulu, promised to call if anything broke.

It was late, almost 8:00 a.m. I piled on the clothes and stepped into a crystalline blue morning. I breathed deep, letting the dry air cleanse me. Ordinarily, these were my favorite days, the ones after a mad storm, the sky so bright, the cold so bitter, the air snapped with energy.

The barn was deliciously fragrant with animal smells. I peeked in at Nott and Delling, amazed at their lack of verbal abuse given the lateness of the hour.

They'd been grained up, their water replenished, their stall tidied. I walked down the row. All the animals fed, all the stalls pristine.

Larrimer. *Again.*

I inhaled deeply. The fresh barn scents eased my heart that squeezed tight. Too tight.

Back inside, I found him warming his hands by the woodstove.

"You need a decent pair of gloves," I said, almost finished with knitting him mitts. "Not just those thin leather ones. You wear them or don't at the oddest times, too." *That wasn't what I'd wanted to say.*

"I feel more alive without them."

He wasn't going to talk about last night, damn him. "Were the barn chores an apology for your disappearance or a thank you for the kiss?"

He turned to me, a large man more distant than the coldest moon. "Maybe a little of both."

No way would I put myself out there. Say things that couldn't be unsaid. Feel things that couldn't be unfelt. *Coward.* "Are we ever going to talk?"

A battle raged inside him and burst over me. Yet it showed neither on his aloof face, nor in his relaxed stance. "Words. I'm not sure I have them."

"I hope you'll find them."

"Not really an option."

Downstairs in the cellar, I tugged on my gloves and pounded the heavy bag hung from the ceiling. I punched and kicked and punched some more.

I'd saved those kids with fireflies of power. That power. The feeling. Insane. Intense. Glorious. Boy, when Dave said I was the magic, not an overstatement.

Then again, there was my cotton ball fail.

Magic was useless if I couldn't help Lulu.

My mind twisted and turned, but I couldn't find a way in. Punch, kick, punch, kick, kick. I ran a mental data scan. Dave's words, "take the chest." Dave's secret calligraphy. Punch, kick, twist, kick, punch, punch.

He had to have a case for his calligraphy tools. Lulu would have cherished that case of her father's. Sure, why couldn't the case *be* the chest?

So where was it? If it had been at his home, it was long gone. At the Feed and Seed, or maybe in Lulu's room?

After a quick swipe of the towel, I trotted up two floors to her bedroom, with a detour to grab a pair of nitrile gloves and a couple of small baggies. I'd be invading the girl's privacy. I'd live with it.

I shut her door behind me. My breath caught. Everything looked so normal. Stuffed bear on the bed, PJs crumpled at the foot, running shoes tossed near the closet. A picture of Ronan tucked into the dresser mirror. Pens and a pad and an Ilona Andrews paperback on the bedside table, with a pair of tiny silver post earrings shaped like stars atop it.

That necklace in the snow. How cold it had been yesterday.

I started with the bed. Felt the bear, smoothed the coverlet, looked under the mattress. Nada. I trolled her pink Bean backpack and her suitcase, found more teenaged girl stuff.

No surprises in the nightstand drawers.

I walked over to the dresser. Atop it sat a small, plastic jewelry box, the one Larrimer had rescued. I lifted the lid. Inside the box lined in pink velvet, a ballerina twirled in a voile tutu as it played *Swan Lake*. A few trinkets lay in the small compartments on the top level, earrings, two rings, an amethyst pin.

She wore an amethyst pin.

The room dissolved.

I stand in a bedroom, have to look up to see my mother in a tweed suit bent over my brother, maybe three-years old, pale and ill beneath the covers, one of his small hands scrabbling on the crocheted comforter, blue veins and bones a roadmap of sickness.

My mother, a tall slender woman with an auburn pageboy, taking him to the doctor.

I smell camphor and Witch Hazel and...

A whisper from far, far away. *Clea.*

I blinked, looked around. No one there.

I'd always had these brief fugue states, where I'd drift off into memory, my ADD and all that. But never about things that didn't exist.

I had no brother.

CHAPTER TWENTY-FIVE

I shook myself, the way a dog does when it's soaking wet, and got on with it.

Shoes lay on the closet floor, and a dress, a few skirts and shirts hung on the bar. I ran my gloved hand along the shelf above the bar, acquiring a nice clump of dust in the process.

On the floor, I found two boxes of shoes, and in the deep hidey-hole in back, a lighter box. I pulled it out, said a little prayer, and lifted the lid.

Letters. From Dave and Ronan and an old one that smelled of the attic. From her mother.

My own mam. Was that a true vision of my mother? A long-ago brother? Had he died with them in the accident? Except my Da didn't die in an accident. A stupid tear landed on the envelope. I wiped it away, replaced the letters, and snugged the box into its original spot.

A breeze. I glanced over my shoulder. Larrimer, arms and legs crossed, leaned a hip against the door frame. "Digging for treasure?"

"Why don't you help?"

"Because there's not enough stuff in here to warrant it."

I moved to the bookshelves that held so little of Dave's epic library. "At least I'm *doing* something."

"I am, too. Watching a beautiful woman acting crazy."

He thought I was beautiful? "I am not crazy. And get that smirk off your face."

The muscles in his jaw bunched, then broke. He burst out laughing. I whipped a book at him, which he easily caught, his eyes dancing.

"Damn you, Larrimer."

"Crazy has its appeal. So, get on with whatever you're doing."

"I'm looking for Dave's calligraphy case."

"Why?"

"Because it's important."

And eyebrow raise was all I got in return.

After my not-unexpected failure to find the case, Larrimer accompanied me to the Feed and Seed, which we scoured, and, again, no joy. If the calligraphy case was the cause of Lulu's abduction, I doubted *they* had it, either.

As I locked the store, SAR called. The dogs found no scent of Lulu and ten inches of last night's snow obliterated any trail across the ice.

Larrimer and I stood in the cold, he with no hat, no gloves, statue still.

"Ronan," he said. "Let's go talk to the kid."

We parked on the white farmhouse's gravel drive and walked up the small path.

"I called him," I said as we approached the door. "He knows about Lulu."

"The kid's tough." Larrimer gave a decisive nod. "He'll do okay."

"Geesh, guy, they're in love. You must remember what that felt like."

He chuffed out a breath, but said nothing. After I rang the doorbell, long minutes passed before Ronan's dad cracked the door and invited us inside. Today, he wore jeans held up by suspenders and topped by a neat blue sport jacket, his sparse hair tidied in a comb-over. I hadn't taken him for the Sunday churchgoing type.

I asked after Ronan, and, apparently a man of even fewer words than Larrimer, he led us down the center hall to the back of the house and pointed to a window. Outside, a group of kids played pickup ice hockey on the pond.

We slipped and slid down the icy path, crossed a field, and walked onto the ice where the kids batted their puck. Only Ronan, the largest player by far, seemed to have that Bruins ferociousness.

"Ronan!" I shouted.

The boy looked up from where he was guarding the goal, notched his head at us.

High on the hill, his father barked, "Ronan! Now!"

Oohhs and *bummers* from the kids as Ronan removed his helmet and gloves and skated toward us. For such a lumbering guy, he was elegance on ice.

The puck launched off the stick of a girl in blue. "Shit!" she screamed.

The bullet flew toward my head. A hand blurred and snapped it out of the air.

"Sorry!" The girl skated over to us, frantic. "My aim sucks. Sorry. Sorry."

"Not a problem." Larrimer returned the puck to her.

Ronan patted her on the back in that awkward teenaged way.

Sadness touched my smile. He was a good kid.

"How did you do that?" Ronan asked Larrimer as he traded his skates for work boots.

"I used to play hockey, too," Larrimer said.

"Cool catch." Ronan stood, stared at his feet. "I'm pretty worried."

"I know," I said. "Me, too. We'll find her."

"Yeah." He sighed, face drawn. "I... I miss Lulu. She's, well, she usually texts all the time, and I feel like, um, empty."

"Empty," Larrimer said. "Yes."

"We need to talk to you, Ro," I said.

Ronan's eyes brightened. "How can I help?" He tucked his helmet and mitts under his arm, slung his skates over his shoulder.

I gestured toward town. "How about we talk over lunch at Mandolins?"

Ronan toed the snow with his boot. "Can't. Dad made lunch."

Can't, huh. Hummm. "After lunch then?" I asked. "An hour? Come over to the restaurant."

"Okay. And Agent Larrimer," he said. "It's not my place, but you should wear more clothes. You're gonna freeze that way." Then he hocked a loogie on the ground.

At Mandolins, Larrimer and I ordered sandwiches, hot drinks, and oatmeal cookies, and found a seat at a corner table where I could watch the door. Larrimer had no problem having his back to it, which would drive me nuts.

Black-and-white animal photos decorated walls painted a soft yellow, the conversation—low murmurs with occasional bursts of laughter. Patrons greeted each other, the atmosphere convivial, almost like someone's home.

And any of them could be involved in Dave's and Jason's murders.

I checked my phone. No messages. No calls. Nothing from the kidnappers, the cops. Just nothing.

Two hours later, Ronan entered Mandolins wearing a blue watch cap and sporting a bandaid across his cheek, one that hadn't been there before lunch. When he spotted us, he walked over.

He took a chair next to Larrimer and swiped off his cap. His lips were raw, and his psyche lacked its usual joy.

"Are you hanging on, Ronan?" I asked.

"Sort of, I guess."

"About Lulu's kidnapping."

His stare turned glassy.

I covered his hand with mine. "Here's what we need."

He squared his shoulders. "I'm a crack shot."

"We need information, Ronan," Larrimer said. "Not Wyatt Earp."

I rubbed my fingers across Ronan's fist. "Try to relax a little."

"We believe the men who killed her father took her," Larrimer said. "They want something."

Ronan sighed. "If I'd been there for Dave that day—"

"Then you'd be dead, too," Larrimer said.

I wrapped my hands around my mug of hot chocolate. "We think Dave had something or knew something that a man named The Master wants."

"Never heard of him." Ronan huffed. "Stupid name."

"Yes, but lethal," Larrimer said.

"We're guessing Dave died," I said, "because he wouldn't tell them what they wanted to know. And now, they believe Lulu knows what 'it' is. Maybe she does. Maybe not. She's a great secret keeper."

"Yeah," Ronan said. "She is. Will they hurt her?"

I forced myself to meet his eyes. "I, we hope not. Do you know anything about Dave's calligraphy? Or any of his secrets? Anything?"

I watched him battle the beast as tears pooled on his lower lids. They didn't fall. He swiped at his nose. "Her dad was a good, good dude. He... man, he was nice. Treated me like I was a responsible guy, ya know. Like I could be trusted. I was over there lots. Helped out at the Feed and Seed until Lu told me to stop. She was scared, and scared for me, too."

Larrimer nodded. "Of what?"

Ronan shook his head. "She couldn't, wouldn't tell me."

"His calligraphy was important to him, Ronan," I said. "Do you know anyone who hired him professionally?"

He pursed his lips. "No. Dave was—"

"Hey, Ro!" A couple of teens beelined for us. One of the boys slapped Ronan with his ballcap. "Your pop's looking for ya."

Ronan's nostrils flared. "You tell him I was in here?"

"No way, bro." The boy's face darkened.

"Thanks for the heads up, man."

The teens sauntered around the corner.

"Dad's got a lot of chores for me to do," Ronan said. "No biggie."

"No," Larrimer muttered under his breath.

"Can you think of anything else?" I asked.

Brow furrowed, Ronan glanced at the door. "About a week before, you know, he died, he gave me a gift. It was sorta cool. A box. Said he'd made it for Lulu and me. Nice, y'know. He got how much I love Lulu."

I sucked in a breath. "Can we see it?"

The door opened, and Ronan's father stood in the doorway, face flushed with anger, a chaw of tobacco bulging his cheek.

The kid froze.

"Ronan?" I whispered. "We need to see the box."

"Gotta go." He pulled his knit cap onto his head. He rose, a huge boy dominated by a small man.

"Pop," he said.

"Need you, Ronan."

"Coming."

His father waited.

Ronan turned back to us. "It's somewhere in the house. Can't tell you where." He shrugged. "My pop said he'd keep it safe. I don't know. Please find Lulu. Please."

Ordinarily, I'd wait until the following day, when Ronan's father left for work, but I needed to get inside that house *now*. Was the chest there? Oh, I hoped so. It could be the key to everything. Larrimer caught my eye and nodded.

Almost March, and each night, the sky darkened later. Normally I would relish that. Today, I cursed it.

"Why don't you take the truck and check on Bernadette," Larrimer said as we exited the restaurant.

"Oh, right," I said. "While you break into Ronan's house. *Alone.*"

His eyes narrowed. "Yes, alone. Not your area of expertise, babe."

I chuckled. "My ass. I was in CI. Think again, *sweetcheeks.*"

He growled. "So what do *you* think we do, *honey bun*?"

"I'll keep the old man busy, while you hunt for the box."

"The man's a beast," he said. "I'm not letting you within ten feet of him alone."

"Letting me?"

He crossed his arms.

"I don't need this bullshit. We wait until they're asleep, and we both go in."

Mr. Dragon Dude, for sure. I'd swear smoke poured from his nose. And then he smiled, tightlipped, slow and mean, like he was cooking something nasty. "Fine."

It was after 2:00 a.m. when capped, booted, gloved, and dressed in black, we slid through one of the Miloszewskis' rectangular cellar windows and found ourselves surrounded by the detritus of a farming life. Shadow and light carved the large cellar, with a frozen dirt floor that would be damp come spring. An ancient plow, boxes, old harnesses, a pile of plastic shipping popcorn: a jumble. There were rooms, too, one with a huge metal door.

We wove our way toward the cellar stairs. They were old and worn and the door whined as Larrimer eased it open onto an old farmhouse kitchen right out of the fifties. The linoleum groaned as we skirted the table toward an archway. To my right was the living room where I'd talked with Lulu, to my left, a parlor. I swept my beam left, over a room crowded with rugs and easy chairs and a china cabinet and, front and center, a recliner that faced the darkened flat screen on the wall. A charming contrast to the mounted animal heads that surrounded it.

I peeled off into the parlor, while Larrimer took the living room.

I walked the perimeter of the room, shining my beam into cabinets and drawers and closets, over the mantle and across the desk. I paused. A card lay carelessly strewn among the papers that littered the desk, but enough like the gala invitation to make me snap it with my phone and email myself the image. I slid the card down the front of my shirt and turned the corner toward the bow-fronted glass cabinet. And almost screamed. Ronan's father slept in the recliner aimed at the blank flat screen.

Shit. I continued my circuit of the room, awareness heightened of the man in the chair.

I aimed the narrow flash into a glass cabinet. Assorted doodads, much dust, and there, on a shelf, a graceful black box carved with the initials R and L entwined on the lid.

Of course, the case was locked.

Currents of air brushed my skin in the old, drafty house as I slid my picks from my jeans. The simple lock took seconds. Just before I opened the case, I glanced again at Ronan's father. Drool dribbled down his chin. I slid my fingers into the case and lifted the box, opened it, and inside, nothing. Perhaps, it was a puzzle box. I photographed it, emailed the photo, and slipped the box into my small backpack.

I relocked the case, turned to escape the room, but a soft thud, the sound familiar, froze me.

The gray cat had leapt onto Miloszewski's lap, and a reflexive hand rose and stroked its head.

I flew toward the door on silent feet.

The snick of a bullet being chambered stopped me.

I reached for my gun, spun around to face the older man.

"Wouldn't do that," he said.

I lowered my arm. He stood less than three feet from me, a small bully wearing a mean smile and holding a Chief's Special aimed at my face.

"I knew you were a nasty one." He held the gun with a careless authority, like he used it a lot.

"Not so nasty, old man. Just curious."

He stepped closer and thwacked the back of his hand across my face, knocking me sideways. I steadied. "Asshole."

He hit me again, with a fist this time, and I staggered as pain shot from my jaw through my head. I could take him, but chose to play helpless for a moment longer.

Through my aching jaw, teeth gritted, I said, "Is this how you treat Ronan?"

He grinned, gleaming white teeth at odds with his leathery face. "It's how I treat any burglar. Guess my pal's dropped your big friend already."

"Not possible."

"'Spect he got the drop on him 'cause a you." His chuckle really pissed me off. "We knew you'd come."

I wanted to ask how. Chose not to give him the satisfaction.

A sly look. "Oh, my pal, he's got his ways." He seized my shoulder and pinched.

He knew just what nerve to press, and I fought the pain, powered through it, and grabbed the arm with the gun as it moved past me, started twisting, going with his movement, the flow of it giving my move energy.

The creak of a board, someone behind me. Pain exploded the crown of my head, and the world disappeared.

CHAPTER TWENTY-SIX

I didn't want to open my eyes. I was hurt, woozy, and freezing my ass off—where was my coat? my backpack?—and damned if I could remember...

Reality snapped back *fast*.

I lifted my lids. Nothing happened. I was engulfed in blackness.

No gloves, no jacket, no hat.

My jaw ached, and the back of my head felt like a frigging bomb had gone off there. I touched it gingerly. Sticky blood clung to my fingers. Bastards. I'd been coldcocked.

A groan from somewhere in the room.

"Larrimer?" I ran fingers across the floor. Cement, not dirt.

No answer. Miloszewski's "pal" must have some moves to have brought Larrimer down.

I reached into my pocket for my phone. Gone. Of course it was. Crap. Nothing was ever easy.

Freezing air tickled my nose. My mouth was dry, and I was at once oddly hungry and nauseated. I'd better get up.

I pushed to my feet. Dizziness threatened to slap me to the floor again. I groped, found something hard and cold to keep me upright. It swayed, and I gripped it tight to stay vertical.

"Larrimer!" I hissed.

Nothing.

I needed a light. *The box.* I'd stashed it in my backpack. Dropping to the floor, I groped, no backpack, but my fingers found splinters, shards. And a prickle of power. I lifted a piece and smelled. Wood. The box. Destroyed. Ronan's father, the bastard. I bet the bastard hadn't thought much of the box until I took possession of it. But it wasn't the chest, a thing I suspected not so easily destroyed by a rabid man.

I pushed cold fingers down my shirt for the invitation. Gone, too. Miloszewski feeling me up while I was unconscious. *Gross!*

The wood, the power. Dave's gift to the kids. I slipped the slivers into the pocket of my jeans, then stood again, one hand on a wall, shaky, but better. I followed the wall, every so often bouncing into something cold. And creepy. I stoppered my imagination.

Fingertips numb, I felt around a tall object, tripped over a lump on the ground, and found what I thought might be a door. Next to it, a switch. I flipped it.

Another groan, and I stumbled across the room, much of it in shadow given the dim bare bulb hanging from the ceiling. In the corner darkness, a slumped shape on the floor.

"Larrimer." I slipped to my knees. "Larrimer. Wake up." I bent onto my haunches and shook his shoulder. He didn't stir. Another groan.

His face—Ronan's father and accomplice had beaten him bloody, lip split, cheek cut, right eye swollen shut.

I pulled him to a sitting position and cupped his bruised cheek. "James."

Nothing. I hugged him close, trying to warm him, and turned to face the room.

"No."

The faint light outlined an enormous carcass, an antlered moose, hung from a hook chained to the ceiling.

We were in some kind of refrigeration unit.

"Oh no," I said aloud, gut punched by the second carcass. I gulped in a breath, fighting my damnedest not to freak or puke or both. A naked man—headless, handless, and footless—hung by another hook that curled into his upper back. Beneath his leg stumps, an icy metal bucket of what had to be blood sat below. I clenched my jaw, trapping a scream.

I saw us—Larrimer, me—swinging from those hooks after we'd frozen to death.

I'd seen horrors in my work, plenty, but nothing like this. How did someone *do* that to another human being?

Out. We had to get out.

"James." I shook him. No response. Dear gods. And then I kissed him, kissed his lips, his cheeks, his forehead, his ear, and I reached for our song. More wet, sloppy, hot, kisses. "Wake up, *please*."

A groan, and I kissed him again, sucked on his lower lip, amped up our harmonic resonance. When he answered the kiss, my blood fired.

"Larrimer, wait."

"Nice," he mumbled, deepening the kiss, parting my lips, tongue thrusting.

Holy shit. I pulled back. "Larrimer, wake up!"

"Sure," he slurred. "Mmmm. One more." And he kissed me with the whole nine yards, arms crushing me, tongue inside me, cock hard against his freezing jeans.

I was plenty warm now, and I'd bet he was, too.

"We need to leave *now*. Wake up. Hurry."

"Getting there," he said, his voice a granite rumble.

I unwound from his arms, stood, and inched my way to the horror on the hook. I wouldn't need any snapshot to recall this.

I closed my eyes, couldn't look. Not a person. Not a person. Dead. Dead. Dead. *Okay, I can do this.* I opened my eyes.

A heart tattoo on his shoulder read Mom. Torso with a small pot belly, uncircumcised, lean muscular legs. I walked around him. A long scar jagged just above his butt cheeks. He wasn't old. I reached for his hand—right, no hands—fisted mine instead. And they'd drained his blood into a bucket.

Had I known him? I hugged myself. No, no, no. He shouldn't be up there. He shouldn't. I reached to lift him off the hook, take him down.

Firm arms wrapped around my waist and lifted me away from the corpse.

I looked up at Larrimer. "What?"

"Let's go. Now."

"But I have to—"

"No, you don't. He's long gone, Clea. He won't care."

I leaned my head against his chest. "It's so wrong in every way."

"Jesus Christ, obviously. But I don't want us to end up like him."

I let out a breath. "No," I said, voice thin.

He squeezed my hand. We felt like two popsicles.

"How did they get you?" I asked.

He blinked.

"Larrimer?"

"Said they had you. Yeah, I know. Then my head exploded, and I woke up kissing you. Sleeping fucking Beauty, that's me." He walked toward the door that lacked an interior handle and put his shoulder against it. "Care to join me?"

"There's no way, Larrimer."

"Perhaps there is."

I leaned my shoulder against the frigid metal door.

"On three," he said.

"Set."

We pushed against the door. Nothing. We tried again. Not even a budge.

He moved me out of the way, walked to the far end of the room, and I felt him gather strength. He flew across the room and rammed his shoulder into it. And again. It bowed. But it didn't open.

"Shit." He turned to me. "Be nice if you could do those light things right about now."

Blood drained from my face. He'd seen, and said nothing. Then again, he'd just bent the door with superhuman strength, and I'd kept my trap shut.

"I can't. Not on command. I, um, I don't know how."

"Try?"

I held up my right hand and pushed, while I begged the magic to come. Nothing but a lot of cold air between me and the door.

He kissed my cheek. "Okay, Plan B."

Larrimer snapped the antlers off the moose as if they were toothpicks.

"What are you doing with those?"

"Making do."

A sudden fit of shivering stole my legs, and I banged into one of the walls and down on my ass. Breathing hard, the effort to rise felt impossible.

"Clea," Larrimer said.

"What?" I sounded like Marilyn Monroe with the sniffles.

"When you hit that wall, it made an odd sound."

He was losing it, too. "Meaning haha odd or weird odd?"

He staggered closer. "Not like steel odd."

I thought about it, then gave the walls a closer inspection. "We're in the basement inside some kind of meat locker."

New Hampshirites are inventive. We wouldn't *purchase* a professional meat locker if we could build one. DIY are us.

I knocked on the wall, covered in insulation board. He was right. It sounded different. I picked up the saw and moved it back and forth, again and again. The insulation was plastic foam, but it wasn't seamless, had been riveted to the walls.

He swung an antler.

"Wait!" I stopped his arm before he hit the wall. The only noise was the persistent blower pushing frigid air into the room. Gods, I was cold. And sleepy.

His hand brushed my face. "Don't go to sleep or I'll leave you here."

"Huh?" Oh, right, think, think. Synapses triggered. "A cellar window. Like the one we used earlier to break in."

He peered down at me. Blood had dribbled from his right eye onto his cheek. "Good."

I stumbled past the hanging man and moose to the darkened far corner, and touched where the walls met, barely feeling them with my frozen fingertips. I moved a few feet down the outer wall, judged where the half-window might sit. It had to be there. It just did.

"Try here," I said.

He lifted one of the antlers to what I pictured the join of wood between the ceiling and wall. They clattered to the floor.

"Goddamn, fucking, lousy—" He opened and closed his hands a couple times.

"Ssshh." I rubbed them, trying to bring back circulation. We listened.

Nothing but the blower and our chattering teeth.

He bent at the waist, rested his hands on his knees, wavered for a minute, then braced himself against the wall. "This level of cold does things to me." Then, he retrieved an antler and wedged the spiky side into the board's join.

In seconds, he'd pried the plastic away from the wall. It made a horrible noise, and we stilled, heard nothing. He pulled at the plastic and the pink fiberglass insulation beneath, tossing it like cotton candy.

A spurt of joy. Pale almost-light exposed a modern cellar window maybe three feet wide by two feet high, with a swivel lock handle at the top of the inner sash.

Perfect for lowering dead men through. Ugh! Horrible image.

I looked at Larrimer, my smile triumphant. Except Larrimer's eyes closed, and he slid down the wall.

I knelt in front of him, ran my hands across his shoulders, his arms. "What's wrong? Larrimer! Where did you go!"

He was out, and even if I could reach the window handle, which I couldn't, there was no way I could lift him out of there. I pressed a hand to the pulse in his neck. Slow, so slow. We were freezing to death.

I began warming his hands. Tried kissing him again, massaged his arms, legs. I dug for our song and found... silence. He sat in front of me, torpid breaths puffing the air. I was watching him die.

Please. Please wake up.

Nothing.

If I could somehow get the moose down, climb onto it, use it like a ramp, I could crawl out the window, and bring help.

I tried to get the moose off the hook. I tugged and jerked, and there was no way. I looked at Larrimer, barely breathing.

Stop. I was going at this all wrong. The window wasn't that much higher than I was. I tried jumping, but couldn't reach the handle. A stepstool. Maybe...

I turned Larrimer and lay him face down on the floor, positioned his butt beneath the window, removed my boots, and stepped onto him. *Sorry!* Stretched on tiptoes, I wobbled, then bent my knees and jumped. Yes!

My icy fingers caught the lock's handle and in one motion, I turned and pulled downward. Open!

I stumbled backward off Larrimer, silently begging for forgiveness. Air spilled in from outside, cold, but not as cold as the meat locker's, and far fresher.

Boots back on, I got my hands under Larrimer's armpits and lifted. I barely moved him, so I sat him up, back against the wall.

I wrapped my frozen arms around him and blew hot breath on his lips, his cheeks, his ears, whispering, singing, kissing his neck, mumbling incoherent words.

He didn't respond.

With or without the window open, we'd die of hypothermia.

Another brush of sleepiness wrapped me in warmth. I could do that, cuddle with Larrimer and slip into that comforting, numb world. So easy.

Except we hadn't even made love yet.

I slid down beside him and tucked my arm through his, rested my head on his shoulder. "It's pretty easy, isn't it? Going off this way. I read that somewhere."

A picture of Tommy, smiling, dealing a hand of Texas Hold 'em. He'd cheat, again. Always did. I peeked at my cards. Whoa. Except he transformed into Lulu, red hair aflame. Why was Lulu playing cards?

I tumbled down, down, and wrenched awake. She was trapped, too, kidnapped. She needed us.

I tugged at his shirt. "Wake up, dammit. Lulu needs us. Wake up!"

Nothing.

Focus. I pictured the burn from eyes blue as the Pacific, and reached deep, deeper for that otherness in him that echoed mine. My soul sang the song, grasping, straining for that resonance, that harmony.

And he moved.

I wheezed, coughed. "Are you there? I got the window open. We can do this."

He nodded. "Here," he mumbled. "Shut down for a minute. A reset. Sorry."

"I thought you were dying." It crushed me.

"Not a chance."

He stood on his own in one supple, fluid movement. He cupped my face with his hands and kissed me, and I tasted his blood, felt his power flicker over me, building and building like furnace under pressure.

Just then, voices outside, faint, in the snow, but getting closer.

CHAPTER TWENTY-SEVEN

I **leapt toward the light switch, more like a stumble, but** managed to flick it off just as the voices grew louder as they neared the window. Time to pray that they didn't notice.

Oh gods, do not let them hear or see.

"Is the moose ready?" said a muffled male voice.

"Yup." Another male voice, one I recognized as Ronan's father.

"And George in there?" Muffled, but a ping of memory. Gone.

"Just about."

"I'll need his blood this weekend."

"It'll be ready," Miloszewski said.

"Good." A smile in that voice. Another ping, but not enough.

Bile surged up my throat. I swallowed hard.

Their boots boomed like cannon fire. I held my breath. Just past the window, they paused. *Crap.*

"You know what we must do to that boy of yours," said the voice.

"Nope. Can't."

"You haven't kept him in check, like we agreed. The Master—"

"He's my *kid*."

"Not for long." A pause. "All right, all right. Let's talk about this later."

"Won't do..." And they walked on, voices fading, the crunch of the snow beneath their boots drowning out their words.

The thought that they'd kill Ronan staggered me.

We waited moments longer until the only sounds were the trees clacking in the wind.

Larrimer braced his hands on the sill and slowly lifted his torso. "It looks clear." He curled out the window until all that was left in the room were his booted feet. Then, they disappeared, too.

I waited in silence. And waited. And thought I'd lose my mind if I had to wait any longer.

Hands appeared at the window, then forearms. I jumped, snapped my hands around his wrists, and he did the same for me. And pulled.

I dangled a foot from the snowy ground, his arm banded around my waist.

"You good?" he asked.

"Better than good." Almost-dawn smoothed the world's edges, and I paused to listen, interminably glad to be free of that nightmare cellar.

Free. We were free.

We had to get to Ronan, except we were barely functional. We needed to warm up, so we raced down Station Road, thankful for the near darkness.

It had to be six-ish. My numb feet protested, threatening to spill me onto the road. I tripped over a rock, bit my lip to stop my shout of pain as I landed on my knee. Larrimer pulled me up.

We ran again.

The glow of Mandolins and of the Inn and the General Store brought a slow smile. Death had felt close and intimate and inevitable. I couldn't stop picturing 'George' dangling on the meat hook.

The town twinkled, lights from cozy houses leading us on in the pre-dawn murk. So much beauty, so much horror.

I bit my chapped lips. Past the pond, the post office, the church. We crossed the street holding hands, frozen. I felt nearly paralyzed. When we slipped into our front seat, I retrieved my spare key from its niche, started the truck, cranked up the heat. Then I unlocked the glove compartment and removed my backup Glock, knife, and flashlight. The gun felt icy, but comforting.

Larrimer dug his hands through his hair and looked straight ahead. I wished I could see his eyes.

"What's wrong?"

"Mandolins is open," he said. "We need something hot."

Minutes later, the scents of coffee and tea filled the cab. He drank swiftly, his face granite-still, staring at nothing.

He'd had problems in the cellar, but so had I. He looked shaken, disturbed. As if he'd failed himself or someone.

"James?"

A pause, then, "Yeah. I'm cool."

"We need to get Ronan. I'm going to call the police, Balfour. We need backup."

"No. They could kill the boy while we deal with red tape." His bunched muscles relaxed as he downed his tea.

"So we go in first." I angled myself to face him. "They'll arrive and back us up. We don't know what crazy stuff Miloszewski's got going on there."

"No." He looked at me, eyes near-fever bright. "Do you trust me?"

"Yes." My knee-jerk answer surprised me. "Yes, I do."

"I've been investigating these people for months now. There's more going on here than meets the eye. It's deeper. Complicated. Deadly, in ways you haven't dealt with before."

"But I—"

"The last person we should call in is Balfour."

My jaw tightened. This wasn't about their pissing contest. This was more. And it played right into my fears about how my boss had taken to acting. "The Staties? The local cops? Why not them?"

"You realize Miloszewski's people most likely have Lulu, too."

The thought chilled me. "Yes."

"Afterward. After we deal with Miloszewski. Alert them then."

I had my suspicions about how he'd handle Ronan's father, too. All of this a-tangle with Dave's bizarre death. I gnawed my lip.

"Call now, and the echoes will aid Cochran's killer." He took a sip of tea, giving me time to think. But his eyes held mine, and his conviction burrowed deep inside me.

Larrimer wouldn't stop me contacting the authorities. Trust. It always came down to that. "All right. I'll wait."

I finished the coffee, slipped on my spare vest and mitts, and handed Larrimer a fleece I'd tossed in the way back. As I warmed, the pounding in my head matched the one in my jaw, reminding me how much I despised Ronan's father.

"I wish you had your gun," I said.

218

"Not as much as I do."

I held up mine, but he took the knife. "This will do just fine."

Again, we dogtrotted up Main Street, avoiding the lights splashing onto the gravel sidewalks and stopped across the narrow dirt road from the sprawling white farmhouse that had almost killed us. We crouched behind a juniper.

"Kids are skating already," he said.

"It's New Hampshire."

"Think he'll do the kid the way he did us?"

I shook my head. "The father, you heard his reluctance."

I was able to see over the small rise.

"A couple kids with glow sticks," he said. "Ronan's one of them."

"Let's just take him and go," I said.

"No," he said, voice iron. "The father tried to kill us. He'll try again. We've got to take him out of the equation."

"I hear you." I wouldn't let him kill Ronan's father. But he didn't have to know that now.

He gave me a hard stare. "I'll do this alone. You look for the boy."

So aloof. So cold. I paused. "No. Together."

We moved forward and chose the shed connected to the end of the elongated house to slip inside. Old hay bales and rusty farm tools lay scattered about the small room.

We walked through another shed-like structure attached to the house, and I almost tripped over a pile of dirty clothes. I kept my flash out, but shielded and pointing downward.

Listening for the sound of voices got me nowhere. It was too quiet. When I stood before the kitchen door, I pushed out my senses, reached for Ronan's father with my mind.

A hot poker knifed my brain. I clung to the doorknob, bit my lip so I wouldn't scream.

I snapped my mind away, back from that horrible place. *What had done that?*

"What's wrong?" he asked.

"Nothing."

A few more beats, and I tasted only the pain's bitter aftermath.

He moved in front of me and tried the door. Eased it open. Pale light dappled the worn linoleum. Not a light on in the place. Where was

Ronan's dad? I refused to believe he'd carry out his son's death sentence.

A groan, from the room next to the kitchen. A trap? The floor squeaked as I crossed, bent at the waist, gun ready. Larrimer flowed forward, velvet smooth.

"Help."

A whisper. A moist wet one.

I knew that sound.

"Help," moaned the voice.

Gray light on the parlor floor. A man lay supine, fingers scrabbling at the carpet, lips painted dark, glistening. Ronan's father.

I handed Larrimer my gun and crouched down. "Who did this to you?"

"Save... him." A red bubble formed and popped, dotting his nose and chin with blood. He pointed toward the pond.

I knelt. "He's going to kill Ronan, isn't he?"

He nodded, lips forming an indecipherable word.

I leaned closer. "Who? Who's going to kill him?"

"Master..." Then, a soft whoosh of breath and empty eyes. That metaphysical moment when the spirit leaves and the shell remains.

I closed his lids. Larrimer was already racing out the back door.

I skidded down the icy slope. Larrimer had vanished. Dawn's rays fingered across the pond. The skaters were gone. I scanned the iced-over terrain. Where was Larrimer? Ronan? The killer?

I crouched on the slope, a target, then dashed to where the pines met the hill, slipping behind a large tree. Still no one.

My breath in harsh puffs, I rested my hands on the rough tree bark and inhaling the piney fragrance, opened my senses.

Silence.

So, pulse pounding, I raced like hell down the hill.

There, a man, silhouetted against the snow. I leapt for the trees.

My back to a pine, exhilaration throbbed in my blood.

"Goddammit, Clea," came the disembodied voice that hummed anger.

"What?"

"You should've stayed put." Disgust bit his words.

"My ass," I said. "And don't sound so damned superior."

He emerged from the trees.

"Ronan?" I asked.

"Can't find him."

"Wait." Again, I quieted my mind. Pressed harder, reached out.

HIM. A clamp of pain, fell to my knees, clawed my scalp. It shook me, a wolf shaking prey, again and again, that crippling pain. And I pushed, slapped up my shields, and I was suddenly free, on all fours, panting in the snow.

More shielding practice needed. Check.

Two hands reached to lift me, and agony speared through me.

I shook my head. "Hurts." I clawed to my feet using the nubby pine bark and leaned against the tree, catching my breath, dizzy. And there was Larrimer covering me, stance protective, my gun in his hand.

"What the hell was that?" he asked.

Took a minute, but I finally caught my breath. "I suspect whatever's hunting Ronan. It won't happen again."

He handed me my gun.

All was silent, empty. Then the crunch of snow and snap of twig boomed the air. Whistling? Oh, swell.

Larrimer charged up the hill, me after him. There, on the path where the old train tracks had lain, walked Ronan, casual, hands in pockets, whistling "You Are My Sunshine."

"Down!" Larrimer shouted.

Ronan raised his head.

"Ronan!" I pumped my legs and leapt.

A gun barked just as I flew into the six-foot bruiser. We fell sideways and rolled together, arms and legs a-tangle.

"What the fu—"

"Sshhh!" I sprawled, gun drawn, pointing down the slope. "Stay down."

I didn't see Larrimer, who must have gone after the shooter.

Ronan's whole body vibrated.

"Are you hit?" I asked.

"I don't think so." He snorted.

221

It sounded suspiciously like… "You're *laughing*?"

"Never been tackled by a hundred-pound girl before."

"Very funny. Not!"

We skittered to the tree line before we climbed to our feet. Well, I climbed, he bounced, much like Tigger.

"Ouch," he said. "Shit." The tips of his gloved fingers shimmered red.

I checked Ronan's shoulder. Only a flesh wound. Thank you, gods. "Maybe you'd better sit down again."

Minutes later, Larrimer strode over.

"Gone," he said. "As well as what was in the cellar."

On our car ride to the hospital, a shudder went through Ronan when I told him about his dad. I tried to draw in his pain, sensing I could that, but I hadn't the understanding of how. Or maybe that was just another batso idea.

"He tried to save you, Ronan." I gave a quick squeeze to his fisted hand. "He's the one who told us someone was stalking you outside."

Ronan turned away and leaned his head against the window.

His father was a beast, but he'd tried to save his child in the end.

"Come stay with us at the farm," I said. "After the hospital. Please. I've got a spare room."

Ronan peered out the window. Another kid's world ripped away. In a town like Hembrook, change didn't come often or easily.

At the hospital, Larrimer remained with Ronan, while I phoned Balfour about Ronan's dad, then went to visit Bernadette. I sat beside her bed as snores wuffled from her lips. Her bandaged head looked like a poster for some war movie.

Confounding woman. At least her cheeks had lost that awful pallor. I stood and covered her feet where the sheet had slipped.

"Don't!"

I jumped. "Bernadette, I—"

"Uncover me. *Maintenant!*" Her lips thinned, her accent again deeply French.

I undraped her feet, exposing the incongruity of veined, scaly feet and bright red toenails.

I hid a smile. "Who painted your nails, Bernadette?"

The anger softened. "And what's it to you, Viviane?"

My fingers curled, nails biting my palms. My mother's name. "Who?"

"That sweet Lulu did it. She's nothing like that willful child of yours."

She was talking to my mother. "No," I said. "Lulu's nothing like Clea."

"*Ça va.* She's a good child. But what a handful. I was a warrior, not a caretaker, and you, sending me off to New Hampshire. Now the time shortens. Viviane, why did you give her to me?"

As far as I knew, my mother had *not* given me to Bernadette. "Because you were my best option."

"*Mon dieux!* Why not her own kind? I've weakened, my power thinned. You, of all people, know that. Your *métis* expressed as Mage, not Fae. Yet you laid her burden on me."

Fae. Mage. Da called me his little Mage. A half-breed. "Was my mother Fae? Am I part Fae?"

She grunted with disgust. "What are you talking about? You're a nurse. I need to go to the bathroom. Help me up."

I helped her into a sitting position.

"And that curly mop of yours. Unconfined and unhygienic! Shame on you."

She was firmly planted in loopytown.

After our toilet run, I wrangled her back to bed and sat beside her, the vinyl chair making that squeaky noise on my ass.

"*Enfin!*" she said.

"You're welcome," I said, knowing the "thank you" was seldom in her vocabulary.

I rubbed my forehead, trying to erase the deja vu. Four-plus years earlier, it had been the almost the same.

I'd just gotten out of the service. Tommy, too, except he hadn't come home like I had. He emailed us, saying he'd met someone amazing, who was schooling him, loving him.

Typical Tommy, off on one of his toots. *Passion,* he'd say. *The key to everything. Follow your bliss, Clea. Let it sing.*

He was supposed to go back for his Masters, had gotten into Worcester Poly. He'd promised Bernadette and me to finally use that amazing brain of his. This new woman, he said, was encouraging him to do just that. But he'd deferred one semester. Just one. He couldn't be apart from Tanya, not quite yet.

But he *had* come home, when I'd written, panicked about Bernadette's small stroke and her resulting mental instability. I'd tried to reach her, but, unsurprisingly, hadn't been able to. She needed her Tommy.

A day later, he'd breezed through the door. And he'd stayed for a week, high on his "training," nattering about his Ty, how much she knew, how much in love he was, how happy.

He worked so hard with Bernadette, bringing her back, helping her remember, doing familiar tasks with her over and over, reacquainting her with the present, shedding the past.

At night, when she was in bed, those crisp fall nights, we'd start the woodstove, drink mulled cider, his favorite, and he'd talk about how Ty was so much more than he'd ever imagined. He refused to get specific, but wore that smug look on his face. Knowing Tommy, that look had to be about sex. No way was I going to ask for particulars.

I chuckled, then stilled. The memories sifting through my mind, my emotions, morphing from joy to sorrow.

That was the week we'd planned our cross-country trip to the Grand Canyon. I'd said he should bring his new girlfriend. And he'd laughed, saying she'd find that funny.

He'd been so good with Bernadette. So warm to me. I wished I'd pushed him, learned more about his Tanya, her last name, what she did, where she lived. Now I never would. And the hole that never filled, deepened. He wasn't here now to bring Bernadette back. He wasn't anywhere.

CHAPTER TWENTY-EIGHT

The final straw—**Ronan had to stay overnight in the** hospital. I was beat, my bouquet of crazy overfull. I slid onto Fern's passenger seat, earning a frown from Larrimer. He swiped the keys from my outstretched hand and started the truck.

We drove in silence to Sparrow Farm, and once the hysterical greeting of our dog pack subsided with their dinners, I gathered the feed to take care of our animals.

"I'll help," Larrimer said.

"Thank you, but I'm good."

Hearing my critters greetings, feeding and watering them comforted me. The movement worked out some of the kinks in my body, and I breathed in the restorative farmy smells. No need to think. Just *do*.

So blissfully normal.

Larrimer would be showering or tapping on his computer or dancing with his swords. A beautiful way to stay in shape. *I* wanted to stay in the barn. Hide there.

Lulu, Lulu. I had to stop thinking about her or my head would explode.

It almost had at Ronan's house. The pain. The possession. After all today's creepiness, that *IT* crawling around in my head had scared me the most.

Cold finally drove me into the house. Padding on silent feet, I climbed the stairs and gently closed my bedroom door.

Each step I took felt odd, as if not simply my legs, but my entire body was asleep. I sat on my bed, crossed my legs in the half-lotus, rested one hand on my knees, and with the other, I rubbed my fist across my chest again and again. But it didn't help. Why was that? Why did nothing help?

The sound of my bedroom door cracked like a gunshot.

Larrimer stood there looking feral, as if he'd doffed some costume to present his authentic self. Sweat coated a body clothed only in those loose workout pants. Arms crossed, stance wide. It was as if he'd shed his human husk to become something "other."

"What?" I asked, voice like a ventriloquist's dummy, as if it came from a piece of wood. As if I'd turned something "other," too.

"I'm concerned about you," he said, his words quiet, at odds with his persona.

"I'm fine."

"Then what's with the tears?"

I raised a hand to my face. "I don't know."

He stepped inside and kicked the door closed, then walked over and plucked a couple tissues from the bedside table. He handed them to me, and I wiped my face, then blew my nose. I chucked the ball into the wastebasket.

The silence grew and grew. "I had my door shut for a reason," I finally said.

"You always have your door shut."

I notched my chin. "So?"

His jaw clenched. "You hate letting anyone in."

"That's why I shut my door."

Flesh stretched taut over cheekbones, he snarled. "I'm not fucking talking about the door."

He reached for me, and I shrank back. A weight on the bed, his arms around me, lips hungry and hot pressed to mine.

Did I want this? Yes.

I opened to his greedy kiss, wove my fingers through his sweaty hair, cupped the contours of his bruised cheeks, answered his tongue with my own. Intoxicating.

I'd wanted this from forever ago.

"Godsdammit!" I gasped for a breath. "You're a pain in the ass."

He growled low in his throat and licked me.

I moaned. "James." I caressed the word with all the caring, the longing I felt for this man.

He nudged me away. "You tantalize me."

My heart bruised at the flatness of his tone. I searched his face. "Cold. You can be so cold."

"You just noticed?" He sat back, a nasty smile tugging at his lips.

I scooched away. "Cut out the 'cruel and ruthless,' Dragon Dude."

"Why? Take off those pretty blinders."

I smiled. "They're not blinders. The opposite. They're windows into you."

He was in my face in a blur. I froze, and he ran a knife so close to my cheek, it chilled me. Eyes mocked, razors of cruelty. "See? *This* is me."

I bit his shoulder. Hard.

He threw his head back and laughed. His lips hot against my ear, voice a cold whisper. "Do you like it?"

His heartbeat, thudding. Breath warm, so warm. His shoulder muscles bunched, an ooze of blood, teeth marks, *my* teeth marks. *Dear gods, I really bit him.*

And he was one scary shit. Huge and muscled. Fierce, with a scarred face and hands and torso that spoke of battles won and lost. But it was that contained power. You just knew if he ever unleashed it, it would be nuclear.

In for a penny, and all that. I grinned. "It's kinda sexy."

He was off me in a flash, stood beside the bed, body vibrating. "You're a fool," and almost to himself added, "And what am *I*, then?"

"More," I said. "You're more."

He paced, hand scraping his chest. "Oh, I'm more, all right." He stilled, a bow strung, brushed a finger down the scar at his temple. The cruel grin returned. "Ever hear of nanotech?"

"Not much."

"Nanotechnology. The manipulation of matter on an atomic and molecular scale. You can Google the rest. There was a bomb."

I shuddered. "You were injured. I heard—."

His snarl, a bitter sound. "I wasn't injured. I was hunks of meat and splintered bone. What was left was taken to... that's not important now. In any event, none of this is from memory. I was told bit by precious bit.

They took me to the lower levels, to their underground research facility."

He sat cross-legged at the far end of the bed. He wasn't breathing. I waited and waited. His chest neither rose, nor fell, his body inhumanly still. "I can control my breathing, if need be. I breathe normally, but I don't have to."

I groped, unfurling my senses, but he had those damned shields up. He breathed again, and I now wondered how much was artificial, a costume he wore to appear alive?

He crossed his arms, a wicked smile tilting his lips, eyes a burning indigo. "I'm a creation. Frankenstein's monster. The beast under the bed. Every centimeter of me except my brain; that part is mine, from before. They would have replaced that, too, if they had the science to do it. They haven't figured out how the brain becomes the mind, how it generates a sense of individual consciousness. The rest? They recreated me, remade me, down to the scarred bullet holes."

Like from a horror novel. I leaned forward and ran the pads of my fingers across the raised mark on his shoulder. Smooth and rough. Skin and scar.

"That's why you don't want people touching you. You're—"

"No one should touch me."

"But—"

"I'm toxic."

My eyes narrowed. "No, you're not."

"Stop!"

A hand clamped around my throat, a finger stroking my carotid. I hadn't even seen him move.

"Hush," he said, low, cruel. "See how fast I am, little girl. I could kill you using less than a hundredth of my strength."

I forced myself not to flinch. "Hey, dragon dude, you realize you're touching me, right?"

He whipped his hand away and again leaned against the footboard, arm resting on one bent knee. "You're really something else, babe. They enhanced me."

"This is most definitely not Fish and Wildlife stuff. Who are 'they'?"

He said nothing. I could only imagine what "enhanced" meant. His speed. His strength. His resilience. What else? Did he ache for human touch? Or did it no longer matter?

"You've touched *me*." More than just physically. "Kissed me."

He frowned. "Only you. I can't seem to help that. I'll do better."

"Please don't."

He snorted. "They tried to program emotion out of me. They screwed up, can't fix it. You may have noticed I sometimes overreact. A flaw."

"Not to me." We sat there for long moments staring at each other. I finally said, "In the cellar, you shut down. You said that."

"Yes. That was literal." A hint of confusion. "I don't understand how you awakened me. This body," he said with disgust. "It shuts down when it overloads. The cold. I was out too long. They warned me. It's never been a problem before.

"With great pride, they said it took more than a year and millions to create me. Fifty million. A hundred. A billion. I don't give a damn. They stole me."

I ached to touch him, to soothe his hurt. He'd never let me. The stubble of beard, face bruised from the beating, one eye still badly swollen. He looked real. Felt real. Yet he could have been a sculpture. I wanted to understand this Larrimer, too, all of him.

"What happened to you? While they remade you?"

He blinked. Once. "That year and half is gone." He paused. "You can tell no one."

"I know how to keep secrets."

"That, I'm aware of. I have little family left. My parents are dead. Friends, comrades in arms. I've been warned off them. Bad things would happen if I ever reconnect with them. After the bombing, they were told I was a vegetable."

What a terrible and lonely thing. "That's monstrous!"

"That's what I am."

It was like talking to a machine. No affect. Nothing. I shivered and tucked my old cashmere blanket around my legs. "What are you called?"

"Freak," he said. "Monster. My terms. My handlers, the government, they love names, acronyms. I ignore them all. To them, I'm a highly useful and expensive weapon they need to control."

"Fish and Wildlife? The endangered animals?"

"All part of the op. A real one. But they're not the puppeteers."

"Who then?"

He remained silent.

So much I didn't understand. "Why you?"

"Timing. I was highly trained. A mercenary who—"

"But you were in the FBI."

He nodded. "Things got a little too hot, so they unleashed me, and I was recruited by a corporate mercenary group."

Men like that fought, killed, raped with no government oversight.

My revulsion must have shown on my face, because his next words came sharp and very slow.

"Some *do* rape," Larrimer said. "Some murder. And some *don't*. Some protect. Most don't even carry weapons. In Afghanistan and Iraq, thousands of my brothers and sisters died in service, as many as U.S. troops. More were maimed. And since we're unofficial, we receive no cheers on our return. No flags waving. No parades. We get no VA benefits, no support. We stand in harm's way and are silent."

"I had no idea."

"No one does. We are the unacknowledged."

I tried to breathe deeply, but the air felt still and thick. "So why remake *you*?"

"As a human, I was faster than average. Stronger. Smarter. I've never asked. They've never said."

"Between living and dying, if you'd been able to choose, would you have—"

"Never. *Never this.* I'm a fucking monster."

Whatever shield he was using shattered. His lips pulled into a snarl, his face savage.

The primal part of my brain screamed, "run!"

I was more than my primal part. Screw it!

"Ever see *Blade Runner*?" he asked.

A favorite of mine. I nodded.

"That's who I am. A replicant. One of those messed-up things. All science and..."

"What?"

He shook his head.

I searched for words, meaningful ones, not platitudes, the ones that would make him see sense.

The room held notes of my patchouli incense, the musk of his sweat, the scent of my fear. I saw the curl of his hair, the curve of his shoulders, the blue of his eyes, the laugh lines, a shade lighter than the bronzed skin surrounding them. I knew the beat of his heart, the brush of his spirit, the light of his intelligence.

"A replicant?" I paused, took a breath. "Not a chance. It matters not, flesh or construct, bone or steel, human or other. We're spirit. We think. We *feel. You* feel. *That* survived. Nothing else matters. I'm glad you told me."

His lips moved. A whisper. "I needed to." A large, scarred hand reached for my cheek, then dropped. "You. You make life... bearable."

"James."

He was at the door before I blinked. Turned back, his smile grim. "Some mindfuck, isn't it?"

Gone. And I hadn't tried to stop him.

I sat stunned, attempting, and failing, to process. My fingers stroked the blanket's cashmere over and over.

When the phone rang, I was thankful I'd found both mine and Larrimer's in a drawer at the Miloszewski farmhouse. When I looked at who it was, not so much. Bob. Calling, *again*, worried, except...

A snarl. Mine. Larrimer was mine. And Bob *knew* about him and saw him as a thing. And he hated him, and, maybe, envied him, too.

I bottled my anger and declined the call.

I could do one thing, finish one thing. I knit several rows, then cast off the stitches. Larrimer's mitts were complete. They would warm him.

Around six the following morning, well before a watery sun peeked over Mt. Cranadnock, I rolled out of bed. I was exhausted, had barely slept. My mind had traveled over and over Larrimer's words.

How could they do that, transform death into a man? The science, I'd never understand. The cruelty, that I got. Users. They were users.

I ached for him, for his grief at a lost life, for his lack of choice, for his self-loathing. For the spirit inside him that he failed to see.

I thought, too, about his touch. I longed for it. The pads of my fingers traced my lips. I wanted him more than any man I'd ever known. Not one word he'd told me had changed *that*.

Maybe, because it didn't feel real. Maybe, because it was another freaky thing atop all the others. Maybe, because I didn't care *what* he was, but *who* he was.

In the middle of the night, I'd heard him dancing with his swords in his room beneath my bedroom. I'd felt him, too, his energy, his passion, his anger, above a low thread of desperation. Oh, his shields were titanium, not that I'd tried to get inside, but his leaks of emotion, they'd been precisely what Dave had trained me to read. I could have blocked them out, but Larrimer made me hungry. So very hungry.

I pulled on some cargoes and a turtleneck, then reached for my gun on the night table, my backup Glock.

Larrimer coffeed me up, and we slipped into a routine in the barn. He was good with the animals. Being Larrimer, he said nothing about our conversation. Questions bubbled my brain, about his past, where he was from, a thousand things. But I respected his silence.

I caught him looking at me. Covertly. After what he told me, was he wondering if I found him disgusting? Saw him as a thing? A monster? The Freak.

In fact, I found him a little bit magical. Boy, he'd be horrified if I told him that.

"What are you smiling at?" he asked.

I snuck a hand into my pocket and pulled out the large, black mitts I'd knit for him. Made from a fine, hardy wool, I'd soaked them in Eucalan last night and let them dry. They were soft now, yet strong, like the man.

"Here." I handed him the mitts.

He put them on and flexed his fingers. "They fit."

"Of course."

He turned away. Blam went the rubber mallet on the next bucket of ice. Crackles sounded as he topped off Clem's water.

"You knit them," he said, not looking at me.

"I did." I added fresh hay to Clem's hayrack and slipped him an apple.

"They feel good. Thank you."

I didn't need to be an empath to feel his quiet joy.

Back inside, Larrimer disappeared into the office. I refilled the woodstove. Someday, I swore, I'd have oil or gas heat. I was sick of emptying the ash in the morning, lugging it outside to a burn-safe container, then filling the woodbox.

Lulu. Something would break soon. It had to.

After I showered, I sat on the sofa with my coffee and iPad, and pulled up the emailed images of the invitation and the box I'd taken at Ronan's house. The picture told me nothing of the box. But the invitation was pure platinum.

An invite for The Adept's Den, the address, Asheville, a mere two towns away. I mapped the street view. The old brick factory they'd transformed into condos and commercial space.

Coupled with Roberto, the calligraphy, and Ronan's father, I liked it. I liked it a lot.

So did Larrimer, who said his techs would duplicate a card. He was even sort of excited.

Next, I called my sometime wood supplier, Buzzy Benhoff, my Asheville local who knew all there was to know about the town.

Given Asheville's size, there wasn't that much.

Buzzy said the private club was a chi-chi place, mostly out-of-towners, but everyone who entered wore "pricey duds." Jewels, fast cars, big money. After much cajoling, he admitted he'd tried to get in once, but failed. He swore a blue streak about the bouncers. If they were like Blondie, I could imagine.

The club held a supper party, invitation only, once a week.

If they kept to the pattern, the next one would be on Wednesday, two days hence.

Would the techs be able to duplicate the card that quickly and get it to us? Larrimer assured me they would.

Whoooeeee!

In the laundry room, I retrieved my bloodied jeans and pulled the splinters of Ronan's and Lulu's box from a pocket. Feathery tingles zipped up and down my hands, making me drop them. I massaged my hands. They felt fine. Normal. Like hands.

Gingerly, I used my thumb and index finger to pick up the largest fragment. More tingles, not unpleasant, like a gentle, soft wave undulating up and down my skin, reaching for my wrist.

It might not be the chest, but it was a *something*. A thing of power. Yes, that fit.

"Shit!" The Celtic spirals crawled around my right wrist and glowed. They freaking glowed.

Determined. Insistent. I pushed power out. Dammit, I *would* see those glowy fireflies.

Not one appeared. Gurrr. Next time. I might be sick of failure, but I wouldn't give up.

I had knowledge in this brain of mine, and memories, and they'd surfaced at the most unexpected times. Someday, I'd grasp all of it.

Well, listen to me, all Ms. Magic about stuff. Whatever was happening to me, whatever extraordinary thing was going on, I vowed to matter-of-factly accept it, learn from it, absorb it.

I was a Mage. Yes, a Mage. *Own it, kiddo.*

Hell, next I'd start spouting life-and-death pronouncements and profound haiku.

Dammit, I needed Anouk to tell me the real deal. The retwining worlds. The hows and the whys. After. Yeah, after we found Lulu and the chest and The Master.

I continued to clutch the splinter of wood, its feathery tingles almost pleasant, and watched my glowing spiral for a long, long time.

When Larrimer materialized behind me, all cool intensity, I pocketed the wood and looked over my shoulder.

He wore a navy t-shirt, jeans, boots, jagged hair almost brushing his shoulders. Gorgeous. Lethal. *Mine.*

"What's up?" I asked, going all casual.

"I'm getting Ronan from the hospital. He wants some stuff at his house, too."

I stood on tiptoe, slipped a hand around the back of his neck, and kissed his chin, which was all I could reach. After a long moment, he wrapped his arms around my ass and lifted me, and we kissed, long and deep.

I finally broke the kiss. After all, *I* needed to breathe. "Be safe."

"You, too."

You're going down, mistah. I baggied the wood splinters and tucked them into my top dresser drawer. *You just don't know it yet.*

CHAPTER TWENTY-NINE

y Wednesday, we'd gotten everything into place, including settling Ronan at Sparrow Farm. Given her level of confusion, Bernadette was now in Pine Valley Rehab on the hospital campus, undergoing further tests. They said it *might* be a bleed in her brain, but it could have a bunch of other causes, too. My thoughts went to magic, which sounded less and less nonsensical these days. About Lulu, we'd learned or heard nothing. Forensics gleaned precisely zilch from Bernadette's Jeep or the icy lake. Her kidnappers had gotten away clean. The barn was almost as bad, offering little but some ubiquitous industrial carpet fibers and a few hairs that produced no DNA matches.

In a few hours, Larrimer and I would attend the weekly "do" at the The Adept's Den. I was nervous, jittery—we were finally *doing* something—but once I started my transformation, I'd settle.

I'd always been a chameleon, inherently cool with dress up and roleplay, which was why I often used costumes, along with my knitting, in my work as an interrogator. Plenty of people in the area knew me, so I'd deemed it wise to radically change my appearance.I polished my toes pink and applied fake nails, also pink. I donned a wavy brunette wig crowned by a topknot, a darker base, brown contacts, pink lipstick, and a rented green satin evening dress that arrived, along with the invitation, from Larrimer's agency. I'd Amazoned a pair of topaz chandelier earrings, dripping with stars—my homage to Lulu. I dabbed on perfume and, voila! Sofia Vergara! Okay, not exactly. But still.

Two hours after that first flick of polish, I walked down the stairs, all tentative steps and care, having squished my feet into a pair of loathsome spiked heels. I now stood an acceptable five foot nine. At the bottom of the staircase, Larrimer waited, looking every inch the suave desperado in a black suit, unlit stogie in hand, hair curled and enhanced with product. His clipped beard and mustache, and a small gold ring in his left ear added to the jaunty effect. Different enough that any folks from the gala wouldn't recognize him.

And a misty image of another man, hair honied blond, Roman-nosed, laughing eyes, wearing a gold earring.

Not again. But there it was in Technicolor.

Da. He wore an earring, too, when he'd argued with Mam about my calico kitten. He'd won, and I'd kept her. She'd found me after the explosion.

Meow. Our calico kitty threaded through Larrimer's legs. Different markings, but so like my kitten.

"Clea." Larrimer held out his hand.

I smiled. "Don't you look the pirate." I gave him my five digits and he bent, turned my hand and kissed my palm.

Like a flaming arrow, heat shot from those lips to the juncture of my thighs. Not tonight. Sigh.

"Not so bad yourself." His eyes promised the devil.

"I'll show you mine," I said with a purr. "If you show me yours."

He grinned, and pointed to his ankle. "Gun, right, knife, left. A semi tucked in my shoulder holster."

"Sexy." I licked my lips, pointed. "Thigh knife, right. Gun, left thigh." I showed him the slits in my gown, so my weapons would be in my hands in seconds. I held my topknot in place and pulled out my five-inch-long "sticker." "I hope I don't have to use it and ruin my coif."

"That would be a shame." He winked and handed me the invitation.

"It looks perfect." I tugged on buttery leather gloves that reached above my elbows. "No gloves tonight?"

"In my pocket." He thrust out his arm, I took it, and we were off to the ball.

Twenty minutes later, we turned right off Main Street in our rented

Beemer and into the Asheville Mill complex. A man in a tux checked invitations before admitting cars through the gates to the lot, where valets parked them. In minutes, we made it to the first checkpoint. Larrimer handed over our invitation. I held my breath. Mr. Tux flashed two lights, one ultraviolet, at the vellum. He waved us on.

"Your guys used blood in the invitation ink," I said.

"They did."

A blazered young man took our keys and gave us a retrieval tag.

"Do me a favor." Larrimer slipped the boy a fifty. "Don't block us in."

"You got it, mister."

I hooked my arm in Larrimer's and we headed toward the dimly lit entrance with the discreet sign *The Adept's Den* above the door.

Laughter floated on the night air, infused with contained excitement and high anxiety. I snuck glances at the guests. Vibes of entitlement enveloped me like a prickly cloak.

Voices grew louder as we neared the entrance, where a greeter bent over each woman and kissed her hand. Next he shook the hand of her escort. When he spoke to a man in a black scarf, I stopped.

I dragged Larrimer into the shadows beneath a balcony. "You can't go in. The greeter. It's Blondie from the gala. Even with your altered appearance, he might recognize you."

He stiffened. "I doubt it."

"It's not worth the risk." I stood on tiptoe and patted his cheek. "I'll go in alone."

"Fuck it." Larrimer stilled, his gears churning, possibilities being born and discarded. "Let's go. We'll come back for next week's party. I'll wear a thorough disguise." He wrapped a hand around my upper arm.

I dug in my heels. "This is our only lead on Lulu right now. It took me two frigging hours to get this dolled up. Blondie won't recognize me. I'm going in."

His eyes incinerated me. "No."

I kicked his shin, snatched the invitation, and ran down the drive toward the entrance and Blondie. Well, ran as fast as I could in a pair of five-inch stilettos.

Larrimer's wrath burned a hole in my back. But he didn't follow.

I bit my lip. I felt bad for kicking him. Sort of. Oh hell.

A faint glow from faux candles lit the path as I walked to the back of the line. Two couples queued behind me, chatting softly, and in front of me a woman dripped enough emeralds to fund several Habitat for Humanity homes. Her partner, wearing a tux so ill-fitting it hurt, had a fleshy face, an orange tan, and a look of hungry greed I'd seen before.

Blondie nodded them in, and then, it was my turn.

I'd danced with this man. He'd held me close, kissed my shoulder, tried to kill me. Little things like that.

"M'lady," Blondie said. My gloved hand held steady when he lifted it to his lips. His eyes never left mine.

I smiled, not too broadly, as if a flunky kissing me was tolerated, but annoying. Like I was privileged. Like I mattered more than anyone here.

He pointed to the glam girl standing in the shadow, who held a basket lined with velvet.

"Phone, please."

I wasn't thrilled, but I'd anticipated the move and brought an unused, but carefully populated, burner. After I deposited the burner, I handed Blondie my invitation.

He lost his obsequious smile, all business as he shone two lights on it. "Your invitation is for two?"

I sighed, and in a sweet Georgia accent said, "Yes. Unfortunately, at the last moment, my Ronnie couldn't make it." I looked straight at him. I'd told him the truth. Mostly.

His lifeless stare almost undid me.

Eons later, Blondie nodded again and laid my invitation in my outstretched hand. "Enjoy."

I let my smile peek, just a bit. "I intend to."

He turned to the couple behind me, and I stepped inside, relief flooding my system.

I passed through the anteroom, where a woman took my wrap, then into the main salon, all old brick and weathered floorboards and twinkly lights. An intricate crystal chandelier hung from the ten-foot ceiling crossed with sturdy beams.

Stunning. But I'd expected nothing less. A maître d' guided me across the first dining salon, filled with about seventy-five guests, through a brick archway and into a second, smaller salon. Here, I counted a dozen tables, and wondered what differed on my invite to get me ushered into this more exclusive pasture. My money was on the blood.

Ivory linen draped square tables set with thick napkins, delicate porcelain plates, Sterling flatware, and cut-crystal stemware. The lighting was soft candlelight, the ambiance soothing. The room dripped elegance, simplicity, and refinement, as opposed to the overdone opulence of the diners.

I followed the maître d', and we threaded our way around banquet tables piled high with hors d'oeuvres and bottles of wine. He waved toward the place settings and indicated I could take whichever I wished.

I scanned the room. Far to my right, Mrs. Funeral Director Shatzkin sat across from a breathtaking man with ebony skin. Surprise, surprise. So much for a widow's grief.

Across from her, wearing a smug smile, Selectman Kip Alvarise touched his wineglass to his lips. His sadness for his wife had been real. People were never simple equations.

I gestured toward the back, to my left, and we arrived at a corner table set for four, all the seats empty. The maître d' drew out a tapestried chair that faced the wall. I shook my head and took the one facing the room. "My preference, if you don't mind."

He smiled and bowed, then removed the fourth place setting.

"For you," I said and slipped him a fifty. "Thank you."

On occasions like this, when I inhabited a persona, I could do meat. But I said a prayer that a place of this quality would also serve vegetarian fare.

Everyone else in the room must have paid a small fortune for entrance to tonight's "party." A Cabernet sat on the table, and I filled my glass and sniffed. I was no wine aficionado, but it smelled "off." Or maybe it was the vibe of giddy excitement that leaked into my personal space. So far, nothing felt strange or special. But Blondie was here, and that equaled danger.

To keep my profile low, I didn't bother with the hors d'oeuvres, but a side of Larrimer would've helped. I'd have liked his take on the room, the setup. Then again, he'd ticked me off. *No,* he'd ordered. *My* ass.

Of course, I'd pissed him off and kicked him. Maybe he'd strangle me on the way home.

The room continued to fill, and a couple joined me at the table, a woman in floor-length red velvet gown and a man in a bespoke suit. They ignored me, although the woman's lips parted when she spied my earrings.

Cubic zirconia at its finest. I smiled my airhead smile, and she sniffed and turned to her date. And that was that.

The atmosphere ratcheted up a notch.

The brick wall almost directly behind me had two arched alcoves, one on each end. I assumed one led to the kitchen, but the other made me curious. From time to time, the maître d' would walk a singleton or a couple to the arch. I reapplied my lipstick, using my mirror to watch the alcove. A couple approached with the maître d'. Hidden in the alcove, I caught the outline of a beefy man cradling what looked like an Uzi. The maître d' held out their invitation, as if showing it to the hidden guard. Then the couple walked into the darkness. I angled the mirror as light spilled across the alcove when the goon held the door, and I glimpsed a room with a single banquet table. And just before the door swooshed closed, another beefy tuxedoed man standing sentinel. Heavy muscle.

So there was yet a third tier to The Adept's Den. One guarded with goons and guns.

I snapped my compact closed.

When I raised my eyes, I caught Alvarise staring at me like I was a prime side of beef. *Shit.* Except then he bit his lip and returned his attention to his date. Interesting. He hadn't been longing for me, but for the arched alcove behind me.

At nine sharp, a hush fell over the crowd of about thirty souls. Lights dimmed, and with the ring of a sweet chime, a man walked from the far alcove to stand between the two. I had to turn my chair a bit, so I could see him clearly. Ah.

Roberto. Mr. Portly, dolled up in a fresh tux, greeted the crowd. Interesting new job.

Blondie, Roberto, lots of vibe. Oh yeah, something foul lived here.

Roberto greeted us effusively. He jabbered on, and I listened, but it was hard work, given the level of bullshit and gush. I rested my chin on my hand, fighting tendrils of boredom. *Get on with it, dammit.*

Continuing, Roberto again assumed the mantle of the Man in Charge. Except he was merely a mouthpiece. Blondie, on the other hand, was the real deal. I found him standing guard by the entrance to this second dining salon, loose limbed, casual, but filled with import. Those in the outer first room were apparently persona non grata in here. Interesting.

I allowed my mind to open, and tasted harsh tendrils of greed and need, waves of insecurity and pulses of ego. I closed my mind fast.

Portly droned on, something about tonight's menu, and—praise heaven—a cadre of waiters finally streamed through the room, placing discreet sheets of vellum—our menus—onto the porcelain plates.

I was starved. Thank the stars we were about to eat.

"Ta da!" said Roberto.

Everyone looked down at their menu. So did I. And stifled my gasp.

—*Tonight, at The Adept's Den*—
  Appetizer:
Fine strips of Coleocephalocereus purpureus, an endangered cactus from Brazil. Served en croute.
  Salad: Spring Greens, Quinoa, Sunflower Seeds and Pecorino
  Soup: From the tender meat of the severely endangered Hawksbill Turtle.

I took a breath, then another, trying to even my pulse. I toughed it out and smiled, shaping my face into a haughty, yet eager look.

  The Entree: Mountain Gorilla, Critically Endangered, from Bwindi Impenetrable National Park Uganda, with Bacon from the Critically Endangered Visayan Warty Pig, Potatoes and Caramelized Onions

  OR

  Indochinese Tiger, ours from Myanmar, with Israeli Couscous, Smoked Tomatoes & Guajillo Chili Sauce

  Dessert: Adept's Den Chocolate Cake
  Peaches in Absinthe
  Alice B. Toklas Brownies

I was supposed to eat a gorilla or a tiger? *Holy moly shit, with a serving of screw me.*

My pulse wasn't slowing, and I told myself, mantraed the words *breathe, breathe.* It wasn't working, and I crushed the drape of the tablecloth beneath my hands. *What was this insanity?* Dizzy, I lifted my purse from the table, hands shaking, put it in my lap. I opened it as if searching for something, head throbbing, and when I reached into the purse, I swear-to-gods I saw those stupid fireflies seeping from my palm, the scent of citrus and the spiral, glowing *outside* the glove.

I shattered back to reality. Fireflies gone, spiral fading. *Goddammit, get it together.* I had to suck it up or soup it up, depending on how I looked at it. This mission was no different from any other.

I might be a vegetarian in real life, but tonight I was a sick-fuck predator who ate endangered species for the fun of it.

Something concrete at last—The Adept's Den—this horror—was offering illegal and endangered species as food to the privileged. A prestige dining experience. Talk about messed up.

Hurrah for Larrimer. We'd found the endgame for his trafficked endangered species.

New goal—to get out of the damned place without hurling all over the tablecloth.

I snapped my purse shut and lay it back on the table. I smiled at the couple across from me, who smiled back as if they had hemorrhoids.

Time for a little journey. Off I went to the ladies' room, hoping to troll for juicy conversation and interesting vibes. I gleaned several things. First, the diners were pretty much self-important assholes, with too much money and too little sense. I also learned that just about everybody, but especially the men, would kill to get invited into that third room. Apparently that was the ultimate. In what? Not gonna go there, not when I had to focus my will on getting through the meal.

CHAPTER THIRTY

T he night *would* end, I kept telling myself, as I slid yet another chunk of tiger meat between my lips and chewed. My eyes burned, and I stuffed the revulsion down deep, knowing that if I gave myself away, I was dead.

I made it through the evening, which I counted as much a victory as the shootout at the Feed and Seed. As I exited and retrieved my phone and wrap, Blondie bid me goodnight and again kissed the tips of my fingers.

"*Enchante*," he said.

I nodded, haughty as hell, which was all I could do without barfing in his face.

I compelled myself to walk, when I itched to sprint up the incline to where the stream of cars idled. I desperately looked for Fern, remembered the BMW, and saw its halogen lights swing my way.

Larrimer stopped the car, and I clamped my jaw while he walked around and opened my door. We pulled away and followed the line of cars headed toward home.

"Well?" he finally said once we'd made it through the gates, that one word crisp with anger.

"Find a deserted side road. Fast!" I slapped my hand across my mouth, and counted one-potatohead, two-potatohead in a raging battle to hold off my stomach until we were out of sight of the club and any cars whatsoever.

He drove like a banshee, never questioning me, and suddenly swerved to the left, crossed the road, flew down a steep dirt track that stopped by a burbling stream.

I leapt out of the car, fell to my knees, and puked, shaking, sweating, hair cascading around me, more vomiting, and then a warm hand pressed against my forehead, while his other held my hair. When I'd finally emptied every last drop of vileness in my stomach, I gulped several deep breaths and staggered to my feet.

He offered me a water and a pristine white handkerchief. Skin clammy with aftershocks, I swigged and spit, wiped my mouth, and blew my nose.

I knew what a horror I must look like, what I must *smell* like.

Earning dozens of good-guy points, Larrimer folded me into his arms and held me, silent, minus a barrage of questions he must be dying to ask, until I stopped shaking.

I was finally able to say, "Thank you, partner."

"You're welcome, partner."

Back in the car, I gave him every gruesome detail.

"My gut says to wait, but do you think it's time to call in your people?"

His lips twitched. "I like your gut. Let's talk it through first."

"My gut concurs. We'll talk it through."

The following day, I still hadn't eaten a thing, although I'd barfed two more times, the second only producing dry heaves.

I was slow to action, but Larrimer had been busy on the phone, and I heard words like zoonosis and parasitic worms and trafficking, none of which thrilled me.

We finally convened in the living room around one.

"Have you told anyone?"

He frowned as he scanned a web page. "Not the specifics. Not yet."

I released a breath. "Good. Talk about sick bastards."

Unable to get comfortable, I finally picked up my knitting, and the sticks flew in my hands as I knit, knit, knit my fur babies' spun cashmere.

Larrimer cultivated the art of patience. I was glad.

"I've heard of stuff like this before," I finally said. "But mostly served in exotic locales, in Africa and Asia."

He grunted as he tapped the keys of his laptop. "That's a cliché."

I shot him a dirty look.

"Not what I mean. Places in the states do it, too, mostly exotics, not so much the endangered animals. Too big a risk."

My stomach tangoed. "It was one of the most horrible experiences I've ever had. How could a human being eat a gorilla, which, I might add, I didn't."

"This from a woman who's pried open the minds of rapists, torturers, and serial killers."

"What's that got to do with it? I love opening up the bad guys. Animals, they're not like that. They deserve our protection."

"I agree."

I put down my knitting and leaned forward. "We should move slowly on this—"

"Lulu," he said.

"Yes. There's more. About last night, I mean. I heard whispers, hints." I pulled the legal pad closer and began to sketch The Adept's Den.

"Here." I swiped a line across the rectangle and detailed two rooms. "This is where most of the club's patrons dine. I'm guessing it's high-end, but legal food."

"And here." I swiped another line across the rectangle. "This is where I dined. Maybe twenty-five, thirty people. The diners were there for prestige, to make themselves important. That they'd eaten the forbidden, the illegal, the illicit. That they were special, entitled."

He nodded and laced his fingers together. "And...?"

"*Here.*" I stabbed the pencil so hard, it pierced the center of the third portion of the rectangle. "Here's where the elite dine." I looked at him. "I heard whispers of how some patrons longed to get admittance into that most exclusive room and what they'd do to get the invitation. I read them, James."

I relived last night's desperation, the lust, the evil. My mind howled.

Warmth spread through my arm, pet my neck, skimmed my throat. Soothing. Gentling. Comforting.

I ran my hand over the back of his. He stilled and moved away, his face betraying nothing. I wondered if he knew how much he gave.

I put moxie in my voice. "Thanks. The night was horrible, and it wasn't just the food. Those people: anger, avarice, craving. I could taste it. Which brings me to the elephant in the room."

His curled his lip. "Human flesh."

"Yes," I said. "That man, George, in the refrigeration room. I'm guessing he was on the menu. The question isn't what, but how and why does The Adept's Den connect with Dave, The Master, and Lulu?" And the chest.

He crossed his arms. "Cochran was involved."

"And his investigation into the animal trafficking brought him to the attention of The Master."

"All right, let's say that's truth."

"Then doesn't it make sense to wait before you bring in the troops? That would give us a chance to go back and get Lulu."

"What if they kill her in the meantime?"

For long moments, I thought about that. Hard. She was a pawn in this. I suspected they were bent on kidnapping, not killing her in the bus crash. That the bullet that creased her head was a stray. She knew stuff, info they wanted. She was her father's daughter, and he'd trained her, maybe differently than me, but she'd resist. Lulu would also know that once she gave them the information, she'd most likely die. I raked my fingers through my long hair. I could picture it—a bunch of FBI and Fish and Wildlife enforcers descending on the Adept's Den. Her kidnappers would end Lulu in a minute. "We have to wait."

"I can't, not for long. My people need to know. You going to inform your boss?"

"No," I said. "But *you* could. After all, you're the one who's been working with him."

He barked a laugh. "I told the bastard to tell you."

"His mistake." Bob's duplicity ripped at me, but I was getting used to that feeling.

Larrimer leaned forward, as if he were about to say something, then stood abruptly.

So much between us now, layers upon layers. What wasn't he saying? What truths was he refusing to share? What truths was I?

"Where are you going?" I asked.

He waved a hand as he climbed the stairs. "To take a bath."

"Really," I deadpanned.

"Helps me think."

A mystery, wrapped in an enigma. Around James Larrimer, I was never bored.

Sounds of the bath running came from upstairs, so I ended up calling Bob. Instead of his normal anger when I'd been in danger, I got sympathy. Oodles of it. I almost asked about my enforced leave, but something was going on here, something that was all twisted up in this FUBAR.

Signing off a call with Bob had never been easier. My bets were on Larrimer not telling him that I knew they were working together.

I rummaged cabinets for some crackers, my inner Bernadette chiding me to eat. I hoped for a call that said she was back to herself. She was a pain in the ass, but she was *my* pain in the ass.

I missed her madly.

"Ha!" I'd found her secret stash of Oreos. As I reached for them, an oily evil brushed my senses. The kitchen door blew open and a muscled arm clamped around my neck.

"Got her!"

I knew that voice.

I curled my legs to my abdomen, pulled my boot knife, and stabbed the bastard in the arm. A shout of pain. Free, I crashed to the floor and rolled to a stand.

I faced two men, one of whom was Blondie, the other, Mr. UPS. "Todd?"

A nasty grin. "A guy's gotta make a living."

"You prick." I held my knife in a loose, comfortable grip. So, why they were here? Had Blondie sussed me out last night?

Blondie's gaze lit on my breasts. "Come, and we won't hurt you."

"Seems to me the only one hurt's going to be you." I lifted my chin toward Todd. "He's already bleeding like a stuck alligator."

If I threw the knife, I'd lose my weapon and the guy left standing would massacre me. If they moved in close, I could take them, maybe. But Blondie was holding back Todd, who obviously wanted to gut me.

"Our Master wishes to speak with you," Blondie said.

A spurt of relief. No, not about last night. "Why?"

He shook his head. I was so tempted. I'd meet The Master. "Tell him to get in line."

Spittle flew from Todd's mouth. "Once we fuckin' get you, we're gonna blow the pretty boy's brains out, and the damned dogs, too. I'm sick of those fucking dogs." He raised his gun.

I threw my knife. It sliced through Todd's carotid like butter. Blood spurted, but I didn't wait for Blondie's response. I rounded the corner, and zoomed out the mudroom door, the air parting behind me with the zing of Blondie's shots.

I guessed meeting The Master was no longer the plan. I dashed across the driveway toward Fern, my back itching from exposure. Any minute I expected the bite of a bullet. I'd replaced my backup Glock and knife in the glove compartment, and aimed to get them before Blondie got me.

Instead of chasing me, Blondie ran into the barn.

Shit. I retrieved my gun and another knife and headed after him. This was so messed up.

My back to the barn, I slid to my right, braced myself, and leapt over the fence into the first pasture. Keeping low, I crept toward one of the stall doors.

I realized what Blondie intended, and panic threatened to blind me.

"I've got Nott here," Blondie shouted. "That's what the brass plate says. I'm holding her."

I opened my mouth to answer. Slammed it shut.

A horrible squeal of pain, and then, "She's gone. Dead. I'll slit each animal's throat the same way unless you lose your weapons and come with me."

Time slowed. Decision made. They say fear is good. It felt like shit.

I lay on my belly, slithered my way through manure-dotted snow, inching forward.

A squeal of pain. "I'm gonna snuff the second one. Delling, right?"

I was one stall away. The pasture door stood open. Fool, telling me which goat he had. I pictured his exact location.

"I'm about to cut her throat. She'll live if you come out."

I gathered my legs beneath me and leapt. I focused my mind, imagined exactly where the bastard was, and squeezed the trigger over and over and over. He flew backwards, a bloom of blood spreading across his shoulder.

I landed on my feet, and his gun stared back at me, barrel to my heart.

My breath stuttered. Was this it? The moment faced by every human? *Talk, babble, stall, say some...*

A blast from the barn door. Blondie's gun flew from his mangled hand. Larrimer.

I managed to move forward, Glock aimed at Blondie's head, Larrimer paralleling me.

Damaged arm tight around Delling's neck, Blondie held his knife to her throat. She struggled, and he strained to hold her.

"Let her go," I said to Blondie. "It's over."

He gave Larrimer a flat look. "You. You understand."

"Where is Lulu?" I asked, using my skills, managing my voice. "Who's The Master?"

Blondie smirked, and his knife flashed lightning fast. He slit his own throat, severing both carotid arteries.

Blood sprayed as we raced to him, and I slapped my palms to his neck, tried to stem the flow.

"It won't help, Clea," Larrimer said.

Blondie's malicious glare dissolved. He was gone.

I released him, and his body flopped on its side.

Larrimer looked at Nott—dead, empty—then back at me. "I'm sorry."

I peered up at him, in jeans, but bare chested, barefooted. My lips wobbled. "No more afternoon baths."

Back in the house, I washed my hands, but stayed in my gross clothes, covered in dung and blood, to take care of Nott.

Mr. UPS was the first person I'd ever killed. I should be feeling... Pity? Guilt? Regret? No. I'd save those emotions for those deserving of them. Or, at least, I would try my best to.

I stepped over Todd's body on the way back outside. "Dickbrain."

The sun was dazzling, the sky impossibly blue and clear, one of those spectacular winter days.

It was hard to remember that beauty and goodness existed.

On the way back to the barn, I stopped short. Larrimer had dressed and was piling wood out in the first pasture. Building what? I shook my head. Delling needed me.

Two stalls over, I found her munching some hay beside Thor and Sif. He'd moved her so she wouldn't be alone. I smiled, just a little.

I ducked through the stall, patting the goats as I passed, and walked across the pasture to Larrimer. Sirens blared in the distance. We'd informed the state and municipal cops, along with Bob, and any minute they'd be swarming the property.

"Lemme guess," I said as I reached Larrimer. "A bonfire for s'mores."

He dropped a broken two-by-four onto the pile. "We can't bury Nott, so I thought we'd give her a good send off, Viking style. No boat, but a pyre. After the troops leave."

Yes, I saw Larrimer, but he saw me, too.

While Larrimer dealt with the MEs and the techs and a special agent sent by Bob, whom I discreetly avoided, I showered and dressed in a black turtleneck and leather vest to go with my leather pants and my shitkicker boots. The wig, a severe black helmet and bangs, fit perfectly. I carried two knives, plus my trusty Glock secreted beneath my vest, and a sweet little spare in the small of my back. Not that I expected to use my arsenal. But the more the merrier.

I had a selectman to visit.

CHAPTER THIRTY-ONE

Of the two I'd known at the dinner, Kip Alvarise seemed a better quarry than Mrs. Shatzkin. His eyes had been ravenous when he'd focused on the entry to that third room. I'd also recalled the night of the gala, when we'd danced. He'd been wearing one of those Old Man of the Mountain lapel pins. A lot of men had. But those men weren't eating tiger at the Adept's Den.

Alvarise was a lawyer with his own firm in town, and I Googled him and learned that his focus on the selectboard was planning, government, and taxes, all suitably vague. I saw, too, a photo of his wife. Small, like me, a blond, but there the resemblance ended, her face drawn and tired. Would she have liked the exotic dinner or loathed it?

Everyone but Larrimer had left by the time I came downstairs two hours later, to find him standing at the bottom of the steps.

He didn't blink an eye at my getup, just held out a glass of what I guessed was bourbon, neat.

I quirked a smile I'd labeled *sardonic*. I took the bourbon and slugged down half. "Thanks."

He raised his matching glass and nodded. "To surviving."

We clinked. "You got that right."

"So what's your twisted mind cooked up now?" He waved his hand so I'd take a seat.

I didn't. "I'm going to play with a selectman, and I don't want him to recognize me."

His laconic pose belied a snap of anger so powerful I almost stumbled backward.

I straightened my spine. "Problem?"

His glass shattered, bourbon and shards raining the floor. Pain washed over me, *his*. With notes of fear and longing mixed in.

I stood on tiptoe and pressed a hand to his chest. "Hey, dragon dude." I kept it light. "You're sexy when you're pissed. Didja know that?"

He blinked, then took me in a bruising kiss, all lips and tongue and hunger. I answered the same way, struggling to grasp why his control had shattered so completely.

But right now my body cried for something different. Needing his hands on me, I ran mine across his back, his waist, lower, where he pulsed hot and hard.

He cupped my breast, squeezed, and I moaned into his mouth. I wanted us skin to skin, so I tugged on his shirt and worked my hands beneath it. He felt good, warm and smooth, ridges and planes. I reached for the song, found static instead.

Muscular arms wound around my back, but he pulled away just enough to rest his forehead on mine. "No," he ground out. "The first time we're together will not be in anger."

He utterly disarmed me. I rested my cheek on his chest, tracing his broad back with my fingers. "No. Not in anger." I breathed, husky with unfulfilled need.

Not releasing me, he sat in the chair and pulled me onto his lap. He buried his face in my neck. "This is me. With my freak on. And you, you're going out begging for violence."

"It's Kip Alvarise. He was at The Adept's Den, in that room. I can manage him." I wove my hands through his hair again and again. Gods, what this man did to me.

"And you're incapable of staying out of trouble," he said.

I pulled back. "Goddammit, Larrimer!"

Face stoic, but eyes laughing, pleased that I'd buzzed when he'd pressed that button.

I smiled, gladdened by his banished pain. "Ah, but look where it gets me."

He brushed my cheek.

"Geesh," I said. "I forgot you're bleeding."

I plucked the purple handkerchief from his front jeans pocket, neat, folded as expected, and wrapped it around his hand. "Now I know why you carry those things."

"Blood's a bitch," he said.

My fingers traced his face. I'd wanted to do that forever.

"Tell me what happened today," he said. "And where *we* are going."

Cool, collected Larrimer was back. But not completely. A small part of Mr. Demented was still with me. I liked it.

I gave him the full Todd-and-Blondie Adventure.

"Who slits their own throat nowadays?"

"Given Blondie's dominance," he said, "it seems The Master isn't short on power."

I cupped his cheek. "What are you still keeping from me? Don't lie. Please."

"They're lovely, you know," he said. "Those haunting pale-green eyes of yours."

"Please."

"The secrets I hold close," he said. "That knowledge is lethal."

I made my smile slow and sexy. "Oh, you'll tell me. Yes, you will." I brushed a kiss across his lips. "What did Blondie mean when he said you understood?"

"He was a stone cold killer. He saw that in me."

I didn't give a frig what Blondie, or even Larrimer believed. "That's not who you are now."

He shook his head, as if I were a fool.

Now wasn't the time for that battle. "If we don't leave soon, we'll miss him."

"This selectman. You think he's got answers."

"Maybe," I said. "He's the best bet we've got."

"I'll go up to his office with you."

"No way. One look at you, and he'll wet his pants."

"You annoy me occasionally." A hint of a smile.

I gave him big eyes. "Only occasionally? You stay in the truck. You can be my getaway driver."

He tapped his ear. "A wireless ear bud. I've got one just your size, babe."

Still on his lap, a place I enjoyed immensely, I said. "Manipulative. You never intended to go to his office."

"Perhaps."

"You won't always win, you know."

His laughter followed me out the door.

The large brick building on Glade Street held the region's biweekly newspaper, the offices of several lawyers, and two shrinks. This late in the day, the place felt empty, although a few people remained, hidden behind their office doors. I checked the board for Alvarise. His offices were on the third floor, and I hoped he hadn't left for the day as I trotted up the smooth granite steps dithering between two types of entrances.

Going for the second, I checked the door, found it unlocked, opened it, eased it closed behind me, and turned the old-fashioned latch.

No receptionist. Good.

Alvarise must have heard me, because he appeared seconds later.

"Sorry, we're closed," he said. "Heading home early."

I tried not to think about his ill wife as I put on my best Slavic accent. "We need to talk. In your office, okay?"

He puffed up. "We're closed."

I stepped forward and hooked an arm through his. "C'mon, Mr. Alvarise. Just a small chat. Let's talk in your office."

"No."

I drew my gun. "Yes."

Alvarise stumbled back, and I closed the door and snapped the lock. "Most definitely we're going to talk."

He moved behind his desk, as if the mahogany edifice could keep him safe from big, bad me. I slid into one of the client chairs, crossed my legs, my gun aimed at his chest.

I took in the heavy maroon drapes, plush velvet carpet, leather captain's chairs. Everything felt big, except for Alvarise. He felt small, with high notes of arrogant and low notes of scared. I needed a Tums.

"Wouldn't you like to sit down?"

He ka-thunked into his chair.

I waited for him to settle. He straightened his vest, smoothed his hair, gathered a sprawl of papers into a neat stack.

"I'm bored," I said. "So let's get this done fast. Spill everything you know about The Adept's Den."

His handsome face drained of color. "It's not much, really," he said, his voice a whisper.

I smiled, predatory. "Do speak up."

Alvarise cleared his throat. "It's a place I go for dinner."

A spurt of bile filled my mouth. "Interesting fare."

Sweat beaded his face. "I... I... Yes."

Crap. He was going mute on me, his nerves spiking.

When I was so invested in a case, I sometimes misread my prey. Shame on me. I needed a different way in. I holstered my gun and allowed the atmosphere to subtly change.

After a few beats, he visibly relaxed. "Look, Mr. Alvarise. Kip." I sighed. "I'm not here to judge." My ass, I wasn't. "But I'd like you to share just a little more. Who runs the place?"

His head shook back and forth. "Never met him."

Truth. I modulated my voice, adding just enough warmth to imply confidence in him. "Okay. Any ideas, thoughts?"

He shook his head again. This was getting me nowhere. I leaned forward, projecting trust. "There's a third dining room, correct? You'd like to be invited in, wouldn't you?"

He nodded.

"I'd like to be invited in, too." I smiled, all conspiratorial. "Tell me more."

"I've heard the talk," he said, his grin smug.

"Of course you have. You're an important person." I nodded. "Someone of stature."

He puffed. "I am." His voice was eager. "They say eating in there gives you power. Lots of power. From the food."

He'd drawn the word "food" out. Alvarise was in a different place now, dreamy, lusting. I plowed on, all chummy.

I pitched my voice low, sharing a secret. "Eating human flesh can do that."

"That's what everyone says."

"So, what's the key to getting into that room?"

"Everyone who wants in has to sign a contract. To perform a gift for The Master." He leaned forward. "We're the select few."

"Perform a gift, huh. Have you given your gift?"

His face flushed. "Not exactly, but..."

Humm. "What did you do, Kip?" I reached out a hand, ran a finger over his. "Impress me."

"We were supposed to find some chest."

"We?"

"The three of us." His hand trembled as he played with a letter opener.

"Who, Chip?"

"I..."

"Chip, c'mon. Indulge me."

He plucked at his watch band. "Some guy from away and Mary, the Bronze Printing babe." He cupped his hands above his chest, in that age-old "big boob" gesture.

"The three of you—a dynamic trio."

"Yeah!" He puffed out his chest. "But I was the leader."

I kept my cool, projecting a quiet interest. "And did you find the chest?"

His eyes slid away from mine. "We went in as a group. It wasn't in the stupid barn. Guess their intel left something to be desired. But I did something better. The guy took off, but Mary helped me." He rushed his words. "We were sure The Master would appreciate the gift, so we offed some goats, y'know, blood sacrifice."

I couldn't breathe. My fingers itched, aching for my knife. In seconds, it would be in my hand, and I could slice his throat just the way he'd cut through Loki's and Lofn's. "Goats?"

His shrug said it all. "And some chickens. A move like that, shouldn't that get us inside?"

Bastards. "Wow, that's intense."

He cracked his knuckles. "I'd say! They made a hell of a lot of noise and mess, and the shotgun setup should've worked."

My muscles quivered, primed to leap across the desk. "Impressive. The Master's or your idea?"

"Mine." He thumped a fist on his chest. "All mine. Well, mostly. The shotgun was supposed to be a 'lookout, lady!' That was Mary's idea. And where did it get us? Nowhere."

"Unfair. A warning to the barn's owner, a good plan." Some warning. The shotgun would've killed me. "It didn't go well with The Master?"

"It was that big blond guy. It was *him*. He's the one who talked about killing the goats in the first place. Y'know, if we couldn't find some chest of bone. Fuck him. He said The Master was really 'displeased.' Stupid word."

Chills skittered across my shoulder. *A chest of bone.*

"Wow. You did good, and they dissed you. Not fair. You're a man of action. You know important things. You see, I'm looking for my friend. I think she goes there. Red hair and—"

A hiss in my ear. "Cops. Get out. Now!"

Go? No way. I'd hold my ground. I was FBI, goddamnit.

Except I'd been masquerading and intimidating, both of which would earn the ire of not just Balfour, but the SAC. I was already on leave, on shaky ground with the Bureau. This op could be the final nail in my coffin. Blast!

I flew out of the chair. "Gotta go."

Did Alvarise have one of those buzzers under his desk? I didn't know, but he'd somehow alerted them. His smug smile vanished when I beaned him on the head with the butt of my gun. Out cold. A cacophony of noise, then shouts from downstairs. I hadn't checked out escape routes. Larrimer would shoot me, or call me a fool. He'd be right.

I flung open the tall double-hung window. Except it didn't move. Latched, high up.

Thunderous pounding on the stairs.

I jumped once, unlatched the window, pushed it open.

Crap. A three-story drop. No fire escape, no balcony. Nada. It was darkening, the sun almost set. A monster oak towered five feet away. Could I land the jump?

Bashing at the door of the outer office.

A groan. Alvarise was coming to.

Jump, it was.

I stowed my gun and pulled myself up onto the deep windowsill.

Shouts, splintering wood.

I leapt.

Arms outstretched, except the oak was coming too fast.

I smashed into the tree, head bashed into a branch, a burst of pain, but I clung like Curious George. Voices. Would they shoot me in the back?

My breath caught. I let go, dropped to the next branch, then the next, clung with my hands. Little monkey me.

"She's there!" someone shouted. More shouts.

I looked down. Still too far, but I had to drop. Bit my lip so I didn't scream as I fell.

Flat on the ground, breath knocked out of me, I got a knee beneath me. *Ouch*. Got my other knee up.

Steel arms lifted me from the waist and slung me around across his shoulders, around his neck, arms pinned, legs pinned, tight. Larrimer, damn him! I wasn't a freaking pretzel.

Except the guy was tall, but not tall enough. *Shit*!

He ran like fate chased him. I could barely see, couldn't kick, couldn't grab, couldn't do squat except squirm. Down a hill, across a parking lot, into an alley, and through it.

Listerine. The scent in my nose, my mouth. Alarm bells. I wriggled harder, which did zip. He flung open the back of a truck and tossed me inside.

An arm pinned me down, hard, then banded my neck, while fingers crawled from my shoulders to my breasts, squeezing, pinching. I waited, playing possum, until he reached for my waist.

I pulled back a leg and kicked—hit air—scratched the arm, deep. He backhanded me. Head ringing, I bit, snagged flesh, and chomped.

He leapt atop me, the arm pressing my neck. He put his lips to mine and inhaled, sucking the air from my lungs. I couldn't breathe! I punched and pushed, hitting his shoulder, his back, doing nothing as black spots danced before my eyes.

His hulking body covered mine, immobilizing me, and he punched me over and over—my head, my side, my stomach—and then he wormed an arm between us, unzipped my pants and wrestled them down to my thighs.

He jammed his fingers inside me, pumped, again and again, and then he slid them to his zipper.

"Nobody said I couldn't sample the goods. For Ivor."

"No!" I screamed, a wave of panic, head shrieking, a mini-cosmos of fireflies swirling in my palm.

"Shit!" An uppercut to my jaw, blazing stars as his weight vanished, and he relieved me of my guns and my phone and leapt backwards, shoving me away, hard, vicious. I slid across the floor of truck.

Gasping, I lifted my palm. Nothing. I pushed onto my elbows, legs bent, about to leap to my feet, to jump forward and out and...

A grinning gargoyle, washed in the glow of the streetlight, stared back at me.

Blondie! Impossible.

"Twins, bitch!"

The doors slammed, and I sat in blackness.

CHAPTER THIRTY-TWO

With shaking hands, I slowly pulled up my pants, zipped, and buttoned. Except the button was gone, the leather ripped. I got quiet inside, very quiet. I bit my lip, tasted blood. *Okay.* I was okay.

Pain screamed back that I wasn't. Face throbbing, arm... belly... alien fingers digging at me, into me, and... I reached a hand and touched... *No, dammit.*

I was quiet. So very quiet.

A ghost. I'd just been kidnapped, almost raped by a horrible, monster ghost.

The earpiece.

I checked. Gone, gone, gone.

A grinding noise, a rumble, and the truck jerked into gear, and moved backwards. More gear grinding, and I swayed as we drove forward.

Locked in a truck. No Larrimer. No windows. No escape.

As we thundered somewhere, I scooted sideways and braced myself against one of the truck's walls. I rested my head on my knees. Just for a sec. He hadn't taken my boot knife, which was wonderful, actually. So why hadn't I used it? I'd forgotten it when I saw that prick.

I was an idiot. No Glock, no little gun. I was losing a lot of guns these days.

Now was the perfect moment for the fireflies. Perfect.

I held my right hand up, palm facing the back double doors, thumb out, and fireflied.

Not even a dribble.

He'd seen them, though. They were real, and they scared the hell out of him. So why couldn't I do it?

Okay, Larrimer knew I was missing. And maybe this wasn't all bad. Maybe I was off to meet Master HooHa, and I'd learn what the hell was going on and find Lulu. Except I'd most likely be chopped chuck. Oh, bad image.

Burrr. Maybe I'd just freeze to death in the damned truck.

There *was* a way out of here. I just hadn't found it yet.

Think. Think. I inched close to the double doors and pushed down the inner handle. No movement. Locked from the outside. I slid my knife from its sheath and pushed the tip against the thin gap between the doors. Metal scraped against the tip. The overlap. Not a chance.

I stood, swayed, then crawled around the inside of the box. As I'd guessed, it was simply that, a metal box. Or a prison.

I punched the wall and slid onto my bum. I'd better speed up this big escape, or we'd arrive, and I'd be mincemeat.

Why did I keep thinking in food metaphors?

Since I believed the fireflies were real and powerful, why did they never appear when I just asked, summoned, whatever? What did I know. They were somehow connected to the pressure in my head, except if I replayed the times I'd created them, more than summoning was at work.

Forcing myself, I relived the UPS accident, which, given the revelation of Todd as a shit, wasn't an accident at all.

Running down the driveway hill, Lulu helping the boy, me trying to reach her, but so far away and—voila. Then the horror at the Adept's Den and the thought of eating, consuming tiger. Now, a man hitting me, touching me, about to rape me.

The truck wobbled, downshifting, grinding, a right turn, slow, then picking up speed again.

I played the movie of those three events over and over.

Panic. Each time I'd fireflied, I'd been compelled by panic.

And a memory. Larrimer and I had flown out the window of Dave's home. It was murky, but someone, Larrimer, he'd held my wrists, and I'd felt such panic, and the swirls of fireflies. That voice in my head, too. I'd heard it then.

Panic had to be the trigger.

Well, crap. Here I sat, anxious, fearful, upset. But I wasn't panicked. That was the key.

I'd recreate it.

I focused, reached out, and found a meditative state. I pictured racing down the driveway, seeing the UPS truck slide, the bus, the traffic. Reliving it. *Feeling* it. Move, Lulu! Move! My breathing sped up, sweat formed in my palms, a pulse in my head.

Beautiful fireflies swirled in my right palm, a mini-cosmos. And the scent, that divine scent.

I lifted my hand, thumb out, focused on the rear doors. My head throbbed lightly.

The firefly swirl never budged.

We thudded to a stop, and I braced so as not to slide. If we'd arrived. Shit.

I scrambled to a corner into a crouch, pulled my knife from my boot. When Blondie2 opened the doors, I'd jump.

And I almost fell on my ass when the gears ground and we started up again.

Not there yet. I sighed, sat back down, leaned against the side of the truck.

Swirling in my palm wasn't enough. The fireflies had to project outward, like the stream of a comet.

What was wrong with my last effort? Maybe I hadn't evoked enough emotion. Those events were over. Lulu was safe. Well, she had been then. I had to *feel* the panic.

Oh, this was nuts.

A voice, my own inner devil, whispered The Dream. I shut it down. I didn't want to do that, relive that, go there.

Which was why it was perfect.

I placed my hands beside me on the floor. My breathing sped and terror glided up my spine. I closed my lids and sank deep, deeper, inside The Dream.

The helicopter...

No...

YES, dammit...

Tommy's laugh... blades thud-thud-thudding... the canyon... the tail

262

plunges down and down and down.
A jagged boulder... stabbing metal.
Exploding shards...
I scream.
I scream and scream and...

I raised my hand, dazzled by pain and pleasure, leaking tears and fear, swathed in cedar, as a river of fireflies formed and knit into the arrow pattern that glowed. Arrows streamed from my palm, and I aimed my hand at the double doors.

We hit a bump, swerved hard, and I flew, and the white-gold stream swiveled forward, right at the driver's cabin.

Burning metal, a scream, and I fisted my hand to stop them.

Except they kept coming.

The truck careened, and I was flung in the air.

And the stream changed direction and encircled me and flew 'round and 'round as the world topsy-turvied and thundered, with me cradled inside a cocoon of light.

A boom, and I sensed movement around me, eve inside the twirling, whirling light.

The thunder stopped with a final groan, a creak.

I'm cushioned in my bright golden cocoon. How to get out? A niggle of fear. *Now what?*

I again curled my hand into a fist and thought, *Stop!*

The cocoon vanished, and I dropped onto the metal floor of the box. Ouch.

Well, swell, easy enough to stop now I knew what to do.

I hurt, and a wildfire of exhaustion swept me away.

Metal beneath me. Hard. Unbending. I had to rise, to move, took a deep breath, another. Just a few more minutes. My Celtic spiral glowed, and faded.

My eyes adjusted. I wasn't on the floor of the box, but on its side.

The whole truck lay on its side. There was watery light, too. It seeped in from the front of the box, where my fireflies had ripped through the metal and into the cab, a frisbee-sized hole. Which was upsetting, given I was definitely larger than a frisbee.

I crawled toward the cab, stood, and peered through the hole. The dome light was on, and my stomach flip-flopped. Blondie2's head was a bolognese of blood, brains, and bone above his stump of a neck.

I slid onto my ass. I'd done that with things that came out of my hand. *I'd* done it. Stopped the bastard from kidnapping me. Launched the fireflies with *intention* for the first time.

Now what was I supposed to feel—happy or horrified?

Except I was still stuck in a metal box with no way out. I was spent, I couldn't crawl an inch further, and I somehow knew I couldn't call again on the fireflies anytime soon.

For endless minutes, I sat in the metal box. Maybe if I rested long enough, I could get the fireflies back. Maybe.

A gunshot blasted the back of the truck. I skittered forward, knife at the ready.

One of the doors swung open.

"Clea?"

"Larrimer!"

"Don't move!" he said, voice a granite command.

A flashlight beamed into the truck, and an arm appeared.

"Ease into my arm," he said. "On your belly."

"I don't...?"

"Come." He waggled his fingers toward me. "Come and get me. Slow and easy."

I inched toward the muscled arm and touched his fingers with mine. He was warm and alive. Oh sweet gods! I gripped his hand.

"Let go for a minute," he said, then slid his arm around my waist. He lifted me from the box and curled me into him.

He pulled me tight. "Put your arms around my neck, legs around my hips, and don't let go."

I did as asked, face smooshed to his chest, and hung on. He released me, and I felt him pull on a rope, muscles straining as he sidestepped us away from the truck. Clear, arm over arm, he climbed us higher and higher. Then he lifted us up and over a barrier and stood. His breathing harsh in my ear, I dropped my legs to the ground and he octopussed around me.

I drank him in, inhaling his sweat, his fear, unsure what had just happened. And we stayed that way for a long moment, until he broke us apart.

"Look." He pointed.

The full moon was round and bright when I peered over the guardrail, down the precipice. Dots of light twinkled across the valley far, far below. Fairy lights.

The truck lay on its side, the box where I'd been imprisoned facing the drop, its one wheel caught on a boulder. If I'd managed to open those doors, I would have slid out and plummeted into space, falling until the earth broke me.

"Shit," I said.

"Yeah." He moved away, freeing the nylon rope from his waist. The rope was mine, the one I used to fasten my kayak onto Fern's roof.

"I don't feel so good," I said.

"You look worse." Larrimer at his most pragmatic.

"Nice." I slipped my hands around him and stroked his back. I couldn't help it.

"Like I said, incapable of staying out of trouble." He bent his head and nuzzled my neck, and in a husky voice said, "I'm glad you didn't die."

We sat in Fern, the heat cranked on high.

"What happened to the guy?" Larrimer said. "You shoot him?"

I shook my head. He'd seen them once, but how to tell a rational, concrete sort of guy that I'd taken out Blondie2 with fireflies coming out of my hand? "Not exactly."

Sirens blasted the air. In the rearview mirror, a firetruck barreled toward us.

"I'm not up for this," I said.

"Me, neither."

He put the truck in drive and we peeled away, more than happy to let Balfour make excuses for why we'd left the scene. Wasn't much, but the Old Man had to be good for something.

On the way home, I thought of Bernadette. "It would be good to stop by and see her."

A twitch of Larrimer's lips. "You have no idea what you look like, do you?"

I pulled down the shade flap and slid back the vinyl hiding the mirror. On went the light, and I scared myself. I closed the flap and crossed my arms. "Maybe after dinner."

By the time we pulled into the dooryard, my teeth chattered, and I couldn't seem to stop shaking. Dammit. The door barely budged when I pushed against it. Dumb thing.

And Larrimer was there. He lifted me out, kicked shut the door.

"I don't need—"

"Yeah, you do."

"I have to shower."

"Understood."

Amidst an exuberance of dogs, he carried me upstairs and into the main bathroom. He set me down on the floor, on the fluffy white bath rug, and began to divest me of clothes.

"Larrimer, don't." I pushed at him with the muscles of an infant.

"Let me."

That honeyed-granite voice crumbled my will. With exquisite care, he unpinned my black mess of a wig and tossed it aside. He lifted off my vest and undid my empty shoulder holster.

He drew off my boots, first the left, then the right, went to unbutton my pants, paused—I wouldn't look at him, couldn't—and unzipped them. I knew he'd see the bruises. Big ones.

Blondie's hands groping. I stiffened.

"Hey," he said, all gentle and calm.

Pants gone, turtleneck off. Ugly black-and-blues mottled my body. He stood to turn on the shower, and I just sat there, fingers plucking the flokati rug. Water and steam began to fill the room.

This was *not* how I pictured the first time I got naked with him.

He moved to unhook my bra.

I pushed his hand away. "I can—"

"Let me."

"All right."

He slipped off my panties, lifted me, and sat me in the tub. The pounding spray felt good. *I'm alive. I'm alive.* And Blondie2 is dead. Dead. Dead. *Dead.*

But now I'd killed *two* people. Put a period on two lives, two humans I'd erased from the earth.

I seized up, pulled my knees to my chin, wouldn't look at him.

"Ssshh."

Larrimer shampooed my hair, laved my face, my arms, all of me, his callused hands gentle, so gentle, and I steadied and watched that hard, scarred face for a long while until I finally relaxed and just felt the blessing of it, a soothing balm. No one had ever taken as much care with me. No one.

He rinsed me with just as much deliberation. My body, my hair, my breasts, my left arm, my right.

"What's that?" He held my right hand.

I knew what he was staring at. The black spiral remained. "My tattoo."

"Pretty." He kissed my wrist and set it free.

He stood beside my bed, looking down, dripping water and oozing that familiar fortitude I'd come to appreciate.

"Why don't you try and sleep," he said.

I wasn't eager for the dreams, for the feel of Blondie2's hands on me again.

He crouched down on his haunches. "Mind if I join you?"

His understanding, it broke me. "That would be nice."

He stripped, rubbed some of the towels over his body, and climbed onto the other side of the bed. He curled around me, so I was enveloped in him, his warmth, his scent, his calm. He drew the covers over us.

"I'm tired, James."

He stroked my wild, curly hair. "You're a warrior. Remember that. Now sleep, Clea."

And I did.

CHAPTER THIRTY-THREE

When I awoke, it was after nine that night, and Larrimer was gone from my bed. I forced myself to do the postures of an abbreviated Sun Salutation. Everything, and I mean *everything* hurt. But the feel of his hands surrounding me, I remembered that, too, and tucked it away in a safe, warm place.

I eased sweats over a body I'd slathered in Bag Balm and walked downstairs to find Larrimer setting two plates at the kitchen table.

"The animals?" If I moved too fast, I'd shatter.

"Fed and watered."

"The brouhaha at the cliff?"

"Taken care of by that ever-efficient prick Balfour, along with the headless corpse."

He didn't know. "My kidnapper was Blondie. Well, his twin."

"Shit."

"He was taking me to The Master. Where's Ronan?"

"Practice. I made him some burgers."

"That was nice."

"We need to talk."

"About...?"

He gave me a hard stare.

"All right. But after dinner."

"Deal." He held out my chair, and I chuckled. "Thanks. I know this chivalry won't last."

His smile flowed to his eyes.

It felt almost normal, if I could forget the feel Blondie2's hands on me and golden glow of fireflies that decapitated a man.

Vegetarian chili, baby greens salad with avocado, and homemade bread from the market. Except I played with my food, more than ate it.

"Eat," he said, the word dark with command.

"There went the chivalry." But I swiped a spoonful of chili into my mouth, did it again, and suddenly the chili, the salad, were gone.

After dinner, my ribs screamed when I reached into the tall cabinet for a bar of chocolate. I slid the milk from the fridge, got down the sugar, vanilla extract, and cocoa powder, and cursed because I had nothing for whipped cream.

"What are you doing?" He sounded annoyed.

I turned on the front burner, bent down for a small pot.

He loomed, yes, *loomed* behind me.

"I want to make us a treat," I said. "I'll be in, in a sec."

He cursed, but I felt him leave.

In minutes, I'd prepared two mugs of hot chocolate. I lifted them, and my arm tremored. Cocoa sloshed onto my hand, burned. I steadied myself, licked off the cocoa, and carried them into the living room.

I handed him his mug, set mine on the table beside the red chair, and eased into the seat.

"No one's made me cocoa in a long time," he said.

Our companionable silence unnerved me.

I didn't want to do this. Didn't want to explain or tell him about the fireflies. I just wanted to sit and be silent for a while, pretending Lulu and Bernadette were upstairs and Ronan was coming up the drive.

A vroom, and then a screech in the dooryard. The dogs' barking commenced.

Instantly, Larrimer bristled with guns. He stood with his back to the doorway, peering into the mudroom entrance, weapons up. I retrieved my small Glock and knife and crouched behind the red chair, which gave me a good sightline to the mudroom door.

A curse, the knob turned, and the door flew open.

"This place is a damned hellhole."

Bob?

Gun at my side, I stood. Larrimer hadn't moved.

Bob stomped his feet, then strode into the living room. Larrimer lowered his guns, stepped away from the wall.

Balfour twirled on him. "What the..." His wave of disgust rolled across the room. "Oh, it's you."

"In the flesh," Larrimer holstered his weapons.

"Yeah, right." Bob sniggered.

Cruel, and so unlike the old Bob. I laid my gun beside my mug.

While the dogs bounced around Bob—a new toy!—he shrugged off his FBI jacket and slung it onto the back of a dining chair. He patted his suit, as if he could erase the wrinkles. A stain marked one knee. I'd never seen him so unkempt. It was almost shocking.

Tension bloomed, with high notes of crazy and low ones of testosterone. As I got Bob a Scotch on the rocks, I spied him headed for the red chair.

"That's *her* chair," Larrimer said, his tone a whiplash. "Take the couch." Cocoa in hand, he thumped into the chair opposite.

"Fuck you," Bob said, but took the couch.

I handed Bob his drink and sat in my chair, their hatred for one another an acrid taste on my tongue. The dogs sensed it, too, pacing like confused chickens.

"Settle," I said, and they curled by the woodstove.

I picked up my knitting, felt the soothing presence of Loki and Lofn. Alvarise. I imagined filleting his flesh off...

"Clea?" Larrimer said.

"Uh, sorry." Knit, purl, knit, purl. Filleting him very, very slowly. "What are you doing here, Bob? Come to put me back on active duty?"

He took a hit of Scotch. "What the hell has been going on here today?"

"This and that," I said lightly.

When the tension between the men dulled, I filled Bob in, including The Adept's Den kerfuffle. I avoided the chest of bone, my fireflies, and the near rape. Those... I no longer trusted him.

"His head," I said. "His gun must have gone off. Pity."

"Pity," echoed Larrimer.

Bob downed his Scotch, smiled, and held out his hand toward me. "Another, Young Pup?"

In one fluid motion, Larrimer stood before him, swiped the glass from Bob's hand, and strode into the kitchen.

Bob looked like he'd chewed a lemon. "You two have been busy campers. Have you fucked yet?"

Shock rippled through me. In the kitchen, Larrimer stiffened.

"Bob," I said in a quiet voice. "That's totally inappropriate."

He frowned. "Have you?"

His jealousy and disgust washed across my senses. "None of your damned business. What's your problem?"

He swiped his face. "Don't do it. Promise me you won't."

I smiled, sweet as pie. "I don't make promises I can't keep."

Ba-boom. "Dammit, Clea, you—"

"Balfour." Larrimer towered before him, holding out another Scotch.

Oh, this wasn't good.

Bob made a point not to touch Larrimer when he took the glass. Larrimer leaned down and rested a hand on his shoulder. Bob's lip curled, Larrimer grinned. "My pleasure."

Seconds passed, elastic, ugly.

Grace barked, and the elastic snapped. Larrimer walked to his chair and raised his mug. "Good chocolate."

Bob's eyes tracked from Larrimer's to mine. "Too bad we don't know what he wants with this girl. The food thing. God, Clea, that must have been hard for you." Sympathy leaked from his pores.

That was the man I knew. "At least, Agent Larrimer has some answers on the endangered animals." Knit, purl, knit, purl. "Anything on the men who attacked me this morning?"

He held the glass to his lips and sipped. "No prints in the system, no DNA, no nothing on any of the dead guys, not even in your foster mother's car. Invisible enemies."

Lies. Did he think I wouldn't catch them?

Bob tapped his phone, whistled. "It's been decided. In six days, the next dinner party, we surround the place, and if we're lucky, get the girl, and take this Master down."

I shook my head. "It feels wrong."

Bob bristled. "What the hell's that supposed to mean?"

"What if Lulu Cochran isn't there?" Larrimer said.

"We'll have The Master." Bob shrugged. "We'll find her."

"And what if you can't?" I asked.

Bob slapped his thighs and stood. "It's done. Nonnegotiable. I've got to be going."

"That wasn't a discussion," Larrimer said. "Nor was it meant to be one." He rose to his full six-foot-four. "So what's your real agenda here, Special Agent Balfour?"

"Assistant Special Agent in Charge."

Larrimer folded his arms across his chest, eyes dancing.

"Get out, Larrimer," Bob said. "I need to talk to Clea alone."

With a look of disdain at Balfour, Larrimer turned to me. "You okay with this?"

"Are you her damned puppy?" Bob barked.

Swirls of anger figure-eighted around the two men. Larrimer stepped forward, deceptively relaxed, eager.

Bob's body tightened, an old bear about to pounce.

"Guys. Guys?" I rested a hand on Larrimer's bicep. "James," I said in a whisper. "It's okay. Go walk the dogs for me? Please?"

Whatever he saw in my face relaxed him.

"My pleasure." He nodded at Bob, a promise of violence, and whistled. The dogs trotted after him.

"So, Bob, is this where you tell me you're putting me back on the roster?"

He drew in a breath, released it. "I can't. The Bureau can't. The SAC won't have it, not until this case is closed."

I notched my chin. "What is it really, Bob? Why are you holding me back?"

He snared my eyes. "Soon, Young Pup. I promise."

Lies. Too bad my lie-dar didn't offer the meaning behind them. Now, one of the truest friends I'd ever known was gone, replaced by no-idea-what. "Your plan for the Adept's Den feels wrong."

He straightened, donned that familiar mantle of authority, and spread his hands. "It's the higher-ups plan."

"What do *you* think of it, Bob?"

He shrugged.

"You're playing politics with the poohbahs again. Be present in your own right."

He notched his head toward the door. "Is *he* present?"

"Always."

A flush mottled his face. "You don't know the half of it."

"So tell me."

"He's a *freak*!"

That's when I got it. That, which made up Larrimer, he wished for it, too. Wanted it so bad, it ate at him from the inside out. "You used to be kinder than that, Old Man."

Of course, Bob told me nothing. Crawling beneath the sheets before Larrimer returned with the dogs, I rubbed my belly. Sore. Blondie2. His hands, I still felt them. There. The invasion. The pain. His fingers jammed inside me.

I wanted Larrimer to come to my bed again, to tell him what Blondie had done, to have his comfort replace the pain.

He never appeared.

Senses on fire, I jerked awake, grabbed my gun. I wasn't alone. But I was. Except beneath me, in my office, Larrimer stormed with cold fury as he danced with his swords, so I reached for LoTR beside my bed. No way could I sleep through his passion.

More than an hour later, he stopped, paused, started talking. I shouldn't. I really shouldn't.

I lay on the floor, my ear pressed to the boards. Handy that our timberframe had little but wood between the floors.

"Now is *not* the time to bring her in." He might be roiling with anger, but his voice was honied smooth and calm.

He laughed. "Flaunting your authority? What authority? You're my *handler*, nothing more."

Even through the boards, I could hear screeching on the other end.

"We're closing in on The Master," he said. "Yes, she knows about the chest. She's hunting it. That's why it's too soon." A pause, then, "Involved with her?" A chuckle. "Balfour is an asshole with daddy issues."

Pause.

"Go ahead," he said, precise, cool. "Send Geirr to 'assist' me. Fuck up the mission royally. I don't give a shit."

The phone clicked off, then something hit a wall. I leapt into bed.

Tomorrow came, and my body screamed at me. After a scorching shower, I slathered on another round of Bag Balm. I should buy a stock. I plundered the pile of jeans on the floor, donned fresh underwear and a t-shirt, and downed three ibuprofens.

And got the shakes.

I slumped to the bed. Dammit, it was over. I wasn't kidnapped, wasn't raped.

But that wasn't it. No, it had been Larrimer's phone call. Apparently, I was a *mission*. I should confront him, confront Bob. Except, whenever confrontations happened, people died, most often the confronter. My trusted sounding boards—Dave dead, Bob involved in "the mission," Bernadette unwell—were gone.

Larrimer was my best bet. But he was torn between helping me and doing something that was shredding him from the inside out. I could use that, except I sucked at deceiving those I cared for. And yeah, my feelings for Larrimer were dark and complex. And I would not use the "L" word.

Every time I used *that*, someone died. My parents. Tommy. Dave. Lulu?

Shit.

Bottom line, Larrimer would never deliberately hurt me. Soul-deep, I knew that. So I'd have to pick an opportune time and get him to open up. Sure, like using fingernails on a tin can. Yippee.

Bernadette's *Buck it up, cookie* made my head ache. Grouchy old woman. Maybe I *was* still too soft.

No. I was strong, strong enough to survive Tommy's death, and Dave's. To defeat Blondies. To find Lulu.

To love James Larrimer? A man who cared, but one I doubted would ever love me back. I scraped a hand through my shoulder-length curls, which had started to feel like silky dreadlocks. My hair seemed to grow each time I fireflied. Geesh, I could end up a reggae Rapunzel.

Bernadette was right. Time to buck it up.

The aromas of coffee, eggs, and toast drew me downstairs. Larrimer sat at on the couch shoveling food into his mouth, eyes focused on his computer.

"Damned Bruins." He slammed the thing closed. "Lost again."

So normal. Like we were regular folks having a garden-variety morning.

"How do you feel?" he asked.

"Nothing's broken. It could be worse."

Eyes focused on the screen, he waved a hand toward the kitchen. "I made you a plate. It's in the oven."

"You'd make a swell wife," I said as I beelined for the food.

He chortled, then coughed.

"That's what you get for laughing at me."

He closed his laptop and carried his plate to the kitchen table. "C'mon."

I retrieved the plate and my coffee, and joined him.

"How do you not miss this?" He chomped on a piece of bacon.

Beside his chair, Grace, Mutt, and Jeff sat at attention, a rope of drool dripping from Grace's muzzle. They liked bacon, too.

He chewed slowly, thoughtfully, and swallowed. "Wife, huh?"

"You'd be ideal." I put perky into my smile.

He didn't return it. I caught a simmering *something* beneath the morning routine. Something bad.

"Tell me," I said.

He set his fork on his plate. "Ronan never came home last night."

I sucked in a breath.

He nodded once.

Maybe we were wrong, maybe Ronan stayed over at a friend's. But my gut knew he'd been taken.

"Balfour knows," he said. "His guys are on it."

"You should have told me right away."

"And what would you have done?"

"Why haven't they contacted us, dammit?"

He tilted his chair back. "They keep trying to steal you. They want *you*."

"I guess I'm not so stealable, huh."

His eyes iced over.

"I don't know why!" I said.

The ice cracked. "Did he rape you?"

The fork I threw at him bounced off his chest. "You've been waiting to ask that, haven't you? Haven't you? Would it disgust you because we haven't screwed yet? Because you haven't..." *What was I spewing?* "I'm sorry. I didn't mean those things."

His phone played, and played and played and...

He exploded from the chair and crushed the phone into a hunk of metal and glass. Fury blew from him like a tsunami, stealing my breath.

I stood, hand outstretched. "James."

A hard stare so primal, waves of fury so intense, I stumbled back. He wrapped his hands around the chair. It snapped in two.

"I wasn't there to protect you." His voice, a guttural growl. "Didn't have your back. Someone touched you. Hit you. Hurt you. He *hurt* you. And I wasn't fucking there to stop it."

"I'm okay," I said. "It's okay."

"No," he ground out. "It's not."

He ignited, his gaze, lethal blades aimed at me. Except he wasn't seeing me, not a bit.

I took a step toward him.

"Stay the fuck away." His voice, gravel low, filled with savagery. "I'm a killer. They created me for violence. Stop."

I moved closer, and he was a blur, slamming me against the wall.

Pain arced up my back.

His hands splayed beside my head, body pressed against mine in some hideous parody of making love. Confining me, smothering me, imprisoning me, and I pushed and pushed against his chest, a mouse trapped by a tiger.

"Stop this!"

Deaf. He was deaf to everything but some inner howl, his rage seething, his flames biting me. I wasn't Clea, but a foe he ached to erase.

I couldn't breathe, couldn't see, couldn't escape. Had to. He pressed me harder, deeper against the wall, our bodies fused. In this mindless fever, he'd kill me.

Then I felt them, the fireflies, swarm my palms. I'd be *free*.

I inched my trembling hands up his chest, flattened them above his pounding heart, to stop it beating, to end this. *Yes*, I could do that.

Never.

With all that I was, I projected outward, pain and pleasure and power, cycloning my thoughts, my feelings, my heart, while inhaling his terrible anger, pulling it to me, drawing it in.

And in a blinding rush, fireflies, citrus and light, streamed from my fingertips to swirl and dance and tornado around us, gaining power, leaching the pain, drinking it in, deeper and deeper, his rage, splinters beneath fingernails, razors on palms.

Fireflies knit together, to form a Tree of Life pattern, thick-trunked, wending branches that bowed and swayed, meandering roots that met the branches to form Celtic knots. The fireflied tree mantled around us, speed blurred.

Dizzy, I pulled the cyclone impossibly tighter as the golden fireflies vortexed, until a scream bubbled up, my body shaking with its force, scalpels scything flesh, scoring bones. Release it. Release it. I must.

I would *not*.

The tempest intensified, and I screamed, silent, the blackness, malevolent, hungry, sucking me in, swallowing me, blinding me.

And I saw it then, down in that deep and dark place inside of him, a red-gold dragon, keening and writhing and screeching in pain.

And the blackness absorbed that, too. No light, no scent, no fireflies. Only a dragon's agony. Except, there, a spark of magic that flickered—almost out—and I fanned that flame so it brightened. Brightened to a warm, comforting glow. The dragon chuffed twice, then settled. Watchful, but appeased.

Pain bladed my spine. And I leashed my mind, fed the calm, evoked James stroking my cheek. Surrounding my body. Soothing me.

A hint of light, a flicker, a stream, then a billion stars exploded the blackness.

CHAPTER THIRTY-FOUR

The kitchen. Standing in the kitchen. With Larrimer, the true Larrimer, a massive man, sweaty, chest heaving, eyes aglow with a blue fire that dissolved to confusion. He relaxed his muscles, and I moved my hands up and around his back and held him tight.

He rubbed his stubbled cheek against the curve of my neck. "Sorry. Sorry."

"No biggie," I said, digging for humor.

He snared my eyes and scowled. "You are the one person who can wind me up like that."

"Just a girl of many talents."

He released me, and I felt chilled.

He scraped his hands through his hair, face tight, cheekbones blades. "I said I'd have your back, and I didn't."

He reached for the mudroom door.

"Don't you dare!" I gripped his forearm. "I'm a big girl. We deal with lots of crap. Things happen. We survive."

"What you just saw," he said, words a clipped whisper. "That's who I am. That *thing*. The anger. The violence. That's me."

"Kinda sexy."

He shook his head. "You are *blind*, woman."

"Twenty-twenty, big guy." I wasn't having any of his bullshit.

There went the eyebrow. "I've killed dozens, Clea. Without a blink.

I almost killed you."

"My ass, you did," I said, with an arrogance I didn't feel. I swiped my coffee and tossed a snarky look over my shoulder. Somehow, I made it to the living room couch. I sprawled, my back against the arm, needing the support. Tired didn't come close to describing my state.

But no nosebleed, eyes okay. Just a residue of pain. My body was acclimating to the fireflies.

Please don't leave, James. Please. I listened for the click of the mudroom door.

Long minutes passed, and when he appeared, he took the other end of the sofa, matching my position, his long legs surrounding mine.

Mr. Cool and Calm and somewhat Ironic was back.

"That was... different," he said.

"What?"

He snorted. "*What?* Those light things swirling around us."

In for a penny. "Oh, you mean my fireflies."

"Fireflies."

I shrugged. "That's what I call them. Could you smell them? Um, they're what took off Blondie's head."

He winced. "Jesus. And I'm not charbroiled because...?"

"Um, I'm not sure. I never did *precisely* that before. Every other time—"

"Every *other* time."

"You saw with the bus," I said, a little snippish.

"Not really," he said. "Not like this."

"Mostly, I project outward. This time, with you, I pulled inward. It worked."

"Christ."

"I don't think he's involved."

He pinched the bridge of his nose. "You didn't fix me, not permanently. But it helped. Did something good. What did it feel like?"

Pain. The horrible pain. The pleasurable power. The blackness. The dragon. Worth it. "Different."

Before he could respond, I told him about the fireflies. The vague memory at Dave's house. The dinner. Blondie. My tattoo. The cobrathings and the wolves.

His lips thinned. "I knew something was wrong that day."

"I have no idea what any of it means, but I've accepted it, the

279

weirdness, the magic." I paused, took a plunge. "You have magic, too."

He frowned, nodded, silence.

"And?" I finally said.

His finger traced his scar. "A spark. A Fae animated me. Without him, they couldn't have brought me back."

"I can feel it. The Fae. I've felt it from the beginning." I leaned forward and rested my hands on his knees. "And..."

All I got was one of those flat stares I really disliked.

"I saw it," I said. "Um, *him*."

"You saw the Fae," he deadpanned.

I shook my head. "The dragon. *Your* dragon."

"Not possible."

"He's red-gold. Pointy things along his spine and rounded scales and razor teeth dripping drool like Grace. The drool part, I mean."

"The fuck."

"I really did see him. He was in a lot of pain. But not by the end."

He swiped a hand across his face, fisted it. "He was a wyvern, not a dragon. They used wyvern blood to make me. He was much as you describe. Beautiful. Deadly. Powerful."

"Where is he, er, when he's, um, not inside you? Oh, geesh, I don't understand this at all."

He flexed his fingers. "He's not anywhere. They took his blood. Again and again. Tried to infuse it into others. They failed. People died. All of them, except for me. The wyvern withered. They kept taking. The wyvern died."

He reached out and swiped a tear from my cheek. "He's worth your tears."

"He's not dead." My voice sounded rough, a whisper. I strengthened it. "He's inside you."

A calloused hand cupped my chin. "I don't see how that's possible, but if you say so... And he had a name, one I couldn't pronounce." His smile was slow and warm. "He was something to see."

"Tell me more," I said.

"They bribed the Fae or more likely tortured him into reigniting me with a spark of magic. My magic is drawn to yours."

I prowled across the couch on hands and knees to sit on his lap, and he held me loosely as if he wasn't sure if he should. I tucked my head into his shoulder. "Your magic's drawn to mine, huh. That's sort of nifty."

"You continue to confound me with the things that pop from your mouth." He took my wrist and turned it this way and that, his eyes focused on my tattoo.

"It glows when I firefly," I said. "It's pretty cool. I don't have much control. I can't go puff and they appear."

I felt his smile.

"So, just now, that was an experiment. You're lucky you didn't fry the both of us."

"Not to worry. It would've been quick."

His bark of laughter did warm things to my innards.

"You are a ridiculous woman," he said.

"Ridiculous, am I? Humph."

He quieted. "I should have had your back."

"You rescued me off a frigging cliff."

"I'm fucked up."

"And I'm not?" I kissed his throat.

He stilled, that statue thing he did. "I've got to make a call."

Damn. Damn damn damn. I kissed his throat again, tasted the salty-sweetness of him with my tongue, and sat up. "I'll go take care of the animals."

"Need help?" he asked.

"Why don't you call whomever was hot to talk to you? Use the landline. Please don't crunch that to death, too."

Chores complete, I phoned the diner, hoping Anouk had returned. She knew *stuff*. No joy, but I left another message. Damn that woman, creature, whatever.

Minutes later, rehab called and said we could pick up Bernadette. *Yes*. On our way, and after a quick trip to the Verizon store for a new phone for Larrimer and some new burners, I laid out my plan for the night at The Adept's Den.

"ASAC Balfour's plan," I said, "is set for late in the evening, after everyone's been seated and served. We go in disguised well before the FBI does."

"They'll make you," Larrimer said.

"No way. I'll wear a different costume, you'll be in disguise."

"*Yours* worked well the last time."

"Blondie did *not* recognize me from the dinner. By the way, sarcasm is never appreciated."

"Says she who's the expert at it."

Gurrrr. "Blondies are dead. We're golden."

"Christ, Clea, he wasn't the only one who saw you that night."

Grace barked from the car's backseat, probably agreeing with him.

"No," I said. "But he was the only one with a functioning brain."

"Alright. Given our options, it's a solid plan. We'll get in before the FBI."

"Into that inner sanctum."

"Yes," he said. "That's where The Master will be. Where Lulu and Ronan will be, too, if they're there."

"They will be." I waved a hand. "I suspect he loves an audience. So theatrical. I bet that's what the food thing's all about. He'd be keeping Lulu close. Ronan, too."

His sidelong glance said he didn't like it. "You realize they could be killed, either in the assault, or when we go after The Master. What he really wants is you."

My gut agreed. The Master knew I'd come. If he wanted me, he'd have me. Hell, yeah. He'd underestimated me so far. He'd do so again. "Yes. What other choice do we have?"

Frustration rolled off him like scalding oil as he turned off 202 and took the hill to the hospital campus. He rammed the truck into park, and it bounced once. "I can think of several different ops, all of which include taking you out of the equation."

Larrimer wasn't a fool. He knew I'd never agree to that. "So I'll be bait. And you'll have my back." He would. More than anyone I'd ever known.

Bernadette's room at rehab smelled antiseptic. She slept in a green vinyl recliner beside the bed, her things in a clear plastic bag on her lap. I'd taken her derringer, but she still wore that silly turban.

Her attending physician peeked in. "Mrs. Sevaux is doing very well. She needs rest, but gives every indication of a complete recovery."

"Her memory?" I asked.

He removed her chart from the foot of the bed. Nodded. "Good. It's good. All except for the assault. It may return, but very possibly won't. That's common with this kind of trauma."

"You talking behind my back, Doctor?" came a voice from behind us, with, thankfully, only a trace of French accent.

We turned. Her teasing smile flirted with the sixty-something doctor. She turned to us, wrinkled face pleating with joy. "You kids here to take me home? Wonderful."

My mouth moved, but nothing came out. Bernadette had been replaced by an alien.

She rose, hooking the bag across her arm. "Clea." She took my arm.

Then she turned to Larrimer and beamed. "And my boy. My sweet Tommy."

Shit.

Four days later, we'd cemented our plan for The Adept's Den. Four long days with no phone calls, no messages, no breaks on Lulu or Ronan. On the plus side, no one had tried to steal me, shoot me, or stab me.

Larrimer, of course, stuck to me like white on rice. But not in the good way. Oh, he'd touched my cheek, smoothed my hair, patted my shoulder. But it was all affection, like you'd touch a friend. No kisses, no heat, no sizzle.

When you want to jump someone's bones, this was torture.

I insisted that each day we go to the diner to see if Anouk showed. She didn't. We also visited Shatzkin and Bronze Printing. Both were "on vacation." Convenient.

The world stretched tight in anticipation.

The evening prior to The Adept's Den costume party, we got lucky. I spotted Anouk entering the diner. Larrimer would watch the place while I hid in the ally anticipating her smoke break.

She didn't fail me.

Light spilled from the back door, then the woman who conjured thoughts of Amazon warriors and giant panthers followed. The door closed, and darkness enveloped us. The outline that was Anouk paused, a moment's hesitation, then she sauntered toward me. Seconds later, a lighter flared. Those sloe eyes took me in, snaring mine, and she fired up her cigarette and inhaled.

"It is about time," she said, in that precise, not-quite-English accent.

As if I'd kept her waiting. "You were supposed to get in touch with me."

"You are damaged since we last met."

"Funny, I don't feel damaged."

"But there is more to you this time. Much more."

I wasn't in the mood for cryptic. "A chest of bone."

"Shush." She took my hand. "Come, let us walk. Your shadow, he will not see or hear us."

I had every faith that Larrimer would.

We walked down the alley and onto the street, Anouk apparently unconcerned as we strolled beneath the streetlamps. Bundled in down, the night wind didn't chill me, but she wore no coat.

"You must be freezing," I said.

"No."

We'd better move past the monosyllable stage. Fast.

Few people were out, and when a couple passed us, they appeared wrapped in their own warm world. We headed toward the closed shops of Station Square, and at the shuttered Garner Deli, she led me up the steps and indicated we should sit on the porch bench.

We sat side by side, and Anouk kept her grip on my hand.

"Anouk, the—"

"Wait." She held up the cigarette between her two long, slim fingers.

So I sat there silent, inhaling secondary smoke, while she puffed away, slowly, as if it wasn't twenty degrees out.

She finally dropped the cig, squashed it with her boot, and slipped the butt into her sweater pocket.

I waited.

Her tongue swiped her lush lips.

Finally, I failed the patience test. "Who are 'we?' You never told me."

CHAPTER THIRTY-FIVE

She shot me an annoyed look. "We, *creatures of magic,* thrived in our world."

I chuffed out a breath. "I know there are Fae, which I've looked up online."

She snorted. "Some truth there, but also much garbage."

"And Mages. I'm one, right?"

Her eyes glowed, that panther color. "You have been busy. Yes, you are Mage. Have you looked that up, too?"

"I found a lot of gaming stuff, and books, novels. What I need is an encyclopedia." I grinned. "Have one handy?"

"You are a smarty pants."

"And no one's used that term since forever."

She lit another cigarette.

"You're not going to stop talking now, are you?"

She waggled the tip at me. "No, but you are."

I clenched my jaw.

After a slow nod, she continued. "The chest. You see, we of the magic realm could manage without the chest with the worlds' unplaited. We had no choice, as without it, we could barely reach into your reality and—"

"The mundane world."

She cut me a sharp look. "Where did you hear that term?"

My Da. "A memory."

She took a drag. "It is the correct one. To continue. The chest was powerful, but with the worlds separate, not essential. As time passed, so we have learned, the chest transmorphed into a simple box. For a thousand years, this has been. Mundane on one skein and magic on the other. Always parallel, on occasion touching, but only with the delicacy of a lover's caress. Ah, a lover's caress." She took a deep inhale and blew smoke out her nose. "Then, fifty years ago in your timeframe, the strands began to reweave."

"Why? Why then?"

"We have our suspicions, but that is, as you say, above your 'clearance grade.' Now, the braiding is becoming chaotic, different, the fabric warped without the chest. The new Guardian cannot find it."

New Guardian. "Who was the former Guardian?"

Her lip curled. "Your friend, Dave."

"But I thought the chest was lost. The Storybook—"

"A metaphor... of sorts."

Metaphor, my ass. She wasn't telling me the half of it. I plowed on. "Explain more about this chest of bone. That's the right name, yes?"

"It is the Chest of Bone, all capitals, my dear. You should not name it aloud." She hissed, and her head tilted sideways. She listened.

The world lay still, breathless. A few errant leaves, autumn leftovers, rustled the parking lot. The rumble of a car. Voices, laughter, but distant. So distant.

"The chest is a thing of magic. Of power. As the skeins continue to intertwine, the chest orders them, melds them. Without it..." She bared her teeth. "It is really quite simple. In safe hands, the chest helps weave the plaits together in pure symmetry. In evil hands... Well, you have read the books about what happens then."

One storybook in particular came to mind. "Who is The Master?"

"We do not know. We do know he feeds on power, and we suspect he has serious help from the Magic realm. With the chest..." She shook her head, then flowed to her feet, as did I, except when I tried to release my hand, I failed. Superglued together. Swell.

"How can you not know who he is?" I asked. "Is he a Mage? A Fae?"

She shrugged.

"What are *you*?"

"For now, my dear, I am your guide."

Swell again. "Are you or are you not a panther?"

She did the glowy eye thing. "Remember the wolves."

So she was a wolf? They were shapeshifters, too? Oh, why not. I saw those all the time. They sold them at Target.

"You, Clea Artemis Reese, must find the chest, and you must keep it safe, until *you* hand it over to the new Guardian."

Which was all well and good, but... "What I need to do is find Lulu and Ronan."

"You do not see. You still do not see. Why, my dear, do you think you were named Clea? You're The Key, of course."

She released my hand, lit another cigarette, and vanished.

Yup, she vanished. Right up that damned column of smoke. Helluva guide.

I dropped back hard onto the bench, expecting Larrimer to emerge from the shadows.

Instead, a man towered over me, costumed in calm. Oh, great. Sure, he looked relaxed. Like the Mummy before it grabbed you.

"What the fuck," he said in that slow, low voice. "Two seconds ago, when I climbed the steps, you weren't on this bench."

"Of course I was. Why don't you sit down before I strain my neck?"

He didn't.

So that was the way it was going to be. All right. I slapped my thighs and got to my feet. When I tried to take his hand, the icy fist didn't budge. I crooked an arm through his. "C'mon, let's walk."

Down the steps, we crossed the parking lot to the path that ran by the river. "What's your problem, Larrimer?"

"I'm contemplating the plusses of strangulation. Of you."

"I'd rather you didn't." Was that teeth grinding I heard? "Now, aside from throttling me, what—"

"You vanished."

"All we did was walk from the—"

"No," he said, with a preternatural calm. "You did not. You disappeared. I couldn't find you."

"She held my hand the entire time." I patted his arm. "I guess she made us invisible, which goes with the whole psycho shebang. Ready to listen?"

He fisted his hand in my hair, tilted my head back, brushed his stubbled cheek against mine. He inhaled deeply. "You scare the shit out of me." He used that low, honeyed voice that turned me to goo. I wanted a kiss. Where was my kiss?

He released my hair and took my hand.

We walked, and I regurgitated Anouk's tale. "When I was a kid, I loved reading fantasy, sci-fi. Still do. *Lord of the Rings, The Once and Future King, Dune,* Asimov, whathaveyou. I never once imagined any of it was real. How much of fiction and myth is real?"

He was taking this all pretty well, until I said, "Anouk's a shapeshifter, by the way. Maybe a wolf. Although that doesn't feel exactly right."

That stopped him dead. "Doesn't feel *right*?"

"She implied the wolves who helped me were, too."

"Shapeshifters." He nodded.

He'd gone somewhere far away. Wherever he was, he'd never tell. I squeezed his hand, wanting him here, present, with me. "Oh, and she vanished in a puff of smoke. Wish I could do that."

He squeezed my hand. "Me, too."

"I think of those tales about thin places," I said, "Where the otherworld is closest to ours. That idea always intrigued me."

"Never heard of them," he said.

"Maybe they were places the magic always touched, and where the reweaving started. Humm. Some say people under enchantment create the greatest art and beauty. Mysterious ancient books exist, like the *Voynich Manuscript* at Yale and the *Oera Linda Book,* that I learned about in school. Adder stones, the Lothar Crystal, the Chintamani Stone, Zuni fetishes. Protective wands, healing, curses. Synthetic apriori."

He paused, a flash of a smile. "Immanuel Kant?"

"Why not? Doesn't our situation fit the idea that what we experience as humans is only appearance, and not the things themselves. Didn't Kant hypothesize that space and time are subjective forms of our human intuition?"

"You're wading pretty deep."

I grinned. "It was a good college course. Maybe magic is also a science, just one with its own set of rules."

We stopped beside the river. Moonlight danced on the small crests, and the scents of water and pine and snow drifted to me. Stars crowded the sky, distant points of light.

"Pretty." Larrimer raised our joined hands and kissed the back of mine, grounding me in a much simpler reality. "'There are more things in heaven and earth, Horatio, than are dreamt of in your philosophy.'"

"First you know Kant, now Shakespeare? Should I be worried?"

His soft laughter echoed on the empty path as we walked to the car.

The Audi we'd rented for The Adept's Den dinner party purred. Earlier, Larrimer, sporting a hooked nose, wrinkles, bags beneath his eyes, and a mustache had passed my inspection. He looked nothing like James Larrimer, a fact that added hope for the evening's outcome. My gold-lame pants itched, and my loose velvet blouse, hiding a knife strapped to my waist and my gun's shoulder holster, showed enough of my pink pushup bra to make me blush. Oh, screw it. I plumped my breasts up even more. Ballet flats, gold-painted nails, Cleopatra eyes, and a red wig with bangs completed my transformation.

I looked like a hooker on crack.

I'd already slipped my FBI badge, a second knife, spare car key, and cash into my dainty purse.

Larrimer's lab—which was certainly helluva lot more than Fish and Wildlife—had recreated the original invitation, changing only the date. It would get us through. Where it wouldn't get us was the inner sanctum. The diners I'd seen enter that alcove to the third room had *always* been escorted by Adept's Den staff. No one had walked in alone. No one.

So, we just had to do it the hard way.

Before leaving, I tucked Bernadette in for the night, telling her we were going to a costume party. She found that quite marvelous and laughed with delight just before she'd kissed "Tommy" goodnight.

Her tiptop physical shape contrasted sharply with her mental fragility. Of course, her doctor hadn't known Tommy was dead, so to him, Larrimer as Tommy made perfect sense. Still, he had to be right. Her brain could heal, *would* heal, from a minor bleed. For now, her confusion made my life easier, but also made my chest ache.

"I figure I'm pretty safe calling you James tonight." I stared out the window into the cloudy night that threatened snow.

"Sure. I'll call you Artemis. It suits you."

I flushed, oddly pleased that he liked my middle name.

"What happened with her grandson, Artemis?" Larrimer put the Audi in gear.

"I was orphaned young." I told him about my childhood and how I came to be with Bernadette and Tommy. "Anyway, Bernadette was disgusted when Tommy joined the Army."

He turned the corner, headed toward Asheville center. "And were you disgusted?"

I shrugged. "I didn't want the military, but it was the only way I could afford my college of choice. I majored in psych. Tommy majored in beer and broads, with a minor in philosophy. I went to Clark, did my ROTC training at WPI, deferred the Army, and got my Masters in counseling at Northeastern. Tommy went to UMass on the six-year plan, so we both enlisted at the same time, to Bernadette's horror."

"You have nightmares about him."

My eyes widened.

He took a cigar, a prop, out of his pocket and threaded it through his fingers. "You cry out sometimes. Shout. Say things."

"The dreams," I said. "We'd driven cross-country, and stopped at the Grand Canyon. I'd always wanted to take a helicopter into the canyon. Tommy bought us tickets. A surprise for me. Actually rented a special copter so he could fly it. He'd learned in the army." Oh, how he loved flying.

"I bitched at him like crazy, wanted to go with him. But his was a two-person machine, and a company guy had to accompany him. I went in a second copter. Tommy's crashed. Exploded. Burned. Gone. All while I watched."

"And you could do nothing." His warm fingers threaded through mine. "An accident. But you haven't forgiven yourself yet."

"What about you, your life before?"

He chomped on the cigar. "We're almost there."

Goosebumps crawled up my arms, and I rubbed them.

As before, we left the car with the valet. I tucked my hand around the crook of Larrimer's arm, and we crossed the parking lot. The closer we got to the door, the more my nerves prickled. Just under the skin, excitement bit me. I massaged the dangling star earrings, the second, different pair. We'd be fine. Nerves were good.

I lifted my chin, pasted a smile on my face, and in minutes we were through the entrance. No Blondie tonight. I thanked heaven they weren't triplets.

When we entered the first dining room, a maître d' bustled over, his hair in a trendy man-bun that pulled his features tight. Larrimer handed him our invitation, and we threaded our way through the diners. I appeared to talk to Larrimer, and he to me, but we both were checking out the guests, the servers, the beefy goons decked out in tuxes.

The maître d' flashed our invitation to the guard as we entered the second dining room. Same number of diners, same hum of excitement and entitlement, same nasty, potent brew.

He steered us toward a table to the center left. Well, lookie lookie— the Bronze Printing bimbo. Vacation. Right.

"Last time, I sat in that corner." I smiled at the maître d' and pointed to a table for two in shadow near the entrance to the third dining room. "More private." Slick as anything, Larrimer slipped him some bills.

We followed the maître d' to the requested table. Larrimer assisted me into the seat that faced the third room's entrance, while he took the one opposite.

A crystal carafe of red wine sat on the white linen, and Larrimer started to pour. "I'd swear there's blood in it," I said. "Don't drink."

"I don't intend to."

"I'm too jacked up, dammit."

"Look at me."

Larrimer sure didn't look like himself, except for a moment, I lost myself in those Pacific-blues. Their touch was warm and calm. Such perfect calm.

His grin spelled danger, and I laughed.

"I'm glad you're on my side," I said.

"Always."

I lay the thick linen napkin in my lap. "We should wait for Roberto to announce tonight's menu," Thank the gods only Larrimer could see my revulsion. "They'll be distracted, filled with excitement. When we disable the guard in the alcove, we can head for that third room. I saw three guards the first time."

Larrimer had given me one of two tiny aerosol sprays he said would instantaneously knock out each guard. He had the other one.

The sprays niggled at me. Contrary to movies galore, I knew of no on-the-spot drug that could do that. But I was betting those clever guys at his mysterious agency did.

He nodded.

Easy peasy. Sure.

I opened my senses, reassessing the crowd. Emotions popped with fizzy excitement, and low notes of fear and anxiety. I closed down and focused on the wine, pretending to sip. Not even liking the stuff near my lips, I surreptitiously poured some on the floor.

"One teensy thing," I said. "I meant to mention it earlier."

Larrimer stifled a groan. "That is *not* a good phrase."

"Blondie2 saw my fireflies."

He cursed under his breath. "Think he told his boss before you took off his head?"

"I don't know."

"We'll handle it."

Long minutes later, Roberto bounded out from the far entrance, all smiles.

The room hushed.

"Tonight, we're serving extra-special delicacies. Our appetizer is fresh dugong from Palau."

Applause.

"Chimpanzee from the Congo!"

Enormous applause.

"And, for something really unique, the Maned Wolf from Argentina!"

I applauded, mantraed composure, and imagined how my shapeshifter wolves would react to that little treat. Larrimer smiled broadly, clapping like mad.

Waiters swarmed the room, and one placed a thick sheet of vellum in front of me, then Larrimer.

He lifted his. "Wow, looks delicious, doesn't it, darling?"

I reached for mine. "Divine, honey pie."

The room was abuzz.

Wearing that fake smile, he said, "Now, I think, darling."

To impress the gun-toting thug, I undid another button of my blouse, spilling my breasts out further. "I couldn't agree more, sweetheart."

I started to rise. Larrimer stood swifter than I, and the room went silent. Two goons had emerged from the rear alcove, one flush against Larrimer, who went ice still. So, a gun. Swell.

Larrimer could take them, but that wasn't the point.

The taller one nodded to me. "Someone wants to speak to you. Wait here."

They flanked Larrimer, who threw me a wink, then the three stepped backward, into the alcove, into darkness.

Larrimer. That crazy man was frigging pumped.

On high alert, I resumed my seat.

I dipped the fingers of my left hand beneath the hem of my blouse, slid out my gun, and held it under the table.

Whispers filled the room, like smoke from a smoldering pyre. Candle-flames flickered, shadows dancing, then blazed bright. Nettles scored my skin, my wrist itching like crazy.

He was coming. I streamed out my senses, crashed against hunger and excitement, greed and lust. Too much.

My right hand spasmed. Quiet. The room was so very, very quiet. *Focus. Focus.*

That voice, *Da*. My mind calmed. I forced my fisted hand to unclench, reach for the water. I sipped. Cool. Refreshing. Sipped again. Drained the glass.

He was near.

I was ready.

A medium-sized man in a silver-gray suit took shape beside the table. I didn't raise my eyes, but sensed when he waved a hand. The room's hum recommenced at a frantic pitch. I thrust my shoulders back, poised for battle, and aimed my gun at the man taking Larrimer's seat.

I looked up.

And the world vanished.

CHAPTER THIRTY-SIX

Tommy filled my world. He was here. Alive. My lips moved, but no words came. The ghost seated across from me folded his arms, his chocolate eyes bright with delight.

Light brown hair, a strong nose that tilted up just enough to make him hate it, stubbled chin with that sweet cleft I always loved. He had the grace of an acrobat, a man who could fly through the air and catch the brass ring. And me. He always caught me.

"Impossible," I whispered, unsure of whether I'd said it aloud or to myself.

A pale hand reached across the table, lifted my icy one and kissed it, soft and gentle and real. "Possible, dear Clea. Long time no see."

The voice, always a little rusty and sharp. I'd know it anywhere. The burning behind my eyes intensified, and I cursed. "Not Tommy. Can't be."

The grin that was my sun for years shone from his lips.

"No? Remember that night we were supposed to be studying, but snuck out to go joyriding instead? When you leaned too fast into my old Fiat's door? The open flap window caught you below your left eye. Your blood gushed everywhere, and you used my new shirt, dammit, to wipe it up. Bad girl." He chuckled.

I withdrew my hand and raised a finger to the small heart-shaped scar that testified to the event. "I saw you die."

"But I didn't!" He smiled. "All fakery, theatrics."

Not for the dead copilot, nor the other corpse in the helicopter.

"Like your old mentalist tricks," he said.

Which were hints of my nascent powers. Powers that were murmuring things I refused to hear.

"It's really you," I said.

He nodded. "Of course."

"How did you—?"

"Not now."

He kissed the back of my hand again, and the intensity brought fresh tears.

"Why don't you put that gun away now?" he asked.

Zombie-like, I slid it into its holster. "I've missed you *so much*."

He frowned, nodded. "Not as much as I've missed you."

"Why the charade? Where have you—"

"Later. We have all the time in the world."

"And Tanya? Are you—"

His eyes twinkled. "Still together."

But he'd hidden from *me*, from Bernadette. "Why are you here, in this—"

He waved a finger.

Power bathed me in silence. My ears rang. The world, a tunnel of light, shining around Tommy.

I knew. Of course I knew. The moment I'd seen him. But I hated the knowing. Didn't want it.

Tommy was The Master.

I forced myself back, pulled reality around me, cloaked myself in it. I lowered my lashes. He'd always been able to see the truth in me.

Acid surged up my throat. I swallowed, hard, reached for the pitcher of water with its graceful lemon slices floating on top. He beat me to it and poured. I couldn't look at him. Wouldn't.

How had my universe shattered so utterly?

He waited for me to drink, then ran a finger up and down my hand. "Look at me, Clea. Hear me out."

I stared at him, my mind galloping across scenes from our childhood. Tommy and me playing He Man. Riding Clem. Building a fort of sheets. The boy I knew better than myself. "It just can't be. The Master."

He bubbled with excitement. "It is. And, yes, I'm The Master. But there is *so much* you don't know."

And so much I did.

He leaned in, lowered his voice to a whisper. "As a team, we could help the world. The Chest of Bone. That's all we need."

"What?"

"Wondrous power. A grail wrapped in a box." He sighed. "You don't understand. Look, magic's just..." He tapped a finger on the table. "Like the Internet. Magic's just a tool."

"No it's not." I thought for a moment. How to get through to him. "It's more like nature, elemental, organic. It's becoming rewoven into our world, a *part* of our world. Integral."

"You don't get it." He shook his head. "It's a device, and someone needs to wield it to keep things in order. On an even keel, right? Control the flow so others don't abuse it. Why not me?"

I could think of a thousand reasons I wasn't stupid enough to utter.

He leaned forward. "We'll be getting in on the ground floor of The Next Big Thing."

"The magic, you mean. If anything, Tommy, the magic is ours to protect, not to exploit."

"No no. It doesn't need *protection*. Control the magic, control the world."

Which sounded like a slogan for a bad TV show. "So you're telling me you can control the magic."

His finger tapped faster. "Some of it. A lot of it. See, it's like Amazon. Yeah, Amazon. And I'll be Jeff Bezos."

"I don't recall Jeff Bezos killing anyone, like the way you butchered Dave and murdered Jason. Or kidnapping teenagers. Or—"

He held up a hand and donned a solemn face. "Unfortunate. Dave interfered, and not in a good way. That other guy, he got in the way, too. You have to keep focused on the big picture. We knew those two kids would draw you out."

He was right about that one. "That thing that attacked me in Mt. Auburn? The attempts to kidnap me? Blondie almost raping me?"

His face froze. "I only wanted you here, with *me*, like we used to be. Warnings. Threats. Some escalated out of control."

"Why not just call me? Draw me out?"

"It's complicated."

Tommy-speak for, "I had my reasons." Ones, he knew, I wouldn't find palatable.

"When I realized..." He shook his head. "I would never hurt you."

I blinked. "But you did."

"And I'm sorry. I am. Think of it as a trade, since you took out two of my top associates." He folded his hands as if in prayer. "This is a great quest. Join me, sweetness."

I jerked at the familiar endearment. A cut that would never heal. "In what? Finding some box? Controlling the magic? What?"

His fingers danced over mine. "The chest is the key to everything."

Anouk had called me the key. He obviously didn't know that. "What chest?"

His eyes mocked. "Don't play coy. You know about the Chest of Bone. It's near. I can feel it. You'll help me find it."

There it was, Tommy's truth. Our bond, gone, consumed by some mania I failed to wrap my head around.

"Let me show you." He rose, and so did I.

He was always a talker. I'd let him unwind the threads of his truth.

His arm wrapped around my waist, hand resting on my hip, casual and light, and the gesture felt the same as always. But at my core, the difference scraped like sandpaper.

The room stilled, all eyes on us, breaths held. We moved toward the alcove.

"You can lose the chameleon act, sweetness." He chuckled.

I hadn't realized I was still in character. I buttoned my blouse. "Right. Guess my costume wasn't so effective."

"Oh, it was tremendous." That slow meandering smile of his appeared. "One of your best. But I have my ways."

He always had.

My shattered heart skipped a beat, then began again, and I consciously sheathed it in steel. I could do this. *Had* to do this.

We walked past a goon cradling an Uzi who whispered a reverent, "Master."

Tommy nodded.

Master, my ass. Yeah, Jeff Bezos did that, too. Not.

Endorphins fired through me, heightening my senses. Time became supple, and suddenly we'd arrived at a wooden door that arched at the top.

James and Lulu and Ronan. I said their names over and over.

As we entered the innermost dining room, I locked on Larrimer. Two goons supported his slumped figure a mere ten feet away, face bloody, out cold. They'd beaten him with more than fists. Bastards.

"Was that necessary?" I asked.

"For that drone? Yes."

"He's the antithesis of that." But he knew about Larrimer.

"Oh, my dearest girl, if you only knew the truth."

Truth. The word rang in my ears, a hollow sound.

A snapshot—a smallish room, twelve-by-twelve-ish, one long dining table, center stage, perpendicular to where we stood. Crystal chandeliers, golden chalices, and a dozen diners, who looked up, whispered, "Master." He nodded to them, dismissing them back to their gorging.

The diners sucked in their food, and at table's head... Lulu! She wore indigo satin, a rose pinned to her hair. To her right sat Ronan, his enormous body encased in an ill-fitting tux. Of all the guests' faces, hers was the only one turned toward us. Ronan looked downward, eating like the others, but Lulu's violet eyes tracked us. They howled terror, and she shook her head and mouthed a silent "no." Her hands weren't on the table, she wasn't eating. The bastard had tied her down.

Some costume I picked. Lulu recognized me, too.

To the left of Larrimer and the goons, a brick arch spanned a raised stage. Soft, classical music wafted from speakers, and sprays of my favorite sunflowers flanked the arch.

No one seemed in charge. Diners ate like animals, fingers greasy as they shoved food in their faces. Lulu's eyes grew wider still, and she mouthed, *run*.

A commotion by the stage. A small man wearing a chef's cap stood on the low platform holding an enormous domed silver platter. He stepped down into the room and headed for the trestle table.

The chef placed the tray in the center of the table and raised the lid. My stomach lurched, but I couldn't look away. On it lay a footless *human* leg, roasted, the ends dressed in a paper ruffle, like the kind on fancy turkeys. Rows of sliced meats lay in an artfully presented circle around the leg, dotted with parsley clips and evergreen sprigs. He began carving the leg. The diners ignored him, kept shoving food into their mouths.

Who was on that platter? George in the basement? Someone else?

I bit my cheek hard enough to taste blood, trying to bring some order to my mind. But it was frantic, darting from Tommy to the human leg to Lulu to Larrimer.

Wrong screamed at me in so many ways I couldn't breathe.

Clea. Larrimer's honeyed voice compelled my attention.

Had I imagined it, that soothing voice in my mind?

Didn't matter. Focus. *Focus.*

"Why, Tommy?" I asked. "Why this horror show?"

His lips pursed. "A small enterprise, an important one that, I confess, didn't result in what we anticipated."

I whirled on him, pushed hard, backed toward Ronan and Lulu.

A blur, and Larrimer bristled with guns. A goon crumpled to the floor, Larrimer pointing one gun at the other goon, the second tracking Tommy's calm amble to the stage.

Larrimer counter-moved, materializing beside me.

"Clea," was all he said, and I settled further into an iron calm.

"Isn't this something?" Tommy said. "You, and that *thing* beside you." He splayed his arms in front of him. "All I wanted was to talk to you. To explain. Please come here. Please, sweetness."

A crack in my steel exposed our childhood, our adventures, our intertwined lives. Tommy was love, caring, home. Confusion, thoughts so muddled, and I wandered the hills and valleys of our past.

Tommy. My Tommy.

"Clea!" Larrimer said through gritted teeth.

James. Tommy.

Larrimer's arms were rock still. "Babe, come back."

His heat combusted those beguiling memories, and I slammed my shields up so hard it hurt. "I'm with you," I said so soft only he would hear. "Completely."

"Clea!" Lulu said, her voice pleading. Tears splashed her face, now twisted in pain.

"I told you not to speak, girl." Tommy flicked a finger, and she moaned.

The scent. Just a hint. Rotted geraniums, cat urine.

My thoughts jigsawed into a picture—his thirst for power, his pleasure in pain.

But had I sensed this part of him? And ignored it?

I opened my mind and reached for Tommy.

His arms dropped, and he leaned a hip on the wall. "Nice parlor trick, but you can't get inside me."

But I could, and I found anger and elation and righteousness. He actually believed he was in the right. That was rich. And lust. For me, for my abilities. Fat fucking chance. But the guns, he didn't fear them. And he seethed with power. A hurricane's worth, gathering.

Except he was unaware I could taste him. Score one for us. "We're here for Lulu and Ronan."

"So you think," he said.

"Why aren't these people reacting?" I asked. "What's wrong with them?" Other than eating human flesh.

His cocktail of disdain and pleasure was vile. "Entranced. They're sheep. I couldn't entrance the little redhead, though. Annoying. Zip ties work just as well."

"I don't care what they are," I said. "What you are. Just give us the girl and the boy." Bob's troops would be on site any minute.

He nodded, a sage, considering my request. But he wasn't. This was some sick game, and it was delighting him. Why? Why wasn't he afraid of Larrimer's guns?

He flicked out a hand, and a river of silver quills bristled across Larrimer's chest. A grunt, then blood.

I gasped.

Lulu screamed.

Larrimer fell to one knee, guns steady.

I stepped in front of him. Tommy wouldn't hurt me. Except this creature wasn't my Tommy.

"Move away from the freak," he said.

"No."

Larrimer sagged against the backs of my legs and fired both guns. The bullets never reached Tommy, but the goon to my right fell. Then, Larrimer collapsed at my feet.

Tommy's shield had stopped the bullets. They lay on the floor, rolled sideways. What protected him? I saw nothing.

Tommy smirked, that same damned look when he'd won a game of Scrabble or done a triple flip.

Back then, I'd found his pleasure funny and endearing. Now, it was sick. He was sick. No. He was a monster.

"We adepts don't fear bullets," he said, with grating grandiosity.

Little taste here, Tommy? I forced myself not to glance at Larrimer, bleeding out at my feet. I chuckled. "Reading too much fantasy fiction, Tom?"

His face darkened. "You don't believe."

"In what, that you're an adept? C'mon." He only guessed at what I'd learned, had no idea what I could do.

I had to get Larrimer out of there. But I wouldn't leave without Ronan and Lulu. In one motion, I drew the knife from my boot and leapt, landing beside the boy.

"Ronan!" I slapped him. "Ronan!" He shook his head, as if awaking from endless sleep.

I moved to Lulu.

"Oh no, you don't, sweetness." Tommy waggled a finger, and as I reached for Lulu, I met resistance, like a viscous wall. Thorns of pain pierced my fingers. Panic twisted Lulu's face, and she shouted, "Clea!", but it was muffled, like she was underwater.

"Please join me, sweetness," Tommy said. "I want you with me. Imagine what we could do together."

I could. That was the problem. "In your dreams."

"That's the girl I remember!" he said with manic glee.

I groped for Lulu, or tried to, but the barrier held. Pain scoured my hands, moved to my wrists, my elbows.

"She's coming with me, sweetness. Until I have the chest."

Screams. Bursts of noise. Gunfire. The FBI!

"Ronan!" I said. "Ronan!"

The boy struggled, raised his head, blinked.

"Take Larrimer. Get out of here!"

But he reached for Lulu, and his body shook, his hands not penetrating the wall. And mine were frigging stuck inside it. Tears of pain sluiced down my face.

"Go!" I said. "The FBI are here. I'll bring her! Take him!"

Ronan scooped Larrimer up and lurched out of the room. And the diners kept eating, cocooned in the nightmare they'd brought unto themselves. The wages of sin.

The slime climbed higher, rising to my biceps, burning me, blistering me.

"You'll bring her?" Tommy said. "And how, sweetness, will you do that?" He glanced at his watch. "Three minutes. I am cutting it rather close, but oh, this is fun."

I absorbed the pain, goaded it, forced it to center my mind. "I *will*."

"No," he said. "She stays with me, and you will bring me the Chest of Bone. Find it! You don't want to join me? Fine. I'll trade. The girl for the chest."

His lips pulled back into a mockery of a smile, and he sauntered toward Lulu.

Closer. Closer. The pain in my arms expanded. Live it. Absorb it. Make it *mine*. Ten feet, nine, *now*. I went feral. Fireflies glittered, swirled in my palms, and dissolved.

CHAPTER THIRTY-SEVEN

Ohhh, poor Clea." Tommy paused. "**Can't make the** mojo happen, can you?"

What a flop! I tracked him as he closed on Lulu. My vision blurred, saw Larrimer broken, his blood, his essence draining away, dyingdyingdying.

Golden fireflies burst, cutting the slime, incinerating it, forming the feather and fan stitch. I aimed the torrent straight at Tommy.

Face frozen in shock, he stumbled back. But his shields held.

I grinned, didn't give a shit. I laughed, pure energy pouring from me, scorching, scything. I pressed harder, faster. More. I wanted more.

His shields cracked.

Yes!

Tommy's hands, a conductor's.

Lulu screamed, flew through the air.

She smashed into him, knocking him backward, but he clamped her to him, turned, and vanished.

I fisted my hands and raced after them, through the alcove—and into a wall.

I fell on my ass, stunned.

Tommy and Lulu were gone. *Gone.*

I leapt to my feet, groped for a handle, a clasp, anything. Fingers scraped the brick, clawed, punched, but the wall was solid. Tried to firefly. Nothing. Where the hell was the catch? None. I could find none.

An image of Larrimer choked my fury.

I swiped my bloody hands on my pants, ran to snag my purse, slung my FBI badge around my neck, and flew through the dining rooms. Agents swarmed, blurred as I passed. I flashed my badge over and over. No one gave me a second glance.

Bob. His momentary stare slid past me, my costume at last effective on someone.

Outside, chill air bit me. I paused. There, Ronan in the parking lot, talking to a young agent, waving frantic hands at the guy. I raced to him, waved my badge at the agent.

"He's with me," I said, thinking *time*, precious time.

"Sorry, Agent. No one can leave."

Shit!

Ronan gripped my arm. "Where's Lulu?"

I shook my head. "I'll bring her home. I will." I turned back to the agent. "Look, Ronan's my nephew. ASAC Balfour authorized it."

The agent held my badge, then flipped it around, checked my ID. Slow. So slow.

"I'm Special Agent Clea Reese. Out of Boston headquarters. ASAC Balfour will be most unhappy if you detain us." A confidential smile. "You know how he can get."

If he confirmed on his walkie-talkie to Bob, we were screwed.

"He's a kid," I said. "A high school kid. C'mon. He's hurting. "

Ronan managed to look hangdog, and the young agent made awkward noises.

I turned back toward the club, shook my head. "Ronan, let's go find Agent Balfour."

"Wait," the young agent said. A pause, then he flapped a hand.

He was letting us go.

"Thanks," I said. "I'll make sure the ASAC knows what a help you've been." I dragged Ronan away. "Where's Larrimer?"

"The car."

We raced to the Audi.

Larrimer, supine on the gravel, eyes closed.

I beeped the car open with the spare. "Hurry!"

"No hospital," came Larrimer's voice, rough and faint.

Oh James. "Put him in the back. Gently!"

Ronan heaved and slid Larrimer onto the seat.

A spike of fear. I'd seen guys talk a blue streak, then die. Larrimer. He wouldn't dare.

I tore off my shirt and wrapped it tight around his torso to stem the bleeding. Then I eased into the backseat, lifted his head and shoulders onto my lap. I handed Ronan the key. "Drive."

Moonlight spilled into the car, across his battered face. Larrimer lay like the dead, and I smoothed the hair from his forehead, threaded fingers through the midnight strands. My lips trembled.

There's no crying in baseball. No crying.

The car flowed forward. At each checkpoint, I showed my badge, and we passed. Once on the road, Ronan accelerated to a mighty thirty-miles-an-hour.

"Speed it up, Ronan."

"But I don't want to get a ticket."

"Gods save me," I said. "Faster. *Now.*"

I looked down at Larrimer, a faint smile on his face.

"James."

"No... hospital," he whispered hoarsely.

Deja vu, tables turned. "You're bleeding out. You need blood."

"Trust... me," he said. "Home. Trust..."

"James."

He went limp. He was out of his mind. He was dying. I knew the signs. But he'd asked me to trust him.

"Ronan," I said. "Back to Sparrow Farm."

"Are you—"

"Do it."

We zoomed up the driveway, jerked to a halt.

The mudroom door flew open. Bernadette, limned by the porch light, hair turbaned, eyes wild, derringer in hand.

She holstered her gun. "Do you know what time it is, cookie? You have school tomorrow!"

With great care, Ronan hoisted Larrimer into his arms.

I gripped her shoulders. "Larrimer needs your help. *James.* Your nursing skills. You're a nurse. Remember. Please remember."

Forehead creased, brows caterpillared, she stared for endless moments at the blood-drenched man.

Dammit, I would *drag* her back to reality. Fireflies glowed beneath my hands and around her shoulders.

She blinked furiously, her gaze snapping to my fireflies. Her eyes blazed with pleasure, then cooled.

"On the couch," she barked. "Wait. A sheet. More hygienic."

Thankyouthankyouthankyou.

Dogs prowled at our feet, silent for once as Ronan carried Larrimer into the living room.

Helpless. I was drowning, breath coming in gasps.

Bernadette spread a white sheet dotted with bluebells across the sofa, then Ronan lay down Larrimer, a groan slipping from his lips.

Bernadette slid a pillow beneath his head. "I'm going to get some things."

I knelt by Larrimer. Amidst the bloody bruises and cuts, his face was gray. Blood pooled on his chest.

Trust him, he'd said.

Was I a fool? Had I killed him?

"Lulu?" Ronan's voice broke.

"I *will* get her, Ronan. I failed. I know, but—"

"Didn't fail."

"James." I took his hand. "Why here?"

Bernadette reappeared.

His lips twitched a smile. "Needed the Lady's kind ministrations."

She glared at him, then me. "Well, are you just going to look at the man or are you going to help me fix him? Go wash your hands."

I ran to the kitchen. Pins flew as I ripped off the wig, now tipped in blood. *His* blood. I threw the wig into the trash, lathered my hands, and scrubbed.

"*Vite*, cookie!"

I moved. She'd already cleaned his face of makeup and blood, butterflied his facial wounds, and covered his legs and hips in my knit afghan. I knelt beside her.

"Where is that boy?" she asked.

"Ronan!"

"Stop the bleeding," Bernadette said, as if chanting to herself.

"Clean the wound. Probe for fabric. Sterile gauze."

Ronan appeared beside us.

"Now." Bernadette thinned her lips. "Clea, turn his head to the side, in case he has trouble breathing."

My fingers shook as I moved his head, brushed the hair aside at the back of his neck. A tattoo I'd never seen—a lightning bolt with a star at its end. Beautiful. I'd ask him about it when he...

"Ronan!" Bernadette pointed to the end of the couch. "Stand there. Can you hold his shoulders and arms still, boy? Careful, not too hard. Don't press, just restrain."

He looked terrified. "But."

"Now, please." When Bernadette used this tone, stronger men than Ronan folded.

He placed his arms across Larrimer's shoulders, his hands circling his wrists.

"Ready?" Bernadette said.

I ripped open his shirt, exposing his blood-soaked chest. Tommy's quills had vanished, leaving dozens of gaping holes.

Bernadette wiped away the blood. No fresh pooled.

\\She cleaned the area with Betadine, then with a nasty stainless steel tool she probed a hole. Larrimer's muscles flexed, but he didn't move. Ronan held on. In seconds, Bernadette pulled a shred of bloody cloth from the wound, released it into her tray.

Bernadette clucked. "Deep."

Again and again, she dug. He held rock still, but his pain scoured my senses.

She let out a sigh as she finally lay down the probe. "Hand me the Neosporin." She circled his wounds with the antiseptic.

"Clea, the sugar box."

She scooped sugar onto the wounds, keeping it inside the ointment circle. Was she still loopy?

She unwrapped several antiseptic bandages, smeared them with more Neosporin and placed them on his wounds. She sealed the bandages with tape and rocked back on her heels.

Larrimer lay limp, unmoving. I could barely sense him. My eyes burned as I wove my fingers through his hair.

"Get my heating blanket," she said.

We covered him with the blanket and plugged it in. She ran her hand across it. "Good. Warm. Going into shock will kill him."

When she struggled to stand, I took her elbow.

She gave me a wan smile. "I'm fine."

"I know you are," I said. "Sugar?"

Her eyes snapped. "Sugar and honey have been used to treat battle wounds forever. Have you forgotten I was a nurse in Vietnam?"

"No, ma'am," I said, like when I was ten.

She nodded, pursed her wrinkled lips. "Had to make do, since you failed to take the man to the hospital. Shame on you for bringing him here."

"He asked me to. I trust him," I said, voice firm.

"You're too trusting, cookie." She harrumphed. "I'm going to bake some buns."

Ronan watched over Larrimer while I got him a fresh t-shirt for later.

When I returned, Bernadette stood over him. "He's lost too much blood. Whatever hit him, his lungs, heart, liver..." She shook her head. "A shame, cookie."

She walked away.

I sat on the floor, holding his hand, watching his chest rise and fall, shallow, barely taking in air. My breaths synced with his, as if I could help fill his lungs, as if his next breath wasn't a hope, and I could make it a reality. He was far away, a mere wisp of life. Fading, fading.

Do not let this be. Please.

Grace curled up beside me and slept.

I warmed his hand, icy in mine, and rested my head against the couch.

How would I ever tell Bernadette about Tommy? He was her alpha and omega. I desperately tried not to picture what we once were to each other. But the slideshow continued.

I wished I'd never known him.

But of course, that was a lie.

My heart ached, that special place where Tommy always lived. It had been secure, safe, home. He'd loved me unconditionally. And I, him.

That was gone now, too, and the emptiness gaped black.

Time passed. Larrimer had lost too much blood, damaged too many vital systems.

Had science failed him? Was he truly shutting down? Ending? Had *I* failed him? Because I was too soft, felt too much?

Oh gods, *please*. I needed this man. I loved this man.

Like a flower waiting for the sun, the realization bloomed, beautiful and terrible. He could not die. Could. Not.

Resting my head on his hand, I dozed.

Barking dogs and Bernadette's, "Get up!" awakened me.

James. His face, serene, glassy, like a pond awaiting a pebble. He breathed. Deeper. Or was I imagining it?

"*Vite! Vite!*" she said from the kitchen.

I pushed to my feet. *Who?* Had Tommy come after us?

Voices shouting orders. A booming, "Wait for me."

Bob. *Shit.*

He couldn't find a vulnerable Larrimer. Okay, we had to keep Bob in the kitchen. He couldn't see through the half-wall to the couch.

I ran into the kitchen, smoothed my... damn! I was still in costume, and now it was covered in blood. "Stall him," I said to Bernadette. "I've got to change."

I flew upstairs. Had Ronan moved the rental car? A peek out my bedroom window. Gone. Garaged. Good boy.

As I whipped off my clothes, a knock at the back door, then voices. I scrambled into jeans and shirt, raced to the bathroom, scrubbed my face, poked fingers through my wild hair, forced myself to calmly walk down the stairs and into the kitchen.

"Bob!"

He stood by the counter talking with Bernadette. He looked exhausted. Vertical lines creased his face, the bags beneath his eyes smudged purple.

"Don't you look like crap," I said. "Come. Sit." I walked him to a chair at the kitchen table, one facing the mudroom. Risky, but riskier to leave him just standing there. "Ssshh. Not too loud. Ronan's asleep on the couch."

Bernadette bustled around. "So good of you to visit, Captain Balfour."

"Special Agent," we both said simultaneously.

"Special Agent, then." Her smile could have melted chocolate. "Can I get you some coffee? Tea? Scotch?"

He waved a hand. "Just coffee, Bernadette. And thank you."

"I'll have some, too."

A covert look of worry. "Of course. Let me take your coat, Captain."

Minutes later, she placed a carafe of coffee, milk, sugar, mugs, and a platter of cinnamon buns on the table. She vanished into the living room, sat by the woodstove and picked up her knitting. Just like anyone's sweet granny. Ha!

He frowned. "You were there tonight."

"Yes." Why wasn't he barking at me for going in on my own? For squirreling away Ronan?

Bob's hand drifted across the table and covered mine. "You could have been killed, Young Pup."

"But I wasn't, Old Man."

I moved my hand to reach for the carafe, poured him a mug, and did the same for myself. Where earlier I'd begged the powers-that-be for a movement, a word from Larrimer, now I pled for silence.

Bob swirled sugar and milk through his coffee, studying me. "So tell me about it."

One false step. *Hell.* I smoothed my face.

"I'm not sure you're going to believe this, but..." I recounted a much-edited version of the night's events, leaving out any mention of Larrimer and magic, my fireflies and the Chest of Bone. I explained The Master, sidestepping Tommy's name and all he meant to me. He'd use me as a wedge with Tommy and view Lulu as a side issue. Not gonna happen.

"I ran out of the place," I said. "Just as your people came in. I had to get Ronan out of there, to safety. He was already hurt and—"

"Hurt?"

"He'd been imprisoned and his girlfriend has vanished with a monster. He'd been compelled to eat that meat." My stomach flip-flopped.

He leaned back in his chair. "You were always tough, Clea, but ever since—"

"My breakdown? My panic attack? The doctor cleared me, something you seem to have conveniently forgotten. You're talking to Clea 2.0."

His eyes warmed. "So I see. Rest assured, we'll find this master and the girl."

They didn't have a prayer. "Could you open the brick wall behind the stage?"

He nodded. "There was some screwy secret latch. Took us a fucking half hour, which is why we lost him. This guy's got a payload of tricks. He's making buckets of money with his endangered animal scheme. Sick bastard, but clever. I'm surprised you didn't see that. You usually cotton on to things goddamn fast."

"Yes well, I admit it, I was scared. Everything got muddled."

His sympathy flowed over me, then sharpened. "And where was the mighty Larrimer in all of this?"

"He was going to come with me," I said. "But he got a call and said he had to go. Urgent business. He said he'd be gone for a couple of days."

"Is that so?" He stood. "I've got to talk to the kid."

CHAPTER THIRTY-EIGHT

You want to talk to Ronan?" I squeaked. Cleared my throat. "I'm sorry. He was exhausted, but he couldn't sleep. I gave him an Ambien. Ouch. Tomorrow?"

"*Now*, Clea. Even if—"

"I Shot the Sheriff" wailed from somewhere. *Shit.* Do I get Larrimer's phone? Shove Bob out the door?

And Bernadette appeared, fawning over the agent.

I jumped up. "My phone. Be right back."

I started to search Larrimer's pants. *Hell!* Of course it wasn't there, we'd taken the burners.

The damned song kept playing. Where?

I ran into my office, dove for the phone on the daybed. "Hello?" I asked, shooting for high and breathy.

"*Who* is this exactly?" said the woman.

I knew that voice, knew it from... *Holy shit.* Taka. Special Agent, my ass.

The identifier photo had shown a pixie-haired, lab-coated, black-lipsticked woman, glasses askew. Just like that trippy 3-D flash I'd gotten of her weeks ago.

I further enhanced my faux voice. "I'm sorry. Mr. Larrimer isn't here."

A pause, then, "I see. Have him call me ASAP."

Staying in character, I made sure to ask, "Who's calling?"

"He'll know." She disconnected.

Why was Taka calling Larrimer, and at three a.m.? I checked the phone's recent calls. Taka's call said DarkPool. What was *that*?

I powered down the phone. A haggard Bob sat in my kitchen. He was up to his neck in this sewage. How? And that "agent wanting to study me" bit. Yeah, right. Like I was a frigging lab rat.

Larrimer was their lab rat, too, except he wasn't following their protocols.

I collected myself, then returned to the kitchen table. I didn't sit.

"A friend," I said to Bob. "Saw a car come up our driveway. Wanted to see if we were all right. I checked on Ronan. The kid's out cold."

Bernadette tsked. "3:00 a.m. Terrible time to phone."

"They were worried about us, B," I said. "Bob, I'm exhausted. How about you give us a break?"

Bernadette stood. "A fine idea. I'm quite tired, too, dealing with that unfortunate boy. I'll get your coat."

Bernadette disappeared, and Bob rose. "I'll stay. That maniac could come after you."

"Thanks, but we're fine, Bob," I said.

He put his hands to his waist. "Now you listen, Young Pup, dangerous stuff's going down. You're out here in the middle of nowhere. You're not safe."

Shit on a shingle. Now what?

His phone rang, "Balfour." He frowned, nodded. "A tip. He's been spotted in Fantin, with the girl. It seems you'll get your way, after all. Take care."

I stood a far better chance of stopping Tommy and getting Lulu. I'd follow.

Bernadette reappeared and handed him his coat.

I smiled up at Bob, trying to ignore the acid tension souring my belly. "Thank you. Now, get that bastard."

"I'll come back out tomorrow."

"You needn't, Bob. You're exhausted, too." Me, all molasses and light.

"I'll be here."

After Bernadette closed the door, she turned to me wearing a Cheshire grin.

"What?" I reached for my keys.

"I like those, what do you call them, burner phones. Handy."

I didn't get it, and then the lightbulb lit. *"You* called in the tip."

Endless hours passed. Too many. Larrimer hadn't moved, hadn't awakened. At 6:00 a.m., I shrugged into my barn coat. Watery morning light streamed across the dooryard. Each day we gained a few minutes. A red squirrel spotted me and scampered off. Grace at my heels, I walked through the barn, feeding and watering our critters. I whistled for Clem, who frolicked in the pasture. He sensed spring was coming, too. Oh, not this week or next, but it always did, and with it, longer days, baby green leaves, the sounds of peepers, and an excess of mud.

I longed for it all, even the mud.

Damn. I'd scheduled the farrier to do Clem's hooves today. I'd reschedule, but, gee, it would be fun to mix her with Bob.

Finished up, I flicked off the lights and dragged my ass back into the house. Checked once more. James Larrimer still breathed.

I showered and dragged my sleeping bag to the living room, pushed the table away, and set it beside the couch. If he awoke, he'd need something.

Sleep eluded me, and I had this crackbrained idea. I sat up, placed my hands over his heart. He felt warm and real and alive. I called my fireflies. *Oh, pleasepleaseplease.*

Nothing. Either I was tapped out or not panicked enough. Who the hell knew. I lay back down, my busy mind fogged with exhaustion.

James stands tall beside me, a gun in each hand pointed at Tommy.

Tommy raises his hands, and a river of silver quills arcs toward James.

His face splits, his torso, his legs.

Blood, blood everywhere, splashing, frothing as the quills rip him apart!

His head rolls across the floor, comes to rest, eyes blank, mouth open, neck red and jagged with bone and flesh.

Nooooo!

I sat up, screaming, imagined James on his haunches, holding his side, shirt in tatters. I breathed a sob. Still dreaming.

Calloused fingers warmed my cheek. I held them there.

"Are you all right?" he asked.

That voice, honied granite. Eyes burning, I blinked twice. Real. "Yes. Yes. Sit before you keel over."

A grin. "Still giving orders?" He eased onto the sofa and stretched out his legs.

"Absolutely." I sat beside him, nuzzled my face close to his. He felt so good. *So* good. I settled. "You shouldn't be up, you're—"

"I'm fine." He frowned. "Getting there. Thank you for the trust."

"Okay. Now, how are you really feeling?"

He grimaced. "Like shit, but I'll live."

I skimmed my fingers along his jaw. "Nanotechnology at its finest." Arctic stillness.

Stupid, stupid mouth. I leaned closer and nipped his ear. "I'm glad you're tough."

"Comes in handy."

"Bob was here. He's coming back today."

"Fuck."

"I agree." Time to tell the tale. "Tommy's The Master. My Tommy."

He nodded. "I heard as much before I passed out."

The ache in my chest grew as I filled in the blanks. Like I was betraying my best friend. My emotions better catch up to my brain. Instead, the ache grew. "Tommy wants to trade Lulu for the chest. And he wants me."

His face tightened. "He can't have either."

"I don't care what the thing does..."

"No."

Except, it was the only thing that would placate him. If that. I churned with scenarios of how to deceive Tommy. He was too sharp, too canny. His power terrified me. His shield. Those silver quills. He'd frozen me for long minutes in that goo. Had he been trying to kill me, I'd be dead.

Somehow, some*when*, Tommy had tapped into the magic retwining with the real world. What did "real world" mean anymore?

How many years had Tom known about the magic? When had he learned? He'd have practiced, hard. He was methodical, my Tom.

As a freshman, when he'd been cut from the basketball team, he'd been so hurt. Afterwards, he'd shot baskets, endless baskets, and as a sophomore, become their star point guard. I admired his doggedness, yet he'd never meshed with the team, always held a germ of a grudge from that original cut.

How hard must he have worked to fake his own death?

What I'd never seen, or, what I'd refused to acknowledge, was how his determined streak could bleed to obsessive, his unyielding notes to pitiless, his perception of some people as beneath him. His ability to lie—to me, to Bernadette, to *himself*—when it came to what he wanted. Perhaps those behaviors stemmed from the loss of his parents, the way they'd left him with his grandmother one day and disappeared. That sense of abandonment could warp a child. Or maybe it was just *him*, hardwired into who he was. I didn't know.

Yet loving him back was like breathing.

"Clea," Larrimer said. "Where did you go?"

His eyes filled with concern, his worry undid me. My eyes burned.

He pulled me onto his lap and folded me into arms warm and strong.

The burning turned to tears, and became a torrent. "He's done horrible things. Terrible. Because with me, he always loved. Unreserved, fierce, loyal. No one, not Bernadette, not even Dave, loved me as Tommy did."

And I couldn't stop crying for a loss more devastating than when I'd seen him "die" in that copter.

When I finally wound down, Larrimer's tattered shirt was damp, and a quiet sort of numbness smoked through me.

Last night, my fireflies had affected Tommy. But they hadn't brought death, not when his resurrection was so new to me. I'd held back, too.

When I fireflied, I'd begun to note subtle differences, the distinctions controlled by my emotion. To draw a thing to me. To protect. To attack. To kill.

The path was clear, but I hunted for a way out. Like a rabbit caught in a leg-hold trap, the only escape—to gnaw off my leg.

I must, I *would* kill Tommy.

He'd never see it coming. I was the only one who could get that close to him.

Here I was, contemplating ending yet another life. A third life. No other way. All exits blocked. No escape route. Tommy would die. And so, most probably, would I.

Larrimer couldn't know. He'd try to shield me, and Tommy would end him. Alive, he'd keep Lulu safe. Bernadette, too. *He* would be safe. To do this, to kill Tom, I needed to know James lived.

"What's going on in that twisted mind of yours, babe?" Larrimer said.

I took a deep, stuttering breath, and smiled. "Nothing too diabolical. Tommy's a master of some kind of magic. He built a wall of ooze that contained me. It hurt. Until I fireflied." I looked up. "I wish you'd seen them. They were amazing. Fierce."

"I wish I'd seen them, too."

Those probing eyes saw too much. "Tommy will get in touch with us. With me."

"He said that."

"No, but he will."

"What about telling Bernadette?"

The pressure hurt. "No, I can't. Can't tell her what he is, what he's become. Her mind, it's better. She fixed you up."

He raised an eyebrow. "Did I imagine sugar?"

"Nope." I pushed the button on my phone. "Geesh, it's one in the afternoon."

"You had a good nap, until the end."

I smiled. "Yeah, the ending's always a bitch. Oh dear, Ronan." I started to get up.

His arms tightened. "Still sleeping. Bernadette's in her room. I was on my way to take a shower."

I pictured him showering, wished I could join him.

He leaned forward and kissed me. He tasted of salt and honey and *him*. His mouth moved gently, but I felt his storm.

I wanted more, and I ran my tongue over his lips, combed my fingers through his hair. He held me to him. Rock hard. Solid. Divine.

All while my thoughts devised ways to kill my best friend. I slipped from Larrimer's embrace and off his lap.

He cupped my face. "What?"

"You had a phone call around three this morning. I answered. Sorry, but it came when Bob was here. A woman. She sounded annoyed. She said you'd know who she was."

He ran a finger down my cheek. "Did you tell her who you were?"

"No."

"Good."

Secrets and lies, words knit like an intricate lace shawl, obscuring the truth.

A quick kiss, and he stood. "After I shower, mind if I borrow the

Tahoe, er, Fern?"

"You can't drive yet."

The eyebrow again. "But I can."

"What's DarkPool? I thought Fish and Wildlife was—

His eyes flared, then cooled. "I'll explain when I get back from town. Promise."

Hours later, I was alone for the first time in what felt like centuries. Outside, I threw my knives, then I trotted to the cellar, slipped on my gloves, worked my kickboxing routine.

Punch, kick, punch, punch, kick. Muscles liquefied, gliding into the familiar, and I sank into the zone of dancing and movement, then segued into my ballet workout. I flew.

The world felt near normal. Ronan at practice. Bernadette going to her bridge club. Larrimer off to Boston.

Yet I walked on quicksand, reality having become a capricious thing.

Tommy controlled his power. I could control *him*.

I rested my hands on my knees, panting.

No. That way led to madness.

I trotted upstairs.

Time to stop stalling and find the chest.

Showering again, I pictured Lulu in that indigo satin dress, felt her anguish, her blazing hope when she saw me, her terror *for* me. And her horror as Tommy trapped her in his arms.

Ronan felt that same pain. He adored her, and she, him. She admired him, too. Trusted him.

Ronan *was* a special young man.

Humming with hope, I snagged a pair of nitrile gloves, walked to the room at the end of the balcony, and turned the knob.

The tiny bedroom—all lodge plaids and bear lamps—was dressed with military precision. For such a big fellow, Ronan didn't take up much space. A few pair of jeans, along with several button-downs and t-shirts hung in the closet. His hockey gear, some doodads, a PlayStation. That was it.

At the end of the bed sat one of our seamen's trunks. I lifted the arched lid. His duffle bag lay inside. I unzipped it.

A tool-sized box, maybe a foot long by six inches high, sat inside.

All nerves, I slipped on the gloves and pulled my scuffed find out of the bag. Made from red leather, the lid bore the letters DC in faded gold. I traced them with my fingers.

I carried the box to my room and sat it on my bed, feeling as if it were a snake about to strike. If this thing was so powerful, would monsters leap for my throat when I opened it?

The box felt good beneath my hands. This was Dave's. He'd used it, loved it, cared for it.

I unsnapped the brass fittings. Would anything pounce out and get me? I took a couple breaths and lifted the hinged lid.

Nothing leaped. Or even hissed. The box's top tray, lined with red felt and stained with ink, was filled with calligraphic pens. Some with what looked like ivory handles and brass or gold nibs. The divided tray also held assorted sized and shaped nibs, some dabbed with dried ink. Lulu had entrusted her father's calligraphy box to Ronan. Smart.

I lifted the tray out, and found a row of inks in glass bottles and three glass vials with colored powders inside—green and red and blue. Small sheets of blotting papers lay against the side of the box. Sure, this could be it.

The final test.

I drew off a glove, felt the brush of magic.

The door banged open. Knife in hand, I whipped around.

CHAPTER THIRTY-NINE

L**arrimer, gun drawn, crouched in the doorway.**

"Shit." He straightened, then tucked the gun behind his back. "I could've shot you."

"Really." I snorted. "Who else would be in my bedroom? Paranoia anyone?"

He nodded at my knife, and I slipped it back into my boot. "Point taken."

Laugh-lines crinkled as laughter tugged at his lips.

My breath hitched. This complex man held my heart. He'd never hurt me, not intentionally. But he could destroy me.

I turned away.

"Clea?" He walked into the room.

"How was your meeting?" I slipped my gloves back on.

"Interesting." He strode to the bed as if tethered. His scarred hand traced the case's open lid. "The Chest of Bone."

"I believe so." We'd talked about the chest, but I hadn't told him its full name. I stood. "You know the Chest of Bone because...?"

He lifted a bone-handled pen. "So this is what it's all about. Pretty unimpressive." After long moments, he looked up at me. "I have to take it."

I snapped the lid closed and stood, glared at him. "What? No way."

He held my gaze. "Why are you holding your knife, Clea?"

I glanced down. I hadn't realized I was. "Oh."

"And you'd gut me for some chest?"

"Yes." Not exactly the truth.

"Christ, you're insane." He nipped my lower lip.

"Ow!"

"Of course you wouldn't, but you talk a good game."

"Screw you. I mean, really, I'm not kidding."

He licked the lip he'd just bitten. "Yum. You're delicious when you're fired up. Babe, you don't have it in you to kill someone without provocation. You're too gentle for that."

"My ass I am," I said.

"And you do have an adorable one."

That voice, it sizzled with heat. "Off topic. It's our trade for Lulu. This is what Tommy wants." *Which is what he'll* think *he's getting, before...*

"Put the knife away, sit down, and we'll figure this out."

I locked the chest in my trunk, then sat on the bed, legs folded, leaning against the headboard. Larrimer took the foot, and I gave him a pillow to soften the footboard's hardness. That amused him, too.

He pulled off his boots and dropped them to the floor.

"Red socks?" I asked.

"I like red. So shoot me." He stretched out his legs, surrounding me.

I flipped my knife, caught it, flipped, caught it, flipped...

Larrimer blurred, and he was on his knees in front of me, handing me my own knife, a smart-alec smile on his face.

"Wiseass. The chest is powerful, dangerous. Why do you want it? You're many things, Larrimer. Power hungry isn't one of them."

"What happened to 'James?'"

"I'm seriously pissed."

"I can see that. It's cute."

"*Gods.*"

A long pause, then, "The people I work for. They instructed me to get it."

I masked my shock. "Obviously not Fish and Wildlife. DarkPool?"

"Yes." He did his Iron Man thing and closed up tight.

"From the beginning?"

"Yes. DarkPool is a military-for-hire corporation. Security services, private investigations, with an arm in technology and the sciences, as well. I was working for them when I was blown up."

What a fool I was. A clueless fool. I laughed. If I didn't, I'd cry.

Finally, the truth. How much more was there?

I locked the bedroom door. "I need to know. Everything, dammit," I said, voice cold.

He seeped pain.

"Your wounds hurting?" I asked.

A bitter laugh. "No. Hell no. Only you, Clea. It's always been only you."

Words threatened to bubble out. I mustn't. I rubbed my chenille bedspread, back and forth.

Silence.

"Waiting," I said in a sing-song voice.

He inhaled a breath, deep and long. "Twelve years ago, two researchers messing around—"

"Messing around?"

"I don't know what the fuck else to call it. Not my thing. These two DarkPool geeks noticed energy anomalies popping up around the world. Think small volcanic bursts."

"So this isn't about the recreation of you?"

"Not directly. They sent a team to investigate, and, much as they despised their findings, they concluded the rifts were pockets of magic." He chuckled. "They don't use that term. Their scientists came onboard and termed them Unnatural Energy Anomalous Incursions. They could quantify them, but failed to understand them. Believe me, they tried. Now, they're paranoid and scared. So DarkPool got into bed with the government. They call their consortium The Union. They began mapping these, what they call, incursions. I've seen the Las Vegas-style map on the wall. High-tech. Colors. Razzle-dazzle. Looks like a neon sign. The colors move constantly.

"They keep trying to grasp the magic. They continue to fail. Which scares the shit out of them. They've used those who possess it—Fae, the wyvern, others—but they can't create it. They've succeeded in tracking these anomalies across the world. Places of eruption. That mess in Sedona was one."

"A disaster. I saw the footage."

"The Golden Eagles were another. The Great Victoria Desert."

"Where's that?"

"Australia, by the Nullarbor Cliffs. Overnight, five thousand acres of flowers appeared."

"Flowers?"

He nodded. "Tulips and orchids and gardenias carpeted the desert. Right after a pocket of magic exploded."

"Wow."

"Not just places and events." His voice hardened. "People, too."

"People."

"Your friend, Dave. A bright incursion. He was magicked to death. Something black and evil sucked the life out of him."

The clarity of it hurt. "Tommy."

"Yes. I'm sorry. You're not immune, Clea."

"I never thought I was."

I stared at the seemingly everyday calligraphy box. Of course, The Union wanted the chest. I bet they were dying to distill the magic down to zeros and ones. Then recreate it, manipulate it, control it. Hadn't they done just that with the earth's resources? Gluttony and greed at its finest.

Could magic be deconstructed, catalogued, categorized? Did humans even have the tools?

The magic needed to be protected, cared for, so we didn't mess it and ourselves up.

Tommy, The Union—two different aspects of the same Janus face.

"And you?" I asked.

"My remaking was connected to the project. I'm their creature."

The urge to lay a hand on his thigh, to comfort, almost undid me.

"Six weeks ago," he said. "They handed me this mission. My cover, the endangered species threat, which was real, and one they suspected was connected to all of this. I was to find the Chest of Bone and bring it in."

I closed my mind to all that meant. "How did they learn the name of the chest?"

He shrugged. "From the Fae who reanimated me. Or it could be another from the other side."

"The magic side."

"Yes. He may have taken one of The Union there. My handler—"

"You mean, Taka."

He ran a finger down his temple. "Yes." Strong. Cool. Dispassionate.

"Go on," I said.

"Their instruments can't read the chest."

"Anouk said it changed, being so long in the mundane world."

"Or maybe it's shielded, much like the Fae taught me to shield." He paused, quirking a smile. "I can feel you sometimes, probing my mind."

"You're the song, aren't you? The shadow?"

His brows scrunched.

"When we met in the Feed and Seed. The watcher when Taka and Bob first came here."

"My clever Clea. I needed to do recon on my own. They told me little."

As if he were some unthinking machine.

"At the store, that was the first time I felt your magic," he said. "It astonished me."

"Outside the house and again, at Mt. Auburn."

"Yes. I felt your fear and cursed myself for being too late." He leaned forward and his thumb grazed my lower lip. "My poor little Mage, how you've hurt. I promised myself I'd protect you, keep you safe."

I would not cry. "I'm not anyone's poor little anything."

"No, you're not. I was called in today because you've gone off the charts. You're a blazing star on their fucking map."

The Union was tracking me, trapping me. Like an animal.

My face must have shown something, because he moved up the bed to settle beside me. I wouldn't look at him, no way.

He caught my chin and turned my head to face his. "I won't let them get to you. I promise this. They will never have you."

I imagined myself—their personal Ms. Magic in the bowels of a tech-flavored hell, picked over, tested, probed by faceless beings in white coats. No, not faceless. By Taka.

"I've got you, Clea," he said.

I searched those Pacific blue eyes. "Do you?" Whispered words. "I won't give you the chest."

His look, all resolve and desire and... more. His arms moved around me, and he pulled me close. "Yes. Always."

My mask cracked. This was real. He was real. His heart beat beneath my palm, his body warm and comforting, his scent honey and pine. What he said, his feelings, that was truth.

Everything else was just white noise.

He pulled me to him and kissed me, just the way I liked. I softened, felt his lips tease, then he deepened the kiss. His tongue entered my mouth, and I answered with mine. Kissing, touching, he eased me back, to where I lay stretched out, his torso atop me. I ached, and I rubbed against him. We kissed and stroked until I was dizzy, his hardness straining against his jeans, pressing my mound, my cleft. I moaned, wanting to feel him, needing him touching me, all of me, his skin hot on mine.

"Your wounds," I said.

"I'm fine. Count on it."

I snuck my hands beneath his t-shirt, and my fingers glided over warm, hard muscle. He tore his shirt off and tossed it. His pants, too. I did the same. And we were naked, and I could feel all of him, his warmth, his hunger, his song.

Gods, he felt good. My nipples ached, and my cleft throbbed, and his hands moved, and his tongue laved my breasts, his mouth greedy, sucking. He nipped, and pricks of pleasure arrowed down me.

I needed. "More, James, more."

And then my hips were in his hands, and he spread my legs and kissed me there, where I needed it most. His tongue, piercing, penetrating, sucking, flicking back and forth across my clit.

I scraped my nails down his back, and he growled. I'd wanted this for so long, this man, inside me.

He raised his head, eyes wild, a Pacific storm. "Now, Clea."

"Gods, yes."

He kissed me again, there, and then he slid up me, his heat scorching my skin, his weight—delicious. And he took my lips as his cock probed my entrance and he slowly, evenly dug into me.

The song. Our song. There it was.

I was so high. *Move, move.*

I arched, but he paused, not inside me yet, not all the way, and I wanted him deep, deep, slamming into me hard, moving.

Then he stilled, petting me, nibbling my neck, licking my breasts, sucking, and I touched him everywhere, his carved arms, his broad back, desperate. I needed him deeper.

I wanted him so damned much. "James."

He started to move and with each undulation, he thrust deeper, and oh gods, he felt fine. So fine. My fingers wove through his long, black hair, and I kissed his lips, his face, his neck, anything, everything. He tasted of salt and honey and *him*. And it wasn't nearly enough.

And he thrust.

A moan slipped from my mouth, and he pounded hard and heavy, over and over, our song blending, complementing, heightening. Fast, oh, so fast, and I met him, again, and again, and the world spun, the song crescendoed, and my heart spiked, faster and higher and...

I splintered, the release, oh, gods, yes, I came, my back arching as surge upon surge of orgasm bathed me in pleasure.

A gasp, one breath, and then another. I couldn't move, didn't want to move, but I had to kiss him again, savor his musk of sweat and honey, our song's coda. I licked him. Oh, so yummy.

"Killer," I said.

"Lethal."

"You didn't come."

Through harsh breaths, he replied, "Still savoring."

And he shifted, just a touch, a feather. Mmmm. Divine. I smiled. Okay, I grinned like a bastard.

"More," he said.

"Oh yes."

Eyes never leaving mine, he moved inside me, slow and steady, a metronome of power, the smoke of pleasure curling again within me, and the slickness of him, the sweat of him, again and again and again, so even, so measured, and I spiraled tight, tighter, until he barked his release, and he didn't stop, but kept thrusting, pounding, and I fractured a second time. And I held him fast as we rocked in sweet satisfaction, panting like runners, high, so high.

"My Clea," he said, voice hushed and rich. "Mine."

I ran my hands up his slick back to curl them around his neck, fingers toying with his sweat-dampened hair. My senses opened, and, his shields down, I drank in his satisfaction, his joy.

And our song, that harmonic resonance I'd first heard weeks ago— us, together, sang with synergistic beauty.

He went to move off me, but I refused to let go, relished his weight atop me, his sweat mingling with mine, legs entangled, bodies slick. He rolled us, so we lay side by side.

"James," I said.

"Clea."

He kissed me. And we lay together until our breathing slowed. I nestled in the crook of his shoulder, my hand mapping his face, his petting my back, for long, long moments, one after another after another.

Sounds of a car pulling into the dooryard. Bernadette. Ronan. I didn't care. Not one little bit.

I would stay like this forever.

"Clea!" came the voice from downstairs, minutes later.

Shit. Bob.

"If only I could end the bastard." Larrimer squeezed me tight, as if I'd disappear.

"I'm not going anywhere, James."

"Never go."

"Bob knows about The Union, doesn't he?" I asked.

"Too much. He's in it thick."

"Clea!" Bob said.

We peeled apart.

"To be continued," I said.

"Yes."

"Down in a minute," I yelled as I flew into my clothes, found a rubber band, and corralled my sweat-sticky mop into a ponytail. Time to buy some scrunchies.

I turned to Larrimer, his gorgeous self sprawled on the bed, a luscious feast. "Stay here. And behave."

He laced his hands behind his head and gave me a shit-eating grin.

I had to kiss him, just had to, and then I zoomed out the bedroom door, closed it behind me, and trotted down the stairs.

"Hey, Bob," I said as I walked into the kitchen, intensely aware of how he'd betrayed our friendship.

He gaped. Okay, maybe I looked like I'd just had the hottest sex of my life. I smiled, going for casual.

"Did you get him? Lulu?" I asked, though I knew he hadn't. I pushed my hands into the back pockets of my jeans.

"No." He looked me up, then down. "Where's the kid?"

"At school. You want some coffee?"

"Sure." His nostrils flared, and I poured.

Oh, the vibes. Bob was not a happy camper. Good. He swiped at his face. He hadn't shaved. Bob always shaved. "What's up?"

He tented his hands and studied me.

He knew something was off. *By the way, Bob, I just had mad, crazy sex. Can you tell?* "Did you learn anything from people at the club?"

A flush blotched his face. No need for the visual aid. I felt his fury just fine.

"The ones eating the exotic meat gave us a little. All useless. Those dining on humans, disgusting."

I would not picture it. And there it was—in 3D.

"They're zombies," he said.

Thank the gods Ronan wasn't. Zombies? "You mean, real—"

"Of course not." He gave me a "you're losing it" look. "The diners in the first room knew squat. Those in the second and third rooms, they're cows. Memories wiped, minds asleep. Lie detectors, threats, we got nothing. The waiters, hired help. Crumbs. All we got are fucking crumbs. However he did it, the guy's good. Even the three goons that were packing couldn't remember who hired them. Long rap sheets, so they're not going anywhere."

"I saw more than three of them," I said.

"In the wind, for now. We'll find them."

I got a mug of coffee, held it up. "More?"

He shook his head.

"Roberto?" I asked. "He wore a tux with a red cummerbund. Round. Florid featured."

He nodded. "Dead. What else can you tell..." His voice trailed off.

Larrimer stood at the foot of the stairs. The man could move like a leopard. He was taunting Bob on purpose, damn him.

Larrimer prowled toward us. Unruffled. Groomed. Menacing. At least, he'd put on clothes.

"Oh, hi," I said. "How was your nap?"

He grinned, all white teeth and satisfaction. "Refreshing."

Bob almost leapt from his chair.

I still had my knife. I could just throw it and wipe the damned smile off Larrimer's face. I swear he could read my mind, because his smile widened.

Bob emitted a sound between a growl and a bark. Larrimer snarled back.

And the testosterone match escalated.

I snatched my keys off the hanger and slipped out the door.

CHAPTER FORTY

I could drive to T-Rox blindfolded. Tommy and I had named the place in grammar school, a secret spot where two dino-sized rocks kissed, and we'd leave each other notes there. Stuff we didn't want anyone else to see. He'd remember. Time to speed things up. Today, I'd leave a new one.

I flipped open the glove compartment and searched for the pad and a pen. Urgency dried my throat.

The world shimmered. Tears, about to slip out. Screw that. I wouldn't cry, not like some sappy eight-year-old whose doll had been stolen by a bully girl.

Tommy had rescued my doll, Brenda. Why had I named her Brenda? After that incident, Tommy taught me how to fight.

I was his Clea.

My palm slammed against the steering wheel. Angry, heavy. Hopeless.

The Master had to die. And my fireflies were the only way I saw to kill him. My Tommy was dead already. Except I was glad he was alive, that he still breathed the same air as I.

I finally admitted the truth. When I killed Tommy, I might die, too.

I swiped the back of my hand across my cheek. So I was crying. So what.

The dirt road I drove lumped and bumped for a mile. When I found the right spot, I pulled to the side, wrote the note, and got out.

Immense silence wrapped me in its arms. Oh, how I loved the woods in winter, the way they comforted me like a hand-knit sweater. I could think, reason, fantasize, explore.

The air was still, as if waiting.

Damn! *Stop stalling!*

I walked down the sleepy, snow-laden path. But the woods told me spring was coming, the bear, the chipmunk, the chickadee would have more food. Plants would push from the earth, their yearly miracle. Sounds would amplify, the rustle of leaves, the chitter of foxes, the clatter of squirrels. Not yet, but soon. Today, my breath still puffed mist and my footsteps crunched snow.

Soon, glorious spring. Would I see it?

The giant granite outcropping, T-Rox, reared just ahead.

A man materialized before me. I backpedaled. As tall as Larrimer, but slender. Jeans, a fitted tee, long braided hair the color of wheat, a faint smile on his long face. And pointed ears. Hello, Mr. Spock. Except—whoa—when he tilted his head, I glimpsed small, pearlescent horns protruding from his skull.

I held up my right hand, palm out.

He stepped forward and took it in his. "No need for that."

Angelic voice. "You're not an angel, are you?"

"No. Better." He reached for my hair, held a long dreadlocked curl on his palm. "You might be Mage, but the Fae in you is strong, too."

I swallowed. "Oh." Could I *be* any more witty? "You can teleport."

"Yes."

"Can all Fae?"

"No."

Well, this was stupid. "What do you want? Are you here to kill me? Take me to The Union?"

"No."

He sure talked like Spock. "I see you're a Fae of many words."

His silver eyes warmed. "Taka called you a viper. I find you delightful."

I jerked back, gathered and unfurled my senses. A strange vibe, one that sang somewhere deep inside me. I sensed no violence. Then again, I'd been wrong before. "So, why are you here?"

He smiled, all sunshine and rainbows. Gods, I'd be seeing unicorns next. Were unicorns real? Shit, off track again.

He sat on a flat rock warmed by the sun. In idiotic mode, I followed.

"To answer your questions, Clea," he said. "My power's faded, been stolen, here in the mundane. I no longer can transport others. Since I now consider The Union my enemies, I don't plan to kill you."

"Gee, that's reassuring. How did you find me?"

"I followed you. It wasn't hard."

He turned his head toward me, and, no, he didn't sparkle. Not much, anyway. Those horns... and out popped, "Can I touch them?"

He shrugged and bent his head.

I reached up and delicately touched the tips of my fingers to one horn.

"Tickles," he said.

I snatched my hand away, the horn's warmth lingering on my fingertips. "Why—" I superglued my lips.

"Why horns?" Those silver eyes laughed. "Very old Fae begin to grow them. In mundane terms of time, very slowly. They're a source of pride, in fact. Since my power has faded, mine have diminished."

The fury pulsing from him literally hurt and snapped me back to the now. "I'm sorry about the horns, about what The Union did to you. Why are you here?"

"I wanted to see you, to see what all the fuss was about."

Ah, that explained everything. Not. But there was more. There was always *more*. "You know my name. What's yours?"

"I loathe when people mispronounce it, which you would. Call me Charlie."

"That's... nevermind. You wanted to see me. So here I am."

He again took a lock of my hair. "You're not like her, yet you are."

"Who?"

He shook his head. "That's forbidden by our queen."

Oh damn. Just damn. "Well, you've seen me. Now go away. I have stuff to do."

He laughed. Swear to gods it sounded like bells tinkling. "I'm glad I amuse you.

"They have no idea who and what you are. None. I have something for you." He pulled out a black knife, all one piece and shiny. "Give it to the man you call lover. Only he."

How the hell did he know that? "Why?"

"It will help him in battle." He tweaked my hair and released it. "He's my child. I gave him the spark of life."

"You're—"

"Yes. James Larrimer. He was my first. I was promised, the last. They lied. Like the wyvern, they drained me. Almost dry. And for that, I despise them."

It sounded horrible. His sorrow and hatred bruised my heart. "Will you get your power back?"

"Perhaps."

His enigmatic smile chilled me. Even so, I couldn't stop myself from asking, "Why? Why did you help them at all?"

"Because we're all fools at one time or another. Be careful, little Clea Artemis. Guard your heart." He nodded toward me. "Our type of Fae, we tether for life, when our sparks harmonize, they sing the same song."

Larrimer and I. Our song. Images of what was and what could be careened through my mind. "What kind of Fae?"

"In your language, a protector. It's in our blood, in our bones, in our soul. That's why the Union chose Larrimer, you see, expecting his Fae spark to resonate with *you*."

Which it had. "He knew," I said.

"No. He did not. The Union understands nothing of the actual tether—your song, Clea. "Resonate" and "harmonize" are two similar, yet different aspects of our spark. Yours and Larrimer's and mine resonate. Yours and Larrimer's alone harmonize, one with the other."

Dear gods.

He smiled, and it was grim. "A grave mistake by The Union, one which, perhaps, may ultimately be their downfall." His sideways glance cut deep. "Or his."

"You gave him the spark. Why don't I harmonize with you, too?"

His face stiffened to porcelain perfection. His bitter chuckle, the brush of leaves on the wind. "Because I am changed. I also suspect each spark received is somewhat altered by that person's soul essence. Plus, Larrimer is *more*."

The wyvern. And in so many other ways. "Yes, he is. The spark thing still bugs me."

He spread his arms wide. "This is all new territory. These Mundanes interfering, acquiring, *corrupting* magic. It sucks."

"Are you immortal? Is he?"

"Not entirely." He shrugged and vanished.

I jerked to my feet. Well, *hell*. I wished I could poof, too. Talk about

TMI and NEI, too much and not enough, at the same frickin' time.

"Know this," came Charlie's disembodied voice. "If I die, so will he."

"Thanks for the PS, Charlie!" I screamed.

I thumped back onto the flat rock where we'd sat, a knife in one hand and my crushed note to Tommy in the other, too stunned to move.

Long minutes later, I got my act together. All righty then. A few steps, and I again stood in front of T-Rox. A bright yellow piece of paper peeked from the join of the two rocks. I withdrew it.

My Dearest Clea, I knew you'd come.

I slammed my back to the cold rock, scanned the woods. Shame on me. I'd been so intent on the Fae, I hadn't paid attention. His men could be lurking. *He* could be lurking. Fool.

Yes, as Charlie aptly said, we're all fools sometimes.

But no, I was alone. This battle had boiled down to just the two of us. I knew it, and so did he.

I sighed, and continued to read.

Tomorrow. 10:00 a.m. at The Bridge. I'll bring the girl. You bring the chest. Fair trade. Be alone, sweetness. Tommy

I fisted the note I'd brought him.

I'd written almost exactly the same thing.

I wish I was more clever. I am fairly bright, but my mind isn't as devious as I'd like. I could deceive, lie, even, but clever eluded me. I had to go AWOL from Ronan, Bernadette, and most definitely, James.

So I came up with a really dumb plan. It was the best I had. Sue me.

When I arrived back home, Larrimer walked outside to greet me sporting a lovely black eye. It added a mean exclamation point to his healing yellow and purple bruises. My imagination supplied what Bob must look like.

Watching Larrimer saunter toward me, lips twitching to an almost-smile, eyes heavy lidded and bright, happiness bloomed.

Just him. Just the sight of him. It occurred to me that I felt that bloom when he walked into a room or when I watched him from a window as he worked on some task. His mere presence offered a quiet comfort and joy.

Such an odd emotion. Such a welcome one.

Ronan waved from the window, and I could smell what had to be a Bernadette Special—prime roast and Yorkshire pudding, horseradish potatoes and buttered asparagus, pumpkin ravioli and mushroom strudel—I'd bet to commemorate Larrimer's amazing recovery. Oh gods, the scent of pecan pie. Heaven. She was mostly back with us. Score one for good news.

Later, bellies full, and after Bernadette trundled to bed around eight, Larrimer and I talked to Ronan, vowing again to find Lulu. We watched as the tormented boy plodded his way up the stairs, shoulders bowed, Mutt and Jeff following close on his heels.

"I'm going to shower," Larrimer said, face stoic, but eyes a challenge.

A sly grin. "Sounds dangerous."

"One could say treacherous."

"Oh dear. I wouldn't want you to get hurt."

"Nor I."

"I'll be sure to protect you."

Once he disappeared, I ran to the barn, found a padlock, and dashed to lock the bulkhead. I raced back to the house, where Grace whoofed an exuberant hello, as if I'd been gone for three hours, not three minutes.

Clothes doffed, I shrugged on my sleep shirt and forced myself to casually walk down the hall.

And there was Bernadette, peeking out of her room.

"Hey," I said, all blasé.

"Where are you going?"

Ah, the drill sergeant. "To the bathroom."

"Agent Larrimer's in there."

In for a penny. "He is."

She mimed zipped lips.

Was nothing normal anymore?

"Nice eye, James," I said as he soaped me.

"One lucky punch."

Since he hadn't mentioned a body bag, I assumed Bob survived.

As we showered, his psyche sparkled. I'd never sensed him so lighthearted. He laughed when Grace scratched at the door.

"She's jealous," he said.

I ran my hands across his beautiful body. Scars in varying sizes mapped his flesh, and I kissed as many as I could find until he lifted my chin and took me in a kiss that curled my toes. Long moments later, I touched his new scars, raised and red, from Tommy's quills, reminding me of tomorrow and what was to come.

"Clea?" He frowned.

"I hate that he hurt you." I lifted my hands to his broad shoulders, down his muscled back, over his ass, relishing his hard erection pressed between our bodies.

"I've been hurt worse." His eyes ate me up. "You're so beautiful."

I wasn't, but hey, if he saw me that way...

He slipped his hand between us, down to cup my mons, and one finger pressed against my clit. I moaned.

"Good?" he asked.

"Oh yes," I rasped. "In the best way possible."

He moved that one finger, and I threw back my head, the spray of water cascading down my face. I groaned, and the slough of his breath touched my neck just before he bit it. I yelped, laughed. He pulled me closer still.

I desperately wanted him inside me, ached for it. Tomorrow wasn't here yet. I wasn't gone yet. And I needed this night and James. Us. I wanted this wonderful, impossible man to know all the passion, all the care, all the tenderness I felt for him. I wanted us to be together, not alone, never alone.

He lifted me, and I wrapped my legs around him. Hands on my bottom, he raised me higher still, and I felt the tip of him touch me. I opened to him.

"James." I hung on, bent my head, and sucked.

He groaned. "Christ." He lowered me onto him inch by inch until I sheathed him.

"Oh, the wicked things you do to me, James Larrimer."

Water flowed over us, slick and hot, and we began our dance, the intensity of our harmonic song almost too much to bear.

Later, much later, after we made slow sweet love again, we nestled warm and cozy in my bed. I lay tucked against his chest, he on his back, his arms surrounding me. I hadn't felt that sense of rightness in forever.

"What will happen when they learn you failed to retrieve the chest?"

He ran a hand across my hair. "Irrelevant. I'm their biggest-ticket asset. Your dreads are glorious. Keep it long."

"Not sure I have a choice. James, if anything bad happens. Look out for Lulu and Bernadette?"

Arctic cold. "Don't even—."

I kissed him. "Not to worry, my beautiful dragon dude. Not to worry."

I rose at five-thirty, slipped out while he slept on, didn't allow myself a backward glance. While I took care of the animals and then showered, I relived last night, the way I'd touched him. The feel of him beneath my hands. The way his eyes softened just before he kissed me. The scrape of his calluses across my breasts, the brush of his lips.

Stop.

I rinsed off, rubbed myself dry, and by the time I reached my bedroom, he'd gathered his clothes and gone. Except for the red socks. He'd left his red socks.

I rubbed a hand across my chest to ease the hurt.

The black turtleneck and leggings I donned were a favorite of Tommy's, designed to spark his memory. I slipped into my Frye boots, which would accommodate the ankle holster I'd strapped on, then slid in the smaller of my two guns.

I'd given myself forty minutes to get to the meet. I couldn't be too early for my plan to succeed, just a tad, because I bet Tommy would be early, too. I emptied my large backpack and began to place the chest inside. Hesitated. What a terrible risk. But, I had to take it. If I brought a fake chest, Tommy would suss me out. With the bait in my pack, I added my Glock, my shoulder holster, the small Bowie knife, and a True Bal. I'd weapon up when I arrived at MacDaniel. I was tempted to take the Fae knife, but suspected it was keyed to Larrimer in some way.

I stretched, got the blood flowing, a freight train through my body. I snapped the lock and opened my bedroom window wide. Finally, I sat on the chair beside the window, focused, and pushed my fireflies.

Whoa! A miniature shower of them erupted from my palm. I projected outward, out the window. They fizzled. Twice more I replicated my moves, and received two more fizzles in return.

Shit.

Memo to Self: learn how to firefly minus the high emotion.

I slung on the backpack and trotted downstairs around eight-thirty to the scents of waffles and eggs. The normalcy of it made me dizzy.

"Isn't *that* the outfit, cookie," Bernadette said when I walked into the kitchen.

I winked. She smiled. I reached in the fridge and took out a yogurt, then refilled my go-mug, my third injection that morning.

"Ronan off to school?"

She nodded as she washed another plate, rinsed, and stacked it neatly in the drainer.

"That's what we bought a dishwasher for," I said, annoyed. Yeah, I was cranky.

"Your idea, cookie," she said. "Not mine. Wastes electricity and water."

No it doesn't. The words wouldn't clear my throat, so I kissed her cheek, which earned me a semi-caterpillar eyebrow. I swiped the keys and headed for the truck.

"And where are you going?" she asked.

"Nowhere. I've got some errands later, and I just want to check the gas. We might be low."

I stowed the backpack on the floor of the backseat. Right. A magic fricking chest just hanging out on the floor of my truck. Sort of like groceries, only more.

I had plenty of gas, as I suspected, and when I closed the door, I pinged the silent lock.

I opened the mudroom door. Now came the hard part.

Bernadette was finishing up with the dishes. James was in his room. I started down the cellar stairs, ran back up, softly shut the door, then shouted up to the men, dosing my voice with fear. "James!"

He blazed down the hall. Bernadette swirled to face me.

"There's someone in the cellar!" My breathing came hard and fast. "Maybe more than one. I heard something. Felt something bad. By the chimney flue." I waved my hand toward the cellar's far end.

They all reacted to my "feeling," just as I'd hoped.

"We need to check." I drew the gun from my boot.

Larrimer whipped out his 9mm.

Such a stupid plan, but... I opened the door and looked behind me. Yup, Bernadette had pulled her derringer and was loading bullets into the double barrel.

"Bernadette, really?" I asked.

She scowled. "It's my home, too, cookie."

"Fine." I put my snottiest tone into that one word. "I'll take point."

Larrimer shot me a look meant to annihilate. "*I'm* point."

I huffed. "Bernadette, get in front of me, then. I want to make sure we're not jumped from behind. Somebody could come in from the bulkhead."

I unlatched the door, eased it open, but didn't turn on the lights. James glided down the steps, silicone smooth, as did Bernadette.

I followed. Well, two steps, followed. The cellar was vast. I waited until they made it almost to the other end, their focus entirely ahead of them. I padded back up the two stairs, eased the door closed, and locked it. Then I dragged the red chair across the room and wedged it between the cellar door and the hall wall.

Shouts. In particular, James' booming voice, "Clea!"

I'm sorry. So sorry.

The chair wouldn't hold them, not with Larrimer's strength. But they'd be trapped just long enough for me to escape.

Just before I left, I placed the Fae knife on Larrimer's bed.

CHAPTER FORTY-ONE

I was back at MacDaniel Lake, only this time, I'd swung around and approached the reservoir high up from the road. I'd taken the burner phone. GPS was a bitch.

When I got out, I donned my weapons. They would do bupkis against his magic, but I hoped they'd prove a distraction.

I stood amidst pines and crept closer to the bridge, up the verge, hugging the shadows of the trees. My watch read nine forty. Twenty minutes to blast off. Gods, that sounded way too literal. I paused, and the early March damp seeped into my bones. Not my favorite type of day. Today might be my least favorite of all—my last.

Pops of adrenaline. I massaged the spiral on my wrist, which was disturbingly inert. I'd been close to death before. He'd kissed my lips, in fact. But this was different. This was Tommy.

We'd come here myriad times. In spring, herons fished the waters. In summer, turtles basked on logs. In fall, ducks flew south.

Today, blotches of dirty ice and snow covered the paths, along with a silence that failed to work its usual magic. All I felt was alone.

Could I *really* kill Tommy?

Having seen his power, would I even be able to kill him? Whispers faint and haunting said yes.

My stomach cramped. For what was to come. For how Tommy and I had gone so wrong. For death. Nobody came back from that particular trip.

Bernadette's bark, *Now is the only moment, cookie. Own it!*

Now. Only now.

I centered myself, readjusted my backpack, then moved, crouching low as I approached the bridge, with its concrete abutments and two-story tower.

Tommy would be on the far side. Beyond that sat a small deforested hill, followed by acres and acres of trees.

I licked my lips. This whole game depended on my knowledge of Tommy Sevaux. That he wanted me, would try to take the chest *and* me. That he loved gambles and trades and one-upmanship, which was how he would see Lulu. She had little value to him. So, by getting the chest and me in trade, he'd one-up me. A childhood game. Our game. He'd won so often, he'd fail to remember that I'd won sometimes, too.

Today had to be that "sometimes."

I took a breath, straightened, and walked forward, out of the trees and onto the wide path flanked by forest. I still couldn't see the bridge. But I knew the way.

I climbed the sinuous path. *Keep walking. Keep climbing.*

Clumps of snow on the bridge and the hill beyond. Gray sky brewed overhead, filled with mean clouds threatening wet snow. Not much wind. A plus.

I stopped and peered across the bridge. Where was Tommy? I squinted, hoping to catch a glimpse of movement. The wind picked up, and from across the bridge, the ugly scents of rotted geraniums and cat urine. Smoke coalesced, darkening from white to charcoal. Lit from within, it pulsed. And chittered.

Oh hell. I knew that sound. A bead of sweat trickled down my back.

The smoke thing banded the trees high up the hill, then flowed down like syrup to the opposite side of the bridge directly across from me.

Yeah, I knew just what was coming.

At the bottom of the hill, the viscous wave paused and coalesced. That woman's face, huge and high-cheekboned, eyes closed, with gray mottled skin, tendriled hair that undulated and soon differentiated into those snake-like things. The Cardillo. She, it, solidified from the mucoid wall, shaping, rising, until the horrible cobrathings spread their pulsing red hoods and black tongues flicked out.

I looked around. Not a wolf in sight. A girl could hope, right?

A primal scream begged to escape. *Focus, focus, little Mage.* My Da's words.

I drew my Bowie.

The cobrathings writhed into a nest and tumbled onto the bridge. Bile in my throat.

Jean-covered legs dispersed the gunmetal ooze, and that nest of repulsive things parted, fawning, glistening cobra-heads bowing.

Tommy stepped from their midst, Lulu clutched to his side, as if they were on some twisted date. She wore that same indigo dress, now dirtied and torn. It ruffled in the breeze.

Hands cuffed behind her, she still struggled. *Good girl.* Duct tape covered her mouth. Wide eyes, a mixture of fear and outrage, stared at me. Lulu might be terrified, but she was also *pissed*.

That fucking bastard. There it was, my anger. I reveled in it, nourished it, bathed in its bright light. My rage spiraled higher and higher. I sizzled.

And my soul knew that I could kill him.

A part of me fixed on those cobrathings. They hadn't moved forward.

"Cle-a." Tommy singsonged my name, slow and strong. It was a lullaby, a call for me to come, a siren's song.

"I'm ready!" I shouted back. "Are you?"

"Have you got it?" he said.

"Oh yes," I said, all husky and warm.

"Then show me."

I rested a knee on the ground, unzipped my backpack, and withdrew the chest. For the millionth time, I wished I could have brought a fake. Knew I would fail if I did. I held it up.

"How do I know it's the real deal?" he said.

"Can't you sense it with your woo-woo powers, Mr. Adept? Maybe those disgusting snaky things can."

He laughed. "Come to me."

There it was again. The call. The cry. The song. "No. You'll just have to believe me that I hold Dave's calligraphy box. The Chest of Bone." I grinned. "With Dave making those invitations, the box was right under your nose. You could have had it all this time."

"I'll have it soon enough." He nodded, and the smoky ooze parted again. Two of his goons, armed to the teeth, stood sentinel.

A spurt of panic, a couple of fireflies escaping beneath hands death gripped on the chest. I took a few steps forward. "Really? I mean, come on. You must be pretty impressed with me, bringing those bozos."

"Not with you, sweetness, your creature."

I refused to turn, but I felt him, immense, his wrath an inferno to my flame.

A cocktail of joy and fear. "James," I said, not turning. "This is between The Master and me."

"Hey, babe, I want to dance, too."

I stuttered in a breath. "You don't understand."

"I do." He stepped beside me. Silent. Savage.

"Take it or leave it, Tommy!" I said with a shout.

We walked forward, which was when my senses caught another person, crouching in the bushes to my left. Tommy would have noticed it, too. Unless that person was part of his cadre. *Hell.*

"Who else—" I said to Larrimer.

"Hell if I—"

"Tommy!" A scream ripped from a soul in torment.

Bernadette! I forced myself not to turn, to keep my focus.

We moved toward the middle of the bridge. So did The Master, wrenching Lulu along.

Ten feet. Eight. Then he stood before me, six feet away, wearing jeans and the blue sweater I'd knit for him one winter. Lulu stilled, eyes saucers, hair wild. She notched up her chin.

Tommy flicked a finger, and a quill of power sliced her cheek. Her cry muffled, she stumbled, but he caught her. Blood trickled from the cut.

I stoppered my howl of fury. *Not yet. Calm, be calm.*

Beside me, Larrimer's cool savagery was a balm to my senses.

"I don't want to hurt this girl," Tommy said.

"You've already done that," I said.

"Give me the chest," he said. "Give me *you*."

His expression gentled, pleaded.

"All right," I said.

Larrimer's feral growl. "No."

"Trust me," I said.

Tommy tugged at me with his power, and I allowed it in. I hugged the chest and walked forward.

Larrimer reached for me.

"No," I said. "Take Lulu, James."

Tommy's smile flayed me. "Not yet."

"*Oui*, Tom!" Bernadette. A wraith beside me, fragile and wild and old. Derringer drawn, her fingers bit into my shoulder.

"Bernadette, no," I whispered.

Then a knife arrowed from Larrimer's hand, swifter than I could track.

Dripping arrogance, Tommy didn't move.

His face seared with shock when the knife drove into his shoulder to the hilt.

He roared.

The cobrathings slithered across the bridge, jaws wide, monstrous fangs dripping venom.

Larrimer reached behind him and unsheathed his swords.

Bernadette fired her gun, and Tommy's shock allowed her to rip Lulu from his grasp, and they tumbled to the ground. I dropped the chest and fireflied, pushing his power away from me.

Streams, rivers of gorgeous gold fireflies answered my call to consume Tommy's miasma of evil, fireflied stitches mimicking my wrist's Celtic spirals, twirling like blades.

Tommy's hands, a cascade of silver quills, crashed against my fireflies.

Mine held. So did his. Stalemate. Tommy couldn't get through. But the cobrathings kept coming and coming.

With the battlecry, "*Aera!*" Larrimer's swords flashed as he danced, a blur, rending, slashing, cleaving cobra head after head after head.

Gods, he was gorgeous.

And Tommy was *mine*. I smiled as I battled, and the pleasure-pain melded, my swirl of fireflies a beautiful symphony of death. Soon, the warmth of blood trickled from my eyes, my nose, my ears. Screw that. "Hell yeah!" I screamed.

Tommy waved his left hand, and the chest flew to him.

"No!" I reached for it, failed to capture it. So I pushed and thrust and rammed that wall of steel, and Tommy staggered back, back, back, his face a bloody mask.

"Now!" Tommy hollered, but nothing happened.

"You're a fucking warrior, babe!" shouted Larrimer.

It was glorious.

Tommy dropped the chest.

"Bitch!" He fell to one knee, angled his hands.

Larrimer kept cutting, slashing, and I, I was pure energy, fireflies boiling, a magic wall of razored spirals.

"Now! You fucking assholes!" Tommy screamed.

The two thugs ran across the bridge and stepped beside Tom, automatic weapons barking. Bullets poured, and I strained against Tommy's rain of silver quills, chanted *warrior* again and again. Bullets hailed, bouncing off my fireflies, ricocheting.

A goon fell. The other, teetered, crumpled.

The remnants of the cobrathings, now a roiling nest, the woman's face, a howl.

Larrimer, flanking me. My world ignited, cyclonic light streaming from me.

And Tommy broke, fell backward into the fog, buried beneath the churning ball.

I staggered.

But his power still pulsed, grew from that writhing mound, as it shrouded Tommy and the men and the Chest of Bone.

Tommy's hand emerged, then his arm, his head, his shoulders, seeking.

I understood, tried to protect them, spread my arms, widened my firefly stream, but I tripped, tired, too tired. And I was late!

A blast from Tommy. Bernadette, cradling Lulu, exploded into the air.

"Catch them!" I screamed at Larrimer.

But I fireflied, more, staggered again, didn't let up, couldn't. And my fireflies began to come apart, unraveling, loosening, deconstructing. *Can't...* I screamed and screamed and...

My heart shattered.

I flew backward, a blur, Larrimer clasping Lulu, Bernadette, pavement, trees, sky, absurdly blue.

Blood. Tasting it, drinking it, *knowing* it, and trying so hard to slow, to soften... killing trees... Try. Try. All used up. All used...

Body on ice, I swim through murky sludge aiming for a surface I know is there, but can't see. Vibrations course through me, tuning-fork fast, as I paddle, seeking the unknown. My focus weaves in and out, wavers, a funhouse mirror. A coppery taste lines my mouth, and my hands slow, my kicks grow lethargic.

The sludge warms, heats, boils with intensity.

Vibrations accelerate, hypersonic.

I can't. I just can't.

Come.

The wyvern. Wings arched in a powerful display.

Come.

I obey.

And fall.

I awakened, sluggish, aching to reach… finding… the smells of earth and pine and honey. Something cradled me, warm and strong. James.

As I reached to touch him, agony. Muscles screamed, something torn, and cold, bitter cold. I moved to rise.

"Don't," the voice filtered through pain and illusion. "Stay still."

"Can't. Must find—"

"Lulu is okay."

I blinked away the blur. Saw his face, scarred and blistered. Fingers moved, clasped mine. I hung on tight, his life pulse intense.

The wyvern. "I died, didn't I?"

His hand tightened on mine. "I don't know."

"You're burned, the cobrathings spittle. Yet you held me."

"Yes. Whatever saved you, it wasn't me."

Oh, but it was. "You saved them, too."

"I caught them," he said, voice gruff. "Bernadette did the saving. C'mon." He rose and carried me to Fern's tailgate.

In the back of Fern, he'd made a makeshift bed from blankets. On it lay Lulu and Bernadette. Both so still.

"Lulu's heartbeat and color are good," he said. "She'll be fine."

"Let me get in with them."

"Clea, don't." A darkness in his voice, one I didn't like.

I crawled between them toward Lulu and brushed her hair from her face. He'd removed her manacles, the tape. They'd left red marks. Her breath sloughed in and out. A steady rhythm.

I turned to Bernadette. She lay on her stomach, face angled toward me, a glaze of red, and I stared at the jumble of blood and flesh and bone from shoulder to waist. *Oh gods.* She wasn't breathing! I moved closer, caught a whisper of breath.

I looked at Larrimer.

He shook his head, face taut, eyes a sorrowful howl. "Everything's broken. Bleeding internally. From The Master's blast. She saved Lulu."

Her turban was off, long, long gray hair pushed to the side, two tiny, pearlescent horns growing from her skull. I started to touch them, clenched my fingers.

I took her limp hand in mine and lay down beside her, my face inches from hers. "Bernadette. It's me, Clea."

Clea Artemis, she said in that voice I knew so well.

"Yes?"

I knew you would hear me.

Not speaking. No, she was inside my mind.

Hear me, child.

"How can I help? What can I do?"

See me.

An image coalesced in my mind of a fierce warrior— armored, with long black hair streaming behind her, sword in hand, eyes flames of midnight suns. Bernadette, young and beautiful and terrible.

You were the soft and he was the hard. You needed strength. He needed love.

"Rest. Please rest."

She laughed inside my head. *No time for that now, cookie.*

I bit back a sob, almost smiled. So very Bernadette.

Hear me. If I erred, I did the best I knew how. You are The Key. La Clé. *You are ready.*

"Because of you."

He is your twin.

I gasped. My brother. "Why not tell me?"

The Fae Queen ordained you be fostered. And so I performed her charade. He was First. Eldest. Thomas Apollo. The boy I loved too well. Adieu, Clea Artemis, *child of my daughter.*

"Bernadette!"

But she was gone.

CHAPTER FORTY-TWO

Moments stretched, elastic, infinite.

Bernadette looked out at the world with an expression I'd seldom seen her wear. Half-lidded hazel eyes, empty with death's embrace, her face softened by a slight smile of accomplishment, as if she'd reached her goal and attained it with pride.

I ran a hand across her hair, touched those newly formed horns, so silky, breathed in a sob and hugged her—still warm—whispering over and over, "I love you. I love you."

At some point, Larrimer loaded Lulu into Fern's backseat. She was asleep, for which I was thankful.

"We should go." He offered me a hand.

I closed those half-lidded eyes and kissed her wrinkled cheek. And I released Bernadette and took Larrimer's hand.

We walked around front, where he tucked me into the passenger seat.

When he got behind the wheel, I said, "Tommy? The two men?"

"Their bodies, that creature, they're gone."

"The chest?" I asked.

"That's gone, too."

My heart clenched. I'd failed, lost the chest. If I did nothing else in this world, I would get it back. At least, Lulu was safe.

We headed home. Larrimer said he and Ronan would come back later to collect the Jeep and the rental. I called Balfour, told him we had Lulu. They wanted to debrief her immediately, but I said she was out, to give us a day or two. I'd call. He conceded, surprising me.

I leaned against the car door and slept.

The following morning, I awakened to pleasure. Not the pleasure of making love with James. But of feeling that glorious power when I wielded my fireflies. It sizzled through me, near erotic in intensity, a cascade of want. My hands shook, and I clenched them into fists.

I swayed, pushed to a sitting position, inhaled a breath.

Nothing pleasurable about my naked body, which told a different tale. My bruises looked like a Jackson Pollock painting. Someone had tended my cuts and butterflied and bandaged my torn calf. Bernadette's handiwork.

No, not hers. Of course not.

Anger bubbled. I swiped a hand through my Medusa hair, dressed, and made it downstairs, where I found Larrimer leaning against the kitchen counter drinking a mug of fragrant tea. He was pissed, too, which only fueled my unsettled emotions.

I walked over. "Where's Lulu? Ronan?"

"Still sleeping."

"And Bernadette?"

"In the barn, covered with her old quilt. I thought she'd like that."

I leaned my forehead against his chest. "I just had the strangest experience."

"To say that after yesterday, it must've been a doozy." He hesitated, then wound his arms around me.

"Yeah." I stood there for a while, battling that bubble of anger until it burst. "How could she not tell me she was my grandmother? That Tommy was my *twin*? And, dammit, we should still be living a life together, not her corpse wrapped up in the barn. It shouldn't have happened that way. She shouldn't be *gone*."

"But she is," he said.

Tears thickened my voice. "She was *forced* to be hard because I was a fricking mooshface."

He bent his head and whispered in my ear, "Warriors can be soft, too."

I stuttered a breath.

Yes. I might be soft, but I was strong, too. A warrior. Bernadette had gotten it right, but not all of it. She'd missed the part of me, which was becoming.

There was so much I didn't know. So what, I could learn. I *would* learn. I stood on tiptoe and kissed his chin. "Thanks, dragon dude." His pine and honey scent mixed with the burn of his anger made a potent cocktail. "You're still pissed at me."

His hand stroked my hair. "Furious."

I stepped back. "Please understand why I went alone."

"Why should I?" His dark look was unrelenting.

"Tomorrow. We'll talk about it tomorrow. Please."

"Tomorrow," was all he said as he walked outside.

Lulu came down later, with Ronan. Her face pale, but her back straight, and her smile, while tentative, appeared often as we talked.

She hadn't been sexually abused, thank gods, or eaten any of the horrible meat. They'd knocked her around a bit, played cruel mental games, but she'd heal. It would be slow, take time. The ripples. Yeah, I knew all about those ripples. Fear had been her greatest enemy, but she'd used a banquet of her dad's "tricks" to fight it. Dave had taught his daughter well. Ripples, sure. But she'd *survived*.

"I'm so proud of you," I said.

She pointed a thumb at her chest. "Me, too." Then she started to weep over Bernadette again, but that pain would ease.

Mine? Yeah, I wasn't gonna think about that. What I did think about, talk about with James, was reporting her death. I was terrified that when the lab techs got ahold of her, they'd recognize something was "off." She wasn't Mundane, but Fae. Did that make her body different? Hell, there were horns.

The Union had appropriated Dave's remains. What if they did the same to Bernadette's? I would *not* have those creeps dissecting my grandmother's body. Since no solution leapt in front of me, I waited.

Tomorrow would be here soon enough.

We did normal things. Tended to the animals. Cooked. Well, Larrimer cooked, I assisted. Played *Boggle*. We talked and we laughed. And cried a little, too. It started to snow around six, and we lit a fire and watched *Alien,* which scared the hell out of me, per usual. Larrimer and I made love. Oh, did we ever. What outside world?

Except a thread of fear wove a spell around me. His mission done, the chest gone, James... He would be leaving. I tried not to think about his absence. The place he'd made in my life, and the resulting hole if he walked out it. Would he stay? Could he stay? Did he *want* to stay? He might hate The Union, but their claws dug into him deep.

The sun came up the following morning just the same as always. When I awakened, Larrimer was no longer beside me, and I ran a hand across sheets still warm from where he'd curved his body around mine through the night. I already missed him.

I felt fewer aches and pains, sensed a little more energy flowing through my veins. I went to slip my feet into my bunny slippers. Except they weren't in the closet.

I went on a hunt, obsessed with finding my fuzzy slippers. The hunt was good. Anything so I didn't have to think.

Barefoot, I slipped downstairs. Larrimer was on the phone, I suspected talking to his powers-that-be, and I paused to watch him. He wore a white t-shirt, was making my coffee, the boiling water singing merrily from the kettle. I loved the beauty of him, of his back tapered to his muscled ass, his movements fluid, as he ground the coffee beans, then added the grounds to his French press.

I expected him to reach for the kettle, but instead he pulled a small vial from his pocket, unscrewed it, and sprinkled some powder atop the ground beans. Then he took the boiling water and poured it slowly, expertly into the French press.

What had he just done?

He ended his call and lay his phone on the counter.

I moved, and he turned and frowned. "I didn't hear you come down."

"Just call me Clea the cat," I said lightly. "I'm looking for my bunny slippers."

"I put them under the couch, so the dogs couldn't get to them."

"They wouldn't dare."

I got Bernadette's tin of walnut chocolate chip cookies and carried it into the living room.

Larrimer had stoked the woodstove. The room was warm, homey, just like yesterday, with the dogs sprawled on the floor, the afghan draped on the sofa, the kitten curled on the chair with lousy springs.

What had Larrimer put in my coffee?

I found my bunny feet, slipped into them, and hunkered into one end of the couch. I waited for Larrimer. Seconds later, he handed me my go-mug and took the couch's other end. Mutt, Jeff, and Grace crawled up and settled themselves between us, with Grace beside me. The only thing missing was my beloved red chair. What was left of it lay in a corner of the living room, broken to bits by Larrimer as he'd freed them from the cellar.

Of course, Bernadette was missing, too, and she couldn't be put back together. My chest ached, and I massaged it with the heel of my hand.

I could hear her say, *get over it, get on with it.*

What had Larrimer put in my coffee?

"How did you find me?" I asked to him.

"I put a tracker on Fern."

"Cute."

"Yes."

Monosyllables. Affectless. Typical.

"Bernadette was frantic for you," he said.

No crying in baseball, remember.

"Somehow she knew," he continued. "I took the Jeep, told her and Ronan to stay. She must have followed in my rental."

I sipped my coffee. It tasted the same. My hands shook, and I stilled them.

"It would have worked," I said. "My plan."

"But it didn't."

"I don't want to argue. I believed doing it alone was the safest way."

"The Master would have killed Lulu and taken you. He wants *you.*"

"Tommy didn't want *me.*" I spat the words. "He wants the magics. The power. Do you think he's dead?"

"If we're lucky."

I curled my legs under me. "He killed his own grandmother. She'd never given him anything but love."

351

"Maybe that was the problem."

"Don't," I said. "She did the best she could."

"I'm aware. Believe me." He added a log to the stove and sat back down. He felt so distant. Again, a stranger.

"So the Fae knife worked," I said. "Charlie gave it to me."

He gave me a long look. "I could have used a fistful." His face darkened, a thundercloud. "The chest is gone. If he's still alive, he's got it."

The chest. A niggle. I put it aside for a more immediate riddle.

"I've got to go do some work." He stood, an enormous presence, muscles taut, fists bunched. A predator on the move.

He was still angry about my going alone to the meet. "Just one question," I said. "What was that powder you poured into my coffee?"

He stilled, shoved one hand into his jeans pocket. With his other, he reached for his mug of tea.

I watched his eyes. Shuttered. But he didn't fool me, not anymore. I'd leveled him, and he was strategizing the best approach. Should he hand me lies? Truth? Half-truth? I didn't need to hear it. I *felt* it.

"You've made me coffee every day since your arrival." I held up my go-mug. "Delicious coffee. The best I've ever tasted. I just saw you pour powder onto the grounds. So tell me, James..." I paused. I didn't really want to know, wanted him to deny it, to say it was just some special flavoring. "Tell me. What have you been dosing me with?"

The room hushed, the only sounds—his breathing, and mine.

Power poured off him. Dominance, demanding my submission. To drop my gaze, to leave the lie, to make like nothing was changed.

"Taka gave it to me," he said in a voice devoid of emotion. "She knew about your morning coffee addition."

Did she know what fucking Tampax I used, too? My jaw ached from clenching it tight. "I was to add a pinch of the powder each day. It was designed to increase your magics, your senses. It worked."

Which explained so much.

I flung the mug at him.

The bastard caught it one-handed.

"I head up a team of five operatives like myself," he said. "The Six. The Freak Team. We work together, often separated by great distances. I coordinate. We're in contact. Always. Informing you about the powder..." He shook his head. "I'm willing to jeopardize myself. But not them. And not you."

"What do they have to do with anything? With us?"

"If I hadn't given it to you, and Taka deemed the powder ineffective, she would have pulled in another member of my team. Geirr. She threatened to, once. He's different from me. He would try to hurt you. Then, I would kill him. Then, they would descend in droves. An unacceptable scenario. Too much risk. Zero payoff."

Larrimer looked at me, straight on, as if daring me to find fault with him.

Find fault? I wanted to laugh my ass off. "How could you do that without telling me? How could you dose me with chemicals that you didn't even know worked? Or what they would do?"

"Pouring it on thick, aren't you, Clea? When I saw it was performing its task, no side effects, I continued. The powder succeeded. Your powers increased. No interference from my handlers."

"Why didn't Taka just take me, dose me herself, instead of having her *minion* do it?"

He flinched. "They want you *and* the chest, so it had to be administered in the field."

Fury stung me. I was blind with it. "Like some date-rape drug. I counted on you. Believed in you. Trusted you."

"I earned that trust."

I was incredulous. "Earned it? You put a drug in my coffee, day after day, *and never told me*. You're working for that bitch Taka and some bad guys just as nasty as Tommy. You betrayed me. Played me. What *are* you, James Larrimer? What *are* you?"

He banged the mug he'd caught onto the table. The table cracked. "A guy who's trying to keep you alive."

"Sorry, but that won't fly. You have agendas inside agendas."

"You're still breathing, aren't you?" His anger lashed me.

"There's more to life than just a heartbeat and breath. Trust, James. It's everything."

I felt violated, a woman who'd been deceived and manipulated and twisted by others' agendas. Bernadette. Tommy. Bob. Even Dave never trusted me with the truth. And James.

My heart stuttered, the pain insane. Soft, was I? Not anymore, boopie.

I would never forgive. Never.

"You may hate me," he said. "But you *will* listen to me."

"My ass—"

"Listen!" His voice boomed. "You have to leave, too. Now."

I stood. "I don't *have* to do anything."

His face tightened, his scars blazing white. But that honey-granite voice I so loved was a low growl. "Yes, you do. DarkPool, The Union, they're coming for you. *Taka's* coming for you. Scientist, yeah, she's a scientist, but also a fucking government kiss-ass agent. She gives the orders. And they'll take you and test you and analyze you. They'll turn you inside out and leave you bloody and broken. If you think what I've done was a violation, just wait until the geeks and Taka get their hands on you. You're special. You'll be their first Mage. A prize. They'll want to know exactly what you are, how you tick, why you tick. They want to control the magic. All the magic. *You* are their ticket in."

"I'm nobody's ticket in!"

"Believe that, if you will."

I opened my mouth with a retort. That I wasn't going anywhere. That no one would scare me out of my home. That I had free will and was a free person.

I said none of those things because I could picture it—trapped, panicked, twisted into a creature to be used for their agendas.

This was truth. What Larrimer had said was truth. He knew those people. They'd made him. *Taka* had made him, and he was her minion.

It terrified me, utterly.

I'd flee. Take Lulu. I was her guardian, after all. And Ronan, he was eighteen, if he wanted to come. The bastard whitecoats wouldn't get them, either.

"I haven't told Taka the chest is lost, so they'll hold off coming after you for a little bit."

My blood bubbled. "They've been waiting for you to take the chest from me."

"Yes. But they have other operatives. Ways of ascertaining the chest is gone. Time your time is of the essence."

And woven through it all was James Larrimer. A chink in my armor. Even now, I didn't want him to go. Pain was always easier to handle after the cut.

"Leave," I said. "Now. Get out of my house, my life, my world."

Lines of strain carved his mouth, and he held out a hand, palm up. "Clea, don't—"

"Now."

In minutes, he'd gathered his things and piled them on the dining table. He shrugged into his coat. "Bernadette."

"My problem. Not yours." All I had to do was figure out how to lay her to rest in ground frozen to granite hardness. I ran a hand across my face.

"Unless you want the geeks to get her, we need to burn her."

I hadn't thought of burning. He was right, of course, damn him. And he'd earned a place beside that pyre. It might go against the grain, but I would stall reporting her death. As solitary as she'd become in later years, I doubted anyone would notice her absence. Another layer of sorrow wrapped around me. "Would The Union take her?"

"Of course," he said. "Taka would love to get her scalpels on a dead Fae."

Never.

In a glade deep in the woods, the four of us each said a few words over Bernadette's pyre. Then we gave her a blazing sendoff and built a cairn above the ash. Larrimer and Ronan did the heavy lifting, for which I was grateful.

Larrimer didn't try to talk to me, nor I to him.

Soon after, he stood by the door, his rental car packed. I was strung so tight, I might snap. Start screaming, beg him to stay, do something I might regret. *Fuck.* I loved the bastard.

Face a cool mask, his eyes beseeched me.

I crossed my arms.

After a heartbeat, he said, "Heed my words."

"You sound like some movie swashbuckler."

He didn't smile. "Leave. Do it. Be safe." And he softly closed the door behind him.

My heart splintered.

CHAPTER FORTY-THREE

Numbness has its advantages. I accomplished a lot the following day. From the piles of money Dave had left me, I'd gotten oodles of cash, and transferred the rest over to his, and now my, lawyer. Client privilege, and all that. I used some of it to purchase debit cards and burner phones. When I explained everything to Lulu and Ronan—all except what Larrimer had told me in secret about himself—they eagerly fell in with the plan.

We packed light, and I hired caretakers for the farm and animals, out-of-towners who'd done that duty several times before. Kind people.

I gathered photos, guns, ammo, knives, Bernadette's account books and journals and one of her baking tins, laptops, my iPad, the Storybook and a few other books, my yarn and needles. My Kermit and my cashmere blanket, a few more treasures, and a heart-shaped rock I'd found years earlier on a hill overlooking the farm.

I'd reluctantly traded Fern and cash for a used Toyota all-wheel-drive minivan, which was now packed and parked in the dooryard. Good lord, a minivan. As I'd driven it home, I begrudgingly admitted the thing was sort of sweet. She needed a name.

The last thing I did before I said farewell to my animals was to enter my office where Larrimer had stayed. When I walked into the room, I could feel him, smell him, almost taste him. I stiffened my spine and got on with it.

My mistake was looking where he'd slept before we'd made love.

In the middle of the daybed, resting in its scabbard, was a sword, the shorter one of the two he used to fight.

I sat on the bed and hugged it to me, a beautiful thing that smelled of sweat and passion and pain. Of James, damn him.

Except. Hasty. *Yes, Bernadette, I hear you chiding me.* Too hasty. But I'd been so pissed off at him, anger toxic in my gut. Not that I'd been wrong. No, dammit, he shouldn't have secretly dosed me with some magic crap.

But I should have forgiven him.

Maybe. I didn't know.

All I *did* know was that he belonged here, with me. And I'd shoved him away.

I was an idiot.

I called him. My heart froze when the mechanical voice said the number had been disconnected.

Minutes later, I used the sledgehammer to smash my computer's hard drive, then did the same thing with the computer itself. I took the drive with me, along with Larrimer's sword, then closed the door behind me.

Earlier, Ronan and Lulu left in the Jeep to run a few errands. Darkness had fallen, and I was glad. Time for farewells.

I jogged to the barn and made quick work of it. My chicken girls, Clem and Claudia, my sweet goats—they'd be cared for and loved, just not by me.

I closed the barn doors. Mr. and Mrs. Hillsdale would arrive in the morning.

I stomped my boots as I entered the mudroom and paused. Electricity crackled the air. I reached for my gun, knowing if Tommy was here, things would go south fast.

I shifted to the balls of my feet, held my breath, gun in hand, and opened the door to the kitchen.

A monster black panther sat at attention beside the kitchen table. Except the panther undulated into a calico kitty, which smeared into a swirl of smoke. When it dissipated, I stared at an immense golden eagle, all bright feathers and noble beak. In. My. Kitchen. I blinked fast. Yup, still there.

The electrostatic crackle dampened to a low hiss.

Stunned into silence.

The humongous bird held up one of its waffle-sized talons.

Like I was supposed to shake it? High five it? I waved instead. "Uh, hi." Brilliant, eh?

A squawk so loud it hurt my ears, then a low chirp.

Imagining a bird the size of a sofa and *seeing* one standing three feet away is quite a different experience. Oh my, yes.

Amber eyes peered at me with what felt like smugness.

Anouk.

The air oscillated, rolled and surged, and again smoke blurred the bird. When it cleared, a six-foot chocolate-skinned woman stood before me, dressed in black leggings, a long turquoise turtleneck sweater, and knee-high boots. Hair the color of midnight, lips full, breasts prominent, she stared at me with that same, smug look. Anouk.

"Quite the party trick," I said.

"Thank you, Clea," the bird-woman said. "May I sit?" A graceful gesture toward the kitchen table.

"Sure."

"Mind if I smoke?" She reached into the pocket of her sweater.

"Not in the house."

She shrugged. "I *am* a shapeshifter, as you believed."

No shit, Sherlock. "But only sometimes a panther."

She drew out a cigarette and rolled it between her fingers. "Not my true form. I like messing with your head."

I slipped into a chair. "Gee, thanks. You're a golden eagle. What happened to—

A shadow crossed her yes. "I told my people to leave. They are safer in the magicworld, for now."

"And the calico kitty?"

She smiled. "Another parlor trick. Your calico is just a kitten."

Her eyes darkened, the electric current surrounding her expanded. My hand holding the gun began to turn away from Anouk toward the floor. I fought it. Not even a wobble.

Panic surged. My fireflies erupted. I held up my right palm even as my left hand was forced down to the table.

Anouk grinned, a nasty one.

My fireflies exploded.

Anouk held up her index finger and twirled, and my fireflies swirled around her digit like cotton candy. She flicked her hand skyward.

They vanished.

My gun hand thwacked onto the table and my gun flew across the room to stop just short of the kitchen cabinets. It dropped to the floor.

"You could have just asked me to put it down!" I said, through clenched teeth.

She released me, two fingers making the victory sign. "This was more fun. You were not really trying, Clea. *Then,* we would have a real battle."

I fell back, goosebumps up my spine. "What the hell do you want now?"

"Many things. Most of all, I would like to help you."

"Oh, like you've 'helped' me in the past, with your innuendos and half-truths. I almost died. Bernadette *is* dead."

"I am aware and am truly sorry about your grandmother. At one time, she was a great warrior. But sarcasm. It is never pretty."

"I wasn't aiming for *pretty*." I straightened my spine.

She sighed, as if that were the saddest thing in world. "Come. Let us move to the living room? I would enjoy a drink. Perhaps one of your special hot chocolates, with some Frangelico added?"

Apparently she'd checked out my liquor cabinet.

Anouk sauntered to the sofa, hips swaying, a small smile on her face.

I began brewing my hot chocolate. As I stirred the cocoa, I peered into the living room. She sat on the sofa surrounded by contented animals who'd slept through everything.

Anouk turned her head. "There are five humanoid species."

"Five? What am I miss—"

"And five chests," she said.

"*Five* chests! What the hell!"

"Well, it makes sense," she said with a dark laugh. "Five species. Five chests. Unfortunately, all no longer resemble chests. The Chest of Bone is but one."

I reached for the Frangelico and poured a dash into her mug, then added a generous amount of bourbon to mine and carried them into the living room. As she took her mug from my hand, she touched my wrist spiral.

Heat shot up my arm, and the spiral glowed.

What *couldn't* she do? "Are you like a special shapeshifter?"

"Perhaps," she said in that silky, smartass voice of hers.

I took the lumpy chair, not wanting to sit anywhere near her. I was ticked *off*.

"Five *humanoid* species, five chests," she said. "Are you listening?"

"My hearing is fine. I can count, too." I sipped. Hooray for bourbon.

She sat her mug on the table, and held up both hands, one with fingers splayed. "Mage. That is you." She ticked off one finger. "Shapeshifter. That is me."

"Yeah, yeah. I get where you're going with this. I know about the Fae, too."

"Ah. Vryko."

"What are those?"

"You would know them as vampires."

"You're saying that vamps exist?"

"Garuda's wings save me, don't ever call them that. Poor things get a bad rap." She raised her eyebrows. "Exist? Naturally."

"There's nothing natural about any of this. Where are these species hiding, under rocks? I've never seen any."

"You *have*." Two handed, she sipped her mug, peering over the rim as if I were a tasty morsel. "Delicious. Finally, the Mundanes, humans, like Muggles." She giggled. "Such as in that wonderful Harry Potter world."

Fiction. Right.

Her face hardened, and she growled low in her throat. "You have a role."

"In what?"

"In the retwining of the worlds. We discovered that when you were three and you took out that demon."

"Another species?"

"Subspecies. You have many things to accomplish."

"Like what?"

"That is for you to learn on your own. You are the magic. You are The Key."

I put down my mug. "You know, you're starting to sound like some bad fantasy movie. Every time we talk, it's cryptic crap. My only role is escaping from the guys who want me to become their lab rat. And to save Lulu and Ronan from the same fate. I plan to do both. That's it. I lost the Chest of Bone, and I'm sorry. But it happened. End of story."

She laughed and cocoa sloshed over the rim of her mug. Caught by her "magic finger," it never made it to the couch. "You are funny."

"I live to amuse," I said. "Just leave, please. I've got stuff to do."

She continued as if I hadn't spoken. "You hold the Chest of Bone."

I shook my head. "It's lost. If anyone has it, it's The Master."

"The Master." She spat the words like poison. "Silly name. He does not have it. You do."

"He's alive?" I asked.

She offered a regal nod. "He thought to control Mundanes by sullying them with human flesh. The fool. Where he got that absurd idea from I cannot image. Yes, he lives, but is diminished."

My brother. My twin. "I don't want to argue about the chest. You say you're here to help me. How? By driving me nuts? To give me an encyclopedia of magic? What?"

"You have left the chest, and you must take it with you."

"I'm beat. You're yelling. Go away."

She tilted her head. "My Voice did not compel you?"

"Only to want you to leave."

One finger tapped her chin. "Interesting. I thought our dossier on you was complete. We must add addenda."

"Who are we?"

"The Guardians."

"Plural? I thought there was only one."

She hissed her annoyance. "Five chests. Five—"

"Five Guardians. Yeah, yeah, okay."

She paused, head tilted, as if listening. "They will be here in forty-five minutes."

Back to that again. "The Guardians?"

"No. Those who want you, and they would love to have me, too." A hiss slipped from her lips. "I will be gone. I hope you are, also."

"Oh, I'll be gone, all right. Why can't you find the chests, if you're so powerful and magical?"

"Because they have changed. The chests lived in the mundane world for so long. I already explained. I can no longer locate my Chest of Stone."

Chest of Stone? I needed some answers. "You're a Guardian, like Dave."

She nodded. "*He* found the Chest of Bone! Locate it and leave, or it will be again unguarded, and they will find it with their meters and divining rods and thumpers."

For all her vagueness about "they" and "it" and "thems," I sensed truth in all she said. Well, some truth. Sensing alleged Guardian shapeshifters was new to me.

"You don't comprehend technology, do you?" I asked.

She cut me a sharp look. "It confuses me! I am all magic. From the other side, now forced to live here because of you."

"Don't blame me, big bird. Too bad you don't have yellow feathers." Ohhh, the look I earned was vicious. "If the Chest of Bone is here, I'll just give it to you."

She shook her head. "No, no, no. First, it is not mine to take. Second, as The Key, it is your task to assemble the chests.

I didn't want it. "I decline. I resign from Keyhood."

She wafted a hand like some frigging princess. "I am afraid you have no choice. You were born such. The chests are drawn to you. And you, to them."

My hands curled into fists. "Not interested. Don't give a crap. I'm going back to being a Mundane."

In a languid motion, she draped an arm across the back of the sofa. A smile ghosted her face. "What would you say if I told you your mother is a Guardian?"

I smiled. "My mother is long dead."

"No." She waggled her index finger at me. "You were meant to believe that. Now, I am telling you differently. And it is truth. Viviane lives."

My mam. I had no photos. No stories. No scent.

But hands, petite hands, tossing me gently into the air.

Hope blossomed inside me. If my mother were alive, how wonderful. But if that were true, it also meant she'd abandoned me to Bernadette's care. There went the tiny violins.

"My father?" I asked, hope blossoming. But I knew the truth. "He's dead, isn't he?"

"Yes, a brave man, a wise one, and a potent Mage." She stood. "I really must go. I need a smoke."

The irony of her smoking wasn't lost on me.

The dogs tear-assed to the mudroom window. A sound in the drive, The Jeep. Ronan and Lulu.

I turned back. "Anouk."

She stood before me. "I have a gift for you." She drew something from her pocket and held out her palm. In it sat a rectangular black box with rounded corners. Plain. No markings. No lid that I could see. "This is keyed to you. A vault for the Chest of Bone. Once you find the chest—"

"Why can't you just show me where the damned thing is?"

"Now, that would be cheating." She smirked. "No, in truth, I cannot. I do not know precisely where it is. Nor would I recognize it. Only you, The Key, can do so. Only you can reveal its true form." She chuffed out a breath. "As I was saying before you impolitely interrupted me, you must activate its magic again."

"And how am I supposed to do that?"

"Do? As The Key, you are the magic. You will know when the time comes."

Could she *be* more obscure? Geesh.

"Then, you will put the Chest of Bone inside this vault, for safety. Thus it will be cloaked from all manner of magical beings, as well as from *them*."

"The Union, you mean."

She nodded. "Take it."

"You just *love* giving orders." But I took the box, and as I did, the brush of feathers tickled my palms. "Oh my."

"Do your job." She took my shoulders and kissed each cheek. "See you around."

Smoke spiraled about her, and dissolved. The great bird looked at me, blinked and vanished. Poof. Another damned poof!

CHAPTER FORTY-FOUR

Long minutes later, the kids barreled into the house.

Lulu's hair—gods— it was short, spiky, and bright purple. "Wow."

She giggled. "A disguise."

It was certainly that. "You all set in here?"

"Everything's in the van," Lulu said. "Packed and ready."

"Your jewelry?" I asked. "Blue Monkey? Bras?"

"Got 'em."

"Super. Check that the stalls are all clean, the water's fresh, and the barn's neat for the Hillsdales tomorrow. Make sure the bird feeders are filled, too. Thanks!"

The Union was on their way here. Time to pick up the pace.

Anouk said the Chest of Bone was here. Since she'd given me the ebony box, she must be certain. Apparently, I'd been wrong about Dave's calligraphy chest. I'd felt power, but he'd handled it a lot, was a Guardian. Wouldn't Tommy have sensed it wasn't the chest? But no, not at first. Anouk said only I could do that as The Key. Golly gee, wasn't I special.

I dashed up the stairs carrying the ebony box. That niggle had grown.

Lulu's room. If it wasn't there, I would eat my Key-ness.

Her clothes, some photos, her stuffed bear, all gone and in the minivan. I'd better name the damned car soon.

My eyes snagged on Lulu's jewelry box. A plastic box with the twirling ballerina. This "chest" had most certainly not been created millennia ago. She said she'd taken her jewelry. So why hadn't she packed the box?

Perhaps something else as work, eh?

Each time I'd touched the plastic box, I'd been wearing gloves.

I held out my hands, then stopped. What if I was wrong?

What if I was right?

I reached for the jewelry box. Magnetic pulses, feathery ones, across my palms, then the backs of my hands and up my forearms. Fireflies swirled, and power fisted into me, my wrist spiral flaring like a frickin' neon sign. The hairs on my arms stood at attention.

Beneath my fingers, the box moved.

I jumped back. It was changing shape.

Groaning, the case morphed from a girl's ballerina box into an oval coffer with a curved lid, about five inches in diameter. Not plastic, but mellow bone that shone with an old patina. It throbbed, like a human heart.

Golden runes slid across its face and down its sides, their swooping letters, Tolkienesque, interspersed with The Ouroboros, The Dragon, The Eye. Dave's tattoo. When the runes and symbols covered the entire box, it stilled.

I touched it again. It hummed, the sound oscillating inside me, a half-remembered melody.

The Chest of Bone.

I lifted the lid, and the overwhelming scent of air just after a lightning strike spilled out. Inside, black. Empty. Unfathomable.

I saw nothing.

I saw everything.

I tumbled into the chest.

Stars on a night field... Swirls of colored chiffon... Scents of oleander, rose, pine and honey... Larrimer, Bernadette, Da... Pegasus, Bobo, Cerberus... Spielberg, Capra, Fellini... Chocolate, bourbon, lobster... Chimes, a Mozart melody, whispers... Wolf-men, vampires, Dave... The Storybook, the Queen, the souls... Golden fireflies swirling around, around, a galaxy, a spiraled nebula, dancing fast, faster, and worlds upon worlds upon worlds upon...

I smacked the lid down.

My fireflies encompassed the chest, hands pulsed once.

A snick. A click. Activated. Alive.

Something had changed, something I didn't understand, but should. I *should*. Because I knew deep in the recesses of my soul. Something had *begun*.

Shaking, my fingertips clutched the box that sang an incandescent song. Centimeter by centimeter, I tugged my mind from the Otherworld back to this one—the bedroom, the house, the farm, the kids.

I quivered, a whisper of breath. What I'd heard, what I'd seen.

One by one, I lifted my fingers from the box. I fisted my hands.

The luminous runes and symbols faded, and with a snap, the box again metamorphosed into a girl's small plastic jewel case.

Chest heaving, I gasped for breath. I laughed. What a frigging *trip*. The Power of Worlds, of those souls who'd gifted a part of themselves to the Chest, its allure, indisputable.

But not for me.

If I was The Key, I should start acting like it.

The jewelry case would never fit in Anouk's black box, but of late, I'd seen stranger stuff. I touched the black box and a hinged lid sprang open. I lifted the chest using a soft pillowcase so I didn't touch the thing, and placed it inside the black box. Of course, it fit. The lid snicked shut. Then I wrapped the box inside the pillowcase.

Anouk said Tommy was alive. He'd gut me once he realized he'd been fooled.

Downstairs, I slipped the Chest into my backpack, zipped it, and slung it over my shoulder, thankful that Ronan and Lulu were still in the barn. I retrieved my gun from the floor, checked it, took my purse and my keys. I tucked calico kitten, the real one, into her travel carrier. Last, I slipped the leashes into my jacket pocket and called the dogs.

I paused, looked around. Bernadette's kitchen, the living room with its vaulted ceiling, the paintings, the ugly sofa. The broken red chair. This was it. I was really leaving.

I dowsed the farmhouse lights and departed, perhaps forever, the only home I'd ever known. I didn't look back.

The minivan stood ready. I pulled open the side door, and Mutt and Jeff jumped in. I lifted Grace onto the backseat. "Stay."

"Lulu! Ronan!"

I put kitty's carrier on the backseat floor and received an indignant meow for my trouble.

The kids appeared, shut the barn doors, and ran to the van.

Ronan took shotgun, and I expected Grace to sidle onto his lap from the back. Instead, she stayed in place, obeyed. Shocking. Lulu slid in back with the dogs, and I handed her my backpack. "Take good care of that, kiddo."

We buckled up. *Here goes.*

A set of headlamps turned into the driveway. No. No. NO.

We were leaving. Godsdammit. We would not be trapped.

"Stay in the car, kids." I slid out of the van and crouched by the driver's side door in the darkness. My Glock was at my hip, my knife in my boot, Bernadette's shotgun in my arms. I waited.

Could I really do this? Shoot up the powers-that-be?

Yeah, I could, but what I really wanted was to firefly. I hoped, prayed, that they would respond.

I would wait until the vehicle crested the drive, just over the hump, to where I could see it. I counted on whoever was inside not shooting me. What use was a dead lab rat?

I faced my right palm toward the driveway's top, and as they hit it, I blasted them.

Not one firefly flew.

"Fuck!" I raised the shotgun to my shoulder.

Moonlight shined across the Suburban. Bob sat in the driver's seat. Bastard. Beside him, that bitch, Taka.

They parked perpendicular to the drive, blocking our exit, and all faces turned toward the minivan. I'd swear Taka smiled.

How could I shoot these people?

How could we otherwise escape?

If I blew out the tires, I'd have no way to get our minivan past the Suburban. And I would not, dammit, run off on foot into the night. Lulu, Ronan, the critters, our stuff. Impossible.

Think, think.

I could ram it. Except the minivan was no Suburban. What the hell. Worth a try. I slipped back into the driver's seat.

A shape detached from the blackness of the barn. Tall and large, with powerful shoulders. It dressed like the night and wore a black ski mask. It glided onto the driveway toward the rear of the Suburban. The passengers didn't turn, didn't see the figure who moved swifter than moonlight.

It rammed the back of the Suburban. The truck lurched forward.

Shouts, a scream, but not fast enough. Shoulder pressed to the truck, the figure pushed the Suburban forward. The passengers scrambled, tried to escape. But the doors didn't open, the glass spidered, but didn't break.

The figure muscled the vehicle across the remnants of snow and shoved it over the hill. The Suburban slid out of view.

The sounds of metal and screams came from below.

It all happened so fast.

And the black figure was there, blocking our way.

One arm flung to the side, the other at its waist, it bowed, saluting us like a courtier of old.

I powered down the window and cried out, "Come with us!"

He tore off the ski mask and trotted to the van.

"James," I said. "Come."

He stood by my open window. His body was stiff, tight, as if to confine all the passion he couldn't, wouldn't express. The moon shined. His eyes glittered. But he was serious. So serious.

Those eyes trap me.

I trap his back.

He says nothing.

I have no words, except...

"Please come." I cupped his cheek.

A slow grin, all white teeth and warmth. He opened his shields to our melodic harmony, so beautiful tears dampened my eyes. Then he dipped his head and kissed me. Electric fire. Bliss.

After long moments, he released me. "I've got things to clean up. I'll find you, Clea. I'll always find you. Promise."

A blur. Gone.

But he'd promised.

I stared into the starry night—wished I could see the future—took a deep breath and gunned the minivan.

I picked a tune on my favorite playlist. Phantom Planet's "California," the Tchad Blake Mix.

"From the OC." Lulu grinned.

I forgave her for that. I loved the song, with its indie-rock oomph woven with those chillaxed vibes. We're coming, California. Watch out.

We all sang—Lulu, her luminous voice giving me chills, me, and Ronan, too, a fine bass. Grace howled along.

We played many tunes that day, and in the days to come. And we sang to keep our spirits up, because, boy, we all knew how bad things sucked, and because we were glad to be alive, together.

We had our critters. Some of them.

I learned the "errands" were Ronan's idea. He'd traded our license plates for a junker's with a For Sale sign on it, parked by the side of a dirt road. Clever boy. That first day, we stopped in Ohio. We took the minivan to a one-day paint shop, and turned the thing from white to dark gray-blue. The place had a drying booth, and so in another day, we were gone.

Somewhere in Indiana, I realized we were becoming a family, the bonds still new, tentative, but evolving, deepening. A second chance for me. Dave's final gift had been his best.

We zoomed our way to Iowa, hoping the Bad Guys assumed we'd take the southerly route for the warmer weather. We drove a lot of back roads, and relaxed as much as possible, playing tunes, talking, snoozing, and eating exotic sausages and fake Chinese.

We named our minivan Janis. Hell yeah, Joplin rocked.

L.A. was our destination. A city with a population three times that of New Hampshire stood a good chance of hiding us. But that wasn't the real reason. A compulsion, one I didn't question, tugged me to L.A.

Maybe it was one of the chests. Or maybe not. I didn't think about that too deeply.

At times, I wished none of this had ever happened, that I was back at Sparrow Farm with Bernadette and my warm memories of Tommy.

At others, this new world excited me, with its shapeshifters and mages, Fae and—shit—vampires. I was a warrior, a badass, The Key.

And always, that song in my soul, James. I ached for him, wished he was with us. He said he'd find me. Promised. He'd better do just that.

The kids and I had stepped into a shitstorm without even knowing it.

We'd been guided and prodded and herded like cows. All the while, I'd been clueless.

I was so over "clueless." I'd learn everything I could about the chests and magic and species and deadly enemies who hungered for power.

One thing I knew. I'd master my fireflies better than Annie Oakley shot her Winchester, and I'd take care of my own. I was done with being a victim. And they'd all better frigging watch out.

A TASTE OF...

CHEST OF

THE AFTERWORLD CHRONICLES
-BOOK TWO-

CHAPTER ONE

The glowing Celtic spiral tattooed on my wrist hurt like a bitch. It pulsed, too. Maybe this time. Maybe...

Plop. Plop. Plop. Dammit to hell. Blood dripped from my nose to plop into the brownie mix. That sucked. My magic sucked. Everything sucked.

All I'd wanted to do was light the burner with my fireflies. Easy peasy, right?

I'd moved a bus with my magic. Beheaded a rapist with my magic. Defeated a mage with my magic.

But for six friggin' months, I couldn't do shit with my magic.

That final battle with Tommy... *I'd tapped out my magic!*

I tossed the brownie pan into the sink. It shattered.

Without my magic, how was I supposed to find the *friggin'* Chest of Stone?

My fingers curled against the counter. Breathe. Think.

I slumped at the kitchen table. My headache spiked. I pulled off the band wrapping my dreads, curled a finger around one and twirled. Nothing was normal anymore, not even my dreadlocks, which were a shiny blonde that glistened so brightly, strangers commented. So *not* helpful to my staying under The Union's radar objective.

Dammitall, I wasn't giving up on my magic. I would not give up.

I entered my bedroom, pulled by the forbidden. My bare feet padded across the cool wood, the lush area rug, until I stood beside my bed before a painting. Danger and desire threaded through me, tendrils that caressed me like smoky wisps.

The Chest of Bone.

A scent tickled me, rosemary and sage.

I lifted the painting that covered the hidden safe and pressed my palm to the safe's door keyed only to my print. The small door whooshed open. There it was, the beautiful ebony box. Deep in my bones, I felt what lay *inside* the box. When I drew it out, the box warmed to my touch.

On the edge of the bed, I set the plain rectangular box on my lap. So smooth, so lush, glazed by the moonlight streaming in from the window.

The box had no lid, no opening. But that was a lie. I was The Key. No other could open the box. None. Not even a Guardian. I touched the top, and the lid yawned like an awakening lotus flower.

There, inside the box—the Chest of Bone. Its curved lid beckoned me. Did I dare?

I'd first glimpsed it as a teen's plastic jewel box, complete with twirling ballerina, not the oval bone coffer sitting before me. I bit my lip. Odd, semi-sentient thing. The five chests changed to suit their environment. Incredible pain and death could have been avoided if I'd only first touched the jewelry box with my flesh. Instead, I'd been wearing gloves, and the chest hadn't responded. Seven months ago? It felt like centuries.

Each of the five chests contained universes, as well as slivers of souls. Each ordered the magic of a particular species, the one before me belonging to the mages, like me. Each only responded to The Key. How ironic, how amusing, how absurd.

My dark mood deepened.

When I reunited the five chests with their accompanying guardians, the magic retwining with the mundane world would synchronize, harmonize, become one, as it once was millennia ago.

Now? The replaiting was chaos—destroyed Sedona and St.

Petersburg, created the flower fields in Australia, vanished the Golden Eagles. *How many other events hadn't reached my ears?*

As The Key, I mattered, a fact I found ridiculous. Because of that, The Union, my brother, others sought to possess me, control me.

But if I opened the Chest of Bone, *I* would be in control.

Wielding its power, I would find the Chest of Sone. The chest would solve all my problems with Lulu and Ronan, too. I would use it to find my lost lover, James Larrimer. We'd be a family, a happy one.

Except the chest wasn't mine. I wasn't to touch it, just keep it safe. It was a terrible and dangerous thing. Anouk said it could destroy me, but...

I set the box on the bed, brushed my fingers across the rich velvet lining. The chest's lid glowed warm and welcoming. It *knew* me. Although I hadn't touched it, pins and needles feathered up my fingers.

Outside its protective container, it would assume a new form. Camouflage. I could hide it on my dresser or in a drawer. Use it at will.

Its ancient patina glowed. It throbbed like a human heart.

My index finger atremble, I touched the chest's lid. A thrill rolled through me. Golden runes slid across its lid and down its sides, their swooping letters, Tolkienesque, interspersed with The Orobus, The Dragon, The Eye. When the symbols covered the entire box, they stilled.

The chest hummed, the sound oscillating inside me, a half-remembered melody, beautiful and inscrutable.

All I had to do was lift the lid, and the cosmos would be mine.

Calm caressed my shoulders, my back, my mind. Delicious melodies wove inside me and coiled toward my pool of magic.

Now. Do it now!

I slid my fingers inside the ebony box to free the Chest of Bone.

"Fuck you, asswipe!" screamed my ward, Lulu. "Kids call me Bloodsuckerhead."

"That's a cool vamp!" Ronan shouted back.

No. Stop fighting. My fingers crept further inside the box.

"You're not my boyfriend anymore!" she hollered back.

"News to me!" he said.

No. I savored the brush of cool velvet, the warmth of the chest.

"They call me Agent Orange, too." A shriek.

"Your hair's copper, a gorgeous shade."

Tingles skating up my hands. Remembered power.

"And Burning Bush!"

"Don't, Lulu!" Ronan hollered.

"Bite me!" Another scream. "Help!"

I snapped back to the now, stared at my hands, which were cupped around the chest.

Shit. Was I crazy? What had I been thinking?

I jerked my hands away, closed the box, shoved it into the safe. I slammed shut the door and raced from the room. "Lulu! Ronan!"

The bathroom door was open, cold light splashing into the hall. I stepped inside. Half of Lulu's luxuriant hair pooled on the floor like a bloody stain as she struggled with Ronan, the scissors way too close to his chest.

"Stop!" I said at her bathroom entrance. "Stop it now!"

They froze, grappling statues.

Lulu, the high school girl, my mentor's daughter—a girl I loved with my whole heart. Ronan, the huge orphaned boy we "adopted" back in New Hampshire, now a college student. Both oozed pain and sorrow, both of their lives as off-kilter as mine.

"Oh, Lulu," I said.

Her freckled face whitened with anger. "I cut it, all right. I cut it, and I'm gonna finish cutting it until it's gone, gone, gone."

I lay in bed, darkness cradling me, so hot I sipped my bourbon on the rocks, rather than neat.

The bourbon was a palliative. Certainly not a cure for the emotions pinballing around inside me. Dave... Lulu's dad, my beloved mentor, homicide victim, and former Guardian of the Chest of Bone. He would've said I'd experienced emotional overload, in that kind-firm way he'd possessed.

Lulu and Roman, acting out, behaving as only teens could. Gods, how could Dave think I'd be a good guardian for his daughter?

Right now, I was so screwed up I'd been drawn to again fall into the chest's cosmos, to feel its magical infinity, to feed on the power of those souls who'd given themselves to strengthen it.

I'd imagined it would fix all our ills. It wouldn't. Of course it wouldn't.

No, only I could do that.

Time to cancel the pity party and get my act in gear.

What had awakened me? My bourbon glass sat empty on the bedside table. The lights were out, and at some point, I'd fallen asleep.

I listened, eyes scratchy with exhaustion, and reached out with my empath senses.

Someone. Some *thing* was in the living room. I tuned my emotional senses, tried to understand. Hunger. Animus.

Grace slept at the end of the bed, her usual snores wuffling her cheeks. The thing hadn't awakened her. Odd. My movement did just that, but I hushed her with a gesture, whispered her to stay.

My hand found the throwing knife I kept between the mattress, then I padded to the closet, eased it open. With habitual movements, I geared up with my gun, several throwing knives, and my small Bowie. I brushed the katana James has gifted me. Not to self: learn to use katana.

James. Where are you?

Knife in my left hand, Glock in my right, I eased into the hall and again unfurled my empath senses.

Shit. Whatever was downstairs wasn't human, its emotional signature off-the-charts strange. It was in the living room, that much I knew, but not moving.

Listening for me? Had it heard me? *Damn.*

I stood still as ice, doffing my emo baggage, while donning that familiar, pre-battle calm.

My bare feet schussed across the wood floor, down the hall toward the three steps that led to the living room. Faint moonlight from the picture window filtered through the stygian dark. I peered around the hall corner, felt a single bead of sweat trace its way down my temple.

Took a cleansing breath.

I slid around the corner, back pressed to the wall. Clear. I had a straight line to the living room's three steps and moved forward.

The closer I got, the more that "otherness" clung to my skin like mucous. *What the hell?*

Ten steps, eight, three.

The living room's darkness yawned. A shape, cloaked in the room's inky black, little more than a shadow, its overriding emotions ones of hunger, desire, death. Tall, maybe seven feet. Shit. Arms, yes, long ones, outstretched, ovoid head, long, long legs, but skinny.

From a crack in the curtains, a moonlit beam brushed the creature's head.

My brain scrambled to process. Splotchy pinkish-red shiny skin, hairless, long canid jaws—a Daliesque version—teeth overlapping, small deepset eyes, and strings of drool stretching downward. Gross. And scary as shit.

What was it doing? Smelling. I could hear its snuffles, like the dogs, only louder, scenting for something.

What would James do?

That pierced my brain just as the creature's head swiveled slowly in my direction, eyes now a putrid glowy lime green, staring right into mine.

It made a chittery sound, like a thousand bug legs scraping together. I hated chittery.

Goosebumps erupted across my flesh. A few fireflies swirled my hands, the first in months. Yeah, but I doubted they'd come through in a pinch.

The creature's head snaked forward.

My fireflies sure caught its interest. "Yeah? You want a piece of me?"

Its jaws opened, a growl. It leapt.

I did the same, shooting as I did, hit its shoulder, knife slicing upward as it plowed into me.

Shit, it weighed a ton.

My gun flew from my hand as the thing plastered me to the ground. I kicked out, twisted my legs around its torso, tried to flip it. Not happening.

My arms, trapped beneath its chest. I pried my hands open just as that canid head, jaws wide, ran up my neck, slow, sniffing, coating me with drool, *licking* me. Gods. Why didn't it bite me? Rip out my throat? Tear my face off?

Screw this.

I head butted it, got my hands open and clawed whatever fricken' flesh I came into contact with.

The creature howled, jumped back, but I hung on with my right hand, tore a knife from its sheath with my left, leapt high pushing off the creature and slammed the knife down on its neck. Rolled out of the way and into a crouch.

A bony hand pressed to its throat, it swayed as it watched me. Assessing its next best move? I didn't wait, but forward rolled, came underneath it and sliced at its femoral artery.

The thing moved, fast, too fast, missed the artery, but caught its thigh. I jonesed on the grate of bone against steel.

"What's going...Eeekkk!" Lulu's scream slammed into me, a deadly distraction. Any second Ronan would join her, and I didn't want the creature anywhere near those kids.

The creature's head snapped to her, hunger in its lime-green eyes, and I threw a knife straight to its...

Damn! Not its heart, but its back, as it turned, snarled, and smashed through the picture window, a trail of drool and blood in its wake.

TO BE CONTINUED...

ACKNOWLEDGMENTS

I must give thanks and appreciation to so many for helping me see *Chest of Bone* through to publication.

To Angela Bell, who guided and informed me on all things FBI.
To Officer Melissa Hetrick, who did the same with guns and knives.
To Rosemary Hill, Michelle Edwards, and Kathleen Ricciardi, who read the manuscript post-Beta.
To my fabulous Beta readers, Abby, Alisa, Debi, Ericka, Kathy, and Richard.
To Ilona Andrews, who took the time and trouble to find me my wonderful Betas. There would be no book without them.
To my incomparable writing partner, Camille Cotton, whom I adore.
To the many Curiosity Quills folks, but most especially Eugene Teplitsky for his breathtaking cover; Nikki Tetreault, for her willing ear; and Alisa Gus, an incredibly skilled and caring editor who added so much to this novel.
To my longtime agent, Peter Rubie—thank you!
To Isis of Helheimen Design, who painted the perfect portrait of Clea and Larrimer. My swoons were real, Isis!
To Grace Draven, Jeffe Kennedy, Tiffany Roberts, Mel Sterling, Lora Gasway, Kimberly Trochesset Ladd, Pilar Williams Seacord, Susan Emans, and Colleen Champagne, who welcomed me into their world of fantasy and magic.
To Monica Lin, who cheered me on, and to Mark Bijasa and Johnny, for their invaluable design expertise.

To Cynthia Michaels, who took me in, and, more importantly, took in Gracie, Penny, and Cranberry.

Finally, to my beloved family: Blake and Ben; Peter, Kathleen, and Summer—I can't thank you enough for your enduring support and for your deep and abiding love.

Please know that any errors, screw ups, or messes are mine alone, and not those of the wonderful and supportive folks named above.

ABOUT THE AUTHOR

My new paranormal romantic suspense series, The Afterworld Chronicles, launches with *Chest of Bone*, (February 2017 Curiosity Quills Press). My mystery/thrillers—*Body Parts*, *The Dead Stone*, *The Bone Man*, and *The Grief Shop*, a Daphne du Maurier winner—feature homicide counselor Tally Whyte and are soon to be ebooks. I co-wrote (with Lisa Souza) *10 Secrets of the LaidBack Knitters*. My late husband, William G. Tapply, and I ran The Writers Studio workshops.

I grew up in professional theater—the Ivoryton Playhouse—and planned to become an actress. Instead, I've slung hamburgers, managed a scuba shop, and am a professor. I'm a mom to two humans and a furry pack. My passions for scuba diving, fly fishing, and knitting pop up in my novels. As do vinho verde and bourbon (not together!) and Maine lobster and chocolate (also not together!). I sing musical comedy scores in the shower, unfortunately not an Equity venue, write daily, and teach fiction and modern media writing at Clark University. I'm currently pounding the keys on the series' second novel, *Chest of Stone*.

VICKI STIEFEL *presents:*
CHEST OF
BONE
THE KNIT COLLECTION

patterns from
KAREN CLEMENTS · NORAH GAUGHAN · ROSEMARY (Romi) HILL

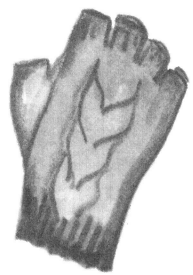

Larrimer's Mitts
by Rosemary (Romi) Hill

Size: Small {Medium, Large}
Hand Circumference: 7 {8, 9} inches unstretched
Materials: Cloudborn Fibers [100% Fine Highland Wool, 221yds/100g]; Worsted weight; Slate Heather; 1 skein

1 - each set US 5/3.75mm and US 6/4mm double pointed needles OR 2 - sets each US 5/3.75mm and US 6/4mm circular needles
waste yarn, stitch markers, tapestry needle, cable needle
spare circular needle, US 3 or smaller, to hold stitches

Gauge (unblocked): 18 sts/24 rows = 4"/10cm in stockinette stitch using larger needles
Every knitter's gauge is different; please check gauge!
Stitches used:
Reverse stockinette stitch: with RS facing, purl every row
Stockinette stitch: with RS facing, knit every row

Abbreviations:

BO: bind off

c6l (cable 6 stitches left): slip 3 sts onto cable needle and hold to front; k3, k3 from cable needle

c6r (cable 6 stitches right): slip 3 sts onto cable needle and hold to back; k3, k3 from cable needle

CO: cast on

k: knit

k2tog tbl: (left leaning decrease) knit 2 stitches together tbl

k tbl: knit through back loop to twist stitch

M1: make knit stitch by pulling up bar between sts, twisting and knitting into loop

M1L: make knit stitch by pulling up bar between sts, twisting bar to the left, and knitting into loop

M1R: make knit stitch by pulling up bar between sts, twisting bar to right, and knitting into loop

p2tog: purl 2 sts together

pm: place marker

p: purl

RS: right side

sl m: slip marker

st(s): stitch(es)

WS: wrong side

Note: instructions are given for both mitts where possible. Where mitts differ, separate instructions are given for left and right mitts.

LEFT AND RIGHT MITTS
Cast on and ribbing:

CO 34 {40, 44} sts using smaller needles.

Arrange sts evenly on 4 double pointed needles or on two circular needles. Place marker and join to work in the round, being careful not to twist cast on round.

Work 3 rounds of reverse stockinette stitch, then work in k1 tbl, p1 ribbing for 2 {2.5, 3} inches.

Switch to larger needles.

Right Mitt ONLY:
Change to working in stockinette stitch with cable pattern, as follows.
Rounds 1 and 2: knit
Round 3: knit 2 {4, 5} sts, c6l, c6r, knit to end.
Rounds 4-8: knit

Round 9: knit 2 {4, 5} sts, c6l, c6r, knit 3 {4, 5} sts, pm, M1, pm, knit to end.
Round 10: knit
Round 11: knit to marker, sl m, M1L, k1, M1R, sl m, knit to end
Round 12: knit
Round 13: knit to marker, sl m, M1L, k3, M1R, sl m, knit to end: 5 sts in thumb gusset
Round 14: knit

Round 15: knit 2 {4, 5} sts, c6l, c6r, knit 3 {4, 5} sts, sl m, M1L, knit to marker, M1R, sl m, knit to end.
Round 16: knit
Round 17: knit to marker, sl m, M1L, knit to marker, M1R, sl m, knit to end
Round 18: knit
Rounds 19 and 20: repeat rounds 17 and 18: 11 sts in thumb gusset

Small ONLY: Repeat rounds 15 and 16: 13 sts in thumb gusset
Work 4 rounds in stockinette stitch
Divide thumb sts: k2 sts, c6l, c6r, k3, remove marker, place 13 gusset sts on waste yarn, remove marker, CO 1 st over gap, knit to end: 35 working sts

Medium ONLY: Repeat rounds 15-18: 15 sts in thumb gusset
Work 2 rounds in stockinette stitch.
Next round: k4, c6l, c6r, knit to end.
Work 3 rounds in stockinette stitch.
Divide thumb sts: knit to marker, remove marker, place 15 gusset sts on waste yarn, remove marker, CO 1 st over gap, knit to end: 41 working sts
Work 1 round in stockinette stitch.
Next round: k4, c6l, c6r, knit to end.

Large ONLY: Repeat rounds 15-20: 17 sts in thumb gusset

Next round: k5, c6l, c6r, knit to end.

Work 5 rounds in stockinette stitch.

Next round: k5, c6l, c6r, knit to end.

Work one round in stockinette stitch.

Divide thumb sts: knit to marker, remove marker, place 17 gusset sts on waste yarn, remove marker, CO 1 st over gap, knit to end: 45 working sts

Left Mitt ONLY:

Change to working in stockinette stitch with cable pattern, as follows.

Rounds 1 and 2: knit

Round 3: knit 20 {24, 27} sts, c6l, c6r, knit to end.

Rounds 4-8: knit

Round 9: knit 17 {20, 22} sts, pm, M1, pm, knit 3 {4, 5} sts, c6l, c6r, knit to end.

Round 10: knit

Round 11: knit to marker, sl m, M1L, k1, M1R, sl m, knit to end

Round 12: knit

Round 13: knit to marker, sl m, M1L, k3, M1R, sl m, knit to end: 5 sts in thumb gusset

Round 14: knit

Round 15: knit 17 {20, 22} sts, sl m, M1L, knit to marker, M1R, sl m, knit 3 {4, 5} sts, c6l, c6r, knit to end.

Round 16: knit

Round 17: knit to marker, sl m, M1L, knit to marker, M1R, sl m, knit to end

Round 18: knit

Rounds 19 and 20: repeat rounds 17 and 18: 11 sts in thumb gusset

Small ONLY: Repeat rounds 15 and 16: 13 sts in thumb gusset

Work four rounds in stockinette stitch

Divide thumb sts: knit to marker, remove marker, place 13 gusset sts on waste yarn, remove marker, CO 1 st over gap, k3, c6l, c6r, knit to end: 35 working sts

Medium ONLY: Repeat rounds 15-18: 15 sts in thumb gusset

Work 2 rounds in stockinette stitch

Next round: [knit to marker, sl m] 2 times, k4, c6l, c6r, knit to end.

Work 3 rounds in stockinette stitch.

Divide thumb sts: knit to marker, remove marker, place 15 gusset sts on waste yarn, CO 1 st over gap, sl m, knit to end: 41 working sts
Work 1 round in stockinette stitch.
Next round: knit to marker, remove marker, k4, c6l, c6r, knit to end.

Large ONLY: Repeat rounds 15-20: 17 sts in thumb gusset
Next round: [knit to marker, sl m] 2 times, k5, c6l, c6r, knit to end.
Work 5 rounds in stockinette stitch.
Next round: [knit to marker, sl m] 2 times, k5, c6l, c6r, knit to end.
Work one round in stockinette stitch.
Divide thumb sts: knit to marker, remove marker, place 17 gusset sts on waste yarn, remove marker, CO 1 st over gap, knit to end: 45 working sts

LEFT AND RIGHT MITTS

All sizes: work 5 rounds in stockinette stitch.
Switch to smaller needles and work in stockinette stitch until mitt measures 1 {1-1/2, 2} inches above separation for thumb.

Little Finger:
Knit 4 {5, 6} sts, and put 28 {32, 34} sts on spare circular needle. CO 1 st over gap and knit to end: 8 {10, 12} working sts. Work in k1 tbl, p1 ribbing for 1/2 {3/4, 1} inch(es) using dpns or 2 circular needles. Bind off loosely in pattern.

Upper Hand:
Place held sts on working needles. Join yarn, pick up and knit 2 sts along CO edge at base of little finger. Work stockinette stitch in the round for 1/4 {1/4, 1/2} inches: 30 {34, 36} sts

Ring Finger:
Knit 5 {6, 6} sts and place 20 {22, 24} sts on spare circular needle. CO 1 {1, 2} sts over gap and knit 5 {6, 6} sts: 11 {13, 14} sts.

Small and medium ONLY: [k1 tbl, p1] 2 times, k1 tbl, p2tog, and work [k1 tbl, p1] to end.

ALL SIZES: work in k1 tbl, p1 ribbing for a total of 3/4 {1, 1-1/4} inch(es) using dpns or 2 circular needles. Bind off loosely in pattern.

Middle Finger:
Rejoin yarn; pick up and knit 2 sts at base of ring finger. Knit first 5 {5, 6} held sts onto working needles. CO 1 {2, 2} sts over gap, place last 5 {5, 6} held sts (from other end of spare circular needle) on working needles and knit sts: 13 {14, 16} working sts.

Small ONLY: [k1 tbl, p1] 3 times, k2tog tbl, p1, and work [k1 tbl, p1] to end.

ALL SIZES: work in k1 tbl, p1 ribbing for a total of 3/4 {1, 1-1/4} inch(es) using dpns or 2 circular needles. Bind off loosely in pattern.

Index Finger:
Place remaining sts on working needles. Rejoin yarn; pick up and knit 2 {2, 4} at base of middle finger: 12 {14, 16} working sts. Work in k1 tbl, p1 ribbing for a total of 3/4 {1, 1-1/4} inch(es) using dpns or 2 circular needles. Bind off loosely in pattern.

Thumb:
Place thumb gusset sts on working needles, join yarn and pick up and knit 1 sts over gap between hand and thumb: 14 {16, 18} sts. Work in k1 tbl, p1 ribbing for a total of 3/4 {1, 1-1/4} inch(es) using dpns or 2 circular needles. Bind off loosely in pattern.

Finishing:
Sew in ends, closing up holes between fingers and thumb, and hand. Wash using wool wash. Remove excess water and lay flat to block. When thoroughly dry, wear and enjoy!

THANK YOU
FOR READING

Please visit http://curiosityquills.com/reader-survey to share
your reading experience with the author of this book!

Kasper Mützenmacher's Cursed Hat, by Keith R. Fentonmiller

Berlin hatmaker Kasper Mützenmacher's carefree life of fedoras, jazz, and booze comes to a screeching halt when he must use the god Hermes' "wishing hat," a teleportation device, to rescue his flapper girlfriend from the shadowy Klaus, a veil-wearing Nazi who brainwashes his victims until they can't see their own faces. Klaus eventually discovers the wishing hat's existence and steals it on Kristallnacht. But even if Kasper gets back the hat and spirits his family to America, they won't be safe until they break the curse that has trapped them in the hat business for sixteen centuries.

Muddy Waters, by Sara O. Thompson

Convicted for murdering her family, and locked up in a psych ward, a Witch makes a deal with the FBI to be their newest Supernormal Investigator--freedom has a price, though it's one she's willing to pay if it means she can track down who set her up for the fall. Solving crimes, doing magic, drinking bourbon. It's dirty work, but somebody has to do it.

51844949R00240

Made in the USA
San Bernardino, CA
03 August 2017